# INTENTIONS OF THE EARL

ROSE GORDON

This book is a work of fiction. All names, events and locales are a product of this author's imagination. If any name, event and/or locale did exist, it is purely by coincidence it appears in this book.



INTENTIONS OF THE EARL



Published by Parchment & Plume, LLC
www.parchmentandplume.com

Other Titles Available by Rose Gordon

*SCANDALOUS SISTERS SERIES*
*Intentions of the Earl*
*Liberty for Paul*
*To Win His Wayward Wife*

*GROOM SERIES*
*Her Sudden Groom*
*Her Reluctant Groom*
*Her Secondhand Groom*
*Her Imperfect Groom*

COMING 2012-2013

*BANKS BROTHERS BRIDES SERIES*
*His Contract Bride*
*His Yankee Bride*
*His Jilted Bride*
*His Brother's Bride*

*OFFICER SERIES (AMERICAN SET)*
*The Officer and the Bostoner*
*The Officer and the Southerner*
*The Officer and the Traveler*

*Dedicated to my maternal grandmother who possessed the worst decorating skills I've ever witnessed.*

*And, to my loving husband who has always supported me, even if it meant reading a copy of my first manuscript by the fire on our annual camping trip.*
*I love you!*

# Chapter 1

*London, England*
*May 1812*

*Smack!*

"Ouch!"

"You deserved it, you lecher," Brooke Banks exclaimed, scrambling to get off the secluded bench where she *had* been kissing Benjamin Collins, Duke of Gateway.

"What was that for?" Gateway demanded, rubbing his cheek.

"You have to ask?" Brooke crossed her arms. "I came out here to see the gardens, not have you maul me in the shrubbery." Why did he, like all men, assume her agreement to go into the gardens translated into permission for him to touch her person—specifically her chest?

"I wasn't mauling you," he spat. His face looked like it had been carved from marble with his mouth clamped so tightly that white lines had formed around the ridges and his eyes had transformed from warm, blue candle flames into hard, cold chips of ice.

"You're correct; you didn't maul me. Yet. I felt your hand drifting from my shoulder. Don't think for one second that I didn't know its intended destination."

Gateway snorted. "And are you trying to tell me you didn't want me to touch you?"

"You know I didn't," Brooke snapped. She clutched her skirt with both hands, twisting the fabric to refrain from striking him again.

"So you say, but your actions suggest differently," he responded slyly.

"What are you talking about?" How could her actions have

possibly been so misconstrued they would suggest she wanted him to grope her?

Still sitting on the bench, Gateway leaned his shoulders back up against a tree and folded his arms. "Well, Miss Banks," he drawled. "I recall us sharing an unusually close dance, immediately followed by you calling me 'Benny'. This not only shows familiarity by calling me by my Christian name, but goes one step further, because someone could think you have a special nickname for me." He shrugged and cocked his head, leering at her. "That's what gave me the impression you enjoyed my company and would further enjoy it in the gardens, where it's dark."

"It was a *waltz*," she cried. "You're supposed to dance close. I'm sorry if you took that as encouragement to make further advances, but they were not welcome." She chose to leave off the bit about calling him "Benny". There was no way she could defend herself on that score.

"You didn't protest my kisses," he said smoothly.

Brooke flushed. He was right, she hadn't protested his kisses. Not to say she enjoyed them, because she hadn't. But she hadn't stopped him, either, which he probably took as encouragement. "Once again, I'm sorry you mistook that as encouragement for your amorous urges."

"I didn't mistake anything. You, miss, are nothing but a tease."

"And you, sir, are no gentleman," she exclaimed, heedless to his sneer.

"I never claimed to be." His eyes flashed fire.

"Well, do try to be one just now and escort me back inside," Brooke said with feigned sweetness.

Gateway pushed up off the bench and offered her his arm.

When they were safely inside the ballroom, she flashed the duke a winning smile and said cordially, "Thank you, sir. The gardens were beautiful."

Instead of responding or even acknowledging she'd spoken, the duke dropped her arm as if he'd been burned and mumbled something about a careless American chit teasing the wrong man as he huffed off toward the other side of the ballroom.

Brooke gave his comment, or what she'd heard of it anyway, about two seconds worth of thought before shrugging it off and greeting her frowning sister. "What is that frown about, Liberty?" she asked innocently.

"You know what the frown is about. If you don't, then you're hopeless," was her sister's low reply.

Liberty might be four years younger than Brooke, but she had a way of acting as though she were the older sister. That was especially true when it came to things like social proprieties. She freely gave lectures, thinly veiled as "discussions," when she felt circumstances dictated such.

Knowing this was one of those occasions, and there was no chance of escaping Liberty's lecture, Brooke decided to get it over with. At least if they had the "discussion" here, in the ballroom, surrounded by a couple hundred people, there was a chance it would be brief. The other option would include being railed against for hours on end once they got home. Turning to Liberty, she flashed another innocent smile. "Whatever do you mean?"

Liberty was no fool; no one could live with Brooke for nineteen years without knowing her tactics. True, Liberty wouldn't make a scene. But she had never been one to forget or to change her purpose just because a crowd was present. Looking at Brooke with all the confidence of a queen, Liberty declared, "You break every rule there is, and you don't give a fig about it."

This wasn't a new concept, and despite their many conversations, nothing had changed. Brooke felt like pointing that fact out, but it would just make this drag on longer. "I know. I'm sorry."

"No, you're not," Liberty snapped, slapping her fan on her palm for emphasis. "You're never sorry. You say you are, but you're not." Her lips thinned. "You must have broken at least ten rules with the Duke of Gateway alone." She let out a deep breath. "And that's just what I saw while you were in here. Who knows how many others you broke while out in the gardens?"

Brooke was ready for this conversation to be over, so she did what she knew she'd regret, but did it knowing it would be the only way to end this here and now. Taking a deep breath and schooling her features to look completely interested, she asked, "What did I do wrong, dear sister, and how should I have done it differently?"

Liberty frowned at her sarcasm; then for the first time in the past half-hour, she smiled brightly. "First, you keep calling His Grace 'sir'. You should be calling him 'Your Grace'." Not allowing a break for Brooke to protest, she continued, "Second—" she ticked off Brooke's second offense on her second finger. "You danced far too close. I know it was a waltz, but even in the waltz there is to be *some* space between partners. You might as well have declared to the whole room that you would like to have him ravish you."

Brooke thought about what Liberty had just said, and how similar it sounded to the statement that the duke had made in the shrubs. Either she really had led him on, or these two were too inept to tell the difference between friendly flirting and blatant teasing. In Brooke's mind, the second option made more sense.

"Seventh, you should never ask a man to claim a dance on your dance card." Liberty's enumeration brought Brooke back to reality for a moment. They were already on number seven, which was good. It meant she had missed four of these crucial life-improving points, and if she were lucky, this speech was almost over. How many things had Liberty said she'd done wrong? Eight? Ten? Brooke tried hard to remember before giving up and mentally shrugging. It was of no account really. It would be over soon enough. Then she could just apologize with false sincerity, as usual, and go about the evening.

Once again, Liberty's voice broke into Brooke's thoughts. "Also, you should laugh a little more delicately. Just a little titter or giggle while in public, not a full-blown cackle. For goodness' sake, you embarrass yourself and your family, while driving the gentlemen away when you laugh that way."

That was the last straw. Was Liberty really going to lecture her about her laugh right here in the middle of Lady Lampson's ball?

No matter how much Brooke wanted to appease her sister by listening to this drivel—from a sister who was four years her junior, mind you—she was done. Interrupting Liberty's tirade, she went on one of her own.

Placing her hands on her hips and adopting not even close to the gentlest tone she had, she burst out, "You know, Liberty, if I embarrass you so much then why are you allowing yourself to be seen with me now? Why is it you want to be accepted so badly, anyway? This isn't our home. We're from New York. We'll be going back after this visit." She stopped for a second to enjoy the look of shock that had taken hold of Liberty's face. "As much as Mama would like to think we're going to marry into wealthy, titled families, we're not. The sooner you accept that, the better your life will be." Unable to keep her irritation for Liberty and her rules under control any longer, her voice rose a bit louder and turned hard as steel. "We're only here for a little fun, and it seems to me that you're not having any. And because you're not having any, you're begrudging me *mine*," she exclaimed, punctuating the last word with a stomp of her foot. Brooke looked smugly at her sister, reveling in the fruits of her labor.

The look of hurt on Liberty's face was proof she'd made her point. The stares from several ladies close by served as proof that she'd been too loud and had once again drawn unwanted attention to herself.

No more than ten seconds later, Mama walked up. The look on Mama's face made it clear it would be a long, uncomfortable ride home. Her voice, however, came out sugary sweet, tinged with a thick, southern United States accent when she exclaimed, "Oh girls, stop being so silly with your little act. I know you like to pretend to argue, but this is not the time." It was a weak attempt to stop the spread of rumors that might result due to someone overhearing what really was being said. But it was an attempt all the same, and with how marriage-minded Mama had become, it was the only thing she could do.

Taking their cues from their mother's face, both girls murmured their apologies.

Once most of the crowd had gone back to dancing, talking or drinking punch, Mama looked to both of them with that stern look that only she could pull off and announced, "We're going home. Liberty, go find Papa and tell him to have the carriage sent. We'll meet you out front. Come, Brooke. We're going to find Madison."

As they walked away, Brooke tried to explain that it wasn't her fault, but Mama would have none of it. Adopting an icy tone, Mama said, "Wait until we get into the carriage; or even better, wait until we get home. You've done quite enough tonight already, young lady. I don't want any more undue attention brought on us right now. Do you understand?"

Brooke knew that tone. It did not bode well for a pleasant ride home, and probably not a good morning tomorrow either. "All right," she said simply. That was all the talking necessary.

The carriage ride from the Lampsons' ball was quiet. Too quiet, to be exact. Nobody said anything. But then again, there was nothing to say. Instead, they all just exchanged looks. Brooke and Liberty shot daggers at each other, while they both received horrified looks from both Mama and Papa. Madison was the only one not interested in the turn of events and stared out the windows the best she could through the little opening in the curtains.

At home, the unnatural silence continued, and Brooke was none-too-gently escorted into the drawing room and told one word: wait.

Wait she did. Not knowing how long she would be waiting or what would happen next, she sat on the pink settee and tried to devise a plan to get herself out of trouble. She only had to wait ten minutes before Papa and Mama rushed into the room to join her.

"Brooklyn, do you have anything to say for yourself?" Papa asked sternly, taking a seat in a wingback chair near her. His eyes blazed into hers, and his voice had taken on the most serious tone she had heard in many years.

Papa used her given name. Now was not the time to trifle with him. "This is not entirely my fault. Liberty was just as involved in the public display as I was. Why is she not here?" she asked with a hopeful smile.

"Stop worrying about your sister," he snapped. "Now answer my question."

Brooke swallowed. Her usually even-tempered father was unhappy and placing full blame on her. Suddenly a thought popped into her head, just the one that could help her escape this situation, if not entirely, then at least she wouldn't shoulder it alone. Brooke flashed him a bright smile. "Papa, I should be worried about my sister. See, she was just as involved as I was, and God punished both Adam and Eve for their mistakes, did he not?"

John Banks, Brooke's father, was a Protestant minister in New York. When in doubt, she had always been able to wiggle out of her problems by using his profession to her advantage. She hoped this time would not prove to be an exception.

A small smile took over Papa's lips. "Oh, daughter, you are so correct. Both Adam and Eve were involved in their fall, and they both were punished. I'm so glad you remember that. Hmm, let's just do a bit of role-playing, shall we?" He paused and tapped one lone finger along his cheek. "In the story of Adam and Eve, who do you think you would play? Adam, the one who was brought the temptation and partook of it? Or would you be Eve? You know, the one who went off alone, did something wrong, then came to her husband and presented him with an opportunity to do wrong as well?" Papa's lips twitched at her frown.

Brooke didn't let his words break her spirit for long, however. "Yes, it's true I could be likened to Eve. I did break some silly rules and create a scene; therefore, I was more at fault." Then, because she thought she had this well in hand, she blithely said, "However, God did not punish Eve more than Adam. They were both punished the same."

"That's true. You make a very good point," he conceded, then paused, letting her bask in the soon-ending moment of success. "However, my dear, you overlook one small detail. I'm not God."

"But—but—" she sputtered.

Cutting her off with a hand gesture, her father continued, "Brooke, I love you. I really do. However, you cannot deny you were at fault tonight." Not letting her talk like she was itching to do, he put on his sternest face. "I know Liberty should have kept her comments until a more private time, such as at home, but I understand you encouraged her, and she obliged. That's when you lost your temper."

Brooke usually took defeat in stride. So tamping down her temper and pride, she ventured, "What shall I do about it now?" The scene had already been made. Everyone had witnessed her raising her voice and stamping her foot like a three-year-old throwing a tantrum.

"There's nothing to be done except wait out the gossip. Maybe there won't be any." That was a hopeful statement; everyone in the room knew that. "You may go to bed now, Brooke. I shall see you tomorrow."

Papa's use of her familiar name reassured her he was no longer angry with her and that all would be well tomorrow. "Goodnight, Papa. I am truly sorry about the way it all happened tonight, and I'll try not to embarrass you again." She desperately hoped that was true. Brooke turned to where her mother was sitting quietly in the corner of the drawing room. Mama's eyes looked worried and her hands were folded primly in her lap. "Goodnight, Mama. I shall see you in the morning."

"Goodnight, darling. I don't think there will be a need to get up too early," Mama responded with a weary smile.

Puzzled, Brooke just had to know what she meant. "Why?"

"Because I doubt there will be any gentlemen callers after the lovely theatrics that were displayed tonight," Mama said dryly.

Papa let out a loud bark of laughter. Brooke held her giggle until she got into the hall, then she let out a great peal of echoing laughter. For as much as Mama hated being embarrassed, she was typically a good sport and saw humor where there was none.

***

"Do you truly believe nothing will come of this?" Carolina Banks asked her husband after Brooke was gone.

"Tomorrow, nobody of any consequence will care about this. Trust me. It's not as if she were caught in a scandalous situation or anything. Sure, someone might remember it forever—" he shrugged one shoulder— "but it's not the kind of thing that will render either of them unmarriageable or cause them to be cut during social events." He stopped talking and gazed at his wife. His face had taken on a contemplative air. "I think the problem could be more that she is dismissing the rules in general, not so much the scene. Liberty, on the other hand, is determined to learn and execute all the rules without flaw, which could be her downfall."

"Oh, John, I worry so about all three of them. I want them all to marry, but I want them to marry happily. For love, like we did," Carolina said quietly.

"I know, but they have their own destinies to make," John said with a yawn.

Carolina got up and started walking across the room to take her leave. Just before she got to the door, she stopped and, in a small voice, asked the real question of the evening. "What did you learn about Madison tonight?"

Closing his eyes, John took a deep breath. "Nothing. I watched her all evening. She refused to dance with every man who asked. She looked as if she were lost in a daydream the entire time." He shook his head as if it would dispel the unpleasant thought from inside. "I just don't know if it's a good dream or not."

Carolina nodded. As she walked down the hall toward her room, she briefly paused outside Madison's door. But instead of going in, she just sighed and went on to her bed.

# Chapter 2

Andrew Black, Earl of Townson, checked his watch. It was quarter after two, which meant he could safely leave without it being seen as he was snubbing the hosts. Making his way to the door, a deep, familiar voice sounded behind him. "Hold there, Townson. I have a new proposition for you."

Andrew knew that voice. It belonged to the man who'd been the reason Andrew had come to this ball in the first place. Turning around slowly, Andrew faced the cold, hard-as-steel eyes of Benjamin Collins, Duke of Gateway. The two were neither friends nor enemies; they were just acquaintances. This was exactly the way Andrew preferred it.

Though Andrew could easily be considered a libertine by the *ton*, the duke had somehow earned the nickname of the Dangerous Duke. He wasn't one anyone wanted to oppose. Revenge was his specialty. Nobody knew that better than Andrew.

Only twice had Andrew found himself on the wrong side of Gateway. But since Eton, Andrew had seen firsthand what happened to both men and women who managed to get on Gateway's bad side.

Andrew had been relentlessly teased from the first day at Eton. After two weeks of close observation, Benjamin Collins decided to do the unthinkable: he befriended the outcast. Even though the teasing ceased, the cost was much greater. In exchange for protection and friendship, Andrew was forced to do Gateway's bidding. From schoolwork, to lying for him when he snuck out at night, to being the "enforcer" of revenge, Andrew did it. He did it well, and with little resentment, because if he refused, his life would be even worse than it had been before.

Squaring his shoulders, Andrew looked him in the eye. "What do you mean?"

"It would appear that I need a favor," Gateway drawled. "Now that we're no longer boys, I cannot offer you my protection from the other schoolboys, but I can give you back your deed." Taking the deed that had changed hands from the earl to the duke earlier in the evening out of his pocket; Gateway gave it a little wave. "Just do me this favor, and I'll give the deed back without any debt attached to it."

Andrew's hands fisted in fury at Gateway's remark about needing his protection from the other schoolboys at Eton. He swallowed a retort and forced himself to think about what this would mean. He had not done a favor for Gateway in more than ten years. After he refused to do one, they had a falling-out that led to someone else doing Gateway's dirty work against Andrew, followed by Gateway taking his own revenge.

After that, Andrew had stayed clear of the duke—until recently, when once again he'd fallen victim to the Great Gateway and was forced to surrender the deed to the last of his unentailed estates.

The estate was in Essex and had accumulated more debt than Andrew could ever pay. Stupidly, he'd agreed to take a loan from Gateway against the estate in order to improve it. The improvements hadn't worked and he'd run out of time on the loan. Tonight was the night he had to surrender the deed to Gateway, which was the only reason he'd come to the ball.

Unlike a normal man who would take care of his business in his study or at a solicitor's office, Gateway had demanded the exchange take place somewhere public. Andrew assumed this was just another way for the duke to gloat.

Silently weighing his options, he let out a pent-up breath and asked anxiously, "Do I get details about this favor before I agree to do it?"

Gateway's smile dimmed and a shadow crossed his eyes. That was not a good sign.

After tucking the deed back into his pocket, Gateway looked around the room. "This is something we should speak about in private. This isn't the place. I suspect you were about to leave, were you not?" When Andrew merely nodded, Gateway said, "Would you care to meet me in half an hour in my study?" Gateway must have sensed there was some hesitancy when Andrew didn't answer and added, "Just to talk about details. You're not committed. Just remember, this could get you back your estate completely free of debt."

Not missing the emphasis on his last three words, Andrew simply said, "A half-hour, then." Then before he could do something stupid, like agree to Gateway's bargain, he walked out of the ballroom.

***

*"Are you mad?"* Andrew asked sharply, gaping at Gateway with open astonishment.

"No, I'm not mad," Gateway snapped. "I don't know what your problem is. You seem to have no qualms with the activity in general. What could possibly be holding you back?"

"I don't dally with innocents. *That* is my problem," Andrew said fiercely. In light of what he'd just been asked to do, that was a rather large problem, indeed.

Gateway strode over to the fireplace, grabbed the poker, and stoked the fire, creating a massive flame. When he was satisfied with his larger-than-necessary fire, he replaced the screen then turned to face Andrew. "Come now, Townson, I'm not asking you to marry her. Quite the opposite. I just want you to compromise her. Everyone knows you're not the marrying type, and she's an American chit. She hasn't a leg to stand on to force you into marriage. It all works out perfectly."

Andrew's face grew hotter, and he wasn't sure if it was because of the newly stoked fire or the fact that he was so outraged by what he'd just been asked to do. Shifting uncomfortably in his seat, he asked the question he wasn't certain he even wanted answered. "Why do you want this girl ruined?"

Gateway didn't answer. His eyes wandered aimlessly around his study. They landed on everything in the room. Everything except Andrew, that is.

Andrew assumed Gateway was doing this in hopes he'd lose

interest in the reasons. Such details Gateway would be loath to share seeing as how he'd never been forthcoming with them before.

Finally, Gateway gave a nonchalant shrug. "I just want them gone. If one of their daughters gets ruined without a marriage proposal, then they'll leave. They'll go home to America and be out of England." His words were spoken casually, almost as if he thought this was nothing more than an ordinary drawing room conversation.

Andrew knew immediately this wasn't the whole truth, but he accepted it just the same. He'd never get the whole story from Gateway, no matter what he asked. But he still couldn't help but wonder how the Banks family's presence could affect Gateway in one way or another. Dismissing his thoughts, he stood and announced, "I'm not interested."

"Not interested?" Gateway scoffed. "How, pray tell, can you not be interested? You're mad to reject such an offer. There's no commitment to the chit. You'll never have to see her again. And don't forget that I'll pay you handsomely. Not only do you get your estate in Essex back, but it will be completely without debt. You get your fun and you get paid for it. Sounds like an ideal situation to me."

"Believe me; I want nothing more than to have my estate back. But there is a fine line between pulling a prank on someone and completely ruining not just one person, but an entire family. I won't do it. Find someone else." Andrew walked toward the door of Gateway's study. He wanted to put as much distance between himself and Gateway as possible. This idea of ruining an innocent girl and her family as a way to get his estate back was the most depraved thing he'd ever heard. It seemed extreme even for Gateway. Andrew had assumed the man still had some scruples. Apparently he was wrong, and this undoubtedly proved it.

"Coward," Gateway called to Andrew just as he reached the door. Gateway's voice was low, almost inaudible.

Andrew's brain told his feet to move forward and walk through the door. He was almost out of there and free. But no, those feet of his just wouldn't cooperate. They were stuck, planted on Gateway's plush, royal blue carpet. His hands were clenching and unclenching into fists at his sides as he tried to ignore Gateway's taunt. Then he heard it. "Funny thing about you, Townson, I really wouldn't have thought you a coward. You've done some brassy things in your life. But maybe all the other boys at Eton knew something I didn't. Maybe they were right, and you are nothing more than a coward who would still go around clutching his mother's skirts if she'd allow it."

All the memories came flooding back—every single one. All the teasing had started because his mother, not his father, had been the one to drop him off at school. That had been enough to garner a bit of harassing anyway. However, it had also given credit to the rumor someone had circulated that evening about an old claim that he was a bastard. From then on he was taunted about being a "bastard mama's boy who clutched to his whore of a mother's skirts" and became the outcast at school. Most likely he would have stayed the outcast if not for Gateway's surprising intervention.

Gateway walked past him and into the hallway, casually saying over his shoulder, "I do understand your position. How could I have thought you'd be able to manage such a task? I should have known you couldn't do it before I approached you. Accept my apologies for wasting your time." He shook his head. "Thank you for the estate. I'm planning a trip there soon. I have been thinking I might even deed it over to my mistress when I'm done with her." He gave a shrug of nonchalance. "Usually, I just give them a cottage or rent them a townhouse for a year. But Sarah likes the country. She'll be happier there."

"Wait," Andrew called. He didn't know if Gateway would really give an estate to a woman who sold her body for money, but it wouldn't surprise him. Gateway was known to do things normal people considered inappropriate. And though impugning one's manhood would generally be enough encouragement to get most men to do Gateway's bidding, for Andrew, knowing his estate was going to be given to Gateway's mistress was the part that made him reconsider.

Gateway halted in the doorway and slowly turned around to look at Andrew. Cocking his head to one side, he asked, "Yes?"

"What do you mean you should have known I couldn't do it before you approached me?" Andrew bristled while he waited for the answer.

Gateway shrugged again. "I hadn't realized you had such trouble in this area. No matter. I'll just go find someone who doesn't." Gateway stopped for a token pause. With a sly smile, he lowered the gauntlet. "If you'll excuse me, I know just the man I need to go see about doing this, since you have indicated for some reason you lack the ability."

"My ability to handle this is perfectly adequate," Andrew snapped before he realized what he had said or what it would mean. In his defense of his pride, he'd just as good as agreed to ruin an innocent girl, all because of his quick tongue.

Gateway could not have looked more pleased with himself. As usual, everything had fallen perfectly into place for his benefit.

Gateway's face changed again. This time he looked slightly skeptical and disbelieving at the same time. He continued to stare blankly at Andrew, not giving any indication to his thoughts.

Andrew knew what Gateway was about: he was picking his next words carefully, so not to allow Andrew a means to extricate himself.

Gateway slowly strolled back toward Andrew. "Townson, I'm glad you think so. I just hope you can prove yourself. How about if we sit down and work out the terms of this agreement?" He gestured toward his desk.

Andrew, and just about everyone else in England, knew Gateway may not be the most well-liked person, but he had always been sharp as a straight pin and he prided himself on knowing just how to trap a person. Andrew had learned this first hand his first term at Eton. Even though they were only boys at the time, Gateway had already developed this unpleasant trait.

"Fine," Andrew ground out, then sent Gateway a scowl for good measure. "Let's state the terms. But if I'm to do this, then I want to be fairly compensated. There will be no reneging."

Andrew resigned himself to the unscrupulous task as he walked across the room to Gateway's desk. His quick tongue might have trapped him into this, but as long as he was trapped, he was going to take full advantage. This was obviously something important to Gateway, so he should be willing to make this well worth Andrew's while. Which was a good thing, because once this was done, he probably wouldn't be accepted into the drawing rooms of polite society for a long, long time.

Taking seats together by Gateway's large, mahogany desk, the two men discussed exactly what they each wanted from the arrangement. Both had lofty expectations, but with a few compromises they both were going to be satisfied in the end.

With a written—and signed—copy of the terms, Andrew felt hopeful about his future. All he had to do was bring scandal to Miss Banks, any of them, in a way that would shame their family enough for all of them to go back home to America.

He sighed. Though they had not determined what type of scandal Andrew was to cause to befall Miss Banks, short of a miracle, only one kind of scandal would send them back to America: one of the daughters had to be ruined. It didn't have to be in truth. The appearance would be enough, he reminded himself again to help tamp down his guilt.

It sounded simple enough when saying it. It seemed easy when reading the words on paper. But the process would not be easy. To start with, he didn't even know who these girls were. He'd never been introduced to them, so how could he get any of them to trust him enough to create a scandal?

Andrew arrived home and went straight to his bed. He had a lot to think of. He should have just walked out of Gateway's study, but that had seemed impossible at the time. And now he was trapped. At least he'd get something that he wanted—no, needed—out of the deal. As guilty as he felt about robbing a young girl of her future, he was going to secure his own.

Thanks to his late father, Andrew was penniless and all of England knew it. His father had accumulated more debt than

Andrew had ever imagined. He knew his father had been a spendthrift, but it wasn't until he had come into the title that he realized just how frivolous his father had been. There wasn't anything the man hadn't bought on credit; and instead of paying it off, he just passed it to Andrew right along with the title.

For the last eight years, Andrew had been paying it down by selling anything of any value to keep the creditors at bay. The estate in Essex was the last thing.

He had tried to save it because not only was it possible that the estate could turn a much needed profit, but also because his mother had been living there. That was another point in his favor for going through with this scheme. He would be able to get the estate back and gift it to his mother, who was currently living at Rockhurst, the seat of his earldom. She deserved at least that for what both he and his father had put her through.

He rolled over. Guilt flooded him. He felt guilty about what he was going to do to the Banks family and about what he'd done to his own mother in the past. Some would say to let the guilt about his mother go, but it wasn't easy for Andrew to do. Not only had he intentionally hurt her with his words, he had essentially sentenced her to a life of solitude.

Even if he hated the idea of what he was going to do, it would solve his two biggest problems. That gave him a bit of a relief, but not much.

For now, he needed to think about his next step. Gateway had told him the Banks family was staying in Lord Watson's townhouse while the baron and his family were staying in the country. Andrew knew Lord Watson—he was the father to one of his friends—but other than that, he had no real knowledge of the family. That would have to be enough, because he planned to start a courtship immediately.

# Chapter 3

The townhouse where Brooke's family was staying looked standard for this section of town. It was three stories high, made of a smooth, light gray stone, and had a white front door. Windows were placed directly above the door on the second and third floors, each with a private balcony. Six large, smooth, stone steps and a black handrail led from the front door down to the edge of the street. When looking from down the street, with the exception of the numbers on the side, the house looked identical to the ones on either side. In other words, it wasn't very original.

Earlier in the morning Brooke breakfasted with her family then decided to go outside on her balcony and read the newest gothic novel she'd picked up in the local bookshop.

She settled into a lounge chair and started flipping through her book. She remembered she was almost to the end and thumbed her way to the back. Aha, here she was, the hero was about to admit he was wrong and beg the heroine to take him back. This was normally her favorite part of novels, even if right after he said his speech, a large boulder came rolling off the side of a cliff and killed him, leaving the heroine to sulk in the sadness of never getting to be with her true love.

Thirty minutes later, Brooke finished her book and shut it with an echoing thud. Not having anything else to do, she was about to go back inside to see what her sisters were doing when a carriage with an unfamiliar crest emblazoned on the side rolled up.

She leaned forward, pressing her face between the bars of the balcony to get a better look at the massive stranger that was emerging from the carriage. He looked like a gentlemen and he even carried himself like one as he walked up the steps to her front door. He gave three swift bangs with their brass knocker. If she were in New York, she would have rushed to the door to open it herself and greet the guest, but that was not the way of things here, and even she was not brave enough to break that particular rule.

She waited in silence for three long minutes before Turner, their usually unkempt and always unprofessional butler, opened the door to greet the stranger.

Unable to bear it any longer, she slipped down the stairs and hid herself behind a potted plant in the foyer just in time to see Turner lead the stranger down the hall to the drawing room.

Deciding it would be best for Liberty to explain to Turner the proper procedure for admitting a guest, Brooke quietly ignored his misstep and tiptoed down the hall behind the pair.

Turner opened the door and showed their guest into the empty drawing room. Brooke stood quietly in the hall and waited for Turner to leave. When he walked toward her, she pressed her fingers to her lips to motion for his silence.

Standing in the hallway, she peeked around the corner of the open door and watched the stranger as he glanced around the ugliest drawing room to ever grace England.

She was sure he blinked his eyes several times to get accustomed to the awful images that were assaulting him. Then without a word, he moved his head side to side, soaking in the painful ambience of their drawing room. The walls were gold—not a pale yellow, but bright shining gold. One settee was bright red, the other was pale pink. He looked over to the far wall where the most hideous paintings she'd ever laid eyes on were proudly hung in glittering silver frames.

The paintings looked like children had taken mud and smeared it around on three canvasses, and not in a somewhat interesting way, either. They were a mix of brown, black, and dark spinach green swirled together. In short, they were eyesores.

He violently jerked his head away, dropped his gaze to the floor, and was greeted by a dark green carpet. "I hope this drawing room is not a prelude to what the inhabitants are like," he mumbled with a shudder.

"I am hurt, sir, truly hurt," Brooke said shrilly as she entered the room. Her words must have caught him off guard because he looked completely frozen in place. Before he could say so much as one word in his defense, she said, "How can you say such awful things about this beautifully decorated room? I worked so hard on it. It is my masterpiece! I spent hours picking the perfect gold wallpaper. Then, I pondered for weeks about those purple drapes. When I went to pick a settee, I was torn between the red and pink settee. So to cure my indecision, I opted to get both."

He was still standing with his back to her. Perhaps he was too nervous to turn around. But slowly, he did turn around. When he was fully looking at her, his mouth dropped open a bit before he shut it with an audible snap. He swallowed loudly then stared at her, not even trying to speak.

Brooke had often been considered attractive with her heart-shaped face and petite facial features. Her hair was a dark mahogany brown and she typically piled it atop her head, with a few curls overflowing her coif and cascading down in the back and on either side of her face. Her eyes were so dark they almost looked black. That was her feature about which gentlemen most often wrote silly poetry.

Seeing another speechless man stare at her was not going to deter her from her fun. She put a look of true pain on her face, one that would suggest he had just kicked a puppy in her presence. She pointed to the back wall where those hideous mud-smeared paintings were hung. "Would you like to tell me your delightful opinion about those portraits hanging on the far wall, sir? I am anxious to hear your thoughts."

"Miss Banks," the stranger hedged. "I'm sorry. I seem to have spoken without much thought. I cannot tell you how sorry I am. Please forgive me."

"Well, you're not forgiven," she exclaimed. "To just come into someone's house and start to criticize their decorations, and then to liken them to the inhabitants of the house is inappropriate." Brooke enjoyed the remorseful look on his face, almost identical to a little boy being scolded for stealing sweets out of the kitchen. Best yet, he had no idea she was leading him on. That drawing room was horrific, nobody could argue with that; and if her family had been allowed to change it, that room would have been changed before the front door shut. But her aunt and uncle would not allow them to make modifications to the house; therefore, all ten of her family's eyes were forced to suffer inhumanely.

Although the drawing room was hideous, it was not the ugliest room in the house. She and her sisters couldn't decide which room took that particular prize, but the drawing room was not it.

Brooke stood stock-still, trying to look like she was still deeply wounded by his opinion, but really she just wanted to see him squirm a minute longer before either of her sisters or Mama came in. She decided to press the topic of the paintings. "Furthermore, sir, you did not do as your hostess asked. You have yet to render your opinion on those portraits."

Their guest flushed with uncertainty.

Those paintings were an unsightly mess that no artist would want to claim—unless said artist was three years of age. If he were to be honest about those paintings, he'd say they looked like a monkey painted them. Her whole family knew she thought so. But no gentleman would dare say such a thing. He would be afraid of hurting her feelings, or upsetting her and being tossed out on his ear.

"They are, well, they are very unique," he said tactfully.

"Do you truly think so?" She suppressed a laugh at his bold-faced lie. "I worked so hard on them. My family doesn't seem to appreciate them, but I think they're just blind to true beauty. I'm so glad you see them as unique! What do you like best about them?" Brooke loved this game. She played it all the time when gentlemen came to visit. Her mother and sisters did not approve, but she couldn't help herself. It was too much fun. She tried to keep a straight face and not laugh at his discomfort. She especially loved that the poor man had no idea that even if he'd kept his mouth shut about the ghastly room, he'd still be having this conversation.

He kept staring at the paintings. Brooke supposed he was hoping the floor would open up and swallow him whole. "I like all of it. It's hard to pick out what I like best," he finally said with as much excitement as one would have when going to the tooth drawer.

"Do you truly mean it? I am so happy to hear you say that. It is very sweet." She took a couple steps toward him and smiled broadly before admitting, "At first, I didn't think I was going to like you very much. You insulted my decorating style and me at the same time, all before we had even met. But now that I know how much you love my artwork, well, I think I have revised my opinion."

Taking a low bow, he said, "I am Andrew Black, Earl of Townson. I do not believe I have had the pleasure of meeting you."

"No, I don't think we've met." Surely if they'd met, Brooke would remember him.

For the first time since she walked in the room, she saw him. Sure, she had seen him before, but now she really saw him. His hair was jet black with a few gray hairs scattered here and there, mostly around his temples. He was tall, taller than most, and had a broad form. In this room he looked positively domineering, but he wasn't using his size to intimidate her like some would have at this point.

Gazing at his face, she liked that it was different than a lot of the other gentlemen's faces. His nose wasn't perfectly straight; it looked almost like it had been broken before. He had a strong chin and full lips. The color of his skin was not pale like most of the English, but rather honey-colored, as if he had seen a lot of sun. By some standards he would be considered handsome, but not to all women—just to the ones who were more attracted to the exotic look.

One of his dark eyebrows rose as if he knew she was mentally cataloging him. But instead of averting her eyes in embarrassment, she met his. When she did so, she was startled. He had the most beautiful blue eyes she'd ever seen. They were not the light blue that was common, rather they were a deeper, darker blue. Looking into their depths reminded her of the deep, blue ocean she'd crossed just weeks before. After seeing those eyes, she realized instantly she was indeed one of those women who found him handsome.

"Have I passed your inspection?" he asked with a hint of amusement in his voice.

His question broke into Brooke's thoughts and startled her. She was generally not one to be embarrassed when caught doing something considered impolite, so she gave a lopsided shrug. "You'll do, I suppose."

The earl shook his head and shot her a half smile. He had a beautiful smile. His white teeth were a startling contrast against his tanned skin. She liked seeing him like this. She'd have to do her best to see him smile again before he left today.

With that decided, Brooke's mind went back to wondering why this handsome stranger was here. Who had he come to see? She had never met him before, nor had she heard either of her sisters talk of him. But he had to be here to see one of them. Surely he wasn't here to see Mama or Papa.

Which sister could it be? Madison was the most beautiful of the three by far. She was tall and slender, with bright blonde hair and clear blue eyes, like their father. Her skin wasn't pale, but it wasn't as tanned as Brooke's either. She had always had a way with wooing a roomful of men just by walking in; and if that wasn't enough to make all the other women jealous, she had this ability to make any dress look fit for a queen, no matter the color or condition of the fabric. Her personality only made her more beautiful. She was always genuine in her friendships and was ready with a kind word when someone she loved needed support. But even though she was the most beautiful of the three, she was also the most withdrawn. She hated to dance, and would hardly say two words to any gentleman that approached her. In fact, she did her best to make it known she had no desire for an introduction. Certainly the earl had not found that encouraging enough to call.

Liberty, on the other hand, was no raving beauty. She was the type who most considered to be plain. Not ugly, not pretty—just plain. Her hair was not considered an exceptional color; it was ordinary, light brown, which matched her ordinary, hazel eyes. Her nose was too big, her teeth weren't perfect, or even straight if the truth be known, and she could afford to gain at least a stone.

Unfortunately, her personality didn't really make up for her physical shortcomings. Normally, when someone wasn't considered attractive, they would have a great personality to recommend them, but not Liberty. Not that she was a shrew, but she was too blunt by far, and usually not in a good way. Brooke knew she was too blunt as well, but most people did not take offense to what she said since it was usually done in good fun. Liberty's comments, though not always intentional, had a way to irritate a person beyond belief. Only her family members got to know the real Liberty—the one full of love and compassion. Surely the earl hadn't discovered that side of Liberty yet.

Still trying to puzzle out which of these demeanors would bring the earl to call, her mother and sisters walked in, startling them both.

***

"You know you're not supposed to be alone with a gentleman, Brooke," broke into the silence from an unexpected source. Andrew would have believed that Mrs. Banks would have said that, but instead, that statement of reproof was made by a young girl who looked barely out of the schoolroom.

"Indeed? I'm not? I had no idea!" Brooke cried with so much bravado, that Andrew almost believed her. But her next statement revealed to Andrew that sarcasm was just part of her personality. "Really, Liberty, you are too obsessed with the rules. We were doing nothing wrong and it was only for a couple of minutes anyway," she said with a dismissive flick of her wrist. Glancing around to read the look on her mother's face, she added, "And we left the door open. I don't see anything wrong with that. Do you, Mama?"

"You're not supposed to be alone with a gentleman, you know that. And exactly, who is this gentleman?" Mrs. Banks asked coolly.

Before Brooke could answer, Andrew gave a low bow. "Andrew Black, Earl of Townson. I have come to call upon your daughters, madam."

"Oh," Mrs. Banks cried excitedly, "how wonderful. An earl

has come to call on *my* daughters!" Then, caught up in the excitement, she asked, "Which one of my lovely girls have you set your striking eyes upon?"

Andrew's lips twitched at Mrs. Banks's outrageously bold question. Her daughters, however, groaned in unison.

Andrew wasn't sure how much they actually knew about polite society and that usually gentlemen did not call on ladies they had never met before. Judging by Mrs. Banks's question, they probably didn't know. Yet, the youngest Miss Banks was looking at him with genuine curiosity while she waited for him to answer. Deciding it best to give an infallible answer, he evenly said, "I have come to call on all of them. They all seem like lovely ladies. How could I leave one out?"

Mrs. Banks tittered and cooed like the young debutante all women of her age yearned to be. With every eye on her, no one remarked on Brooke's quick exit.

Miss Liberty was not swayed. "How do you know we are all lovely ladies, my lord? I do not believe that *we* have ever been introduced before."

She was right of course, but to admit that he had never met any of them would only be greeted by more questions. Questions he had no desire to answer, or dodge. He had to think of something fast. But he wasn't given a chance before Mrs. Banks smoothly broke in and rescued him. "Now, Liberty, don't be so hard on the man. He was just trying to save himself from the sticky situation I inadvertently put him in." Then Mrs. Banks did the most unusual thing—she winked at him!

Andrew stared at her, wondering just what she was about. No matter, he could ponder that and the reason for her odd behavior later. Right now he was trying not to say too much and give himself away. He had a feeling that if little Miss Liberty Banks knew he had never been introduced to, or even seen any of them before, she was going to have a fit of epic proportions. Best keep that little nugget of information to himself.

The middle Banks sister, who he'd barely noticed until now, stepped forward. She gave him the biggest, prettiest smile he had ever seen, and then said the one thing that could only lead to complete disaster. "Oh how wonderful, he has an interest in Brooke," she exclaimed with an expression of pure joy on her face.

Mrs. Banks sent him a knowing smile.

Liberty gaped at her sister. "What do you mean by that? He could be interested in you, you know."

"That's impossible. I've never even seen him before. If he's not here for you, then that only leaves Brooke."

Andrew wished they would quit talking about him as if he weren't in the room, but decided it was best to keep his mouth shut. Opening his mouth is what got him into this mess in the first place. They could all just believe he was here for Brooke, the dark-haired beauty who had decorated this atrocious room. Aside from her decorating skills, she seemed like a good choice, so far. He'd have to evaluate the others before making a final decision, but for now it wouldn't hurt for them to think he was here for Brooke.

As if on cue, the object of both his thoughts and the ladies' conversation, walked back in the room, followed by a footman. How odd.

"Oh, Brooke, I'm so happy for you. To have caught the attention of the earl," Mrs. Banks cooed, once again speaking of him as if he were invisible.

The moment didn't last long enough for Andrew's taste. When Brooke looked around and saw the smiling faces of her mother and sisters, her brows knit in confusion. "What on earth are you talking about?" she asked, shaking her head as she spoke, causing her loose curls to bounce. "I do not have any earl's attentions."

"Don't play innocent, Brooke. Lord Townson has come to call for you," Mrs. Banks said with uncontrollable pride.

"I believe you must be mistaken." Brooke shook her head again. "The earl is not here to call on me. We had only just met right before you all barged in."

# Chapter 4

"This is not proper," Liberty squealed. "A gentleman should not call upon a lady prior to an introduction."

So much for hoping these American heathens didn't know *that* rule. "Well, you see, I have not yet been formally introduced to any of you three beautiful ladies. But I happened to see you a time or two across the ballroom and I thought perhaps if I could call, we could make introductions," he said smoothly. "I know it is terribly indecent of me to just show up, but I simply had to meet you." He hoped that came out sounding intelligent and convincing, but doubted it.

All four women looked one to another, completely confused by his rambling, but it was Mrs. Banks who spoke first. "Oh well, that's very nice of you, my lord. We're not terribly formal here anyway. It's just as well that you've come."

Relieved by Mrs. Banks' response, Andrew relaxed.

However, the relief lasted less than a minute, because Liberty spoke again. "But it's not done!" She had a true look of horror on her face as she protested his presence.

Only vaguely listening to her list of reasons, Andrew surveyed the three younger ladies in the room. Now was a good time to determine which one would be the best choice for the task ahead of him.

Miss Liberty Banks was immediately crossed off his list. Based on how strongly she was protesting his presence now, he had no doubt she'd protest even more if he tried to get her into a compromising situation.

Mrs. Banks and Miss Liberty continued bantering back and forth about propriety. He wondered if Miss One-Must-Be-Proper-At-All-Times knew it was improper to argue; especially in front of a guest, and even worse, an eligible male one at that. With a shake of his head, he surveyed the middle Miss Banks. He didn't know what her name was. Though he had told them his name, none of them had introduced themselves to him. How improper!

The middle Miss Banks was stunningly beautiful. She could even be considered gorgeous, but she looked distant. She had scarcely said a few sentences earlier. Before that, she'd looked unapproachable, almost lost. Even after Brooke made her stunning declaration that she didn't know him, Miss Middle Banks only shrugged and her blue eyes had gone back to their exploration of whatever was just out the window.

Andrew came back to reality for a split second to step backward as a footman walked past him with one of those revolting paintings. Briefly, he listened in on the conversation between Mrs. Banks and Miss Liberty. They were still discussing what was and wasn't acceptable for a gentleman, even a lord.

Andrew shifted his thoughts back to his assessment of the three young ladies. This time he was thinking about Brooke. Wait, when had he started referring to her subconsciously as Brooke? He was slightly surprised to realize he had never thought about her as Miss Banks. From the moment he heard her name, she'd become Brooke in his mind.

He gazed over to where she was. She and her middle sister had taken seats on the red settee. Brooke was looking heavenward, praying for divine intervention if he had to hazard a guess.

Brooke was actually a very attractive young woman when she didn't have that hurt look on her face. She sat there completely relaxed, oblivious that he was staring at her. He studied her. She was thin, but not like a fence post. Her skin was tanned, probably because she was from America. He'd heard people over there didn't put much stock in being pale. Her hair was dark brown and arranged with plump curls spilling over the top of her head; his hands itched to touch her silky strands. Her eyes matched her hair perfectly. They were just as dark, if not darker. He had never seen such large, dark, expressive eyes. He was sure if he were able to look straight into them, he'd see every secret she possessed.

He scanned the rest of her face, his eyes landing on her small, straight nose, the complete opposite of his. Her mouth was a beautiful bow shape. Her pink lips were slightly parted, giving him an excellent view of her pretty white teeth lined up neatly in a row. In no way did she resemble a horse, like a good majority of the Englishwomen he knew. She was perfect.

Brooke must have had heard enough of this ridiculous conversation because she suddenly leapt from her seat. "Enough!" she all but shouted. When Liberty and Mrs. Banks faced her, she drew herself up as tall as her dainty frame would allow and said, "You two are acting like stubborn children. Just let the poor man stay. He apparently has a desire to be here—I cannot fathom why, but he does—so stop arguing, ring for tea, and let everyone enjoy the afternoon."

"You are correct, Brooke. I cannot believe we have acted so poorly in the company of a gentleman. Please forgive us, my lord," Mrs. Banks said, blushing in shame.

With a waving hand gesture, Andrew indicated he had no problem viewing the family quarrel. However, he was glad it was over. That was ten minutes of his life he'd never get back.

He waited for Mrs. Banks and Miss Liberty to take their seats before he looked around the room for a vacant one. Locating an ugly, orange armchair in the corner of the room, he strode over and moved it so he could sit by the ladies perched on their settees.

After he was seated, he gave Brooke a quick smile and a nod of approval, as if to falsely tell her he liked her chair selection for the room.

Brooke's lips twitched at his affirmative nod and she picked up the teapot that had somehow appeared in the room. "How do you take your tea, my lord?"

"How do you take your tea?" Andrew countered. He wasn't picky whether he had milk or sugar in his tea. Today he'd drink what she preferred.

"With honey," Brooke answered matter-of-factly with a sweet, shy smile.

"Honey?" He tried to keep disgust from creeping into his tone. "You mean the sticky substance that comes from a beehive?" he asked to be certain they were talking about the same thing.

"No, I mean a man I just happen to call that term of endearment," she quipped.

"Brooke," Mrs. Banks said, giving her a disapproving look. "Stop that. It's not appropriate to bait him so."

"It's all right, Mrs. Banks. I was just dumbfounded that someone would put honey in their tea." Andrew tried to suppress a little shudder that threatened to wrack his body. Why would anyone taint their tea with honey? "I have never thought to do that before. Must be an American thing," he muttered.

Brooke appeared to be trying not to laugh. He shook his head. She could make jests at his expense all she wanted if this was the result. She looked positively fetching as she was just now. He tried hard to keep his lips from curving up into the slightest hint of a smile and turned the conversation to the girls' homeland of New York, finding himself truly fascinated by their stories.

Absorbed in inane chitchat, it wasn't until Andrew reached into his pocket and removed his pocket watch that anyone seemed to notice how much time had passed. After a quick glance at the time he said, "Ladies, this has been the most excellent afternoon I've had in a long time, but I need to be off. I would like to call again tomorrow. Mayhap I could take Miss Banks on a ride in Hyde Park?" he asked, giving a pointed look at Brooke in case there was any confusion about which Miss Banks he meant.

"That would be splendid," agreed Mrs. Banks. "I can see you have taken special interest in Brooke. She is lovely. It would be delightful if you would take her for ride in the park. She would adore it!"

Brooke shook her head, presumably at the obvious attempt at matchmaking. "That would be splendid. I look forward to it," she said with a smile.

Rising up to say farewell, Andrew cocked his head curiously at Brooke. She looked like she was about to burst. Andrew raked his gaze over her and made a mental note of how attractive she was when she was on the verge of laughter. He would have to get her to laugh again. Soon, he vowed to himself.

As Andrew climbed into his carriage, he couldn't stop the small smile curving his lips. As much as he hated what Gateway had tricked him into agreeing to do, he could take satisfaction that Brooke was beautiful. She also appeared to have an agreeable personality. Best yet, this afternoon he had discovered she enjoyed flouting the rules of society, which would certainly make his goal much easier. This could actually turn out to be a rather enjoyable courtship.

Andrew eased back against the threadbare squabs and stretched out his legs, looking over to the opposite seat at a piece of vellum. Hoping it was from Gateway asking him not to go through with this ridiculous plan, so he could court Brooke in earnest, he quickly snatched up the paper.

*Townson,*

*I have given much thought to your kind words. I hope they were true and sincere. I fear if they were not, I shall perish from embarrassment. However, I am an excellent judge of character, and I believe* every *word you said! Thus, I reached my decision. It may seem rash, but first instincts are usually correct, so I have followed them and have decided to give you a gift. This is a gift from my very soul, so I beg of you not to take it lightly nor dismiss it. Enjoy!*

Andrew tossed down the unsigned note, his face contorting with confusion. Who would have given him such a note, and what gift?

Shaking his head, Andrew dismissed the thought.

When he arrived home, Addams, who recently, because of Andrew's financial situation, had become a man of all trades, met him in the entryway with a baffled look on his face. "It's in your study as you directed, my lord," he said, putting on the air of a butler.

"What are you talking about? What did you put in my study?" Not waiting for an answer, he strode down the hall, opened the door to his study, and for the first time that he could remember since he was a boy, he let out howls of laughter. After several minutes, when he was finally composed enough to speak, he held his sides and shook his head. “That little minx!”

***

None of the women left the drawing room after the earl left. Mama sat at the small secretary by the window and wrote out the guest list to the wedding she was sure would soon be taking place. Liberty was ticking off everybody’s—including her own—improprieties. Brooke tried fruitlessly to concentrate on her embroidery. And Madison sat quietly looking out the window.

It wasn’t until fifteen minutes later when Madison, of all people, with a look of sheer bewilderment broke the silence. “What happened to the third painting that was on the back wall?”

No longer able to control herself, Brooke broke into hysterics.

# Chapter 5

*The next day*

Andrew twisted his lips and drummed his fingers along the edge of his desk, staring at the blank parchment in front of him. What would be the harm in sending her a missive to thank her for that truly spectacular gift? It wasn't customary for men and women to exchange letters without some sort of relation. That could ruin a young lady, for goodness' sake! He blinked. Yes, yes, it could. And *that* was his goal, was it not? He sighed. That *was* his goal, unpleasant as it might be. So with a flourish of his pen, he threw propriety to the wind and made his next bold move.

From the Earl of Townson to Miss Brooke Banks, 11:00 a.m. —

*Miss Brooke Banks,*
*I do appreciate your gift. I will treasure it always.*
*Townson*

***

Brooke stared at the missive in her hand. He'd written her? Surely it was improper for an unmarried and unrelated man and woman to exchange letters. But it was probably more improper she'd given him that "gift" to start with, she thought cheekily as she fanned herself with his missive. Liberty would know these things, but it didn't really matter, because she was going to return his letter whether society allowed it or not.

From Brooke Banks to the Earl of Townson, 11:25 a.m.—
*Townson,*
*I am so happy to hear that. I fretted all last night if I had made the correct decision. I see that I did, indeed, make the right*

*decision. I am glad to know that my art will be treasured by you, and may I presume all the future heirs of the Townson Earldom?*

*Miss Brooke Banks*

From the Earl of Townson to Miss Brooke Banks, 12:45 p.m. —

*Miss Banks,*

*I do not know if all the future earls will enjoy the artwork. But they will at least get the extraordinary opportunity to view the piece.*

*Townson*

From Miss Brooke Banks to the Earl of Townson 1:05 p.m.—

*Townson,*

*Does that mean you have displayed my work in a place of prominence? The portrait gallery, perhaps?*

*Brooke Banks*

From the Earl of Townson to Miss Brooke Banks, 1:40 p.m.—

*Dear Miss Brooke,*

*I would be glad to hang it in the portrait gallery. In fact, I will hang it in the family gallery if you will do but one thing for me.*

*Yours,*

*Townson*

From Miss Brooke Banks to the Earl of Townson, 2:15 p.m.—

*Townson,*

*The family gallery? Truly? Did you enjoy my painting so much you want me to be your countess? I am anxiously awaiting your reply because my mother is already planning the wedding, and I will immediately go pick out my trousseau!*

*Yours Truly,*

*Brooke*

From the Earl of Townson to Miss Brooke Banks, 2:45 p.m.—

*Dearest Brooke,*

*I am charmed that you would accept my wedding proposal, had I made one. But the condition on which I will decide to hang the portrait up in the family gallery has nothing to do with whether or not we marry, but rather another very important question. Who do the initials JRS belong to?*

*Never fear, my dear. I know they are not yours, and that* you *did not paint that dreadful mess, but it has not diminished my interest in you. I will come by your townhouse at four this afternoon and would like you to accompany me for a ride around the park.*

*Yours,*

*Andrew Black, Townson*

"Why would anyone want to claim that? It's a dreadful disgrace to the world of art," Brooke muttered to herself after she reread his note for the third time.

***

At exactly four in the afternoon, a knock rattled the front door, followed by none other than the Earl of Townson being let in.

Skulking about in the shadows, a little smile spread over Brooke's lips. She was glad he'd come.

After a few minutes of drawing room chitchat, Andrew and Brooke climbed into a curricle and were off for a ride around the park.

"My favorite color is red," Andrew stated blandly, his eyes alight with laughter.

Confused by the proclamation, Brooke nodded and shrugged. "Mine's green."

"That's nice. I'll keep that in mind. However, I had guessed that already, seeing as how your gown today is green. I believe the one you wore yesterday was, too," he said, gesturing to her forest green gown.

"I guess I'm very obvious in what colors I like, unlike you. I have yet to see you wear red," Brooke said pertly.

"I said my favorite color is red, not that I like to wear it," Andrew parried.

"Why would you tell me your favorite color? And, if it's your favorite color, why not wear it?" She glanced at him curiously.

"Just because I don't want to wear it, doesn't mean I wouldn't want you to wear it," he countered, putting deliberate emphasis on the word "you". "I'm telling you this so you know what color to choose during your visit to the modiste."

Brooke turned her body the best she could to look him in his eyes. His cobalt blue eyes were looking straight at her as if they could see right through her. She didn't know exactly what it was he could see, or even if it was a good or bad thing he had discovered. "Why would I be going to a modiste?"

"For your trousseau, darling," he drawled. When heat crept up her face, he pushed further, "But if you want, you can spare the expense of building a trousseau." He shrugged with nonchalance. "Nothing is the preferable choice for one's wedding night. But since you think a trousseau is necessary, you should know my favorite color is red. Oh, and I also like things that are filmy and transparent."

"And why would I be creating *my* trousseau with *your* favorite color?" she asked, astonished they were even speaking of such things. Both Mama and Liberty would be scandalized if they knew.

Letting go of the reins with one hand, he grabbed both of her hands with one of his, then grinned at her. "You seem to be bent on the idea of becoming *my* countess. If you are to be the Countess of Townson, that would make me your husband. As such, I thought you should be aware that I will be the one and only to see you modeling said trousseau. Therefore, I thought to tell you what color you should choose for my enjoyment."

Why would he speak to her about such scandalous topics? Suddenly it all made sense to her. He was trying to bait her because of the note she'd written. The fact they'd been corresponding that way in the first place was scandalous enough, but the tone their letters had taken pushed the bounds completely. What started out as formal, polite, and simple in tone had turned very informal and downright scandalous by the time they'd exchanged their last few letters.

"I'm so glad you told me. I'd almost forgotten that I have an appointment on Thursday. I shall remember to get something red and filmy just for you," she said with a sensual smile. Then her smile faded, and she tapped her finger against the side of her head, feigning deep contemplation. "When I go in, should I have these garments and some much needed fashionable ball gowns added to your account?"

Brooke thought something flickered in his eyes, but it was gone before she could name it.

"I have no money, darling. If you agree to marry me and be my countess, we will be known as the Penniless Earl and Countess of Townson," he said jovially with a self-deprecating smile firmly on his lips.

Brooke couldn't stop the little laugh that escaped her lips. "Well then, I suppose I could splurge with my allowance and buy my own trousseau. Don't worry though, after we marry and you get my dowry, which is a whole fifty pounds, we'll be rich and live like kings!" she teased.

"Fifty pounds you say? Well, I don't know about living like kings, but perhaps we could live like princes," he said with a bright smile.

"Oh yes! We could do so many wonderful things. We could go to the opera every night and host huge house parties all Season," she exclaimed playfully. Brooke truly had a dowry, but it wasn't a measly fifty pounds. In American dollars, her dowry would have been larger. However, when exchanged into pounds it came to be about five thousand pounds, just enough to be considered a generous amount, but not enough to be pursued by every fortune hunter. However to be sure, her papa hadn't made known the amount of her dowry.

Andrew pulled the curricle to a halt and jumped down. After helping Brooke down, he led her to an unoccupied bench. "Here, let's sit."

Brooke currently had no interest in the bench. "Oh, look at the flowers. They are absolutely beautiful," Brooke said, walking over to a flower bush. "Back in New York, flowers are rare. Well, not rare exactly, but they don't grow like this."

"Flowers don't grow in New York?" Andrew asked skeptically.

Brooke laughed. "Well, they grow. But with all the snow, ice, and cold, we don't get to spend very long looking at flowers—except roses of course."

"Ah, roses, one of the few flowers that thrive in cold weather."

Brooke took a seat on the bench and waited for Andrew to join her. "The rose is the most common flower found in New York," she said, trying to fill the silence.

"Is it safe to say that you like roses then?"

"Of course, I wouldn't be a true New Yorker if I didn't," she said in the thickest New York accent she could muster.

Shaking his head, Andrew took a seat next to her on the bench. "So, dahling," he drawled, matching her Yankee accent, "what color roses are your favorites?"

Brooke laughed at his imitation of her accent. "Why? Are you planning to buy me some?" She paused a second. "Oh right, I forgot you're a pauper. You can't buy them. Are you going to grow them for me?" She honestly doubted he'd ever given much thought to growing roses or any other type of flowers, for that matter.

"I'd definitely have to grow them, as I don't have the extra funds for one stem," he said earnestly. He placed his fingers under Brooke's chin and turned her head to face him so he could look deep into her eyes. "You still did not answer my question. Which color do you prefer?"

Brooke blinked a few times. Many men had touched her face, tried to hold her hand, and some had even kissed her, but she had never really been comfortable with the intimacy of it nor enjoyed it so much. Andrew's touch seemed to scorch her skin. She wet her lips and stared straight into his blue eyes before answering. "It would depend on who they were from and the reason for the gift."

Her statement seemed to baffle him. "Could you please explain what you mean?"

Still looking into his eyes, Brooke took a deep breath. "Tell me who they are from and why they are giving me roses, and I'll tell you what color they should choose."

Andrew dropped his fingers from her chin and moved them to where her hands were folded in her lap. "From me. Just because."

Brooke gasped. "Um..." She cleared her throat. "In that case, white or yellow would be the appropriate color."

"The appropriate color?" Andrew questioned, lifting his brow.

"Yes, the appropriate color." At his look of uncertainty, she went on. "Different color roses represent different things. White roses represent purity or sympathy. They are often used for bridal bouquets to show innocence. Sometimes white roses are sent to people who are sick or who have suffered a loss to represent sympathy. Yellow roses symbolize friendship or happiness. They can also be given by a friend of either sex. Therefore, from you, a man of my acquaintance or a friend, yellow or white would be appropriate."

Andrew nodded. "Didn't you forget a few colors?" he asked, smiling at her when she gave a weak nod. "What about pink or red? Why could I not give you those colors?" he asked softly, stroking the backs of her hands with his thumbs.

Brooke was distracted by his hands on hers. "In order to give those colors, the relationship and the feelings would have to be different. Deeper."

"Deeper? Does that mean that a lady's intended could give her pink or red roses?"

Distracted by his hands that had turned hers over and were now rubbing circular motions on the inside of her palms with his thumbs, Brooke nodded slightly. Moistening her lips, she said, "Yes. That would be appropriate. The pink ones could be given to your betrothed. Pink roses represent elegance and great appreciation or admiration. The red ones though, are strictly for love—true love. Maybe a betrothed could receive them, or even a woman you want to be your betrothed. A wife certainly could receive red roses—if you love her, that is. You really shouldn't be giving red roses to someone with whom you don't have a strong relationship or you don't love, for that matter. Because then she might get the wrong idea. She might think you love her, when in fact you do not have such strong feelings for her," Brooke rambled on, too busy thinking about the way his touch made her skin tingle to care about exactly what she was saying. At some point during her rambling, she wasn't sure when, his hands had removed her left glove and his fingers were dancing ever so lightly on her wrist.

When his thumb grazed her wrist again, she shivered, then suddenly jumped up and pulled her hands from his searing grasp. "Oh, my. I think we should be going," she insisted quickly, her words flying out of her mouth faster than a bird being chased by a cat. "It's getting late and I don't want Mama to wonder what has happened to us. She does worry so terribly much about us here in London. She says it is not as safe here as we're used to back home. I don't know if she thinks we are going to be nabbed right off the street or what, but she is ever so overcautious. Really, we must be going."

"All right, I shall return you at once. We wouldn't want to risk being accosted sitting here in this vacant part of the park," Andrew joked, taking to his feet.

Brooke gave a faint smile. He probably thought she was a ninny, but the truth was that he was too distracting by far, and she needed to go before she embarrassed herself. She had never felt this way when any of the other gentlemen had touched her. What was worse, he'd barely touched her in comparison to what some of them had tried to do. With other gentlemen, it tickled, or if they had calluses, they'd scratched her skin. But Andrew's touch was different. It was hot and searing. It felt perfect.

So perfect in fact, she might do something she shouldn't if she didn't put a stop to his touching at once.

The ride back to her residence was for the most part filled with companionable silence. "I enjoyed our ride today. If you are agreeable, I would like to go for another tomorrow or the next day," Andrew said, breaking the silence.

"That would be lovely," she murmured. Then she smiled wryly and added, "It will have to be tomorrow or two days hence, because the day after tomorrow is Thursday, and I have my appointment at the modiste."

Andrew shook his head. "You may want to wait a bit on that, at least until I grow you a pink rose."

Most people would be embarrassed by his direct mention of their gaffe, but Brooke was not one of them. In mock irritation she exclaimed, "You, sir, could not be so lucky. I will be waiting for a red one!"

"A red what?" asked a voice from the door.

Both Brooke and Andrew turned to see Liberty standing in the doorway, eyeing them most curiously. "Oh nothing, Liberty," Brooke said trying to turn the attention off of their conversation. How had they gotten back here so fast? "What are you doing outside on the steps?"

"Waiting for you," she stated simply. "You've been gone for more than an hour, without a chaperone I might add." She grabbed her skirt and shook it a little, still looking at them with her big, hazel eyes. "See, even Lord Townson agrees. He's nodding his head."

Andrew was in fact nodding his head, but Brooke highly doubted it was because he agreed with what Liberty was saying.

Ignoring Liberty, Andrew helped Brooke down from the curricle.

"Lord Townson, I did enjoy our afternoon together and I look forward to going again sometime," Brooke told him as a goodbye before this nonsense with Liberty could continue any further.

"I also enjoyed our afternoon, and I shall call upon you again in the near future, Miss Banks," Andrew said, taking his cue and climbing back onto the curricle.

"Wait!" cried Mama, running outside and looking all out of sorts. "Before you go, I wanted to invite you to dine with us tomorrow night. I would be absolutely delighted if you would come and join us for our evening meal." Allowing Andrew no time to agree or refuse, she quickly added, "We eat at eight o'clock, sharp. You'll need to be here a little earlier. Quarter till should be sufficient. We look forward to it." She waved to Andrew and stepped back into the house. "Come girls!" she chirped.

***

Andrew blinked at the door the Banks women had just gone through. Without hinting or directly asking, he'd just secured another approved meeting with Brooke.

At his townhouse, he ate a quick dinner then retired to his study. He had all he needed there to keep him completely occupied for about a half hour.

He glanced at his account books. Still in debt.

He picked up the newspaper. Only crime and social scandals, nothing of interest there.

Ah, a stack of correspondence that had been collecting for more than three months and was about eight inches high. With a sigh, he thumbed through the stack. With the exception of a couple of letters from his mother, it was a bunch of nonsense.

He read the letters of interest and discarded the rest, then sat staring into the fire when a slight knock sounded at the door.

All too eager for the distraction, Andrew ran over to the door and swung it wide open to find a disgruntled Addams on the other side with his mouth agape. "My lord, I do believe it is the responsibility of the butler, which currently is me, to open the doors."

"Addams," he snapped, "this is still my house and I will open any door in this house I wish. Now, what did you want?"

Stiffening his spine, Addams said proudly, "You have a guest, my lord."

"Who is it?' Andrew asked impatiently.

"His Grace, the Duke of Gateway," Addams announced with all due pomp and circumstance.

Andrew groaned, then quickly tried to cover it up when his eyes landed on Gateway not five feet away.

"Don't act so happy to see me, Townson," Gateway said with a mocking smile.

"I'm always ecstatic to see you," Andrew said without any undue sarcasm. "Come in." He gestured vaguely into his study. He really didn't want to invite him in, but it appeared he didn't have a choice. The man was already in his house.

Gateway wasted no time. He made his way into Andrew's study, poured himself a drink, and then sat down on a leather divan with all the grace of a hippopotamus.

Watching from the doorway, Andrew mumbled under his breath, "Just make yourself right at home, why don't you?"

"I think I will," Gateway smugly replied.

Andrew sat behind his desk, crossed his arms across his chest, leaned back in his chair, and just to show the duke how much he respected him, propped his feet up on his desk with the soles of his boots facing the duke. Finally, when he was comfortable, he spoke in a voice dripping with sarcasm. "To what do I owe the pleasure of your company?"

"Miss Banks," was his only reply, but it was enough.

"Yes," Andrew said, raising an eyebrow and making a rolling hand gesture to urge Gateway to continue. When it was clear that Gateway wasn't going to indulge him by saying anything more, Andrew offered, "I met her, if that's what you're asking."

"Good." Gateway nodded in approval. "And?"

Andrew contemplated what to divulge. First, he needed to determine what Gateway was doing here. Was he here to learn that Andrew had started his work, or was he fishing for details? "I found her well," Andrew answered with a sardonic smile.

"Leave off, Townson," Gateway bellowed, leaning forward in his chair. "Do you think you'll be able to pull this off or not?" His face had gone slightly red from rage and he looked as if he were ready to leap across the desk to strangle Andrew for his insolent manner.

"I do," Andrew stated evenly. Years ago he might have been a little uneasy at Gateway's manner, but not now. He learned fifteen years ago that Gateway was nothing more than a bully. But ten years ago Andrew realized that when alone, Gateway wasn't one. Gateway enjoyed giving off the impression he was tough and in control, but really, without an accomplice, he was harmless.

"Good. How soon?"

Andrew steepled his hands up by his chin as if he were in deep contemplation. "Hmm, I don't know. Within the month, I hope, perhaps sooner. Depends on how quickly I can get her to trust me. I know you want this done quickly. However, it won't do for her to be unwilling. If I try to compromise her, which we both know is what it will take—" he leveled a murderous glare on Gateway—"too early in our relationship, it will not be viewed that she was a willing participant. I don't want this to look like I'm forcing her. Then, neither of us would get what we want." Even though he was an earl and a peer of the realm, he was not above the law. Nor did he want rumors circulating that he was the kind to force himself on a woman.

Gateway's eyes took on a new spark, a rather scary spark at that. "So who is the lucky, or should I say unlucky, chit?"

"Miss Banks," Andrew mocked. He didn't like this whole arrangement, and he liked dealing with Gateway even less, so he had to take his fun where he could. For now, that was intentionally irritating Gateway.

"I know 'Miss Banks'," Gateway snapped, his eyes burning with fire. "Which 'Miss Banks'?"

Andrew looked straight at Gateway and with a monotone voice said, "Miss Brooke Banks."

Much to Andrew's surprise, Gateway hooted and snorted with laughter. This drew Andrew up short. He had never seen Gateway behave this way. What could he possibly find funny about Andrew's selection? "Pray tell, what has you laughing like a villain in a bad melodrama?"

"Oh, you'll see. You will see!" was all Gateway would say. After he regained his composure, he added, "I suppose you're going to start 'courting' her, then?"

"Yes, I am. I met all the Banks women yesterday. And I took Brooke on a ride in Hyde Park earlier today." He leaned back in his chair to get a better look at Gateway's face. "Oh, and did I mention that I have plans to dine with the family tomorrow night?"

"Good, all good, Townson," Gateway said and nodded. "You'll be glad to know I've cleared your debt on that estate in Essex. I had no idea it was so much. Nonetheless, it has all been paid. The deed is waiting for you once I get notification that the Banks family has boarded the fastest ship to New York."

"You will be the first to know when they're on their way home." Andrew folded his hands in his lap and examined his nails. "Well, maybe not the first, I suppose all of London will know at the same time. When the scandal sheets tear Miss Banks apart, that is," he amended, fighting a slight twinge of guilt.

"I look forward to it," Gateway said curtly.

"I do wonder why it is that you are so desperate to have this family gone." Andrew idly drummed his fingers along the arm of his chair. "They seem decent enough. Did one of the sisters cut you?"

Gateway's face turned rigid and he sprang to his feet. "That is none of your concern, Townson. Just do what you agreed to. Charm Miss Banks out of her gown and be done with it," he snapped, making a hasty path to the door.

# Chapter 6

"I cannot believe Mama invited him here for dinner," Brooke said, looking around the most distasteful dining room she had ever laid eyes on.

"Brooke, Mama did not invite him. She trapped him. The poor man didn't even have a chance to deny her request," Liberty said.

"Liberty, I'm shocked you didn't ramble on about the improper manner in which Mama handled the invitation," Madison added.

All three of them burst into a fit of giggles.

"She has a point. You take the proprieties all too seriously. You should relax a bit. If you did, then you would certainly have more fun." Brooke tapped her finger against her cheek. How exactly had Uncle Edward come to possess all the dead animals in this room?

"I know. I just want to be accepted." Liberty pointed to the mounted squirrel on the wall that she wanted a footman to haul away. "I don't have Madison's good looks or your outgoing personality. Therefore, if I want to attract a husband, I have to be able to show potential suitors that I'll do a good job performing a wife's duties. Men here care about dinner parties and their wives being perfect ladies out in society. If I can prove to a man that I can do those things, then I might land a husband."

"Dearest, you worry too much about catching a husband. You're only nineteen, you still have plenty of time to find a husband," Brooke reassured her. Then she grabbed the footman by the arm. "Stop. I think our efforts here are futile." Even if they removed all the mounted animals and most of the decorations, and found some way to cover up the table, they would still be left with a hideous dining room. They couldn't cover the sixteen dining chairs, the carpet, or the wallpaper. "This room is hopeless. Let's just leave it alone. We can set up a small table in the parlor and have a cozy dinner like we did back home."

Mama came into the room, beaming. "That is a brilliant idea," she agreed. With a snap of her fingers and a few directives to the footman, a makeshift dining room was created in the parlor. "Why don't you girls go get ready for our guest?" Mama said to Liberty and Madison. "Brooke, I have just the gown you should wear tonight. It may not be a perfect fit in all areas, but I think it just might work. Meet me in my bedchamber in fifteen minutes." With that, the girls were on their way.

Brooke sat on her mother's bed and watched Mama breeze into the room. She was humming a merry tune with a wistful expression on her face that made Brooke shake her head ruefully. Wordlessly, Mama walked behind her dressing screen and came back holding a crimson gown with a silk bodice and sleeves and eight panels of velvet that made up the length of the skirt. The bodice was modestly cut, just perfect for Brooke who had little in the way of a natural bosom. Brooke stepped closer to examine the embroidery. It had little rosettes all along the hem and cuffs, alternating colors: white, pink, and red.

"It's beautiful," Brooke exclaimed.

"It surely is, and you'll look beautiful wearing it. Your cream colored slippers will have to do as I no longer have the original matching slippers."

"Original? How long have you had this gown?" Brooke asked, running her slender fingers along the fabric and wondering if it were even possible to do as her mother asked and wear the dress. Though she and her mother were close in height and build, they were not identical. However, Madison was good with a needle, perhaps between the two they could make a few alterations before dinner for it to suffice.

"Longer than you've been alive," Mama retorted. "I wore this dress the night I met Papa. And as I've always said, it was love at first sight. I hope you have the same luck when you wear it tonight." She gave a quick wink.

Brooke was shocked and a little unsure what exactly her mother meant. "But I've already met Lord Townson."

"Yes, I know," Mama agreed. "But maybe tonight he'll see you differently and fall madly in love with you. Not that I believe for one second he hasn't already started down that path. Wouldn't that be wonderful?"

Mama looked so excited and hopeful that Brooke didn't know what to say. She didn't want to crush her mother's feelings, so instead she just stared blankly at her.

As if sensing Brooke's lack of enthusiasm, Mama went on. "I think he fancies you. I think if you give him a little encouragement —" she shook the gown, indicating it was the "encouragement" she was referring to— "he could develop true feelings for you. Just think of it, you could marry the earl. You would be a countess," she cried excitedly. "My daughter a countess! Oh, you must wear the dress tonight."

Excitement is hard to contain, and it spreads so easily, soon Brooke found herself smiling right along with Mama. "Thank you, Mama."

"You're welcome." Mama shoved the gown into Brooke's hands. "Now go, he'll be here before you know it."

Walking down the hall to her room, Brooke stared at the elegant red gown she carried. A small smile came over her lips and she murmured, "It may not steal his heart, but it *will* capture his undivided attention."

***

Andrew entered the drawing room, his eyes landing on where Mrs. Banks, Miss Liberty, and the middle Miss Banks were seated. Where was Brooke?

The ladies stood. He bowed and they curtsied. Then Mrs. Banks complimented Brooke's middle sister's dress, indirectly informing him of her name. Andrew took a seat on the settee and wondered again where Brooke was. Knowing it would be impolite to ask without at least acting interested in them first, he said, "I trust you have all had a chance to visit the excellent museums London has to offer?"

"Museums?" Liberty asked sheepishly, looking at him under her lashes. "Well no, I don't believe we've been yet."

"Oh, Liberty, don't play coy with the man," Madison broke in, ending Liberty's awkward flirting. "We all know that you have no interest in museums, so stop hedging for an invitation. Your interest in a museum is about as great as my interest in being pursued by gentlemen, and we all know that's nonexistent."

Andrew looked to Madison and ignored Mrs. Banks reprimanding her for her vulgar comment. He was too caught up with the idea that this young lady had no interest in gentlemen. Didn't all young ladies have an interest in men? If she didn't, did that mean she was interested in ladies? He knew that some gentlemen were only interested in other gentlemen, but he'd never met, or even heard of a lady who had those interests. If that were true, he could use that information to send the Banks family away instead of compromising Brooke. Seizing the opportunity, he asked, "What do you mean you have no interest in gentlemen, Miss Banks? I was under the impression all young ladies wanted to marry and have children. Does that not interest you?"

Her face took on an even more distant look, if that was possible, and she shrugged. "That is the dream of most, but not all."

Andrew nodded. That wasn't enough of a confirmation for him to start rumors to the effect that she had "different" interests. He needed hard proof, such as a verbal or physical confirmation. Otherwise it was too risky to try to expose this. She could turn up at a ball the next night and dance with every gentleman in attendance. That alone would disprove any rumors. Besides, he'd never heard of such interests before, so the credibility was already tenuous. Best to leave that cat securely in its bag.

Trying to take on an air of the comforting older brother, Andrew said, "Well, one day you might change your mind. I am sure there are many good men out there who would love to have you as their wife."

Mrs. Banks tittered and cooed.

Liberty snorted.

Madison shrugged.

Andrew cleared his throat. "I'm very flattered you invited me to join you for dinner tonight," he said, trying to get a conversation going. He hated silence.

"We are flattered you agreed," said Mrs. Banks.

"As if he had a choice," Madison muttered under her breath.

With a sharp look from her mother, she murmured an awkward apology and fidgeted with the sleeve of her orange gown.

Andrew didn't much care for the color orange, but on her it seemed to fit. He couldn't explain why. Maybe it was because it was a pale orange and not a bright, vibrant, or burnt orange, but pale, almost like a peach. It suited her well.

Feeling as if he needed to say something, because once again the silence was becoming unbearable with everyone looking at each other and nodding, Andrew asked of no one in particular, "If men and museums are not of interest, what does hold your attention?"

"Reading," Liberty answered quietly.

"Ah, reading," Andrew repeated, trying to think of something to ask to get her, or anyone for that matter, to talk. "What kind of books?"

"Etiquette," Madison answered bluntly for her sister.

Andrew thought she was probably being brutally honest with her answer, but how could he comment? He couldn't. Instead, he just looked around the room, hoping for something to end their torture.

But no redemption came.

He sat with three of the four Banks women for a quarter of an hour, staring, nodding, and murmuring when necessary. All the while he wondered where in the world Brooke was. He hoped she would be there soon. It was not his plan to spend the evening with her sisters and mother. He had come specifically to be with her.

Finally, Andrew decided he'd waited long enough. "Pardon, but are we to be joined by anyone else for dinner?" There, he'd asked, and not in a way sounding too eager or impatient—or so he hoped.

Mrs. Banks was too clever not to see what he really meant. "Yes, my husband will join us soon. He just returned from visiting a country vicar and will be down shortly." She flashed him a knowing smile. "But I get the feeling that is not who you were asking about. Was it?" Not really making him answer her and embarrass himself, she continued, "Brooke will be down any minute. I thought she would have been down by now, but she might have had trouble with her gown."

"Gown trouble?" Andrew asked dubiously. "Surely her maid can take care of that quickly." When the middle Miss Banks laughed outright, Liberty gaped at him, and Mrs. Banks turned red. His brows snapped together. "She doesn't have a maid, does she?"

"No, my lord, she does not," Mrs. Bank replied without a hint of emotion. "In America, people do not usually have a personal servant. Not only does society not dictate it, but the ladies there are usually a lot more independent."

Andrew took in her statement. He wasn't sure how to respond, but didn't want to leave them feeling embarrassed or insulted. Finally, he said quietly, "I can tell that your girls are very independent." He personally had only a scant number of servants, all of whom did multiple jobs, but none acting as his valet—he'd always thought it was uncomfortable having someone else dress and groom him.

Again they sat in uncomfortable silence, continuing exactly where they'd left off: staring, nodding, and waiting for an outside source to put them all out of their misery.

Finally, their redemption came in the form of one Mr. John Banks.

Andrew had never seen John Banks before, but he recognized him instantly when he walked in. He looked exactly like his brother, Baron Watson. Both were slightly taller than average and had pale skin, light blue eyes, and blond hair. While Brooke resembled her mother with her petite frame and dark hair and eyes, Madison undeniably favored their father. Liberty was more of a mix of the two.

As Mr. Banks strolled in, he looked fondly at his wife and daughters before noticing there was a guest in the room. He quickly bowed to Andrew then looked to his wife to introduce them.

"John, this is Andrew Black, Lord Townson, and this," she said, gesturing to her husband, "is John Banks, my husband."

"It is a pleasure to meet you, sir," Andrew said, with a slight smile.

"It is my pleasure, my lord. I wasn't aware we were entertaining such a lofty guest. To what do we owe this pleasure?" Mr. Banks asked with a hint of disbelief.

Before Andrew could answer the question that was clearly leveled at him, Mrs. Banks jumped in. "He was invited."

Mr. Banks' gaze shot to his wife and his clear blue eyes asked her velvet brown eyes an unspoken question: why?

"I personally invited him to dine with us. He's courting Brooke," she said, beaming brighter than a five-hundred-candle chandelier. Then, because she could definitely be termed a matchmaking mama and had the subtly of a sledgehammer, she squeaked, "I believe he has a *tendre* for her. Oh, isn't it exciting!"

Mr. Banks, probably used to his wife's theatrics, just nodded.

Andrew, unused to the same theatrics, could feel heat creep up his neck and face. Now, everyone thought he was besotted with a girl he barely knew. What could he do? Deny it? No, because that could put a swift end to his visits with Brooke and make his mission difficult, if not impossible. Anyway, he liked seeing her. He was not completely sure why, but he enjoyed her company all the same.

Following a mental shrug, Andrew went for it. With his best smile, he looked straight at Mr. Banks and said, "I do enjoy your daughter's company." That was true enough. "I believe she has the same interest in me. So naturally, if you're agreeable, I should like to court her."

"This is highly unusual, young man. You do realize that, do you not?" Mr. Banks asked.

Andrew nodded. He knew he'd misstepped. He may not have been able to help it, but he did know what he'd done and sorely hoped the Banks family was not so high in the instep that Mr. Banks would deny his request.

"Yes, sir. I do know that this courtship has taken place in an unusual manner, and I do apologize for it. I give my word that I will conduct it from this point forward with more attention to what is proper and the respect due you and your daughter, sir." *Stop talking, Andrew. If you keep giving your word to conduct things properly, it will be even more difficult when it comes time to ruin the chit.*

"I am pleased to hear it, my lord," John said, nodding with approval.

They returned to their seats to wait for the missing Banks daughter to appear, and Andrew glimpsed Liberty looking at him with a hint of a smile. He knew what she was thinking without even asking. Once again, he had breached society's mandates by not asking her father for approval to court Brooke. There was a lot Miss Liberty was going to need to learn. Not everything follows propriety. But that wouldn't matter to her in a few months when she'd be on her way back to America. Andrew allowed himself a little smile. In a month, hopefully no more, the Banks family would be on a ship back to New York, and he'd be out of London at his country estate turning a profit. It was a good thing he'd be turning a profit, because he was about to enter self-imposed exile.

Andrew was entertaining further thoughts about what his life would be like in a month or so when Brooke made her entrance. When he saw her, she rendered him breathless—literally.

# Chapter 7

Brooke's entrance into the drawing room was deliberately slow. She was making sure to attract as much attention as she could, and it worked. Andrew had thought her younger sister was the most beautiful of the three, but just now, his opinion had forever been altered. From now on, Brooke would hold that title in his mind.

Belatedly, Andrew stood up and murmured an apology for not rising sooner. He took a deep breath, feeling embarrassed he'd made such a fool of himself by gasping and forgetting to stand when she walked in. Nothing could be done about it now. He would just have to make the best of the situation. He was not the only one so struck by Brooke's beauty that manners were forgotten. Liberty not only did not say anything about his mistake, but her face didn't even indicate she'd noticed it.

Andrew truly felt remiss about not standing when Brooke made her grand entrance. He felt as uncomfortable as if he'd he been at a wedding and not stood when the bride walked down the aisle. He shrugged off the feeling, and continued to survey her. She was breathtaking.

She had on a beautiful gown constructed from different swaths of red material. Some were silk, some velvet. The bodice swooped moderately to give everyone in the room a modest glance at the delicate slope of the top of her breasts. It was obvious the gown had originally been made for someone a few inches shorter, because when she walked, he'd been able to see more of her cream-colored slipper than she probably intended to show. There also appeared to be something a bit amiss around the bodice of the gown. Exactly what it was he couldn't put his finger on, but it didn't matter anyway. She shined like one very well-polished ruby which caused him to strain to think of anything coherent to say.

He swallowed a lump in his throat and waited for someone else to break the silence. Hopefully any comment would be enough to pull him out of this fog.

Brooke appeared proud of the reaction she had created. "I spoke to Turner before coming in. He said dinner was ready." She smiled.

The group nodded their understanding, not bothering to notice or care that their butler was not going to come and get them as was customary. The group formed a line and walked down the hall toward the dining room.

Mr. and Mrs. Banks led the group, and when Mr. Banks tried to make a turn for the dining room, his wife stopped him. "I thought we'd eat in the parlor tonight. It's more conducive for entertaining guests," she murmured.

Mr. Banks gave a nod of agreement about the new dining location and smiled. "Though the parlor is more acceptable, I do wonder if it would be easier on everyone's digestive systems to eat outside."

Mrs. Banks gave a little smile at her husband's remark.

At the back of the line, Brooke lightly rested her hand on Andrew's arm while he brought his free hand up to cover hers and give it a light squeeze. He enjoyed that she became a little less graceful in her step when he did so. Apparently she wasn't as immune to him as she would have him believe.

When they finally made it to the parlor, Andrew abruptly stopped and blinked. Never in his life had he seen such a small dining table. It could not have been more than six, maybe seven, feet long and it had only six chairs. Even when eating by himself, he had never eaten at such a small table. How were they all going to fit? There wasn't a need for more chairs precisely—there were six chairs and six people—but they were *so* close together. There was no way it was going to be a comfortable meal with everyone practically touching each other. Or would it? A sly smile took his lips.

Brooke stumbled slightly because of Andrew's sudden stop. She cocked her head and looked from him to the dining table, as if she were trying to understand what had brought on his reaction. She must have realized that it was the size of the table and how closely they were to be seated because she said, "Unless you want to look at mounted squirrels, opossums, and other wild game while eating, you'll have to get past your discomfort."

Andrew turned to look at Brooke and arched one eyebrow in hopes that she would elaborate as to why he'd have to look at such images while eating if he did not get past his discomfort, as she put it.

But before Brooke could explain, her mother started talking. "Isn't our dining room quaint?" Mrs. Banks studied his face, almost as if she were trying to read his response rather than listen to it.

"Quite," he replied, forgetting about the animals and wondering how everyone was going to gather around this little table. For pity's sake, the seats were so close together, it looked as though all the silverware was running together. How was one to tell which pieces were theirs and which belonged to their neighbor?

Mrs. Banks gave a hesitant smile. "I know this may seem a little irregular for you. However, we are a cozy little family, and we enjoy eating closely together when possible. It makes it easier to all engage in the same conversation," she said with what was clearly a large dose of false bravado.

Silently everybody took their seats. Mr. Banks was at one end of the table with Mrs. Banks seated at the opposite end. Brooke's sisters sat together on one side of the table, while he and Brooke occupied the other.

Once they were all seated, and had said grace of course, they began to eat one of the most delicious and filling meals Andrew had eaten in more than a year. Being impoverished had changed his eating habits considerably, but for tonight, he was going to eat as if he were one of the richest in the land.

"How was your visit to the country today, my dear?" Mrs. Banks asked her husband.

Mr. Banks answered his wife, telling her all about his visit with the country vicar including how the two of them had exchanged sermon ideas.

The conversation turned to the errands that they would run on the morrow. Andrew just nodded occasionally and said yes or no here and there. He was more interested in thinking of how fetching Brooke looked in that gown than in what they were discussing.

"Why do we all need to go to the modiste at the same time?" Liberty asked, after she wiped her face with her napkin. "They only allow us one seamstress. It becomes dreadfully boring waiting for my turn."

"You could bring something to work on while waiting," Mr. Banks suggested.

"Perhaps a book," Madison said helpfully.

Liberty ignored her suggestion and looked only at her father. "Why do we need new gowns anyway? Are we not planning to go home soon?"

"What else would you do with your day if you did not spend it with us on Bond Street?" Brooke asked.

"Girls," their father broke in, "there is no need to quarrel. Liberty, you will join your mother, Brooke, and Madison tomorrow to have new gowns made. You will need them for balls, soirees, and such. I should think we will be here at least another six months."

The females at the table went silent. Andrew assumed they were thinking of what Mr. Banks had said about staying for at least six more months and all the events they would likely attend in that time.

A moment or two later, Andrew turned to Brooke, who was currently more interested in her dinner than the conversation, and quietly asked, "I see you wore red tonight; was there any special reason?"

Brooke blushed slightly before she smiled at him. "It's just a coincidence, nothing more."

"Hmm. A coincidence, you say?" he said, his eyebrow raising and his face full of amusement. "I don't think so. I think you wore that gown knowing I favor the color red and you wanted to get my attention. I must say, well done. You certainly got my full attention."

"I know," Brooke replied smugly.

Andrew chuckled. She probably did know the effect she had on men, specifically when she wore that gown. He leaned over and looked at the hem more closely, then said loud enough for the whole table to hear, "Your gown is very lovely, Miss Banks. I particularly like the roses along the hem." When she glared daggers at him, he smiled. "Miss Banks, I am a bit of a numbskull when it comes to such things as flowers and their significance. Would you please inform me of the significance of the different colored roses?"

The whole table once again examined Brooke's gown, all looking at the various places where rosettes were visible, which just happened to be her bodice. Brooke's face turned pink again, but Andrew didn't think it was because everyone was looking at her. He was sure it was because he was touching her ankle with his foot.

Andrew enjoyed that she had become flustered and unable to speak. He enjoyed it even more a moment later when she jumped a little after he slipped his foot out of his shoe and ran it along her lower calf. Though he kept his foot outside her gown, her face told him it was still causing the desired effect on her. It was making her uncomfortable, which meant soon, she'd be rambling nonsense. His male pride soared.

She turned to look at him with an innocent face and sweetly asked, "What makes you think I would know anything about roses and their meanings, my lord?"

Andrew may not be able to get to her with words, but he was definitely unsettling her with his foot. "I just thought it was something that would be of interest to you, since you are from New York—" he paused in mock contemplation— "which, if I remember correctly, would mean you have seen quite a few. Or was I misinformed?"

"Very true," agreed Mrs. Banks, oblivious to the tension between Brooke and Andrew. "Roses are abundant in the state of

New York. In fact, I daresay that if there were ever to be such a thing as a state flower, the rose would be it!"

The men in the room shook their heads at Mrs. Banks's suggestion that a state would ever be identified by a particular flower or use it as a symbol. Good thing men ran the government. Such ideas were ridiculous! Leave it to a woman to think a state needed a "state flower". What next, a state fruit? Andrew snorted at the very idea. Glancing over to Mr. Banks, he rather thought the man agreed with him, but didn't wish to hurt his wife's feelings by saying anything.

"Mrs. Banks," Andrew said, never taking his eyes off Brooke's pink face while he spoke to her mother. "One would assume that if roses were so commonplace where you hail from, that a person might find them of interest and know what they signify. Right?"

"That is very true. All three of my daughters enjoy roses. Brooke even planted some very beautiful rose bushes in our balcony garden back in the city," Mrs. Banks said, pride filling her voice and face.

"Ah, so my original assumption that you would know about roses and their meanings was not amiss," Andrew observed aloud. His eyes were trained on Brooke as his foot continued to observe her ankle—under her skirt.

"Umm…uh…" Brooke stammered. "I know a little of roses and growing them. However, I cannot begin to know why you would have a sudden interest in their meanings."

"Well, that's simple enough. You see, I was admiring your gown, as I'm sure everyone else in the room has done at some point this evening, when I noticed that you have white, pink, and red roses along the edges. Being a sort that is always thirsting for knowledge, I wondered what, if anything, the different colors meant."

Brooke acted like she barely understood what he had said. Her face took on a faraway look. Her wide eyes were staring across the room, her breathing became shallow, and her mouth hung slightly open. Andrew assumed the reason for her incomprehension was because he kept running his stocking-clad foot up and down her shapely calf.

When Andrew gave a delicate cough, she started. “As it happens, I do know a little about growing roses. I’m not certain I would be the most knowledgeable about their meanings, however.” Her voice was low and held a hint of agitation.

“Poppycock,” Madison said with a wave of her hand, not recognizing her sister’s uncomfortable state. “Brooke knows more about roses than the rest of us combined. She adores them. Not only does she grow them, she also has a book about their meanings, and when certain roses are acceptable to give and receive. On more than one occasion I have been bored to tears hearing all about it.”

Andrew froze in astonishment. Not only did he just learn how much stock Brooke put into roses, but that was more than he had heard Madison say in all of his visits combined. Maybe she wasn’t as featherbrained as he originally thought.

Breaking into his thoughts, Liberty said, “Tell him the meanings. He asked.”

“Yes, I did ask. Please, tell me everything you know. I’m very curious,” Andrew encouraged.

Brooke looked straight into his eyes, which he knew were alight with amusement. His foot, however, was no longer on her leg. “Their meanings are easy really. White ones stand for purity. Pink are for adoration or appreciation. And the red ones, they stand for love.”

While she’d been speaking, Andrew had shifted slightly in his chair. He moved just enough that he could be closer to her without drawing anyone’s attention. Once he was satisfied nobody detected anything, he boldly pressed his thigh against hers. “Are you trying to say you represent all three of these things at once by wearing them all at the same time?” Andrew asked. His voice took on a more silky tone, while his thigh pressed even harder against hers.

“No,” Brooke answered with a slight hitch in her voice. “The gown is in no way a statement about me. It is just that—a gown. I was telling you what the roses would mean if being given in real life.”

"I think the roses on your gown could be considered a statement," Andrew said matter-of-factly. When nobody else in the room said anything, Andrew decided it was time to put on the charm and woo the whole family at once. "I'd assume that the white ones, meaning purity, would reflect you, as you are very innocent. The pink ones could symbolize that there is much to adore *and* admire about you, which I have come to realize in the past few minutes. Furthermore, the red ones, symbolizing love, could be a personal statement of how easy it would be for someone to have that emotion for you."

When everyone was silent after his speech, except Mrs. Banks, who let out a wistful gasp, Andrew realized he had just made a huge fool of himself. Instead of saying something clever, witty, and relatively romantic, he had practically just declared his love and adoration for this woman. A woman he had no business having any kind of feelings for, especially love.

The silence stretched out for a few minutes before Mrs. Banks gave a delicate cough. Andrew couldn't be sure but he took that to mean, she was trying to remind them to close their mouths that were gaping with awe, and for Brooke to acknowledge the compliment. Neither of which happened right away.

It was Mr. Banks who ended the torturous silence. "Well, now that we all have a thorough understanding of how roses relate to Brooke's personality, I should like to inform all of you that we are going to see my brother in a week. He and his wife are hosting a house party and we have been invited. Naturally, I told him we would be delighted to attend."

This was certainly good news for Andrew. The baron's oldest son Alex was one of the few people of the *ton* Andrew considered a true friend, which meant he would be able to secure an invitation to the house party. This could work out very well for him and his plans.

"Are we to go to Bath, then?" Liberty inquired of no one in particular.

"We can go to Bath if you desire, but their estate is actually about ten miles outside of Bath," John informed his daughter matter-of-factly.

"I should like to visit a bathhouse," Liberty said excitedly. "Lady Olivia Sinclair makes trips regularly. She says the baths keep you in good health."

"Lady Olivia needs all the help she can get on that score," Brooke quipped.

"How so?" Mrs. Banks asked. She cocked her head and her brow knit a little in confusion as she looked to her daughters to supply an answer.

"Lady Olivia is always unwell," Madison answered. "Why, just last week when I was to accompany her to buy more ribbons, at her request might I add, her butler informed me she had taken to her room for the day with a headache, backache, fever, and a leg cramp."

"If you ask me, the girl likes to be sick," Brooke added.

"Exactly so," Andrew agreed. "I've known her older brother since we were boys together at Eton. He confided in all of us that she was the sickliest creature he had ever met, and that she loved to take to the sickroom. He even said he believed half of her 'conditions' were made up just for attention."

"I bet her family despairs she shall never marry," Liberty said, shaking her head.

"Indeed, who would want such a sickly wife? Especially if the man in question needed an heir," Mrs. Banks said with true sympathy ringing in her voice.

Andrew knew the answer to that: any man who needed enough money. Her family was one of the richest in England. "Her dowry will help her make a match when it's time," Andrew said smoothly, silently praying that her money wouldn't be needed to secure him as said match.

"Shall we retire to the drawing room? Perhaps we could play a game," Mrs. Banks suggested when silence filled the room once again.

Though her words came out sounding like a suggestion, Andrew knew her meaning was not. There was no mistaking her tone. They were going to play a parlor game.

On the way to the drawing room, Andrew leaned down close to Brooke's ear and whispered, "I do believe you look good in red." He said the words so low that he was sure nobody else could have heard them, but just to make sure, he deliberately slowed his steps so they could put some distance between them and the rest of her family.

"Yes, I agree. Mama says it's my color."

"It's your color, indeed. I do believe anything you don that's red will look good on you. Especially something red and perhaps transparent," Andrew said in a silky tone.

Brooke gave him a sharp look and gestured to where the rest of her family was just steps ahead of them, possibly within earshot.

"It's clear you do not wish to talk about your trousseau any longer. Instead we shall discuss your visit to Bath," he mused.

"It shall be quite refreshing to get out of the city and see some of the country," Brooke responded flatly.

Andrew stopped in the hall and turned to fully face Brooke. "Yes, the countryside shall be refreshing. It shall put some color in your cheeks, I am quite sure." Then Andrew's voice took on a deep husky tone and he added, "The baths your sister spoke of will add some color, too."

At his comment, her face took on some color right there in the hallway of her uncle's London townhouse. Even though she was an innocent, she had understood his innuendo and it made her blush, just as he had hoped.

"I don't think it's appropriate for you to be talking to me about something as personal as bathing," Brooke said in an unsteady tone.

"Not appropriate?" Andrew asked quietly, his voice dripping with mock horror while his hands flew to his chest and his eyes went wide. "I wouldn't want to offend your sensibilities, I assure you. However, when did you begin to care about what was appropriate and inappropriate? Have you been reading Liberty's etiquette manuals?"

"No, I have not," Brooke snapped. "The point is, you have been overly friendly all evening and I would like it if you would stop."

Andrew raised a brow at her. "Overly friendly, is that what you call it? I remember you saying some things that could be considered overly friendly."

"Like what?" is what Andrew expected her to say, but instead, "Stop looking at me that way," was her response.

"How am I looking at you?"

"Like you want to kiss me," Brooke answered breathlessly.

Andrew inched his face a little closer to hers. "Maybe I do." As he said it, he realized it was true; he did want to kiss her. But that was not advantageous. "Maybe I don't."

"Maybe you don't?" Brooke asked disbelievingly. "Every man who has looked at me the way you are right now has tried to kiss me."

"Every man? How many have there been?" he asked, without a hint of shock in his voice. She was a beautiful young woman. He'd be more surprised if there hadn't been any.

Brooke gave a forced shrug. "Not so many."

Andrew decided to let that pass. Who was he to care how many men had tried to kiss her? Just because he wanted to kiss her didn't give him a right to demand the names of all the other cads who already had. "Well then, my dear, you have a lot to learn about men. I, for one, do not intend to kiss you." Then silently, he added, "Yet."

Brooke flushed with what he thought to be embarrassment. She cleared her throat. "I think we should join the others."

Andrew nodded his affirmation and they continued down the hall in silence.

They were immediately accosted by Mrs. Banks when they stepped into the drawing room. "We have just decided on teams for charades. You two shall be a team. Liberty and Madison will be another team, and Mr. Banks and I will make up the third team. Why don't you go sit down on the red settee and wait while Madison and Liberty are out practicing their scene?" she said as happily as a child who had just been given a new toy.

"All right, Mama," Brooke said, walking to the settee.

When they were seated, Andrew turned to Brooke. "Are we really playing charades? I haven't played this game since I was in short pants." He tried to keep the annoyance and disbelief from his tone.

"It's Mama's favorite. There's no use in fighting it. It's better to just indulge her by playing."

Just then Liberty and Madison came in, ready to do their scene. Their faces gave away that they were both quite proud of what they had thought up and were trying extremely hard not to giggle about it. Maybe this wouldn't be so bad after all.

Madison and Liberty walked to the middle of the drawing room where Madison bowed to Liberty, and Liberty curtsied to Madison. Madison extended her hand and Liberty took it then they started to dance.

At first their dancing was very graceful, both Madison and Liberty smiling brightly at each other. He couldn't tell if their smiles were part of the act or because they were on the verge of laughter.

After a minute, Andrew began to wonder what in the world they were acting out. Was he supposed to be guessing? All he could tell was that two people were dancing, that could be anything. That's when it all changed.

Liberty suddenly made a big production of some imaginary object at her feet. She was dancing out of step and swishing her skirts around violently with her hips. Then in a split second, she lost her balance and toppled to the ground, pulling Madison right along with her.

Andrew immediately jumped up, ignoring what he could have sworn sounded distinctly like a dog's bark, and rushed over to them. "Are you all right?" he asked, trying to help Madison off the floor. To his amazement, they were both laughing. Madison was laughing so hard her body was shaking, and Liberty was letting out peals of hysterical laughter, and so were their parents. Apparently everyone in the room, except for him, understood what had just happened. They were all laughing—everyone but Brooke. Brooke's face looked slightly pink, and he could be wrong, but it looked as if she was on the verge of tears. What in the world was going on here?

"We're fine! We're fine!" Madison fairly shouted.

"It was all part of the act," Liberty said in between bursts of giggles.

"What exactly was that act from?" He sincerely wanted to know, too. His understanding of charades was one acted out a popular play, book, or poem, but he had no idea what this specific act was from, or why it would have such an ill effect on Brooke.

"It's Brooke!" Liberty squealed.

"What's Brooke?" Andrew asked, looking back at Brooke who sat motionless.

"The act is about Brooke," Mrs. Banks clarified for a dumbfounded Andrew. "It was one of Brooke's first balls in New York. Prince Nikolai from Russia was visiting and had asked Brooke to dance with him. Before the dance started, Mrs. Clemmens gave Mopsy, her dreadful poodle, to a footman to take him outside for a little walk. The footman lost hold of the dog and it ran onto the dance floor. A few minutes later, Brooke lost her balance and fell to the ground, bringing the prince with her. As if that didn't attract enough attention, she really got full attention when Mopsy started barking and came scrambling out of Brooke's skirt."

The whole room erupted in laughter again.

Andrew swung his gaze to Brooke. She didn't even have a slight smile. Her face was a light red and her lower lip was trembling ever so slightly. Her hands were in her lap, clamped tightly into two fists. She was squeezing them so tightly her knuckles were going white, and her fingernails were digging so hard into her palms he wouldn't be surprised if in a moment there would be a trickle of red running down her palms. What he couldn't understand was if she was embarrassed that it had happened, or that it was being told to a suitor.

He walked across the room and sat down next to her again. The rest of her family was caught up retelling the story. Far too distracted to notice the two of them. He picked up one of Brooke's hands. He uncurled her fingers and with his thumb, then rubbed her palm where she had left four half-moon-shaped marks from squeezing so tightly. A minute later, under his ministrations, the muscles in her hand softened. "We've all had our moments. Some of them are worse than others," he told her soothingly, giving her hand a friendly squeeze.

"It seems my family loves to relive mine," Brooke said very quietly through trembling lips.

Her face was still not back to normal and her eyes looked wet, but he saw no actual tears. His heart squeezed in his chest, but he didn't believe her family had done it with the intent to upset her so much. "You know they only did that because they love you."

Brooke shrugged.

"It's true. I may not know your family very well, but from what I've seen they love you very much. I would be willing to bet my whole fortune, which is just slightly more than forty pounds, that not only do they love you, but I think Liberty and Madison are envious it was you, and not either of them, who gave Prince Nikolai an American experience he'll never forget."

Brooke cracked a smile. A moment of silence passed before she spoke. "I just wish they hadn't decided to act that particular scene out in front of company. It makes me look like an absolute idiot."

Andrew chucked. "It wasn't your fault, you know. And trust me, it could have been worse. Knowing you just the little that I do, I would imagine this incident is probably far from the most humiliating thing that has ever happened to you."

"Perhaps we should play something else?" Mrs. Banks said suddenly, seeming to realize something was wrong.

"Perhaps we should all call it a night," Mr. Banks suggested.

"Indeed," Andrew replied, giving a thankful look to Mr. Banks. "It has been a most pleasant evening. I have enjoyed your hospitality." Then turning to Brooke he asked, "Would you be interested in joining me at the British Museum the day after tomorrow?"

"That would be lovely," Brooke murmured.

Andrew bowed to the family and made his exit.

***

"I shall retire now," Brooke announced immediately after Andrew was gone.

"I would say the evening was a success," Carolina chirped.

"How would you define success, Carolina?" John asked, not unkindly, folding his hands in his lap and gazing at his wife.

"Brooke has secured another outing with the earl. I think that makes it a success," Carolina clarified.

"That's true, but she also ended her evening embarrassed and near tears," John added solemnly.

"I don't think so," Liberty argued. "What is there for her to be embarrassed about? We all know it wasn't even her fault it happened."

"Perhaps it's that she had one of her most humiliating moments put on display in front of a gentleman," John answered. He may not pretend to know the mind of his daughter, but he'd spent enough time in the presence of others during his work as a minister to know enough about feelings to know something was out of place where Brooke was concerned. Exactly what, he couldn't say. But something was certainly off.

"Oh, do be serious, John," Carolina said dismissively. "Brooke found it just as humorous when it happened as everyone else did. She even went around for weeks, telling anyone within earshot about the incident. That includes the countless number of suitors she had back in New York." She paused. "I even heard her recount the story just last fall to that Davis boy we all thought she'd marry. They both found it highly amusing."

"Perhaps this time it's different. Mayhap she has stronger feelings for this one," John mused.

# Chapter 8

Andrew wondered when his life had turned into a giant game. The worst part was he didn't know what piece in the game he was playing: the pawn or the master manipulator. It all depended on which other players were present at the time. For now, he was going to play the manipulator, again.

Andrew had been searching for his friend, Alex Banks, for more than an hour. Finally, he found him at his club, sitting at a table and reading a newspaper.

"Alex," Andrew called, catching his attention.

"Ho there, old chap," Alex countered.

Alex really was a good sort, even if he did talk and act like a simpleton at times. He was highly intelligent but he often missed the obvious, especially when it was staring him in the face.

They'd vaguely known each other at Eton. But Andrew's friendship with Benjamin at the time came at a cost: Benjamin had selected his friends for him.

At Cambridge, things changed. By that time, Andrew no longer felt obligated to be friends with Benjamin, who hadn't even bothered to attend. Andrew had made his own friends, one of whom was Alex.

After graduation, they'd continued to be friends. They traveled together for a while at first, then came back to London and stepped into their roles, Andrew as an earl and Alex a mere mister who was the heir to his father's barony.

Andrew took a seat at the table where Alex was reading his newspaper. "I heard your father is throwing a house party." No point in beating around the bush.

Alex didn't even bat an eyelash. "You heard right. Are you looking for an invitation, Andrew?" At Andrew's nod Alex remarked, "This is a respectable party, Andrew. There will be no skirt chasing, clear?"

Andrew swallowed hard before nodding again.

"I knew I didn't have to worry about you. You have never been a despoiler of innocents, but I do have some cousins who will be there, so I just had to make sure you understood."

Andrew felt those words like a punch to the gut. He was going to lose even more than he initially thought when this was all over. The few friends he had now would also be gone forever, Alex included. He was not likely to forgive a man who deliberately hurt a member of his family, particularly ruining an innocent young lady.

"No worries there," Andrew said roughly. "I'm just looking for something to do for a while. If I meet a woman who I want to make my countess, well, it will just be good luck on my part," he added jovially.

Alex eyed him skeptically, and then snorted. "You had me going there for a minute. You, finding a countess." He shook his head.

Andrew stiffened. "What does that mean?"

"Oh, don't get all worked up. It meant nothing really. It's just that you are a bachelor. Always have been, always will be," Alex said with a shrug.

It wouldn't do for Andrew to contradict this. If Alex thought he was a lifelong bachelor, then he wouldn't be concerned overmuch with Andrew being in Brooke's company.

"You're right, I am not the marrying kind," Andrew agreed. "I had better be off."

Andrew picked up his hat and departed. Walking home, he couldn't help but think about how well things were going for him. Pieces were moving into place better than he would have imagined. If only he could get past his guilt, then everything would be perfect.

***

Benjamin Collins, Duke of Gateway, stared at his guest. It wasn't usual for her to visit more than once or twice a year at most. He'd seen her already twice in the past six months, so her presence today was quite unexpected.

But that didn't matter. He was glad to see her today. She'd once been the closest person in the world to him. But when she ended things, for reasons he didn't understand at the time, he had taken steps to hurt her and the only other person in the world she loved: her son.

Though their separation hadn't lasted long, he'd always been careful not to become too close to her, or anyone for that matter, again.

One reason he'd kept his distance was he hadn't wanted to let slip that he was the cause of her and her son's torment. Occasionally, he'd felt a little guilt about it when she'd spoken of her son and had that distant look in her eyes, but he'd never actually been able to openly admit either his part or his guilt about it. At the time, he had felt his actions justified because of the pain she'd caused him.

At one point he'd even tried to fix everything in a way that would not expose his part in it. But that eventually led to more problems, so he'd washed his hands of it and felt no guilt. At least he'd tried.

"What brings you here today, Lizzie?" he asked, his voice lacking any emotion.

"To see you, of course," she replied cheerfully.

"To see me? Why would you want to do that?" Benjamin took a seat in a chair near her.

Lizzie smiled. "Why, because you are one of my two favorite people, of course. And since you don't respond to my correspondence—" she gave a speaking glance over to where some letters were stacked on the corner of his desk— "I thought I would come and inquire about your welfare personally."

Benjamin gave her a thin smile. He'd never been one for writing letters, and she knew it. At one time, he would have dearly loved to have a letter from her. He had actually longed for one and would have written her back immediately. But not now. No, not answering her letters was just his underhanded way of punishing her for not sending him one when he craved it so badly.

"I am doing well," he said flatly. "You?"

"The same as always," she said with a watery smile.

They were both quiet for a few minutes. Benjamin had never been much of a conversationalist, and Lizzie didn't speak much unless she had something to say or was forced to talk.

"Are you planning to attend the Watson house party next week?" Lizzie asked, breaking the silence. "I hear they have some American relations who are also to be in attendance." She wagged her eyebrows suggestively at him.

He chose to ignore Lizzie's clear attempt at matchmaking. "I will not be attending," he said simply, as if to end the discussion.

Lizzie broke into a wide grin. "Why, Benjamin, I thought you had a *tendre* for the oldest daughter. I did read your name linked to hers in a scandal sheet no more than three days ago. What's wrong, *Benny?* Was the waltz not close enough for you?"

Benjamin grimaced at her words. He knew she was just having her fun. He wasn't going to ruin it for her though. Fun was something Lizzie had very little of in her life. He thought back to the night she was referencing with a crystal clear memory. Brooke Banks had made such a fool of him, and worst of all, he'd let her.

"Maybe I will go to the party after all. Something interesting always seems to happen at house parties. I wouldn't want to miss anything. Will you be going?"

"You mean do I plan to willingly surround myself with a bunch of gossiping old dowagers with fire pokers up their arses? The answer is no." Lizzie's voice was full of conviction.

Gateway couldn't help but smile. Leave it to Lizzie to be so blunt. He could always count on her to be completely frank and honest with him. It is probably why they had stayed so close over the years. They both hated Society and its rules, and neither of them wasted their time thinking about what others thought of them for it.

# Chapter 9

Brooke had always thought she had the perfect mother. As a child, Brooke remembered her mother taking the girls on walks or to play in a nearby park. Even with three girls, Mama had never hired a nursemaid. Mama had taken care to make sure her daughters were dressed to the height of fashion. She had interviewed dozens of tutors to find the most intelligent and disciplined one to teach her daughters. As her girls got older she introduced them to social circles and instructed them on the most valuable points to finding a good husband, like hers.

But even with all of Mama's instructions, Brooke still doubted she would truly capture the attentions of such a lofty man as the earl. And yet, he seemed to be courting her. In preparation for their outing today, she was reading a tome on British history so as not to appear completely dimwitted to the earl at the museum.

Meanwhile, Mama was quietly sitting beside her on the pink settee. She had no book in her hands. She had no embroidery in her hands. She had no sewing in her hands. Instead, she had empty hands and a wistful smile on her face.

"You look like a lovesick debutante," Brooke told her mother, looking up from her book.

"Well, I cannot help it that I'm so happy. I mean how many other women can say their daughter will soon be a countess?" Mama squealed with delight.

"You do not know that *you* can even say that. We are not betrothed, after all," Brooke remarked.

"Poppycock, you know the earl has his sights set on you. He basically declared his love to you in front of the entire family at dinner. And," Mama added, "His words to Papa seemed to indicate that he is most serious about you. If that isn't enough to convince you, he asked you to accompany him to the museum today. I think that clearly indicates his interest in you."

"Maybe he asked me to go because he felt sorry for me after I was so clearly embarrassed in front of him," Brooke parried.

"Stop being absurd. The man has a sincere interest in you. I do wonder why you were so humiliated by that silly little act, anyway. You have never been that embarrassed about the incident before. Why now?"

"I don't know. It just seemed different to tell him," she said with a shrug.

"His lordship, the Earl of Townson," Turner announced, opening the door to the drawing room and keeping Mama from asking any more questions.

Brooke and Mama stood and curtsied to the earl, who reciprocated with a bow which was much lower than necessary. Maybe he did fancy her after all.

"Are you ladies ready to be off, then?" Andrew asked cordially.

"Yes, my lord, let me grab my shawl," Mama answered as Brooke walked over to the earl.

The trio was almost to the front of the house when suddenly the door swung open to reveal a disappointed Madison.

"Why are you not at the sewing circle?" Mama asked her.

"Mrs. Ingram is ill and our meeting was cancelled," Madison said glumly.

Genuine sympathy for Madison built up in Brooke's chest. Madison had no real joy in her life, except sewing. She had fun with her sisters, but her real enjoyment came from helping others, which she did in the form of sewing for the less fortunate.

"We're on our way to the British Museum. Would you like to come along with us?" Andrew asked Madison.

"Are you certain that I won't be intruding?" Madison asked shyly.

"No, I'm not certain that you won't be intruding, but I'm certain it will be a nice intrusion," Andrew replied.

Brooke's heart skipped a beat. He was being so nice to Madison without even being prompted. It would have been rude for her or Mama to invite Madison, but he did it on his own. Most people easily dismissed Brooke's sister, but not Andrew. He'd been kinder to Madison than she'd seen any man ever be. Brooke could have kissed him for it.

Mama linked arms with Madison, and together the four of them walked to Andrew's carriage.

"Thank you," Brooke said quietly when Andrew was helping her into the carriage.

"For what?" Andrew asked, perplexed.

"For inviting Madison. You didn't have to."

"I know I didn't have to, but I wanted to. She looked rather disappointed that she didn't get to go sew for the poor. I thought coming with us might brighten her day. Plus, maybe she'll feel compelled to sew me something," he teased.

Brooke gave him a bright smile then took her seat in the carriage.

With four people in the earl's carriage it felt quite snug. Andrew took advantage of the close proximity and his large size by innocently sprawling out, claiming that he needed more space. Brooke was skeptical, but didn't question it, especially when he lightly pressed his thigh against hers.

Sitting so close to him, Brooke took notice of his masculine scent. He smelled of the outdoors, like woods and trees and such. She had not gone around sniffing an abundance of gentlemen, but had been around enough to know not many smelled this way. And she knew it had to be natural, not an oil mixed into his shaving water. His skin color and actions virtually screamed that he spent a good deal of his time outdoors.

During the half hour ride to the museum from the townhouse, Andrew talked with Mama and Madison, both of whom asked him to use their Christian names. The two of them entertained him with stories of America and their friends and family back home. Meanwhile, she was entertaining herself with thoughts of the earl's body, which was boldly pressing against hers again. Even through her gown and his breeches, the firm muscles in his thigh seared hers. She wondered what they would feel like if she ran her hand over them. She quickly admonished herself for the thought. However, she was powerless to tear her eyes from the object of her imagination. She looked at his thighs. They were practically bulging under his buckskin trousers, yet the seams were not ripping with every move like she thought they might.

She was pulled from her daydream by a light and well-placed tap on her foot. Startled, she looked up and met Madison's knowing eyes. Madison didn't say a word, but her face conveyed a thousand. Brooke had just been caught staring at the earl's legs by her younger sister! She flushed with embarrassment.

Brooke looked at Mama. She clearly hadn't noticed what Brooke had been doing. A quick glance at Andrew's face told her he had. Brooke quickly averted her eyes. She wasn't going to let him get the better of her today.

For the rest of the carriage ride Brooke looked at either Mama or Madison, trying not to let her eyes connect with any part of Andrew.

The British Museum looked magnificent, and so far all they had seen was just the outside. Walking inside, Brooke was overwhelmed. Dozens of people were milling around, going from one exhibit to another. Some artifacts were on display behind glass and others were just corded off with beautiful red velvet ropes.

The four of them looked at the exhibits together. They saw some old maps and compasses sailors had used centuries earlier. They looked at some ancient Greek drawings. Then they walked over to some legal documents several centuries old. So much history was on display here, there was no way they would be able to see everything today. That just meant another visit was in order.

"If it would be agreeable with your chaperone, I would like to show you the sword room," Andrew said, then waited for Mama to give her approval.

"Go on," Mama urged. "Madison and I will be over here looking at these beautiful golden goblets. They are absolutely stunning, don't you agree, Madison?"

Andrew led Brooke down the hall, around a corner, and into a room that had absolutely no swords in it. Instead, the room was completely empty except for a statue in the back corner of the room.

"I thought we were going to look at swords," Brooke said, walking across the room to where the statue was positioned in the corner. Why would he bring her to a virtually empty room?

"I thought maybe we could have a little privacy. That is, unless you truly were interested in seeing some ancient swords," Andrew replied, walking over to stand beside Brooke who was now in front of the statue.

"No, this statue is far more interesting than any old sword ever could be, that's for sure," she managed, looking at the statue in complete awe.

The statue was of a man holding a spear. Other than the spear, there was nothing else adorning the sculpture, which left a very muscular man standing naked, holding a spear.

Brooke had never seen a naked man either in real life or a drawing before. This was the closest she had come, and being as innocent as she was about a man's form, this was fascinating to her. She marveled at how different this man's body was than hers, even if he was made of stone. She was thin and had slender arms and legs, but this sculpture had thick arms and legs that were bulging muscles. His chest and stomach were flat except a few bumps of ripples. She noticed that the man had hair under his arms, a little on his chest and quite a bit surrounding a part she'd never seen before that rested between his thighs. For Brooke, the statue held a higher level of appeal than swords ever could.

Andrew chuckled when he reached her side. But that didn't stop her from looking. She could no more take her eyes off the statue than she could deny a thirsty man water. She looked the statue over up and down, down and up, twice before breaking her line of vision. Then she turned and met Andrew's piercing eyes. He had been watching her stare shamelessly at the statue! She thought he was looking at the statue, too, not at her. She tried to keep a straight face and not show any signs of embarrassment. She'd sworn to herself that he wasn't going to get the better of her today, and she was going to make sure of it.

"See something of interest?" His voice was hoarse, and his eyes were a shade darker than usual.

"Yes, this statue is quite extraordinary," Brooke answered as evenly as she could.

Andrew leaned closer to read the plaque next to the statue. "Hmm, I don't recognize this piece or the sculptor."

"Well, sir, do you make a point to memorize all the naked statues in the world?" Brooke teased.

Andrew smiled at her. "No, only the ones of women."

Brooke gave him a playful swat on the arm. "You're incorrigible."

Andrew didn't answer, probably because it was true and he knew it as well as she did. Instead, he moved a few inches closer to Brooke, closing the gap between them. He reached out and cupped her chin, tipping her face up toward his. "You're really beautiful, did you know that?"

Brooke's lips parted and her eyes went wide. She had never been called beautiful before, attractive—yes, but not beautiful. "Thank you. Everyone always calls Madison beautiful, never me," she said before she'd realized she had revealed too much. A part of her that was vulnerable.

Andrew leaned so close that Brooke felt his warm breath on her face. "To me, you are far more beautiful than Madison." Then he lowered his head and very lightly brushed his lips across hers.

Brooke almost melted on the spot. His kind words had softened her resolve, but his tender kiss was almost her undoing. "You have quite an unmatched skill, my lord," Brooke said weakly.

Rather than responding to her words with words of his own, Andrew moved closer and kissed her again. This time his kiss was not a quick brush of the lips. It was an assault of lips. He started his kiss gently, and just when her lips were used to having his on them, he became more aggressive. Her body relaxed and her lips started to respond to his. He moved his hands around to rest on her back and draw her closer while his lips continued to mesh with hers.

Brooke's hands moved on their own accord up to his neck, and she dug into the soft, black curls that rested against his collar. Her fingers twisted his hair as his lips pressed harder, moving on top and in between hers. Her body was giving up its fight to stay standing, and she would have sunk to the floor if he had not been holding onto her. She leaned against his chest and his hands tightened their grip to hold her in place.

Andrew pulled back and looked down at her. "How do you feel about my skills now?" he asked with a ragged breath, his eyes even darker than they were a few minutes before.

Even with the blood thundering in her ears she understood his question, yet she couldn't form a coherent response. She nodded instead. She knew she was flushed from the kiss and her body felt absolutely boneless in his arms.

Andrew smiled and ran the pad of one of his thumbs across her swollen lips. "You are truly beautiful. I don't care what anyone else says. To me, you are more beautiful than your sisters."

Her heart fluttered at his words. He truly thought she was beautiful. "We should probably return to Mama and Madison before they come looking for us," Brooke forced herself to say before stepping backward and out of his embrace. She wished she could stay in this moment forever, but that wasn't possible, and it really would not do to be found in this position. It could mean they might be forced to marry, which she didn't want to happen—did she?

"You're right," Andrew murmured, offering her his arm.

They barely walked three steps down the hall before nearly colliding with Mama and Madison. "How were the swords?" Mama inquired, acting truly interested in ancient weapons.

"They were not so interesting," Brooke said dismissively, hoping Mama wouldn't insist on going into the room they'd just left. "I'd like to go look at some of those paintings that were mentioned in my book."

"Paintings are down this hallway over here," Andrew said, pointing to a hall on the left leading to where a number of portraits of former kings and queens were located.

Standing in front of the past English kings' portraits, Madison asked, "Did any of these men actually do anything, or are they just up here because they were kings?"

"These here," Andrew said pointing to two different King Henrys, "are responsible for reforming the entire judicial system of England. Before them, the judicial system was a mess. It was based on the whims of nobles or the Pope. However, Henry VIII created the Church of England and ended the Pope's political control of England." Pointing to Henry VII, he said, "His father, Henry VII, made changes by appointing each village a Justice of the Peace or magistrate to keep things under control in each area. Punishments were no longer meted out based on the personal opinion of whoever heard the case. Instead, laws were created and the Justice of the Peace made sure they were followed. If a problem came about that could not be easily solved, or required more proof, a jury would be brought in to keep it fair. You are familiar with the role of judges and juries in the United States are you not?" Andrew asked, raising a brow toward Mama.

"Not personally, I assure you," Mama quickly replied tartly. "But yes, we do use them in our legal system back in the United States. I suppose it is one of the few things the colonists liked about the way their homeland was run, since they included it in the New World." Andrew gave a bark of laughter.

"Stop that. You're drawing attention over here," Brooke hissed.

"Sorry, I couldn't help it," Andrew said unapologetically. He shook his head. "One of the few things they liked," he muttered disbelievingly.

"Wasn't Henry VIII the one who had his wife's head chopped off because she didn't bear him a son?" Madison asked pertly.

Before Andrew could answer, Mama jumped in. "Girls, I believe Papa will be waiting on us. We should be going back now."

In the carriage on the way back to the townhouse, Brooke once again did not participate in the conversation. But instead of concentrating on Andrew's legs this time, she was reliving the torrid kiss they'd shared.

Not letting go of Brooke's hand after she descended the

carriage, Andrew ran his thumb back and forth across her knuckles. "Will I be able to see you again before you leave for the house party?"

"No, Papa said we are to leave tomorrow. We're going to spend a few days in Bath before going to the party."

"Until the next time, then." Andrew bent and placed a slow, lingering kiss on the back of Brooke's hand.

Brooke tried to hide her disappointment at not knowing when the "next time" was as she watched Andrew turn, get back into his carriage, and roll away.

# Chapter 10

The Banks family left London for Bath by traveling coach bright and early the next morning. The family was to spend a few days seeing the countryside before going to the baron's house party.

Brooke and her sisters filled those days spending as much of their allowances as they could on as many things as they felt their lives would not be complete without.

Liberty visited the little bookshop and found a few volumes of interest. To Brooke's great surprise, they were not manuals of any sort, but rather novels.

Madison enjoyed the confection shop most of all. The girls had gone inside searching for tarts and other sweets. One thing they did find was some sort of brown drink that the store owner referred to as chocolate. After only one sip, Madison claimed it was her new favorite drink and had gone so far as to request it with her meals back at the Dog and Fox.

Brooke spent her time looking around a milliner's shop. She'd pause and smile each time she saw something red. She still dreamed every night of that kiss that she had shared with Andrew. No matter what she did, she couldn't get that kiss out of her head. He'd teased her a little after it, but that didn't matter. The kiss itself was like nothing she had ever experienced before. She'd kissed a few gentlemen in New York and in London, but none of them matched the excitement she felt when she kissed Andrew. He seemed to spark something in her that no other had. It was thrilling!

The day before the house party, the Banks family decided it was time to try out one of those bathhouses that were so popular.

"I have made arrangements for us to each have our own private bathing room," Papa said when they were all crammed into their traveling coach riding down to the bathhouse.

Walking into the bathhouse, Brooke spotted a young lady that was ghostly pale with bright orange-red hair sitting in the waiting room. Upon closer inspection, Brooke recognized Lady Olivia awaiting her turn.

"Hello, Miss Banks," Lady Olivia chirped from where she was perched on a chair looking faint, as usual. Her green eyes crinkled at the corners when she spoke. Immediately, her fatter-than-sausage fingers flew to her face to smooth out the wrinkles her smile created on the freckled skin that surrounded her eyes like a raccoon's mask.

"Hello, Lady Olivia," Brooke and Liberty responded in unison. Madison didn't respond, since she was following the attendant down the hall to where her bath was waiting for her.

"It's nice to see you ladies here. I'm about to perish of boredom waiting for my bath. Will you come join me?" Lady Olivia asked with a pout that caused her face to bloat in a way that reminded Brooke of a toad.

"Of course." Brooke sent Liberty and her mother pleading glances, which they ignored as they walked away and took seats on the other side of the room.

Brooke sat down and looked around for any kind of distraction. She didn't particularly like Lady Olivia, but it would seem impolite not to try to talk about something. "Are you planning to attend the house party tomorrow?" she finally asked.

"I should like to." Lady Olivia smiled, displaying her yellowing and misaligned teeth. "I have plans to see a certain houseguest."

"Plans?" Brooke asked, bemused.

"Well, not plans exactly. But I am quite certain I can bag him if I can get him alone for a few minutes."

"Bag him?" Brooke asked, even more confused now.

"Bag him, catch him, snare him, snag him, whatever you want to call it. See, I'm on the hunt for a husband. I am nearly twenty years old now. Far too old to still be single. Before much longer I will be firmly on the shelf and labeled a spinster." Lady Olivia gave a little shudder. "I don't want that to happen, so I've decided to take a husband. The lucky gentleman whom I have selected is planning to attend the party." Lady Olivia gave an anguished sigh. "The only pit in the plum now is I'm not feeling the thing, so I need this bath to take care of my ailment so I can attend."

Brooke just stared at Lady Olivia, her mouth opening and shutting like a fish. She wasn't sure whom she felt more sympathy toward: this gentleman, who was going to be chased by Lady Olivia, or Lady Olivia herself, who clearly was more cracked than Brooke originally thought. The lucky man? More like the poor man. And who was to say that at twenty a lady was firmly on the shelf? If that were so, at almost three-and-twenty, Brooke was an antique.

Brooke couldn't just sit there with her mouth agape. She tried to think of *something* polite to say, and came up with nothing.

Finally, curiosity got the better of her. "Who is the lucky gentleman?" She tried not to let her voice falter on the word *lucky*.

"The Earl of Townson, of course," Lady Olivia said as casually if she were stating the weather conditions.

Brooke was not prepared for that answer, and for the first time in her life she almost swooned. When she got past the dizzy feeling, her jaw opened and snapped shut again. There was no *of course* about it. Brooke had never even considered the possibility. Those two were the most ill-suited people she had ever met. How could Lady Olivia even think it would be a good match?

"I can tell by your pasty, white face that you do not agree with my selection," Lady Olivia said, breaking into Brooke's thoughts. "However, the facts remain that I am an heiress, and quite frankly it's no secret that he's destitute. We both have something the other needs. He'll have my money, and I'll have a title."

"But—but—" Brooke sputtered.

"It's not unusual. That's why most of the *ton* is married to their respective spouses. Some need money, others need connections. It's the way of things." Lady Olivia seemed content that someone would marry her for her money alone.

It was none of Brooke's concern if those two decided to marry, yet she had a sudden ache in her chest she couldn't identify. She tried to gather her wits about her again. "Don't you want to marry for love?"

"No," Lady Olivia said flatly. "I do not believe in marrying for love. Furthermore, I do not believe I could ever love my husband, especially if he were the earl. That man is despicable. He's not even very handsome. That broken nose of his has put off many women, especially after they hear the rumors about how it got broken. Fisticuffs, and with the Duke of Gateway no less, how absurd!" She gave a sniff of disgust to prove her disdain. "I'll just have to make do. I suppose there are some sacrifices one must make in order to be a countess."

Trying not to let on how unsettled she was by what Lady Olivia had told her, Brooke noticed her attendant coming and said quickly, "I believe my attendant is motioning for me. I hope to see you at the house party."

Brooke walked slowly to her room. She was too distracted about all of the things Lady Olivia had said to keep pace with the attendant.

When she reached her room, she disrobed and stepped into the bath. The bath looked like a large hole in the floor that was covered in tiles and filled up with water. It was very unusual looking, but she was still very excited to try it out. This would be one experience she could tell all her friends about back in New York. An experience they would never get to have, she had to make sure to enjoy every minute of it and remember all of the details.

The water was warmer than regular bath water, but not too hot. It felt good on her skin. Brooke sat on one side of the tub and stretched her legs out. She rolled her ankles and relaxed her whole body, which was so easy to do in all this warm water.

She closed her eyes and let her mind travel. She thought about her time in London. All the balls and soirees she'd attended. All the gentlemen she'd met, and there had been many.

Then her mind went to one gentleman in particular: Andrew Black, Earl of Townson. He was different, but she couldn't decide how or why. He wasn't overly handsome or charming, but in her mind he was the handsomest of all the men she had met thus far. She thought about the way he smelled like he'd been outside working in a field or with horses all day. But it wasn't a repulsive smell. It was purely masculine, and for reasons she didn't understand, it made her all the more attracted to him.

Brooke thought about their visit to the museum. During the carriage ride, he'd so brazenly pressed his thigh up against hers. That wasn't the first time he had done that, either. He'd also acted so bold the night he had dinner with her family. She'd felt the same searing sensation that night as well. But unlike the day at the museum, he hadn't kissed her that night at her house, even though she had desperately wanted him to. She had been so disappointed when he'd denied he had that kind of interest in her, she had tried so hard not to let it show. The day at the museum made up for it.

A frown overtook her face when she remembered the conversation she had just had with Lady Olivia. How could anyone not find the earl handsome? Brooke had noticed Andrew's nose wasn't straight when they'd first met. Her first assumption was that maybe he had broken it in some sort of accident, not a fight. It was hard to picture him fighting with anyone. He always seemed calm and reserved. She wondered what could provoke him enough to get into a fight. And why fight with the Duke of Gateway of all people? What was the reason for the fight in the first place? More importantly, why did anyone still care?

Leaving thoughts of Andrew's past behind, she started to think of his present situation. Was Andrew really *that* poor? They'd jested about it that day in the park, but she thought he was exaggerating a bit. Andrew did say someone would marry Lady Olivia for her money. Brooke's frown deepened. Would Andrew marry Lady Olivia for her money?

Then, something that Lady Olivia said finally sank in. The earl was coming to the house party. She had been so upset by the rest of what Lady Olivia said, she hadn't realized she would get to see him tomorrow.

The rest of her bath was spent with a dreamy smile on her

face.

***

Madison walked to the main waiting room and saw that Lady Olivia was still sitting there, probably still waiting to be taken to a room. She visited so often, it was a wonder the bathhouse didn't have a room set aside each day for her.

"Did your bath go well, Madison?" Lady Olivia asked.

"Yes, it did." Madison looked around the room. Nobody else from her family was back yet.

"They had to wait a few minutes after you went back," Lady Olivia said, as if she had read Madison's thoughts. "You may sit by me if you'd like."

"All right," Madison said, taking a seat close to Lady Olivia.

"What brings you here?"

"No reason, really. We just wanted to visit a bathhouse while we were here. You?" Madison really didn't care to hear a whole list of complaints, but it would seem rude not to try to make small talk with Lady Olivia.

"I have been having these dreadful headaches. It feels like my head is going to, umm…uh…" Lady Olivia stammered, waving her hand wildly as if that would in some way help her think of the elusive word.

"Explode?" Madison supplied.

"Yes, explode. I feel as if my head is going to explode, and that is the least of my complaints." Lady Olivia dropped her voice. "The others are not meant to be said in mixed company." Lady Olivia sent a pointed glance over to where Papa was walking down the hallway toward the waiting room.

"I do hope the bath helps you feel better," Madison said truthfully. People often journeyed there from all over the country to take baths in hopes of relieving their complaints. She wasn't sure if it would help a headache or not, but maybe it would help Lady Olivia with her other complaints.

"Are you excited about the house party your uncle is throwing?" Lady Olivia asked after a few minutes, startling a daydreaming Madison.

"Yes, this party shall be the first house party I've ever attended. I am quite excited. I'm also eager to meet some of my other relations." Then belatedly she asked, "Will you be attending?"

"I hope so. It depends on how I feel after this bath." Lady Olivia sighed. "I do long to go though. I hear that the Earl of Townson is also to be in attendance."

"Is he?" Madison asked. She was certain the earl hadn't mentioned it the day they went to the museum.

"Oh yes, I believe his going is a very good sign, too. Between us, I think he's ready to take a wife, and I so desperately want to be there to catch him," Lady Olivia gushed, not noticing the look of disbelief Madison was certain was printed on her face.

"You want to marry the earl?" Madison schooled her face to look only casually interested.

"Of course, who doesn't?" Lady Olivia said airily. "Besides, I think I might have the best chance. The earl is impoverished, and I have a large dowry."

"You don't mind that he would marry you for your dowry?" Madison asked, truly interested in the answer.

"I still get to be a countess, don't I? Besides, that's the way of things here in England. I know that you hail from the land where savages run wild—pardon me for being so blunt. People don't always marry for money. But over here, it's the way of things. I've accepted it. I will find my happiness elsewhere, and I expect he will, too."

Madison suppressed a shudder. Brooke wasn't likely to accept less than a love match when it was time to marry. How else could she have made it to nearly three-and-twenty without a proposal if that wasn't the case? Was there a chance that Brooke would marry the earl? If they did marry, would it only be for Brooke's money? Surely not. There wasn't that much money in her dowry. Anyway, how could he know if she had a dowry or not? Papa hadn't told anyone. If they were to marry, would it be like a business arrangement where he would go find his pleasure elsewhere, leaving Brooke alone? Madison didn't want Brooke to be hurt, ever.

Madison's brain was conjuring up many unpleasant questions and possibilities. She finally decided she would have to watch Brooke and the earl more carefully. She wasn't entirely certain that the earl had the intention of marriage with Brooke, but it appeared that he was serious about courting her, which could lead to marriage. Not that that was bad. She liked the earl—she really did—but she loved her sister more and wanted her to be happy. Brooke would not be happy if she had a husband who neglected her. Of that, Madison was certain.

"I didn't mean to offend," Lady Olivia said when Madison didn't respond.

"Pardon?" Madison furrowed her eyebrows in confusion. She'd been so lost in her scattered thoughts she'd forgotten Lady Olivia was waiting for a response.

"I didn't mean to offend you by saying you were from the land of savages. I mean, you are, but maybe I shouldn't have said so. Please do not hold it against me. You are one of my dearest friends and I would hate to lose you…" Lady Olivia's voice trailed off and a counterfeit expression of sadness came over her face.

"It's of no concern," Madison quickly assured her. Though, to be honest, she wondered how exactly she had become one of Lady Olivia's dearest friends. Liberty was a lot closer to Lady Olivia—not that that said much. This was probably the most she and Lady Olivia had ever spoken. "I was just thinking of something else."

"I see. You do that a lot." Lady Olivia kept speaking without noticing how Madison bristled next to her. "You always seem to be staring at nothing. When I first met you, I thought it was so strange how you were always looking across the room at absolutely nothing. Most unnerving really. But I've gotten used to it."

Madison's face heated and she willed herself not to say something that might embarrass her family. She had the habit, of course, but to have someone else mention it to her and in such a callous and mortifying way made her feel uncomfortable. She was about to excuse herself to go sit next to Papa when she looked up to see that Lady Olivia was no longer sitting in her chair.

"It appears as if my bath has finally been made ready for me. I look forward to seeing you at the party," Lady Olivia threw over her shoulder as she walked toward her attendant.

# Chapter 11

Andrew was making preparations for the next day's journey to the Watson house party with Addams when Gateway's coach pulled up on the street in front of Andrew's house.

"Botheration," Andrew muttered. Just what he didn't need: another impromptu visit from Gateway.

"I could tell him you're not receiving," Addams suggested lamely.

"You and I both know he won't believe that." Andrew shook his head. "Just show him into my study when he finally descends that monstrosity he calls a carriage and decides to grace us with his unwanted presence."

No more than three minutes later, Gateway strode into Andrew's study as if he owned Andrew's townhouse and not his estate in Essex.

"What do you want?" Andrew barked. It was uncharacteristic for Andrew to be short or raise his voice. Normally, he was calm and able to keep control of a situation because of it, but he was tired of dealing with Gateway and his tendency to just show up whenever he wanted to.

"Why so hostile?" Gateway asked with a stiff smile.

"Just say what you came to say, Gateway," Andrew said as he sank into the chair behind his desk and stared at Gateway.

"I do believe at one time we were friends." Gateway put one hand up to his chin and rubbed it with one of his fingers as if he were lost in meditation. "I even remember us calling each other by our given names, Andrew."

Andrew's eyes narrowed. He too remembered those days—the days when they were "friends". He even remembered calling Gateway by his first name even though most of the others called him Channing, his courtesy title at the time. But those were not good memories for Andrew, and the less remembered, the better. "All right, Benjamin. What brings you to call on this lovely day?" Andrew asked with feigned happiness.

Gateway smiled a true and rare smile. The only times Andrew had seen that smile was when Gateway was about to do something unpleasant, or on the rare occasions when he spoke of some woman he was close to. "I was just wondering about any progress you have made with Brooke?" Gateway finally said.

"You mean Miss Banks?" Andrew snapped. The look of interest on Gateway's face informed Andrew his tone was misinterpreted. Andrew unclamped his jaw and softened his tone. "Things are going quite well. Her family seems to approve of me."

"Good," Gateway said, plopping down in one of Andrew's wingback chairs. "I suspect you got yourself an invitation to her uncle's house party."

"Yes," Andrew answered.

"Shall I bring the deed to the party?"

Andrew thought about that. Was it possible to bring about Brooke's ruination at this house party? She had responded to his kisses. That was encouraging. He might be able to persuade her to go off alone with him. The trick would be getting caught in a way that would ruin her, but not completely mortify her at the same time. He had already determined he would have to be careful with the getting caught part. He wanted to hurt her as little as possible. He wanted her ruined and gone, but he didn't want her to be mortified for the rest of her life.

Andrew gave a slight nod. "I think it's possible, but I cannot be sure at this point. I only get one chance at this, and I don't want to push her too quickly."

"Are you concerned you'll be surrounded by several of her male relatives?" Gateway inquired.

"The thought has crossed my mind. I think I can persuade them not to call me out when this is all over." Or so Andrew hoped.

"Would it be so bad to be called out?" Gateway asked with a wicked smile on his lips.

"While you may delight in seeing me cock up my toes, I am

not quite ready to do so. Nor do I wish to injure anyone else," Andrew countered stiffly.

"I see you still have not accepted the circumstances of your father's death eight years ago."

Andrew had no doubt Gateway's mentioning the prospect of a duel was to remind him the way Andrew's father had died and get his hackles up.

It worked. He hated to think of how stupid his own father had been. He'd been a spendthrift drunkard who was caught cheating at cards and died in a pointless duel.

Andrew didn't aspire to do such great things with his life that the details would bore future generations of adolescent boys in history class, but if he could live and die with a little more dignity than his own father, then he'd consider his life a success.

"There will be no duel," Andrew declared. A smile took his lips as a thought formed in his head. "On second thought, if there is to be a duel, you can be my second, since you have taken such a keen interest in my welfare."

Gateway wasn't amused. "No, I do believe my dueling days are long gone. You'll have to find someone else to act as a second for you."

"You've never fought a duel in your life."

"Maybe not," Gateway agreed.

"If that is all you came here to say, I need to meet with my butler about making arrangements for my trip." Andrew got up without waiting for a response from Gateway.

"I'll see myself out," Gateway muttered to himself.

"See that you do, and don't take too long to do it, either," Andrew commented, walking out of the room.

# Chapter 12

"It is such a pleasure to have you here." Aunt Regina hugged her brother-in-law, followed by each of the other members of his family.

"The pleasure is entirely ours," Papa told his sister-in-law before giving his brother, Edward, a hug. "We appreciate your hospitality in having us here to your house and hosting this party. It's quite an honor."

"Think nothing of it," the baron told his younger brother. "We are happy to do it, and very happy to get better acquainted with all of your daughters. They clearly get their beauty from their mother," Uncle Edward said with a quick smile toward Carolina.

"This is Mrs. Morgan. She's our housekeeper. She will show you all to your rooms," Aunt Regina said, directing them toward the staircase where Mrs. Morgan stood on the bottom step waiting to lead them up.

"I have set up your rooms in the east wing, seeing as you're family not just regular guests." Mrs. Morgan was clearly proud of her decision and held her head high as she led them to the family wing.

The house was breathtaking. Everything from the vaulted ceiling to the marble floor was beautiful. Round support columns made of stone so thick Brooke was sure even an adult male could not wrap his arms around them, were located throughout the massive entry area of the house. The entryway to almost all the rooms consisted of an arch that had a scrolled design.

The massive furnishings looked to be in pristine condition and were placed just so, making it look like a picture from a decorating plate she'd once seen. There was nothing out of place, everything perfectly coordinated and inviting. This place had certainly been decorated by a different person than the house in London. The thought made her giggle a little, which she immediately tried to smother.

"I know what you're thinking, Brooke," Liberty whispered. "But please try to stay composed. There's nothing more impolite than to laugh at our host and hostess in their own home." She glanced over her shoulder in the direction of their aunt and uncle who stood by the door to greet their other guests.

Brooke sobered. "I'm sorry." The old Liberty was back. Brooke sighed. All good things must come to an end, and Liberty's failure to point out everyone's impropriety in the past few days had met its end. Too bad it hadn't lasted a little longer.

Mrs. Morgan showed Brooke to her room first. "Ring if you need anything. Dinner is served promptly at seven. You may meet in the drawing room as early as half past six," Mrs. Morgan said right before she left.

Brooke checked the watch pinned on her bodice. That gave her little more than an hour and a half before going downstairs.

She closed the door to her room and wandered over to her bed. She sat down on the edge. The mattress dipped under her weight. It was a nice feather mattress, an improvement from the tick mattress she had slept on in the Dog and Fox.

Pulling off her slippers, she leaned against the headboard and propped a pillow behind her back. She glanced out the window. There were several men down on the lawn playing some sort of lawn game. Bowls perhaps?

Brooke had seen some of the neighbors in New York play five stones. She had even played a few times when Mama had been too busy at the church to know what she was up to. But the game being played down there looked like an entirely different game. Maybe tomorrow she could learn to play.

She squinted her eyes in the direction of the lawn in hopes of being able to determine who the players were. Maybe they were her cousins, or perhaps they were some local gentlemen, or even some from London.

She resigned herself to the fact she was too far away to get a close enough view of any of them to determine who they were.

With a sigh, she closed her eyes and laid her head back on the pillows to take a nap, secretly hoping Andrew was one of the men out on the lawn.

***

Andrew also wished he was out playing lawn games, and it wasn't much of a secret. Not that he had a love for lawn games, but anything had to be better than being trapped in the drawing room trying to explain to Lady Olivia Sinclair why she could not move her pawn backward in chess. "It's against the rules," he said one more time, hoping it would be the final time.

"But why?" she whined, causing her face to twist in the most unflattering manner.

"It just is. I didn't make the rules, I just play by them." Andrew tried to sound polite but she was really aggravating him with her whining and pouting. There was only so much a man could take, and if he had to take much more, he would insist on being nominated for sainthood.

"Do you always play by the rules?" she asked, batting her eyelashes coyly in an attempt at flirtation.

Andrew tried not to let his amusement be known at her poor attempt. Lady Olivia Sinclair was clearly bad at it. That wasn't necessarily her fault though. Some women just were. But nonetheless, her efforts were not going to work on him. "As often as I can," he managed.

"Would you like to play another game? One that is far less tedious and with much simpler rules?" She peeked up at him from beneath her lashes.

"What kind of game do you have in mind?" Did he really want to know?

"Well, it would be an easy game, of course. One where we will both emerge winners, no doubt." She shifted her upper body in a way to best show off her ample bosom.

Andrew's eyes narrowed. What game was she playing? Surely she wasn't looking for a lover. Or was she? What woman would suggest a "game" where both parties can win if she wasn't looking for a lover? The maneuver she kept doing that showed off more of her chest than usual seemed like confirmation to him.

"You see, my lord, we both are in need of something. You need my money and a wife to bear your heir. And I would like to get away from my tedious family. So you see, we both win," Lady Olivia said with a sunny smile.

The pawn Andrew held in his right hand slipped from his fingers and dropped to the floor with a soft thump. His eyes widened in surprise, and he just stared at her.

She was bold, no doubt about that. He could not remember the last time he had been so surprised or shown so much emotion on his face. Quickly, he tried to hide his surprise by arching his brow and acting as if he were really interested in her proposition, though truth be told, he would rather have all his fingernails pulled off than make her his countess.

"You cannot tell me you've never thought about this before. You are in need of a fortune—everyone says so—and I have one," she said airily, her unsightly smile not faltering a bit.

"It's true that I lack funds at present, but I do not intend for that situation to last." There was no point in being cruel to her by telling her that even if he were facing lifelong poverty, he still wouldn't marry her.

Lady Olivia's smile faded a bit. "I did not realize there was another lady already holding your attention. I shall just have to play harder in order to win." She rose and quickly swept from the room.

Andrew picked up the chess pieces, wondering exactly how Lady Olivia thought to change her course of action in order to steal him from this other heiress she had created in her imagination.

With a shake of his head, he left the drawing room in search of more stimulating entertainment.

What he found waiting for him in the hallway was more stimulating, but not necessarily entertainment.

# Chapter 13

"Mr. Banks, it's nice to see you arrived safely," Andrew said with a bow.

"Townson, I didn't expect to see you here," John said with a little bit of curiosity in his voice.

"I had not yet received my invitation when we last spoke," Andrew said smoothly.

"Indeed. I'm rather surprised Regina would not have sent yours sooner." Interest showed on John's face.

"Ah, that is because I was actually invited personally by Alex. He is an old friend of mine." It was true enough. No need to tell him that he'd gone so far as to seek Alex out and ask for an invitation.

"My nephew has a friend?" John said in a half-joking tone.

Alex was a very nice man, but the truth was it was hard for him to make friends. He always had his nose in a book, wore spectacles, and attended a plethora of boring meetings that ranged from plants to bugs to what was dumped into the Thames, and everything in between. His unusual interests and pristine reputation had somehow garnered him the nickname Arid Alex.

It was a common belief among the *ton* that he'd never marry unless the baron, Alex's father, arranged a marriage for him. All of Alex's siblings had drastically different personalities that made them socialites. However, since Alex was the heir to the barony and would one day need to sire an heir himself, it was necessary for him to marry.

"I certainly count myself as one of his friends, sir." Andrew didn't mind Alex's bizarre tendencies. To Andrew, that was what made his friend interesting.

Besides, if Alex couldn't care less about what people thought about Andrew and continued to be his friend, then why should

Andrew care about what interests Alex pursued? The two of them had formed a friendship when neither had another friend in the world, and that friendship was nothing that Andrew would ever want to let go of.

That was part of the trouble with going through with this scheme, most especially at this party. Whatever happened, he would lose his friendship with Alex. He had to swallow a lump that formed in his throat every time he thought about it. He might have let Gateway believe that mattered naught, but in reality it mattered a great deal to Andrew. He didn't want to lose Alex's friendship, and just now he realized exactly how soon it would happen.

John smiled at Andrew. "My lord, you are far less shallow than I originally thought. I am quite certain that Alex values your friendship as much as you value his."

"Thank you, sir. Alex may not be the most entertaining of men, but he is very loyal and sincere, and those are qualities I value much more than popularity and social polish."

"I am very glad to hear that." John gave a genuine smile. "I always admired my older brother. He was different. He was always looking at anything scientific he could get his hands on. He always did experiments whenever he could find the funds and resources. The problem was that nobody but his family accepted this about him. Because of his unusual interests, he was considered an outcast to society. Yet, I admired him."

"I admired him because he didn't care what people said about him. I despaired when I got letters from my brother suggesting that young Alex had the same interests. I think Edward sees things differently now that it's his son being cast out of society. However, I am very glad to know he has at least one true friend. I do believe, in all honestly, I can say I admire you now, too."

Andrew felt like a lead weight was being lowered onto his stomach. John Banks, the man he was about to disappoint on two accounts, first, through his daughter and now his nephew, was telling him that he admired him. It gave him a sick feeling inside. "Thank you again, sir," Andrew said flatly, hoping his thoughts were not in his eyes.

"John," shouted a voice farther down the hall, startling them both.

Both men turned to see who the voice belonged to just as Edward Banks, Lord Watson, came strolling toward them from down the hall. "Someone is here to meet you." the baron said.

"I shall be on my way posthaste. I would not like to keep my guest in your house waiting," John said with a brief smile for his brother. "We'll talk more later, Townson."

As John walked away, Edward called out, "He's in the yellow drawing room."

John raised a hand to indicate he heard his brother and strolled down the hall to greet his guest.

***

Paul Grimes was the second son of Viscount Bonnington. Like other younger sons without titles and very little family money, Paul wasn't given many options: clergy or military. Having never been a very good shot, Paul chose to go into the ministry instead.

That wasn't the only reason he'd chosen the ministry. All of his life he had been preparing for it. Just as his older brother had been groomed to be the viscount, Paul had been groomed to be a minister.

Paul's father was born a second son and had chosen a life in the clergy. He had served as a vicar until Paul was fifteen at which time Paul's uncle died without an heir. After his uncle's death, Paul's father inherited the title. It wasn't an unexpected event. Both Paul's father and uncle had been in their fifties before marrying. The viscount had been unable to sire an heir, so it was always known that Paul's father would inherit the title. Which meant one day, Paul's brother, Sam, would inherit it, as well.

Only three years after Paul's father became viscount, he passed away and Sam inherited the title, lands, and money. That's when Paul seriously began to pursue a career as a minister.

It was all very easy when he first started. He just did what he liked best: biblical research, preaching, helping others, and being spoiled by the all the ladies of the parish baking him bread and bringing him jam.

At three-and-twenty, he was pleased with how his life had turned out and was convinced he had made the right choice. But then he turned four-and-twenty and his life turned into a living hell, so to speak.

The problem was that he found himself the target of gossip. He had a few troublemaking parishioners who liked to add grist to the rumor mill, especially at his expense. And these rumors seemed to be growing by the day.

When he tried to solve the problem, he was met with outrage by the members of the church.

Unsuccessful in his attempts at his church, he had gone to the bishop. The bishop said he was too busy to help mediate small church squabbles and sent Paul back with only a little piece of advice: find yourself a mentor.

After asking a few questions and paying calls to several of the village's most notorious gossips, who of course he knew to be his principal parishioners, Paul learned that the local baron's younger brother was a minister in the United States. And to Paul's good fortune, he was currently in England visiting his brother.

Paul had this knowledge for under an hour before he arrived at the baron's front door. After being shown into a drawing room and waiting for a quarter hour, Paul met the baron. Now he was waiting for the arrival of the baron's brother, who hopefully would agree to mentor him and become the answer to all of his problems.

He got up out of his chair, tossed his hat down and walked to the window where he began to wear a hole in the rug pacing back and forth. His mind was no longer trying to sort out what to do about the church, but thinking about how to ask a man he'd never met to be his mentor. He raked his hand through his blond hair, then took off his spectacles and rubbed his green eyes. *This is a mistake. I shouldn't have come. He may not even agree to do this, and if he does, he might change his mind when he finds out just how bad it is.*

He walked over to where his hat was sitting and was reaching down to pick it up when a creaking noise broke the silence. His fingers dropped his hat and he looked over to the door just in time to see John Banks walk into the room.

"Good afternoon," Mr. Banks said casually as his eyes searched Paul's grim face.

"Good afternoon, sir," Paul replied with a slight bow.

"How can I help you?" Mr. Banks didn't bother to bow.

"I have a small request of you, sir," Paul said timidly, then at John's motion, took a seat.

"Go on," Mr. Banks encouraged him with a warm smile.

"I understand you are a man of the cloth." Paul swallowed. How was he supposed to phrase this? Should he just come out and say it or should he try to make light of it somehow?

"Spit it out, boy," Mr. Banks said, pulling Paul from his thoughts. "I have been a minister long enough to know the more someone hesitates, the worse the problem."

Paul's eyes widened. He let out a deep breath and then the words began to tumble out before he could stop them. "You see, I am the local vicar here, and have been having some trouble at my church. I have spoken to the bishop, but he was of no help and he suggested I find a mentor. I wondered if maybe you could find the time, that is, could you act as a mentor for me?" His face burned with embarrassment. It was awfully uncomfortable asking a favor of someone upon the first meeting, especially when he was asking John Banks to be his mentor because of problems he could not handle in his own vicarage, most of which were directly connected to him.

John's eyes lit up and he jumped to his feet. "I would be honored to do just that." Wasting no time, he strolled to the door and swung it open. "Why don't we go somewhere a little less public and you can tell me about the problems going on in your vicarage."

Paul's body relaxed as they walked down to a private sitting room.

Beside him, John talked excitedly about his early experiences. Just before they entered the room, John looked him square in the eyes and said, "I remember my first few years as a minister. Nothing, and I do mean nothing, could make me want to go back and relive them. But I promise when you get it all figured out and know how to handle people it all gets easier."

"I surely hope so," Paul said with a faint smile.

# Chapter 14

A half hour before dinner was to be served, guests started to congregate in the drawing room to mingle while waiting to be shown in to dinner. Papa had introduced Paul Grimes to his family.

"He hasn't yet mastered all the finer points of the Lord's work, but with a little help and direction he'll be the best vicar in all of England," Papa declared, beaming with pride.

"I thank you kindly, sir. You will never know how much I appreciate what you have agreed to do," Mr. Grimes said modestly.

"Think nothing of it." Papa waved his hand dismissively.

"Good evening, Mr. Banks," interrupted a voice from behind Brooke.

"Good to see you again, Townson. I would like for you to meet Mr. Paul Grimes. He is the local vicar. He came to see me this afternoon. Mr. Grimes, this is Andrew Black, Earl of Townson."

Andrew and Paul bowed to each other.

"So this is the mysterious guest, then?" Andrew asked.

"The very one."

Andrew turned and faced Brooke, her mother, and sisters. "Good evening, ladies," he said with another bow.

"Townson," Mama said cordially.

"Mrs. Banks, you are looking well. And as for the three of you, Miss Brooke, Miss Madison, Miss Liberty, you all look very beautiful tonight."

"Thank you," they chorused in unison.

"Would you like to take a turn of the room with me, Miss Banks, and allow me to introduce you to some of the other guests?" he asked as he held out his arm to Brooke.

"I would like that very much," Brooke said.

When Andrew and Brooke had taken a few steps out of

earshot of her parents, Andrew leaned down and whispered in her ear. "I see those mineral baths agreed with you."

Brooke's face flushed at his innuendo, but she was determined not to let him get the better of her tonight. At least not so early, anyway. "We had a splendid time in Bath. It was quite a wonderful experience," she replied blandly

"You're rather fetching when you blush," Andrew said, ignoring her meaningless comment.

They walked around the room, but Andrew didn't introduce her to anyone. He steered her around the room, avoiding everyone that might want to talk to them. The way he was guarding her, Brooke couldn't help but feel like she was the only woman in the room.

"Have you had an agreeable visit thus far?" Andrew asked.

"Yes, I have. I saw some men out playing a lawn game earlier from my window. It looked like a lot of fun. Tomorrow, I plan to ask if I may join."

"Perhaps I can join you. I know the rules to most lawn games. I can help you learn them if you like," he offered, his eyes dancing with amusement.

"I just bet you do." She did too. He seemed the sort. She'd also bet that him helping her learn the rules would involve their bodies being in close contact. She shivered at the thought.

"Have you seen the conservatory?" he asked, breaking into her thoughts.

"No," Brooke said sadly. "I was hoping for a tour, but when we arrived, my aunt and uncle were too busy greeting guests and neither of them could give a tour at the time."

"What of your father? He did grow up here, did he not?"

"Yes, but he has been busy with Mr. Grimes, talking about the Bible and his church, since shortly after we arrived."

"Ah, what a pity," Andrew said sympathetically. Then his eyes lit up as if he had a breakthrough of some sort. "I will be happy to give you a complete tour of the estate tomorrow if that would please you."

"How do you know your way around the estate well enough to

give a tour?" she asked skeptically.

"I'm rather close friends with your cousin, Alex. He and I attended school together. Then we went on our Grand Tour together. I've been here many times and know where everything of interest is located."

She nodded. "Well, in that case, I should be delighted to go on a tour with you." She looked at his smiling face and added, "We will require a chaperone, of course."

His smile didn't falter. "Of course you require a chaperone." He paused and twisted his lips as if he were thinking about something of great importance. "How about if we invite Alex? It's acceptable for you to be accompanied by a male cousin. He is family, after all. Anyway, at these house parties the rules are more relaxed than they are in London. Nobody would think a thing of it."

"All right then," Brooke said, agreeing to go but still not sure how Mama would react. Even though Alex was a cousin, he was still a man, and none of them actually knew him very well.

As if fate was unhappy with Brooke, she could only revel in her excitement of the promised tour for a mere moment before they were accosted by the enemy: Lady Olivia Sinclair.

"Good evening, my lord," she said, curtsying to Andrew. Then she directed a brief, icy glance toward Brooke. "Miss Banks," she murmured.

Both Andrew and Brooke quickly greeted Lady Olivia.

"I am so glad I found you, my lord. I was beginning to think you had reneged on your invitation to escort me in to dinner." Lady Olivia's accusation was said loud enough to turn heads in their direction.

Brooke was so convinced of her words that her fingers acted of their own accord. They loosened their grip on his arm and lightly hovered on his coat, barely touching the fabric. Was it true? Had he promised to take Lady Olivia in to dinner? If he had, why was he walking with her? Her mind raced with all sorts of questions she wanted to ask but knew she couldn't. She stood still, waiting for Andrew to say something.

When he finally did, it wasn't what Brooke had hoped. "Please accept my humble apologies. I would be glad to escort you to dinner. Let me just return Miss Banks back to her family," he said smoothly to Lady Olivia.

Andrew nearly dragged Brooke back to where her parents were standing across the drawing room.

"You shouldn't be acting short with me. I'm not the one who was caught trying to get out of an earlier promise," she said icily when they were almost to her parents.

Andrew didn't dignify that statement with a response.

When they reached her parents, he disengaged his arm, then turned and stalked across the room to Lady Olivia before any more words could be exchanged.

Brooke stood by her parents. She tried to act as if she weren't bothered with the evening's change of events. She talked to a few of the gentlemen that were around and was escorted down to dinner by Mr. Cook.

On the way to dinner, Mr. Cook tried to make small talk, but even that was too much for her to keep up with. Her mind was too busy thinking of Andrew and why he'd thrown her over like that. If he had previously asked Lady Olivia to dinner, then why did he seek her out? Was he really trying to renege on his earlier promise? As awful as it sounded, she almost hoped that was what had happened. Not that she liked that Lady Olivia had ended up with Andrew as her dinner companion, but she liked the idea that he had attempted to throw Lady Olivia over for her. She knew she was wrong for relishing such a thought, but at least she was honest.

Mr. Cook led her to a pair of seats across from Liberty and Mr. Grimes. Once they were seated, Brooke murmured her greetings to the others then stared at the entrance waiting for Andrew. What was taking him so long? He was an earl, one of the highest ranks in attendance; he should be seated fairly close to the hostess. The Duke of Gateway entered along with his escort, Lady Burbank. She was shocked when they sat down right next to her and Mr. Cook.

Mr. Cook leaned over and whispered, "They are terribly

informal here. Nobody has assigned seats, nor do they arrange anyone by rank."

Brooke nodded to confirm she understood before moving her eyes back to the doorway. That's when she saw them. Lady Olivia came in with a self-satisfied smile as big as the Thames on her face, and when Andrew looked at Brooke, he smiled, too.

A quick, sharp snapping noise rent the air. Looking down into her lap only confirmed Brooke's suspicion that she had indeed just broken her only fan. Not wanting to draw any further attention or questions, she quickly tucked her broken fan into her reticule.

Mr. Cook, the duke, and Mr. Grimes, who were all within hearing distance, clearly had not heard anything. Lady Burbank looked around as if trying to see what it was that she'd heard. But when Brooke turned her eyes in Liberty's direction, a look of sympathy was plainly stamped on her sister's face.

Even with her unseemly obsession with manners and etiquette, Liberty was sympathetic and would do anything for her sisters. Seeing Liberty's sympathetic face warmed her heart.

Brooke tried to put on a brave face. She didn't want her sister or anyone else to know how much it hurt to see Andrew with another woman. She inclined her chin an inch or two, as she had often seen the ladies in London do, and turned to Mr. Cook. "Do you frequently attend parties here, sir?"

"I do." Mr. Cook said jovially.

Brooke hadn't noticed it before, but now she was well aware that Mr. Cook had already started to imbibe the spirits. Both his language and his breath were giving him away.

She turned to look across the table to where Mr. Grimes was sitting. "My father is very excited to have made your acquaintance this afternoon. He is looking forward to working with you." She gave him a small, grateful smile. It was good for Papa to have something to do to occupy himself, and ministerial matters were his favorite hobby.

"I am very fortunate your father has agreed to pass on his knowledge to me," Mr. Grimes said with a hint of stress in voice.

Brooke took his words as a subtle hint that he didn't want to talk about his situation just now. "Well, even if you made up a need for him, it will do him good. He has been trying to find things to occupy his time ever since we arrived."

"I assure you, I need his assistance," Mr. Grimes said stiffly, and then he relaxed a bit. "But it's an honor to meet him anyway. I do look forward to getting to know him and your family better over the next few months."

Brooke caught sight of Liberty stiffening at that statement. Had Liberty already taken a dislike to this man? He acted as straight and proper as a pin. What was there for Liberty not to like? Or did she dislike him at all? Something was off between these two, she could sense it.

"Miss Banks," Mr. Cook said, catching Brooke's attention. He waited until the footman had refilled his wineglass before he spoke. "Pardon me for mentioning this, but I have noticed that you and your sisters have some very unusual names. Do all the colonists give their children such bizarre names?"

Brooke tried not to grind her teeth. They were Americans, not colonists. She was born an American. By her guess, he couldn't be so old that he could have known of the United States as the Colonies, unless of course he was a wee lad in leading strings at the time.

"Actually, I have no real knowledge of what the *colonists* named their children. During my lifetime, I've only known my home country to be termed the United States of America." Her voice was sweet, but her meaning was not.

Mr. Cook was further into his cups than she originally thought. He just sat there and blinked at her as if he had something in his eye he was trying to flush out.

He may not understand what she was saying, but Gateway, who was sitting on her right, did because he was openly laughing at Mr. Cook and his stupidity. "The colonists won their war for independence in 1783, and England formally granted their independence and acknowledged them as the United States of America shortly thereafter. Thus, Miss Banks was not even alive when they were still a bunch of colonies," Gateway said, then cocked his head in mock contemplation. "Come to think of it, Cook, neither were you. It would appear that you missed that particular lecture by Mr. Rawlings at Eton."

Brooke fought to keep a smile off her lips.

Mr. Cook's face colored slightly. "I beg your pardon, Miss Banks. As Gateway so bluntly pointed out, history was not an interest of mine at school."

Brooke was still in shock that Gateway had taken up her defense and set Mr. Cook in his place without making her look bad. Maybe he wasn't such a bad person after all. She looked his way and started. He was staring at her. "Thank you, Your Grace," she murmured.

The duke immediately shifted his eyes and developed a sharp interest in his soup.

Liberty tried to salvage the conversation from across the table. "We do have highly irregular names. Brooke's real name is Brooklyn, which is the name of the town in New York that Mama and Papa had just moved to before Brooke was born. In fact, we still live there."

"Are there any other counties that are close to Brooklyn in New York?" Mr. Cook asked, feigning interest.

"Manhattan, Queens, Staten Island, and the Bronx," Liberty recited promptly. "It's a joke between Madison and I that we're just glad our parents weren't living in Queens when Brooke entered the world."

Everyone in the group gave a little laugh. Brooke personally wouldn't have minded being called Queenie by her sisters. She rather liked the idea.

"What about your name?" Mr. Cook asked politely. "I have never heard the name Liberty before."

"And you likely will not hear it again. It means freedom from external rule. There was a quotation in the Declaration of Independence that begins with 'Life, liberty and the pursuit of happiness'. Anyway, that particular line was very popular among the colonists during the time of the Revolutionary War.

"Mama's family can trace its way back to some of the first

settlers in the colony of Virginia in the sixteen hundreds. Some of them later spread to the Carolinas, hence her name. Anyway, they have always been a very patriotic family and fought fiercely for independence. Her family still says that quote frequently. Mama has a plaque on her bedchamber wall with it engraved on it, and when I was born they couldn't think of a name for me. When Mama looked across the room and saw the plaque, she decided on Liberty right then and there."

This time it was the duke who asked a question. "What of Miss Madison's name? It isn't a place or a definition. I am aware that the current President of the United States is named James Madison, but he has not been in office Madison's whole life."

Brooke decided to answer him before Liberty would ramble on again about a bunch of information that no one, save her family, cared about. "Actually, she is named for the current President. As you pointed out, he was not the president all her life, but he did help to write the United States Constitution. Papa and Mama picked her name because his last name sounded as if it would make a good first name for a girl."

"What I fail to understand is why your English-bred father would allow his daughters to have such American names. It's as if he's not being true to his homeland," Lady Burbank said with disgust and disapproval evident in her voice.

Nobody responded. There wasn't anything to say to that.

It was true Papa was English, and nothing could ever change that. Yet, he had allowed his daughters to take on names that symbolized where they were from and what the United States stood for. It would seem a disgrace to English loyalists.

The rest of the meal was spent trying to avoid the topic of their names or any mention of the United States in general. For her part, Brooke just kept silent. She was too busy trying to inconspicuously glance down the table to where Andrew was sitting with Lady Olivia.

Lady Olivia had worn a smug smile when she entered the room perched on Andrew's arm. Maybe Lady Olivia was right—maybe she would win Andrew after all, if she hadn't already, that is. She had surely started to dig her claws in, and made quite a show doing it.

Brooke remembered how Andrew immediately dumped her off with her parents to go back to Lady Olivia's side. Just remembering it made Brooke's skin grow warm with anger. He probably decided Lady Olivia was a better long-term match and needed to put on his best front with her, which would mean not associating with Brooke any longer.

Brooke wasn't going to dwell on this. If that's the choice he'd made, that was fine with her. She'd just form a new connection and flaunt her happiness in his face, if there was any, that is. If there wasn't, she'd pretend there was.

She turned to survey her options. To her left, Mr. Cook was drinking his wine as rapidly as the footman was refilling his glass. That wouldn't do. She looked across the table to Mr. Grimes. He appeared decent enough, but a little rigid. Something about him struck her as cold and not very malleable. He wouldn't do for her purposes, either.

That only left Gateway, who probably hated her, and for good reason, too. But that couldn't be helped—he was the only one left. She turned her head to look at him. He wasn't looking at her, but he acted like he was clearly aware of her stare.

She opened her mouth to say something, but he beat her to it. "Don't even think about it, Miss Banks."

She flushed. "Think about what, Your Grace?"

"I know what you're about. You haven't tried very diligently to be discreet about your thoughts or future intentions." His voice was low and hard.

"What would those be?" she asked innocently, but her voice was unusually high-pitched.

"I have been told about a little connection that you and Townson have formed. However, now that you've spotted him with that vulture they call Lady Olivia, you've decided that since he has so easily found another lady to woo, you shall find another beau to flaunt before his eyes." He smiled at her slight half-nod. "What I cannot figure out is whether you mean to flaunt that beau, or should I say me, in front of him to make him see reason and come running back to you, or if you want to make him jealous for not making the correct decision to begin with."

"You have taken the thoughts straight from my mind, Your Grace." Brooke said humbly. She bit her lip in aggravation and sighed. "Although, it's not as though I ever really had him to begin with," she finished dully.

"If you want my advice, Miss Banks," the duke said gently, "I believe you are more important to him than Lady Olivia ever could be. I do believe in no time he will return and stick to your side like a bur."

Brooke hoped he was right. She tried to convince herself she shouldn't feel jealous at seeing Lady Olivia with Andrew, but she did anyway. It wasn't as if he had declared himself to her, but she thought he might, and that would cause anyone to be jealous.

Until now, she hadn't realized just how much she had been counting on Andrew declaring himself to her and eventually asking for her hand in marriage. Flaunting another in his face wasn't going to help the situation, nor was it going to make her feel any better. She'd just have to fight for what she wanted, Lady Olivia be damned.

As was the custom, the ladies congregated in the drawing room following dinner while the gentlemen enjoyed their own company for a bit before rejoining the ladies.

"Did either of you have a more pleasant dinner than I?" Brooke asked her sisters when they were comfortably seated on a secluded settee.

"No," Liberty answered without a bit of hesitation. "As you know, I had to sit next to Mr. Grimes. He has the personality of a brick."

"Then you two are well suited, indeed," Brooke quipped. Was it possible Liberty was just pretending not to like Mr. Grimes? The pink tinge staining her cheeks suggested there was more to this than Liberty was sharing.

Liberty rolled her eyes. "I'm being serious. The man is as stiff as a fire poker. He doesn't smile or laugh at anything, nor does he seem to speak unless absolutely necessary. Having a conversation with a person like that is painful."

"I agree with Brooke, you two are a perfect match, indeed," Madison said with a little laugh.

Liberty rolled her eyes again. "That man is not the one for me. Now, tell us what Mr. Thomas was like, Madison."

"He was very nice. More interesting than either of your companions, it seems," Madison said with a slight laugh.

"That's not saying much," Liberty mumbled.

"Who knew that the one of us that is not interested in making a match was matched up with the best gentleman?" Brooke said, imitating Lady Olivia's pout.

Brooke was surprised when Liberty didn't reprove her comment or gesture, but laughed right along with her and Madison. Maybe there was hope for her after all.

At Brooke's urging, Madison told them about Mr. Thomas and his excellent company. "We talked about many fascinating subjects, or should I say people. Mr. Thomas has an interest in gossip and he knows all the most amusing tidbits about all the members of the *ton*. He felt compelled to share all his knowledge with me, which I listened to only out of politeness of course."

"I'll just bet you did," Brooke said with an unfeminine laugh. Madison had always had little trouble listening to and enjoying gossip. Papa had tried to discourage her from this, saying it was sinful, but Madison struggled with it just the same. It was a point in her favor that she didn't further spread the gossip and for that alone, their Papa had sung songs of rejoicing.

"Well, it would have been impolite not to listen, and I would not like to disappoint Miss Propriety over here," she said with a pointed look at Liberty.

"You did well," Liberty assured her, her approval evident.

Brooke was about to ask if Mr. Thomas had mentioned anything about Andrew when Lady Olivia strolled over.

"How nice to see you tonight, ladies," Lady Olivia said in a superior voice.

"Yes, it's nice to see you, too," Madison replied first. "I

suspect your presence here indicates that your complaint was successfully healed during your recent visit to Bath."

"Of course, the baths there are so wonderful. There's nothing they cannot heal."

Except a personality defect, Brooke thought.

"I am glad you are doing better then," Liberty said, shooting a quick glance to where Brooke was sitting quietly.

"I am much better thank you—quite revived in fact. I do believe my energy has been restored and I can now set my sights on loftier things than enjoying the countryside while I'm here." Her words were a bit of a puzzle, but it didn't take a genius to get her meaning. She was declaring loud and clear to Brooke and her sisters that her sights were set on Andrew and she wouldn't be going anywhere until things were settled where he was concerned.

Lady Olivia had said as much to Brooke at the bathhouse, but now seeing her here and declaring it again made it more irrefutable. If Lady Olivia were to be believed, Brooke's time with Andrew would soon be ending. She would have to do something, but what? Hearing Lady Olivia's public declaration was swiftly killing the bravado she had built up after her talk with Gateway.

"I do hope you enjoy yourself," Brooke said stiffly as she stood up, clutching her skirts. She had tolerated Lady Olivia enough for one evening, thank you. She walked over to where Mama was holding court in the opposite corner of the room.

When she reached Mama's side and sat down, she learned this conversation wasn't much better. Lady Burbank was scolding Mama about the names she and Papa had selected for their daughters. Calling it a disgrace and saying it should be considered treasonous toward England. Brooke got the feeling that Lady Burbank thought that *she* should have been consulted when Papa and Mama had named their children.

Even though this conversation was equally uncomfortable, it didn't cause her heart to feel like it was breaking just by listening to it. *Why was that?* How could her chest hurt so badly? She couldn't recognize the emotion attached to the pain. She was very familiar with jealousy, rage, and anger, but this time it was different. It felt like she had lost something, but she couldn't put her finger on what she'd lost. Nor could she name the emotion that was causing her to feel this loss.

After ten more minutes of hearing Lady Burbank's useless and screeching chatter, Brooke couldn't take any more and decided to retire for the evening. She made her farewells and was walking down the hall, looking at her feet as she went when two strong hands grabbed her shoulders.

Her heart skipped a beat, whether out of shock or excitement, she wasn't sure.

When she looked up, she was a bit disappointed to see that the stranger who had stopped her from running him over was none other than her own cousin. "Good evening, Alex," she said.

"What has you escaping so soon?" Alex asked kindly.

"A headache." It was partially true. She didn't have a real headache, not yet anyway, but if she were to listen to anymore from Lady Olivia or Lady Burbank she just might have one very soon.

"There has to be a reason for your headache." His eyes were full of concern. "Is one of the guests causing problems already?" he asked, his voice ringing with sincerity.

She could trust Alex with her secrets. He was a quiet type. He wouldn't tell anyone about their conversation. "There are three reasons for my headache. They come in the form of Lady Burbank, Lady Olivia, and the Earl of Townson."

Alex's expression didn't change at her words. Brooke thought that maybe he had expected to hear those names.

"Would you care to accompany me to the library so we can talk about what's bothering you?" he offered with a warm smile.

"I'm not sure I should," she said hesitantly. He might be her cousin, but surely she shouldn't be going off alone with him.

"If you're worried about propriety, then don't. Nothing is going to happen. You're my cousin. I have no interest in ravishing you." He offered her his arm and waited for her to take it. "Nobody will think anything of it if they did find out, Brooke. It is perfectly acceptable," he added with an encouraging smile.

"All right," she agreed. She followed him down the hall to the library. Once inside, she plopped down on a settee. "It goes like this…"

***

Fifteen minutes later Brooke had shared her secrets about everything—well almost everything.

Alex hadn't said much. He just nodded and occasionally murmured monosyllabic answers as if to say he understood, though she doubted he really did. He was a man. How could he understand her feelings? Nonetheless, she rambled on.

Finally, Alex put his hand up, signaling Brooke to stop. "Let's make sure we understand each other. Andrew had been paying you unmarked attention in London. Not a lot, but enough to make you believe his intentions toward you were honorable. Then, Lady Olivia told you she intends to snag him herself. Finally, you arrived here and he's promising things to Lady Olivia while ignoring you, which makes you think that he has shifted his interest from you to *her*?"

"Yes," Brooke said sheepishly.

Shaking his head in disbelief, Alex stated, "I've known Andrew for many years. Though some may not think so, he is an honorable man. I don't believe he has any true interest in Lady Olivia. By her own admission she's out to 'bag him'. She was probably just playing a part when she confronted him before dinner, and Andrew is too much of a gentleman, he wouldn't embarrass her publicly by exposing her lie."

"Do you really think so?" Brooke asked hopefully.

"Yes. If what you said before about him paying attention to you and making a cake of himself in front of your family is true, then I believe he has an interest in you, not her." He stopped talking and laughed a little. "I'll admit I wish I could have been there to witness him saying those things. I've never seen him embarrass himself. If I remember correctly, he reacts very strongly to being embarrassed or seeing others embarrassed."

Brooke believed that. She remembered the night her sisters had unintentionally embarrassed her. He sat next to her and tried to make her feel better about it, then when it was obvious her family intended to embarrass her more by telling more stories about her, he'd left. She had been too mortified at the time to realize what he was doing, but now that she could think about it more clearly, she realized he was doing his best to protect her feelings.

"What can I do about it then?" Brooke asked.

"About what?" Alex's brows came together and his face looked like he had no idea what Brooke was talking about.

"What can I do about Lady Olivia? How can I compete with her?" she asked anxiously, trying to explain to an oblivious Alex that she did not think the problem had magically solved itself.

Alex leaned back in his chair. "Hmm, I do believe we need to devise a plan of action. If you truly think he was going to ask you to marry him, you could try to get caught in a compromising situation with him."

"I don't think that's the answer," Brooke said disapprovingly. Nor was she sure that Andrew was going to ask her to marry him in the first place.

"Maybe not. But, if you don't do something soon, Lady Olivia might think of the same plan, and she won't be too meek to pull it off."

"She would not!" Brooke said vehemently.

"She would," Alex countered with a simple nod. "You may not know this about Lady Olivia, but as a bachelor, I've become well acquainted with her kind. She isn't attractive or even liked in most social circles, however, she still desires a husband, and I'm willing to bet she'll go about acquiring one any way she can."

"Would he do it?" Brooke's voice cracked on the last word.

"Do what? Marry a lady he was caught in a compromising situation with? Absolutely. He's an honorable man and would do the right thing."

Brooke liked the idea of marrying the earl, but not the idea of a potential scandal. She didn't want to send her family back to the United States in disgrace. Even if she married him, it would still bring disgrace on her family because of the surrounding scandal. She valued her family too much for her to carelessly trample over them just to get what she wanted. "Do you think we could try something a little less drastic first?"

"Yes. Lady Olivia is desperate, but I don't think she will push things that far this soon. She'll try to win him with her money, class, or connections before trying to throw her virtue at him. I'll try to arrange a few activities for you and Andrew to do over the next few days. But you'll have to do your part as well."

Brooke didn't know what her part entailed, but she nodded her agreement. She would do her part and then some if it would help her win Andrew.

"You may not like this, but when I arrange for you two to be alone you'll have to tease him a little."

Brooke let out a nervous giggle. "Tease him? How?"

"Little things really," he said with a dismissive wave of his hand. "When you put your hand on his arm to be escorted, give him a little squeeze. When you're alone with him, act like you're going to let him kiss you, then back away before he does. Do that a few times and he'll follow you like a lost dog in no time."

Brooke giggled again at the idea of the earl following her around that way. "I can do those things. I probably shouldn't say this, but I've been doing those tricks for years."

"No, you shouldn't say that to anyone else, but for our purposes it works to your advantage that you've already had plenty of practice," he said dryly.

"I just hope I can back away when he tries to kiss me," Brooke said without thinking.

"It will be easy, especially if you remember why you are doing it."

"Very true. I shall just have to block the memory of how good our last kiss was and focus on the future good."

"Your last kiss?" Alex asked, his voice taking on a sharp tone. "Just how many kisses have the two of you shared?"

"Jus—just two. At the museum. But one was just merely a brush on the lips, so it doesn't count."

Alex's eyes looked deadly. "He had better not have been trifling with you.

It was time to leave. She had possibly said too much as it was and didn't want Alex to change his mind about helping her. "I think I had better retire now in case Mama checks in on me. Thank you for agreeing to help me. I shall follow all of your advice exactly." Then before he could say anything else, she fled the library and ran up the stairs, heedless to the body that was standing right outside the library door.

# Chapter 15

Andrew was furious as he left Brooke with her parents and stalked across the drawing room to where Lady Olivia was waiting for him. He'd like to shake the silly chit until her yellow teeth rattled. Who did she think she was? And what did she want with him?

"The Prodigal Earl hath returned," Lady Olivia said, looking at him with that miserable, pouty face she always sported.

"Yes, I have returned per your request," he said with a clipped voice. What was she about? Why had she accused him publicly of trying to renege on a promise he had never even made? What was her game? Then he remembered she had gotten upset when he responded to her bold proposal and told her he wasn't interested in marrying her. Her face had changed at his refusal, and then she had declared something about trying to win his hand. This was how she was going about it? Wonderful. Now during the whole party, she was going to plague him and try to put the other girls off, just as she had done with Brooke.

Andrew knew it was wrong, but he wished she'd come down with a complaint tomorrow and return to London or Bath for the remainder of the party. Otherwise, he'd have to spend every last shilling he possessed bribing servants to keep him updated on her whereabouts so he could avoid her like the plague.

"Don't be silly," she giggled. "You said you enjoyed my company and would be delighted to accompany me to dinner. If I were amendable, of course."

Her words were spoken lightly and airily, but her eyes told a different story. She truly expected that he would agree to her charges right here and make it sound like a public declaration of his feelings toward her.

Andrew's jaw worked. This was a mess of the worst sort.

There was only one way out: go along with what she wanted for now in order to keep gossip down, then pawn her off on some other poor sod at the first opportunity. "You're correct, Lady Olivia, I did want to accompany you to dinner tonight," he said loudly enough for the eavesdroppers close by to hear. "Perhaps we shall discuss the rules of chess again and talk more about strategy."

He bit back a smile when he watched her smile slip and disappointment twist her lips into a snarl. He hated being such a heel, but really she was not the least bit fascinating, and if he had to suffer through dinner with her, she would be doing some suffering, too. He was going to make sure of it.

She recovered quickly though. "That would be delightful, my lord. Since you earlier expressed your understanding and penchant for rules, I am convinced you would be the best person to consult about rules and strategy."

Andrew nodded and resigned himself to a dinner companion that might drive him to commit suicide later.

Just then the butler appeared and announced that dinner was served.

Relieved that he wouldn't have to make idle chitchat with just Lady Olivia much longer, Andrew offered her his arm and started walking briskly toward where the butler was leading the party down to dinner.

"Could you slow down? My slippers do not allow me to walk as fast as you," Lady Olivia said sharply.

"Of course," Andrew muttered.

When Andrew and Lady Olivia entered the dining room, he immediately searched for Brooke. Unfortunately she was seated at the far end of the table by Mr. Cook, Liberty, and Mr. Grimes. Brooke's face looked as hard as steel. He tried to give her an apologetic smile, but it did nothing to soften her face

Dinner would have been excellent if not for such poor company. Throughout the whole meal, Lady Olivia cooed, simpered, batted her lashes, and made several other pathetic attempts at flirting. It was enough to make even the hungriest man lose his appetite.

After dinner, the men stayed in the dining room while the ladies went to the drawing room. The separation only lasted an hour, but Andrew felt every one of those sixty minutes.

Andrew walked down the hall with the gentlemen on their way to join the ladies in the drawing room. If not for the fact that he was going to see Brooke when he arrived there, he would have gone up to his room. Just the knowledge that she was in there, maybe even waiting for him, made him walk a little faster down the hall.

He was disappointed when he stepped through the door and his eyes did a quick sweep of the room, revealing Brooke's absence. He wandered around to make sure he hadn't just overlooked her, but that only confirmed that she wasn't there.

It would seem impolite if he were to leave right away, so he made his rounds and politely inquired to Mrs. Banks about Brooke's whereabouts.

"She complained of a headache a half hour ago," Mrs. Banks told him stiffly, watching his face as he absorbed her words.

"I'm sorry to hear that," he murmured, and he was. He had wanted to talk to her and now it didn't look like he'd get the chance. "If by chance you should see her tonight, please tell her I hope she feels better tomorrow."

"I'll be sure to let her know, my lord," Mrs. Banks replied coolly before turning back to the ladies she had been speaking to before he interrupted.

Her demeanor toward him had changed tonight, and he knew why. She probably assumed he was playing loose with her daughter's affections. Any mother who was in her position would treat him the same. The truth was she had no reason to think otherwise.

After making small talk with a few others, he decided he would also go to bed. But first he needed to seek Alex out to confirm he'd be able to join them on a tour of the grounds tomorrow. Thinking of the tour made him inwardly smile. He had made up his mind earlier tonight that he was going to steal another kiss from Brooke on the tour. With Alex acting as the chaperone, stealing a dozen kisses would pose no problem.

Alex had left the gentlemen before they had gone to the drawing room to meet up with the ladies. Andrew looked around. Alex wasn't in the room, either. No matter. If Alex wasn't here, he'd be in the library, most likely with his nose stuck in a book.

Andrew slipped from the room just before Lady Olivia could sink her talons into him again. Walking down the hall, he threw glances over his shoulder to make sure she had not followed him. He wouldn't put it past her at this point to attempt getting caught alone with him. The thought made him shudder.

Andrew put his hand on the handle to the library door and was about to open it when a female giggle erupted from inside. Stunned, he took a step back. He had no idea why Alex would choose to entertain a female companion in the library of all places. Personally, he could think of many better places to enjoy their company, but Alex was Alex.

Maybe it would be best to wait until breakfast to ask Alex. He turned to walk away when he suddenly heard a familiar voice and his body froze.

Getting over his shock, he walked back to the door of the library with the intention of hearing the voice better. It had sounded light and musical, strangely like Brooke's. He shook his head. Why would Brooke be in the library with Alex? And what on earth would she possibly find humorous in that room?

He put his ear to the door so he could hear the voice again, in order to either confirm or disprove his thoughts about the identity of Alex's companion. When he heard the voice again he knew instantly it belonged to Brooke. He couldn't make out what she was saying, but he knew it was her in the library with Alex and she had giggled about something—no, two somethings. He had clearly heard her laugh twice. Now her voice had taken on a different tone and so had Alex's. Alex almost sounded on edge now.

Andrew fought the urge to swing open the door, barge in, and demand to know what was going on, but his feet were rooted to the floor. Did he really want to know what was going on in there? Some people married their cousins, he reminded himself. Was that what this was? Were these two planning to make a match of it? No, that was impossible. They hardly knew each other. Not to mention, their interests were so at odds, they both would struggle in a marriage to each other.

A noise that sounded like a person walking toward the door came from inside the library and he quickly stepped aside.

The door flew open and through the shadows, Andrew watched Brooke dash out of the library and run toward the staircase.

When she was out of sight, Andrew indulged his temper and barged into the library. "What was that about?" Andrew demanded curtly. Tension took hold of his entire body.

"I should ask you what *you're* about," Alex shot back angrily.

"What *I'm* about? I'm not the one secretly meeting with a young lady in a library."

"Calm yourself, Andrew. I wasn't doing anything I shouldn't, unlike you."

"Unlike me? What exactly are you insinuating?" Andrew's voice filled with disbelief.

"You seem to be trifling with my cousin, and I won't countenance it." Alex looked as if waiting for Andrew to deny his charge.

Andrew just stared at him. "What do you mean trifling with her?"

"You were courting and kissing her in London, and now you've thrown her over for Lady Olivia."

"She told you that?" Andrew asked, his anger toward Alex dissolving. His anger in general hadn't dissolved; it was now directed squarely at Lady Olivia for her role in the mess.

"If you're referring to her telling me you kissed her? Then yes, she told me about the museum. If you are referring to you throwing her over for Lady Olivia? Then yes, she told me about that, too." His eyes still held their sharp edge. "Andrew, you might be my closest friend, but that doesn't mean you have free rein to run over Brooke's feelings with no consequences."

Andrew didn't want to know exactly what Alex meant by that

comment, so he ignored it. "I didn't throw Brooke over for Lady Olivia," he said defensively. "This afternoon, Lady Olivia made clear her intentions to woo me. She even had the nerve to propose to me, which, much to her dismay, I refused. Tonight in the drawing room, she made up some outrageous story that I had asked to escort her to dinner and how I was backing out of it by escorting Brooke. I didn't know what else to do. Several people overheard this exchange, including Lady Algen and Mr. Thomas who, as you know, are notorious gossips. I chose what I thought was the less damaging action: I took Brooke back to her parents and escorted Lady Olivia to dinner."

"And you didn't think this would affect Brooke?" Alex asked earnestly.

"It wasn't until I saw Brooke's face in the dining room that I realized how much I'd hurt her, but it was too late. I didn't get a chance to talk to her during dinner. I had hoped to talk to her in the drawing room, but she'd already left by the time I got there. I decided it was best to talk to her tomorrow when I take her on a tour of the grounds." Andrew sat down in a chair across from Alex. "That reminds me why I came to the library in the first place. I need you to accompany us tomorrow on a tour of the grounds. She won't go without a chaperone, and she has no maid."

Alex's eyes looked around the room for a few minutes before they settled back on Andrew. "Andrew, are your intentions toward Brooke honorable?" he asked quietly.

Andrew stiffened at Alex's question. He wasn't sure how to answer. If he were to tell him the truth, Alex would not only refuse to help him tomorrow, but would probably have him thrown out of the party as well. On the other hand, if he said his intentions were honorable, Alex would expect an engagement to be announced soon—especially if Brooke was caught in a compromising situation, which was his plan. What a tangle.

Andrew stared at Alex's probing eyes and quietly asked, "What do you think?" It was the simple way to answer, it wasn't a lie or the truth—he was just avoiding the question and relying on his gentleman's honor to carry him through.

"I believe you have a serious interest in her, and I believe that you will make the right decisions where she is concerned." Alex's tone was still hard, but his face had softened considerably.

Andrew's lips twisted at his friend's none-too-subtle insinuation that if any harm—scandal or otherwise—were to befall Brooke, Alex expected him to do the right thing. He swallowed. He couldn't back out now. He'd gone too far and too much was at stake. He'd just have to ask for forgiveness later.

# Chapter 16

Mama had not been the only one to check on Brooke before retiring for bed. Both of her sisters had come, too.

Between the three of them, she was showered with more sympathy than she'd received in her entire life. All of them said they were sorry about what had happened, they hadn't expected the earl to treat her that way, and how horrid they thought Lady Olivia was.

Brooke agreed wholeheartedly about Lady Olivia being horrid. Even if she had reasons for it, as Alex believed. That was no excuse. She was as much of a snake as Gateway, Brooke was sure of it. She was almost certain all those complaints were just an act to cover up her true personality.

As for the earl losing interest in her and tossing her aside for Lady Olivia, well, that was a different matter. She had a plan. She was going to win him back, and in such a way that Lady Olivia would have to go find another helpless soul to tether herself to. Andrew Black, Earl of Townson belonged to Brooke.

Brooke didn't tell her sisters or Mama of her plan when they came to visit. She wasn't sure they'd approve. Madison might not say anything, but Liberty and Mama would go into hysterics. They'd probably even be appalled at the idea of her flirting so outrageously in order to claim the man she loved. Loved? Could she? Is that why she hurt so badly when she saw him with Lady Olivia? Is that why she had that hurting, angry, empty feeling in her chest? She would have to examine this more carefully later, because for now she had to get ready to go downstairs and break her fast.

All the way down the stairs, she couldn't help but hope he was in the breakfast room and would dine with her. She walked to the grand staircase. Why did this man stir these feelings? Were they truly feelings of love? How could they be? How could she love him so soon? The two of them had only spent a few afternoons together. But those afternoons had been so magical to her. She'd felt differently when Andrew had touched and kissed her than she had when any of the other London gentlemen had. Did that mean she loved him though?

Or were her feelings just an intense amount of jealousy? She was jealous of Lady Olivia. She knew she was—there was no point in denying it. If she wasn't jealous, she would not be trying to win him. But that didn't mean she loved him.

She stuck to her newfound determination for all of ten seconds, because when she walked into the breakfast room her resolution wavered. Immensely.

Andrew was sitting at the end of the long table, his startling blue eyes trained on the door. When she walked in, he jumped up and, with a bone-melting smile, asked her to join him.

After Brooke filled her plate at the sideboard, she sat down next to Andrew, her skin growing warmer.

"I trust you slept well," he said casually.

"I did. And you?" she asked lightly, wishing they could avoid trivial small talk.

"Yes. I spoke to Alex last night," he told her, his lips twitching a little, like he knew a secret he wasn't going to share. "He has agreed to go with us following breakfast to look over the grounds."

Brooke smiled brightly. She had to start thinking of what she was going to do and say during the tour to get his attention back. "I'm glad you remembered your offer," she said shortly.

"I would never forget a promise I made to such a fine lady as you," he replied. His voice had taken on a silky tone.

"Good. See that you are able to keep all your promises in the future," she shot back sternly. Her wounded feelings were not forgotten just because he remembered the promise he had made to her.

"I wanted to take you to dinner last night. I never made such a proclamation to Lady Olivia, but she had me trapped. I did not want to embarrass her by pointing out to all of those people that I had not invited her to accompany me to dinner," he said apologetically.

His words brought Brooke up short. That was precisely what Alex had told her. Andrew's honor would not allow others to be embarrassed, nor would he himself purposely embarrass anyone else. She had believed it for the most part last night, but it made her feel much better to hear Andrew say it. But just to be sure she asked, "Are you telling me you have no interest whatsoever in Lady Olivia?"

"None," he said simply, looking straight into her eyes as he said it.

"I am happy to hear that." And she was, too. Actually, relieved was a better description.

"Now that we have that settled, are you ready to embark on our tour?"

Brooke gestured to her plate where she still had half a pear slice sitting, beckoning for her to eat it. "I should like to finish my pear, then we may be on our way."

"All right, you finish your breakfast and I'll go locate Alex. He finished eating before you came down. He's most likely in the library reading," he said as he got up from the table.

"Where shall I meet you?"

"Just stay here. We'll be back in a matter of minutes."

Once he had left, she finished her pear slice, and thought about their tour of the estate. Would he try anything? He hadn't tried to push his leg against hers during breakfast the way he had done previously, but that didn't mean he wouldn't try anything while they were on their tour. Would he try to kiss her on the tour?

She sat there with a little smile playing on her lips because she had decided yes; he was going to kiss her again. She would see to it that he tried. She was also going to make sure he didn't get his kiss, at least not right away.

Brooke came out of her whimsical trance when footfalls grew louder from the hallway. That must be them. They had returned, and now they could go on their tour.

Nobody else in the room seemed aware of Brooke's

excitement, but several heads turned in her direction when they heard her gasp at the sight of the group that entered the breakfast room.

Alex walked in first, his face contorted in a way that made clear his irritation.

Following him was Andrew, with Lady Olivia clutching his arm as if she were clinging onto a lifeline she'd been tossed while drowning in the Thames.

"A tour you say," Lady Olivia cooed. "I should like to join you. Please allow me this great pleasure. I need only break my fast, nothing more, and then I shall be ready to go." Her words were directed at Andrew, but her smug smile was directed straight at Brooke.

Andrew walked her over to the sideboard to help her with her plate. "All right," he agreed, a hint of annoyance creeping into his voice.

Alex sat down next to Brooke. "I'm just as displeased by these developments as you are," he mumbled and made a sour face.

Brooke took pleasure in his statement. Nobody liked to wallow in their misery alone.

The four of them sat in silence. Brooke was scowling. Alex looked annoyed. Andrew's face was getting more rigid with each passing second. Lady Olivia was the only one who seemed to be enjoying the situation. Of course that was because she was the center of everyone's attention.

When Lady Olivia had finally taken her last bite and wiped her mouth for what seemed like the fiftieth time, she announced, "That was most excellent. I am now refreshed enough to go about our tour."

"You ate enough to be sufficiently refreshed to walk to the nearest village and back without needing any more refreshment," Brooke mumbled under her breath.

Alex heard her and chuckled.

Brooke flushed, but neither Andrew nor Lady Olivia gave any indication of hearing what she'd said.

Andrew stood first. "Alex, I forgot something in your library, would you mind helping me locate it before we go?"

"Is it that important that we find it right now?" Alex asked impatiently.

"Yes, it's of the utmost importance. It will take no longer than a few moments."

"All right. If you'll excuse us, ladies. We shall return momentarily," Alex said irritably as he stood.

They were gone only a few minutes then came back in and strolled over to where the ladies were sitting. "If the two of you are ready, we are ready to escort you about," Andrew said cheerfully.

"Absolutely," Brooke said stiffly. She stood and moved toward Andrew as quickly as she could. When she reached his side before Lady Olivia, she clutched his arm and shot her a triumphant smile.

"I would like to escort you, Lady Olivia," Alex said gently. "If that's agreeable with you, of course."

Lady Olivia's face contorted in a way that suggested she'd just bitten a lemon. "I would like that very much, Mr. Banks," she said waspishly.

As soon as Lady Olivia took Alex's proffered arm, Alex reached into his coat pocket. Taking out his pocket watch, he flipped it open and nodded, then looked straight at Andrew.

"Shall we go to the conservatory first?" Andrew asked with a pointed look at Alex.

"Oh, I adore flowers," Lady Olivia chimed in with her ear piercing voice.

"Very well," Alex said. "Let's be off."

The group started to make its way to the conservatory with Andrew moving so fast he nearly caused Brooke to stumble face-first onto the lawn.

"Why are we walking like Satan is on our heels?" Brooke asked breathlessly.

"Because she is."

Brooke couldn't help it—she let out a giggle. "That is most ungentlemanly, likening Lady Olivia to Satan."

"As far as I am concerned, that's a fair comparison. I asked Alex to keep her busy so we could have a little time without her and her inane chatter. You don't mind, do you?" The last asked as a afterthought.

"No, not at all. I just feel bad for poor Alex." And she genuinely did. He was such a nice person, and Lady Olivia was not.

"Well, you shouldn't. It was his fault she knew about the tour in the first place. When she ran into us in the hall, 'poor Alex' just blurted it right out. He's only giving us an hour, then he said he would dump her off on us whether we are finished or not." Andrew scowled.

"Is that why he made such a show of checking his pocket watch?" Brooke asked.

"Yes," Andrew said tersely. "He said in exactly one hour his 'good friend duties' would cease to exist and he'd deliver Lady Olivia to us no matter if we were done with our tour or not."

She tried not to giggle at the expression on his face as they walked to a large building that was mostly made of large windows acting as the walls and roof. In between sheets of glass there were columns of bricks going from the ground to the roof, encasing the windows. Brooke had never seen such an unusual building up close. She had seen this one yesterday from her bedchamber window. But now that she was closer, she took in the details, including how its red brick siding was crumbling a bit with age and ivy was growing up some of the columns.

Andrew opened the door and she walked inside. She looked around at all of the flowers that were in bloom. She had never seen so many different kinds in one place before. It was magnificent.

"Here we are, the conservatory. This is where Alex spends the majority of his time when the weather is disagreeable," Andrew said as he shut the door behind them.

"He does? I thought he liked the library," she said curiously, walking over to some orange flowers.

"He does," Andrew agreed. "But he has a fascination with biology, physics and even astronomy. When the weather is bad and he cannot study his plants outside or is stumped with a physics equation, he'll come here and study the flowers and trees that are housed inside."

"How fascinating," Brooke said, leaning closer to a plant that she thought might actually bear fruit, not flowers.

"Yes, very."

"Do you have a conservatory at your estate?" Brooke asked innocently.

"No." Andrew's body tensed.

Brooke assumed he stiffened because Lady Olivia and Alex could be heard talking outside.

"Would you like to see the orangery?"

"Yes," Brooke said uneasily. They had barely walked down one row in the conservatory and he was already rushing her off somewhere else. How was she supposed to work her magic?

At the end of the row was a door. When they walked through it, they entered the orangery. "I hadn't realized we were so close to the orangery," she murmured.

"Yes, they are connected, quite unusual really. The orangery was not always here. About five years ago Alex decided he would like to raise orange and citrus trees, but there was no space. His father wouldn't allow a new building to be erected. Alex talked him into a compromise. The conservatory was to be split in half. A wall was put in to divide it. That way Alex could use one of the sides to grow his citrus trees."

A bench was positioned on the opposite side of the orangery, and without a word, Brooke started to walk over to it. Her hand was still on Andrew's forearm, forcing him to walk toward the bench along with her. "I should like to sit a few minutes," she said when they arrived at the bench.

Andrew waited while Brooke took a seat on the bench first. When she was seated and rearranged her skirts around her, he sat down and left only a few short inches between them.

Brooke pretended not to notice how close they were already and swung her right leg, even if it were considered unladylike to do so, slowly brushing his calf with her bright blue skirts with each swing.

Andrew didn't move away. He just looked at her. Then slowly, ever so slowly, he moved his leg closer to hers. He kept moving closer until with one of her swings, she made direct contact with his leg. Well, as direct as one can get through a massive amount of fabric fashioned into a skirt.

Her leg stilled. Heat radiated from his leg all the way through her skirt, petticoats, and stocking. It felt as hot as the iron Mrs. McNaught had used to steam the wrinkles out of their gowns back in Bath. For a moment, they both just looked at each other.

Andrew's eyes changed. They were growing darker and more intense. Desire made them become a new shade of blue. A shade she had only seen once before, in the museum when they were alone in the empty room.

He leaned closer, so close that his face was less than two inches from hers. His eyes seared into hers and his lips were so close she could almost feel them.

Brooke's mind barely registered what was going to happen. The realization he was about to kiss her made her snap out of her lusty trance. This was her chance. She had to be strong. She had to resist. If she didn't, her plan would come to naught and she would be even more heartbroken than before.

With shaky legs, Brooke abruptly stood and moved a few feet away to an orange tree that had several ripe oranges hanging on it. "Do you…umm…think that uh…Alex would mind terribly if we… er…I were to eat one of his oranges?" she stammered.

Andrew was by her side before she even finished her question. One of his bare hands plucked down an orange while the other dug into his pocket. A few seconds later he pulled out a penknife. Wordlessly, he peeled the orange with his knife. In a minute, the rind was gone from the orange and he was breaking it into sections.

Brooke peeked at his eyes. The look was not gone. He still had the deep look of desire in his eyes. Brooke smiled to herself. It was working. He was going to find her, and only her, irresistible by the end of the day. She would make sure of it, even if it drove her crazy in the process.

Once Andrew had the orange completely separated, Brooke

reached for one of the pieces. Andrew was quicker though and pulled them back. "It would be a pity for you to ruin your gloves by touching the orange," he said, looking down at her gloves. "I think the better solution is to let me help you eat this. Come, let's sit back down."

They walked back to the bench they had both vacated in haste just a few moments before and regained their seats, sitting just as close as before.

"Are you ready?" Andrew asked hoarsely.

"Yes," Brooke whispered. Reason told her to put him off a little longer, but her body was screaming something else entirely.

Andrew took one of the orange slices and gently ran it over her lips—just enough to let the juice from the wedge moisten her lips.

Brooke's lips parted a little further and her tongue came out to lick up the juice the orange had left in its trail. Andrew swallowed visibly then shifted on the bench.

After running the orange around her mouth a second time, he slowly slipped it into her mouth.

The slice was a bit too large for one bite, and a little stream of juice came out around the corner of her mouth and dripped to her chin. Embarrassed she was making such a mess on her face while eating the orange, her hands flew up to wipe the juice from her chin. But Andrew was quicker. He grabbed her hands, bent closer to her, and whispered, "Allow me."

Brooke relaxed her hands in his hold. His left hand came up and wiped the bit off her chin, then he brought his fingers to his mouth and sucked the juice off.

Brooke's eyes widened. That was not what she had expected. She wasn't sure what she had expected, but it wasn't that.

All thoughts of holding him off vanished when he leaned a little closer. "It seems I missed a spot." Then, within a blink of an eye, his lips were on the corner of her mouth.

He nipped the corner playfully before moving over to be dead center on the middle of her lips.

Brooke's arms went around Andrew's neck and her fingers

sank into his hair. She twirled her fingers into his black curls, holding his head close to hers. His tongue ran along the seam of her lips. This was new to her, yet it felt so natural. Other men had just tried to shove their tongues inside, but this, this was much better. It felt so good, she gasped.

Andrew took advantage of her gasp and pushed his tongue past her lips. He ran his tongue along her perfect row of teeth before doing a full exploration of her mouth.

Brooke had never been one to only observe. Boldly, she slipped her tongue into his mouth and mirrored all his actions. She explored his mouth just as fully as he was exploring hers. She had never been so bold before. She enjoyed this kind of kissing with Andrew.

Brooke tightened her grip of his hair, and groaned, "Andrew." It was the first time she'd called him by his name, and she hoped she hadn't overstepped by doing so. But at present, she couldn't care enough not to do it again.

Andrew said her name while running his fingers up to her soft brown hair. He grabbed one of the curls that were overflowing from her coiffure and wrapped it loosely around his finger before giving it a gentle tug then letting it go. Then he moved his hands, reached right into the back of her massive knot of hair, and caressed her scalp with his fingers.

Brooke had been aware that it was bad form not to wear a bonnet outside, and had thought to grab hers when Lady Olivia had donned hers, but Andrew had been in too much of a hurry. Now she was glad she hadn't bothered. His fingers tenderly dug into her hair and massaged her scalp.

Suddenly there was a distinct *clink, clink, clink*. Breathing raggedly, both of them drew back and looked around the room to see if they had a visitor. When Brooke moved her head back to face Andrew and his ocean blue eyes, it occurred to her what happened to make the noise they heard.

"It appears that you have dislodged some of my hairpins," Brooke said, her voice still coming in small pants.

Andrew nodded jerkily.

Brooke leaned over and picked up a handful of hairpins that had dropped onto the bench when Andrew had given one of her curls a tug.

When Andrew looked at what she held in her hand, comprehension struck. "I'm sorry, I didn't intend to ruin your..." He broke off and waved his hands around her head.

"It's all right." More than all right in her opinion. "I'll just put these back in real quick." In just a few seconds, Brooke had fixed her hair and it looked as good as it had before.

"You are quite talented at that," Andrew remarked.

"Yes, well, one learns to do one's own hair when one has no one else to do it for them," she said dryly. Why was everyone in England so surprised to learn that a lady could fix her own hair without any help? No wonder they lost the war. Their soldiers probably depended on someone else to load their guns for them, too.

"Of course," Andrew muttered. "Shall we go see something else?"

"Yes, though I'm surprised we haven't been accosted by Lady Olivia yet. How much time do we have left?"

Andrew reached into his pocket and withdrew his watch. "We have roughly half an hour."

***

Andrew and Brooke made their way to the stables, with only about twenty minutes left before Lady Olivia would be foisted upon them.

"The stables?" Brooke asked.

"Yes, I wanted to let you pick out a horse," Andrew said with a smile.

"Pick a horse? Whatever for?"

"To ride, of course. That is what one normally does with horses. I thought we could go for a ride and picnic tomorrow." Andrew laughed as the confusion faded from her face, and joy took its place. He smiled brightly at her. Then his smile slowly faded. It was his turn to be confused. When had he ever laughed, or smiled for that matter, so often? Not for a long, long time. And why did it keep happening in the company of Brooke Banks? What was it about her that made him grin like an idiot? He shook his head. That was not a question he wanted to ponder too deeply.

Brooke took no notice of his facial expressions. She was too consumed looking around at all the horses. She scanned them all. Horses of all different colors, sizes, and dispositions were in the stable yard.

In case he had to help her decide, Andrew came up next to her to look at the horses, too. Some of the horses looked too large and uncomfortable for her. A few of them looked too old and slow to be any fun. A couple were rather high-spirited, which could be hard for her to handle.

"I think that one. The brown one near the back, on the right," she said, pointing to where a brown, medium-sized horse was standing in the far corner of the stable yard, her head bent, eating grass.

"Ah, Bluebell. Good choice. I should think the two of you will get on quite nicely." Andrew's approval was evident in his voice, as well as in the nod of his head.

"Bluebell," Brooke said with a smile. "I even like her name." Then, "It is a 'her', isn't it?"

Andrew chuckled. "Yes, Bluebell's a girl."

Brooke laughed, too. "Not that I have anything against male horses, mind you, but I should think a female horse would be more sensitive to having a female on her back."

"You have no idea what you're talking about, do you?" Andrew accused laughingly.

"Not at all." Brooke burst into giggles.

"I shall tell one of the grooms to have her saddled for a ride tomorrow. We need to be heading back now, before Lady Olivia shows up and invites herself to our picnic."

"All right," Brooke agreed, looking back one last time at Bluebell.

Andrew caught sight of the look she gave Bluebell. The look on her face was pure joy. He was glad to see that. He was glad she took joy in his presence. So caught up in the idea, he leaned down and placed a kiss on the top of her head.

Brooke shot him a questioning glance, but said nothing.

Neither of them spoke during the walk back to the house. When Andrew caught sight of Alex's grim face, he checked his watch. What good timing they had. Only mere seconds more and Lady Olivia would have been thrust upon them. Best to end this while still ahead. "I do apologize that we got separated," Andrew said with false sincerity

Brooke suppressed a giggle. Alex rolled his eyes. Lady Olivia pouted, then said, "Well, if you hadn't been in such a hurry to see everything we could have stayed together. You were practically running when we last saw you. Then you were gone by the time we made our rounds through the conservatory."

"Once again, I do apologize. If you were unable to see everything you would have liked, I am fairly certain that one of Watson's servants can complete your tour," Andrew said smoothly.

"What of you, my lord?" she asked, batting her eyelashes. "Why don't you give me the same tour you gave Miss Banks?"

She was flirting again. He wasn't flattered, nor would he ever *think* of giving her the same tour he'd given Brooke. Knowing her, she'd use the tour as another opportunity to propose. He suppressed a shudder at the thought of her earlier proposal for them to marry. "As delightful as that sounds," he said, trying not to choke on his tongue, "I cannot. I have a pressing affair just now and I fear I'm already late. So without any further ado, I must bid you adieu." He watched in quiet amusement as both Brooke and Alex rolled their eyes at his play on words.

"I must be off, too," Alex said without any preamble, forcefully dropping his arm and causing Lady Olivia to break her hold.

Brooke mumbled an incoherent excuse about needing a nap and ran off, leaving Lady Olivia to find her own entertainment.

# Chapter 17

Brooke practically floated up to her room. Nothing could make her come back to Earth at the moment. Not even an impromptu visit from Liberty could dash her euphoric daydream.

"Where have you been all morning?" Liberty asked anxiously as she burst into Brooke's room without so much as a knock.

"I went for a tour," Brooke supplied, conveniently leaving off who she went with and what exactly the tour consisted of.

"I do hope you enjoyed yourself." Liberty made herself comfortable atop Brooke's bed. "I have suffered the most intolerable morning. *Ever.*" She put so much emphasis on the last word that she made it sound as if nothing, in the past or future, could possibly compare with whatever calamity she had just gone through.

Liberty's misfortune, however, did not so much as stir Brooke. Instead, she just smiled and asked, "What could possibly be as bad as that?"

"I do believe I have found the one person in this world that I can honestly say I hate." The declaration was made with so much conviction that Brooke jumped a little.

"Hate?" Brooke repeated in a questioning tone, her brown eyes narrowed and her brows furrowed. "We've all met someone whom we dislike. I'll gladly admit to disliking a whole list of people, but to actually hate someone…" Brooke trailed off and looked to Liberty who was wringing her hands. "Are you certain?"

Liberty nodded.

"Who is it? What did they do? Who else knows? Do you think we need to tell Papa and Mama?"

"No!" Liberty blurted abruptly.

"All right, we'll keep this to ourselves," Brooke said calmly. It must be bad if Liberty didn't want to tell Mama and Papa. "Why don't you just tell me what happened and we can figure something out?"

Liberty fidgeted a minute. Then she hemmed and hawed a bit. When Brooke started making irritated rolling hand gestures, Liberty got on with it. "It's Mr. Grimes. You know, the man Papa's mentoring?"

"Yes, I am acquainted with him." Brooke nodded her head. She was also aware that Mr. Grimes had been Liberty's dinner companion last night. Brooke was equally certain the two of them had opposite personality types. Liberty liked to talk—blab really—whereas Mr. Grimes was silent, and when he spoke it was brief. But what Brooke was most aware of—which Liberty may not yet know—was she had a sneaking suspicion Liberty didn't hate the man nearly as much as she claimed.

"I know you're acquainted with him," Liberty blustered, bringing Brooke back to present. "The thing is, I was talking to Madison in the drawing room and I thought we were alone. I was embroidering a handkerchief and she was just sitting there. She was woolgathering. You know how she is. She was just staring out the window, and I may have said something to her about it. And, Mr. Grimes was there and he said—"

"Wait," Brooke interrupted, raising her hand to stop Liberty's endless chatter. Her eyes had narrowed even more and were pinned on Liberty in a way she knew scared the wits out of her younger sisters. "What did you say to Madison?" Her tone was sharp and her stare was deadly.

"Oh, nothing really," Liberty said, looking everywhere but into Brooke's eyes. "All right, I'll tell you, but not because I feel guilty or anything. It's that stare you're giving me. Truly, Brooke, it makes me uncomfortable."

Brooke was pleased to hear that. She enjoyed making her younger sisters uncomfortable and bending them to her will.

Liberty shook her head. "I told her to stop, that it's not a ladylike behavior to sit around staring like that."

"Is that all?" Brooke asked quietly. She was starting to feel less sorry for Liberty and her situation, and was rapidly becoming more sympathetic toward Madison.

"I might have mentioned a thing or two about finding a husband, not being an old maid, pursuing more ladylike interests, and suggesting she just hold an embroidery loop and needle for appearance's sake," Liberty said meekly.

"And all of this was said in front of Mr. Grimes?" Brooke asked, knowing the answer, but desperately hoping that by some small miracle Mr. Grimes hadn't heard the entire conversation.

"Yes," Liberty said in a small voice. Then as if a strong wind had started to blow, Liberty put some starch in her spine and inclined her chin a good fifteen degrees. "But that is nothing compared to what he said to me."

"Liberty, you're not looking very good in this story. Are you sure you wish to finish it?" Brooke asked weakly. She didn't know if she even wanted to hear how this was going to end.

"Yes! The things I said to Madison pale in comparison to the beastly things that coxcomb said to me," Liberty said with a grunt.

"Did you just grunt?" Brooke asked with a grin.

"No, I did not grunt," Liberty said defensively. "Ladies do not grunt. It's impolite."

"You would know, Miss Propriety." Then just because she couldn't help but rub Liberty's nose in her misstep, she said, "But just so you're aware of your fall from grace, you did too grunt. My brain knows what my ears heard."

Liberty ground her teeth. "Fine. I grunted. I admit it. Now forget about that for a moment or I will add you to my list of people whom I hate. There may only be one person on the list now, but I assure you, there's room for another." The small hint of a smile on her face told Brooke her sister was trying her best to jest, despite how upset she was.

"Go on. No more interruptions from me," Brooke said, adding a silent, "For now."

"After I had given my advice to Madison, not too unkindly might I add, that beast had the nerve to clear his throat, which scared us both half out of our wits. When I turned in his direction he said the most hurtful thing." She sniffled a little and a single tear rolled from each eye.

Brooke couldn't tell if those were real tears or just theatrics. She was beginning to wonder if she were ever going to hear this "beastly" statement made by Mr. Grimes.

Just when she couldn't take it much longer, Liberty wiped her eyes and said, "He looked right at me and said, 'Leave her be. You're well on your way to being an old maid yourself.' I was so surprised that he said that, I couldn't say anything back. He was so mean to me." She looked to Brooke for confirmation, but her eyes didn't quite meet Brooke's.

"Is that all?" To Brooke's mind, this was not exactly a statement that would compel someone to hate another.

"No, that's not all. If you'd let me finish, I'd tell you the rest. He then made several statements about how I stick my nose where it does not belong." Liberty's face turned scarlet and her voice wavered. "He was so cruel about it! He said I was cold and callous, too. Oh, Brooke, I hate him. I don't know how Papa can tolerate his presence."

"Are you sure you do not wish to tell Papa about the awful things Mr. Grimes said to you?" Brooke asked softly, rubbing her hand up and down Liberty's back to help calm her down.

"No," Liberty said adamantly.

Brooke wondered why Liberty was so set against telling Papa. If Papa knew what happened between Liberty and Mr. Grimes, surely he'd take Liberty's side and end all association with Mr. Grimes. Unless there was something else going on… She didn't know why, but she had a feeling there was more to Liberty's feelings for Mr. Grimes than she was sharing.

"Not to worry, I won't say a word," Brooke falsely assured her sister. Something about the whole situation was off. But before bringing it to Mama's and Papa's attention, she needed to get more facts. That meant asking Madison about what had happened. "Why don't you go join the others on the lawn? I believe they are playing some sort of game out there. I would like to take a nap before tea."

Liberty got off Brooke's bed and left.

Brooke exited right behind Liberty and went straight into

Madison's room.

"What happened between Liberty and Mr. Grimes?" Brooke demanded without ceremony.

Madison didn't even take her eyes away from the window. With a slight sigh she said, "That didn't take long." The words were spoken as if she had expected someone to seek her out.

"Is it true Mr. Grimes said horrid things to Liberty?" Brooke asked bluntly, taking a seat next to her sister on the bed.

Madison started to twist some of the fringe on the counterpane between her slender, pink-tipped fingers. "Yes, he said some wretched things to her. It wasn't very gentlemanly of him, but who could blame him? She provoked him with her blistering set-down."

"Oh, Madison," Brooke said soothingly, moving closer to wrap her sister in an assuring hug. "I'm so sorry Liberty is so critical of you. She just doesn't know how else to be."

"I'm not talking about what she said to me," Madison said, looking at Brooke curiously. "I should have known," she muttered after a minute.

"What?" Brooke asked, scooting backward. What should Madison have known?

"She didn't tell you all of it." She sighed. "My guess is she only told you the things he said to her about becoming an old maid and being cold, callous, and essentially calling her a busybody. Am I right?"

Brooke nodded.

Madison mumbled a few words Brooke was unable to make out, which was probably for the best. Madison might be the daughter of a minister, but that did not qualify her for sainthood. Not only did Madison delight in hearing gossip, but from time to time, a coarse word or two would escape her lips.

"You know about the words she spoke to me, and I'm assuming you heard when she was done, he told her she was on her way to becoming an old maid herself." At Brooke's nod, she continued, "Before he barely had the words out, Liberty jumped up off the settee and said, 'Those are not kind words for a man of God to speak. No wonder you had to seek Papa out to help you with your church. You're probably as ineffective a minister as you are a conversationalist. I have never had such a boring dinner companion.' Mr. Grimes made no response. He just bowed and started to leave."

"Liberty wasn't done though. Oh no, she didn't want him to get off so easily. Instead, she crossed her arms and said, 'If you would be a little more sociable, your problems would diminish. If *I* were the vicar, I wouldn't have near the problems you do. I would have the ballocks to get down to the bottom of the mess and sort it out.'"

Brooke gasped. Her proper sister said a word like ballocks? And she wasn't there to witness it? Life seemed to be unfair at times. But even to hear Liberty say ballocks, she wouldn't have traded her morning with Andrew. What in the world was so provoking about Mr. Grimes to get her proper sister to act this way?

"That's when Mr. Grimes accused her of being too involved in other people's business for her own good. He used me as an example, which I must say was just as uncomfortable as when Liberty pointed out my flaws. That got Liberty's hackles up further and she said, 'You, sir, are a jackanapes. You have no business calling yourself a gentleman.' She took a deep breath and noticed Mr. Grimes was staring at her as if she'd just grown a pair of horns. Then with a sniff to emphasize her distaste for him, she said she wished for him to leave the room, the house party, and to go find another family to bother."

This was worse than Brooke thought. In a way it seemed silly, but in another way, she knew her sister very well. Liberty never spoke to anyone this way, not even her. "Is this when Mr. Grimes said she was cold and callous?" Brooked asked, not sure if she could take much more.

"Yes, although I do believe he said she was cold and had a callous heart." Madison looked surprisingly unsettled by the whole exchange. "I know I shouldn't say this, and do not tell Liberty what I'm about to say, but I think she deserved to hear the things he told her. Maybe not from a stranger, but all the same, I don't believe the words were undeserved. She made some very unkind remarks."

"Yes, she did," Brooke agreed, thinking of what she was going to say to Papa. This was no little incident that could be swept under the proverbial rug. At some point, he was going to find out about it. It might as well be sooner rather than later.

Brooke stood to leave, but when she got to the door she turned back to her sister. "Madison, do you know what sorts of issues Mr. Grimes is dealing with?"

"I've been wondering the same thing all morning," Madison confided. "I tried to ask Mama, but she immediately changed the subject."

"She knows then," Brooke mused. "I suppose it's unimportant just now. We'll need to find a way to sort this out. I'd better be on my way."

***

Paul spent the better part of his morning in a private sitting room staring blankly at an open book. Every time footfalls thudded in the hall, he assumed it was John Banks coming to put an end to their arrangement. It wasn't anything less than he deserved for the hateful things he'd said to Liberty, but he still wanted to avoid it if possible.

He thought about the conversation again. It wasn't that he had intended to be mean to her. He'd wanted to let them know of his presence, then she got angry at him, then before he knew what he was doing, the words just poured out. He should have just left, but he hadn't, and now it was time to deal with the consequences.

With a sigh, he stood and left the room to search for the bane of his existence. There was no time like the present to atone for one's sins.

He walked out of the house and went to the lawn where he saw her sitting in a lounge chair watching some of the other guests play lawn bowls. Her brown hair was neatly pulled into a bun on the top of her head. A few wisps of brown hair fell down beside her face. Her arms were crossed and she was impatiently kicking her feet back and forth. Her face was no more inviting than her posture. Her hazel eyes appeared hard as stone and she was baring her teeth in a way that could pass as a smile or a sneer.

"I have been searching for you," he said, approaching her from the side. "Would you mind if we talked for a moment?"

Liberty nearly jumped out of her skin when she heard his voice. "I have nothing to say to you."

"I think you do, it's just nothing nice," Paul teased gently. He had learned last night this young lady *always* had *something* to say. "I wanted to apologize to you. I am entirely to blame for the unfortunate conversation we had this morning. I should have ducked back out of the room when I saw you and your sister were in there alone."

"We have finally found something about which we both agree," she replied stiffly.

"Yes, well, unfortunately I did not." He took a seat next to her, watching the player rolling the bowl. This was harder than he had anticipated it would be. "I have come to make amends. I said some very harsh things to you, and I shouldn't have. As a man of integrity and as a man of God, I should have known better. I spoke before thinking, and I offer you my heartfelt apologies."

"Apology not accepted," Liberty said simply, glancing at the profile of his rigid face. "Sir, I understand that you and Papa have some work to do. I shall not be in the way of that. I have no desire to tell him about the events of this morning, and I advise you not to mention it, either. If you do, he shall take my side, because I am his daughter after all, and you will once again be looking for a mentor."

"Very well," Paul replied. Coming to his feet, he accepted what she said and decided not to press her. He had no intention of being fast friends with her at this point. But the advice of her father was invaluable, and the thought of losing him as a mentor had been part of what had compelled him to seek her out to do the right thing.

"Why do you need my father's help, anyhow?" she asked, her tone considerably softer.

"That is a confidential matter." There was enough going on in his life with the vicious lies, rumors, and gossip. He had no intention of adding to it by telling her anything. She could ask all day, and he still wouldn't tell her.

Then without so much as a fare-thee-well, Paul vanished.

***

Alex was sitting alone in his library making a list of materials needed for his upcoming experiments when the door opened.

"May I join you?" Andrew asked, taking a seat before receiving an answer.

Alex shrugged.

After the tour this morning, Alex had done exactly what he had told Andrew he would: he'd locked himself in the library and read his latest scientific periodical. There was a writer named E. S. Wilson who wrote some of the most fascinating articles for the magazine. For nearly two years, Alex had tried to get information about this writer, but the publisher adamantly told him the writer was a recluse whom he himself had never met.

He'd finished the article earlier, but was still thinking about it. He made a mental note that he would have to order some new trees in order to do the experiment outlined in the article. Not that he didn't trust this E. S. Wilson fellow, but he liked to do the same experiments to make sure this unknown writer's facts were straight.

"Did you have any success convincing Brooke you have no interest in Lady Olivia?" Alex asked after a few minutes. He knew the reason for Andrew's visit had to do with Brooke. He wasn't sure just how interested Andrew was, but it only took him thirty seconds of Brooke's blabbing the night before to surmise she was in love with Andrew. Alex liked both Brooke and Andrew, and saw no reason to stop them, if they intended to make a match.

"I believe so," Andrew answered. "She has agreed to go riding with me tomorrow."

Alex sat bolt upright and opened his mouth to object, but Andrew cut him off with a wave of his hand. "You're not required to join us. I believe we shall stay close enough that a chaperone is not necessary. If we do wander off, I'll secure a groom."

Alex relaxed. He liked them both, but he did not condone Andrew compromising her, even if he had suggested that very thing to Brooke the night before. What had he been thinking to suggest such a thing? "As long as I don't have to be trapped with Lady Olivia, I don't care how you conduct your courtship. Within reason," he added with a glare. His eyes were piercing into Andrew, trying to communicate the nonverbal message: do not push this too far.

"Of course," Andrew confirmed. "Thank you for keeping Lady Olivia occupied. She can be such a nuisance, at times."

"At times?" Alex scoffed. "Try all the time. I was about ready to tear my own heart out of my chest just to put myself out of my misery during that hour I was trapped with her."

"It's good you did not take such drastic measures," Andrew said dryly. "It would be a waste to throw your whole life away because of something that would be over soon."

"That's what you think. You didn't have to suffer her annoying habits for an hour," Alex said, screwing his face up in distaste.

"It couldn't have been that unbearable."

"It was. Not only did she jabber on and on about you, but the one time she talked of anything else, she threw my past sins in my face."

Andrew smiled. "Your past sins? What could those be?"

"I had her and her cousin, Caroline, thrown out of the *Society of Biological Matters* back in London. I did it at Lord Sinclair's request, but it had to be done in a way they wouldn't suspect he was behind it. Therefore, I became the scapegrace and she will forever blame me for it."

"You lied to her about why she couldn't belong to the *Society of Biological Matters*?" Andrew asked dubiously, his eyes narrowing.

"Yes. I know it sounds bad." Alex thought about it a minute. "All right, it not only sounds bad, it is bad. I should not have done it. But I had a good reason."

Andrew's face took on a look of deep contemplation. "Are you saying you agree with lying if the outcome is for the greater good?" Andrew asked.

"I suppose that's what my actions would suggest," Alex admitted. He never had liked to admit his mistakes, and this was the closest he'd ever come to doing so.

"I'm glad you think that way," Andrew informed him. "Well, I must be going then. I need to make a quick visit before dinner is served."

Alex watched his friend leave. That was the most bizarre conversation he'd ever had. Andrew's reaction to his lie and the following questions made him wonder if Andrew was up to something. If he was, Alex had no idea what it was.

***

Brooke was on her way to speak with Papa when Mr. Grimes intercepted her.

"Mr. Grimes," Brooke said, startled. She hadn't expected to see him. He was now a houseguest at the party and she knew they would run into each other at some point, but hadn't thought it would happen so soon.

"Miss Banks," he said cordially. "If you're looking for your father, he's downstairs."

"Thank you," Brooke returned. "I shall not keep you then."

Brooke had barely walked past him when he spoke to her. "Miss Banks, if you're going to speak to him about the events of this morning, I would like to beg your silence"

Brooke turned around and was face-to-face with Mr. Grimes. "Beg my silence? But why? I love my sister, but what she said was inappropriate."

"I agree with your assessment, but I must ask that you not say anything. I responded to her words in an equally inappropriate manner. I have asked her forgiveness. She has refused to give it, of course. However, we have come to an agreement that we will not speak of the event again nor mention it to your father."

"But…are you…" Brooke stammered. She couldn't help but wonder why he would allow Liberty to say such harsh remarks and not want vindication for it.

"Yes," Mr. Grimes answered for her. "I am certain I do not

wish to involve your father in this. Not that I have anything to hide. I would admit to any of the things I said if need be, but I do not wish to cause any trouble for Miss Liberty."

Brooke nodded. She wasn't sure why he wanted to spare Liberty the tongue-lashing she deserved, but who was she to dissuade him?

# Chapter 18

Brooke was relieved to find dinner that evening a lot more enjoyable than it had been the night before. She would have preferred to sit next to Andrew, but he wasn't present, so she sat with Mr. Thomas, Madison's gossipy dinner companion from the night before.

Brooke and her sisters sat closer together this time, with Mr. Grimes and Lady Olivia seated as far away as possible.

When the men rejoined the ladies after their gentlemen's pursuits, Andrew was still missing.

Brooke was not the only one to notice. "Where's Townson?" asked Mr. Cook, taking a seat near where Brooke and her sisters were sharing a settee.

Alex shrugged before taking an empty chair on the other side of the girls. "I haven't seen him for several hours. The last time I saw him, he mentioned something about a meeting. I don't recall exactly."

"You don't seem to recall much unless it has to do with science," his father gently teased him.

Alex gave a lopsided grin. "What can I say? Science is fascinating, whereas Townson's whereabouts are not."

"Hear, hear," the Duke of Gateway said, holding his glass up in a mock toast. Some of the ladies who had tittered at Alex's remark, burst into full giggles at the duke's.

Brooke didn't think it was so funny. "Should we send someone to look for him?" she asked with a pointed glance to Alex.

"No," the duke answered in a dismissive tone. "He's probably out visiting his mother."

"His mother lives 'round here?" Mr. Cook asked curiously.

"Yes," the duke answered again.

"I always thought she was a recluse," Mr. Cook mused.

"She is," the duke confirmed.

"Hmm…I wonder why that is?" Mr. Cook ventured.

Lady Algen and Mr. Thomas both looked as if they were about to burst at the prospect of spreading gossip. However, Lady Algen spoke first, and because Mr. Thomas was a gentleman, he didn't interrupt her. "She was always a recluse. Her family, whoever they may be, had kept her hidden and away from society until she was of marrying age. Her parents bought her a husband while she was still hidden away in the countryside. Townson brought her to town only on their wedding day. But shortly after they were married, he packed her off to the country where she's remained ever since."

"Why?" Lady Olivia asked, her voice full of wonder.

This time Mr. Thomas was quicker to speak than Lady Algen. "When the old earl agreed to take her as his bride, he was lied to by the gel's family. The details have always been hushed up, but I believe that it is not necessarily about her, but about her real family. Either way, the earl was displeased, stowed her off in the countryside, and sought an annulment. Before the marriage could be annulled, it was discovered the countess was with child. Therefore, the annulment was called off. Townson then filed for a parliamentary divorce, but couldn't prove adultery, nor could his reputation handle such a blow. So he did what any man would do in his situation, confined her to an old, dilapidated estate in the middle of nowhere."

Brooke's stomach lurched. The man she'd come to care deeply about, and even would consider marrying, had such a terrible past. Not that any of it was his fault, but still it was clear that nearly everyone in the room was listening very intently to the gossip about his family.

Brooke sat with her hands in her lap and idly chewed on her bottom lip. She just heard snatches of what was being said around her "…Townson's a bastard, then?" "…no other children…" "…seen her in London once…" her head was swimming with all the accusations and questions. How could people be so cruel about someone who wasn't even there to defend himself?

Brooke's head throbbed and she looked around to see if she could find strength in her family's presence.

Liberty surprised Brooke when she reached over and gave her hand a reassuring squeeze just as Madison leaned over and whispered, "Don't take all of this to heart. People will gossip about anything. You know that."

Brooke tried to respond, but her brain couldn't think of what to say, so she just squeezed Liberty's hand back to let her know she appreciated her support.

After a few more minutes and several additional unsavory comments, it was time to leave. She slipped away virtually unnoticed, as everyone was too absorbed with talk of Andrew's family to care that she was leaving. She could have sworn on the way out the door she heard some reference to his having an unusual attachment to his mother even when he was a boy at school.

She had almost made her way down the hall to the staircase when Alex called after her, "Brooke, wait."

Brooke didn't stop or turn to face him, but she did slow her steps.

"Brooke, Andrew and I have been chums for a long time. He's really a good fellow. You cannot let his past influence what you think about him now," Alex said

Brooke knew he believed he was helping the situation, but he wasn't. "But don't our pasts help make us who we become?" she asked flatly.

"Well, yes, but you cannot hold his mother's past against him," Alex said in defense of his closest friend.

"I'm not."

"Then what part are you holding against him? The part about his strong attachment to her? That's of no consequence now. It was fifteen years ago, nobody cares about it anymore," Alex said, his voice full of conviction.

"No, I am not holding that against him. It's only natural that a child loves his mother. But to say that nobody cares about it is false. I can show you a whole room full of people who still care about it. They're in there right now, laughing at his expense over it." Brooke paused. In the past few seconds Alex's eyes had changed. For some reason, there was a light shining in them now. She blinked, and then continued. "That's not important, nor is it the reason I left. The reason I left has nothing to do with him. I just didn't wish to listen to malicious gossip any longer, that's all."

Alex gazed at her skeptically. He looked like he was going to say something more, but didn't. Instead he just smiled, turned, and whistled while he walked back to the drawing room.

Brooke walked into her room and closed the door. Numbly, she went to the bed and laid face-down across it, burying her face in the pillows. Then before she knew it, tears poured from her eyes so fast no amount of blinking could dam them up.

Brooke was rarely one to sob, but today was an exception. She couldn't understand why people would say such cutting remarks about another. She remembered the speculation that Andrew was born on the wrong side of the blanket. And the accusations that Andrew's mother was nothing more than a common whore who had been lucky enough not to have any more children.

She pounded her pillow, asking herself over and over again how people could be so unfeeling.

***

Andrew left the meeting with Willis, his estate manager, with an optimistic outlook for his finances.

Since he'd come into the title and land eight years ago, he'd failed to earn any kind of profit from any of his estates. All the money that was made went to the upkeep of the earldom and to pay down the debts left by his father. Now all the other estates were long gone, sold to pay off debt, and all that he could hope to make money with was Rockhurst, which was entailed.

Willis delivered some excellent news in regards to the account books. "Last month we paid off the entire balances due to Stimple, Crate, and Greer. If the tenants continue to pay their rents, you watch your spending, and the harvest is abundant, you shall be completely without debt two years from now."

That *was* good news. It wasn't a windfall of money, but the idea of being debt-free made him feel like the richest man alive. "That is most excellent news," Andrew said approvingly.

"But," Willis began again as Andrew got up from the table, "if we were to make some modifications to Rockhurst, you could be turning a profit within three months."

Andrew dropped back into his seat so fast he wouldn't be surprised if he found a bruise on his backside later. "What modifications? How much profit?" he asked with keen interest.

"Before I tell you the modifications, I'll tell you that you will be one of the richest in the land within a year." Willis saw Andrew's arched brow and started to spill his information. "It will cost you one thousand pounds to set up, but in one month you'll be able to pay that back. In less than three, all your father's creditors will be paid. Your yearly income will be approximately fifty thousand pounds."

Andrew let out a low whistle. That was more money than he'd ever dreamed of. He knew some men made excellent incomes of twenty or thirty thousand pounds from a combination of their estates, but he had never heard of fifty thousand from just one before. But he still didn't know what modifications this would require. Most importantly, he didn't have a thousand pounds to start with. Not giving that too much thought, he asked Willis, "What modifications?"

"Nothing really," Willis said, brushing imaginary crumbs from the table.

Andrew felt his excitement deflate. "What are they?" he asked in a low tone.

"Mines," Willis said with a gulp. "There is a record that indicates silver is located on your property. If you were to allow mines built to dig up the metal, you would be very rich."

"No," Andrew said flatly, getting up from the table.

Willis had been in Andrew's employ long enough to know to avoid arguing, so with a nod of understanding, he packed up his papers.

After his meeting with Willis, Andrew met with a few of the tenants to hear their problems and look at anything that wasn't in working order on their homes. Even if he disagreed with the mines, he still felt it had been a productive day and was satisfied with the results.

On his ride back to the Watson estate, he thought more about the mines. He'd told Willis no, but that didn't mean he couldn't reconsider later if need be. The silver wasn't going anywhere. He didn't like the idea of the noise and danger the mines would create though. He might not care that much about the land itself, but he didn't want anyone getting hurt. Nor did he have the funds to build the mine, he reminded himself. That was the bigger issue. He would have to borrow the money to start with. Not to mention, if they drilled in the wrong place, then he'd have to pay to have it moved. It could become a rather costly experiment. And that was not something he was willing to take a risk on just now.

Entering the drive, he checked his watch and frowned. It was past dinner time. With any luck, Cook would still have something for him to eat. If not, since he was hungrier than a bear that just woke up from hibernation, he would gladly ride the hour back to Rockhurst to eat if need be.

All thoughts of eating were gone as soon as he opened the door. "I've been waiting for you," came Gateway's deep voice from the shadows.

"And you will continue to wait. I am off to scrounge for some food," Andrew said without a care for making Gateway wait.

Gateway rose from the chair he had been occupying and strolled to the stairs. Once he was on the first one, he turned his head over his shoulder. "I think this is something you might want to hear, but if you think it's more important to eat than to know what happened with Miss Banks tonight, that's for you to decide." He gave a shrug and walked up two more steps.

"Tell me," Andrew breathed agitatedly. Did he really need to hear this now? Yes, he probably did. Undoubtedly it involved Gateway, which could only lead to trouble.

"It would seem she heard a bit more about your past than is good for your relationship," Gateway said with a smirk.

"What do you mean?" Andrew asked, wishing that Gateway

would just say it and stop playing games.

"It seems that you and your family became the main topic of conversation after dinner tonight. Naturally, Miss Banks was there and heard all about your mother's exile, shame, and your unusually strong affection toward her," Gateway said with a cackle.

Andrew was too stunned to respond. Did any of that really matter? He wasn't intending to marry her, so why should she care about his mother? Then it hit him. She had to believe he cared about her enough to marry her, which meant that his and his mother's pasts would matter.

His appetite was no longer such a pressing matter. "Why was I made the topic of the evening?" he asked through clenched teeth.

"Because you weren't here," Gateway said with a shrug of nonchalance. "Perhaps you should have thought of this before you went running off to your mummy."

Andrew speared him with a look.

Gateway just stared back at him. "It's not my fault Mr. Thomas and Lady Algen decided to shovel out your family's dirt."

"No," Andrew agreed softly. "But you were there and you could have said something to stop it. Do you not realize this hurts you, too?"

"How so?" Gateway asked indifferently.

"Because if she will no longer have anything to do with me, which is likely the case, then you won't get what you want, either."

"Not necessarily," Gateway told him. "I can always find someone else who is willing. You were just easy to cast into the role, but I can find another, more capable man."

"Not now," Andrew hissed. "Either I do this, or you let the whole thing go." It was bad enough Brooke was going to get hurt in the end. But any other man would hurt her far more than necessary, and likely do so in a way that would take away any chance for dignity or self-respect she could ever attempt to gain in the future. Quite simply, anyone else would damage her beyond repair. That thought alone made Andrew's blood run cold.

Gateway laughed his eerie villain's laugh. "I'll give you a few more days, Townson. If you don't deliver by then, the bargain is off. I'll find someone else, and all hopes of regaining your estate will be lost."

Andrew's heart skipped. He'd almost forgotten about his estate in Essex. That was what he wanted, wasn't it? To hold that deed once again? Not only did he want the money that the estate could provide, he longed for the estate as a way to make amends. He'd like to open the doors to that house for his mother, so she could go live there without a backward glance to either London or Rockhurst. That estate in Essex was the only place that held any pleasant memories for her.

He remembered living there with her when he was a boy. His father was always in London or at Rockhurst. Andrew never remembered the earl coming to visit him in Essex. Neither he nor his mother seemed to mind his absence though.

They had no servants, except a cook, and all day he'd play with his mother and one of the village boys named Archer. Though he didn't remember a lot about his early years in Essex, he did remember his first visit to his father's London residence.

He didn't go for his first visit until he was five or six years old and was so nervous about meeting his father, the earl, for the first time, that he had stomach pains the whole trip. Once he arrived and they finally met, he was immediately handed over to a bitter, old nurse who took care of him the entire time. He would only see his father for brief snippets of time every few days. When he did see him, he'd beg to go back home to his mother. When he finally was allowed to go home, his one and only friend had gone away, and his mother started being absent in the afternoon doing countess duties and had to leave him with a nurse.

Even though his mother had been gone during the afternoons, she was there in the mornings and they had remained close. He felt she was all he had in the world, and she acted as if she felt the same way.

Every few months his father would send a letter to his mother asking that she have Andrew packed and ready on the front steps when his servant arrived. She would, and they'd say their tearful goodbyes, then he'd go stay with his father for a few months before returning. Growing up this way, he didn't realize this wasn't the usual way of families.

When he was thirteen and it came time to go to Eton, his father sent a note that he was too busy to take him and his mother would need to do it. She agreed. Leaving the house that autumn morning was the last good memory he had of his mother from boyhood. They had talked the whole way to Eton; both secretly glad Father had decided not to come. But upon arrival at the school, Andrew's world and relationship with his mother fell apart in one fell swoop.

The boys had teased him that evening after she left and continued for a few days. Not only were they talking about him, claiming he had an unusually strong attachment to his mother because she'd brought him to school instead of his father like everyone else, but they were talking about her, as well. They called her a whore and him a bastard. That was when he had decided it was best if he severed his ties with her as best he could. Not because he actually believed the rumors, but for the simple, selfish reason that he was tired of being harassed.

A week or so after the term started, she sent him a package, and he promptly sent it back to her with a letter asking her to refrain from communicating with him any further. She never sent him another note or even invited him to see her until after his father died.

It would be nice to have the money the estate could produce, but at the same time, he wanted to use the house as a grand gesture to mend the rift he'd selfishly created. Not that she had ever refused to see him when he had gone to visit her, nor had she ever acted coldly toward him. She'd even said she held no grudges, but he could see the hurt rooted deeply in her eyes. He'd do anything to take that hurt away, which meant he had to get that estate back. And the only way to do that was to hurt an innocent bystander.

The guilt that he was going to mend one broken relationship at the cost of another was almost enough to make him call it all off. Almost.

Food was the furthest thing from his mind as Andrew trudged

up the stairs. Tomorrow he'd take Brooke on a picnic, honestly answering any questions she asked about his past, and see how far she'd let him go. If she responded to his advances, he'd set up her ruination for the following night.

Andrew lay awake in his bed almost all night long, staring at the canopy overhead and trying to convince himself that the reason he couldn't sleep was due to the gossip about his family, and had nothing to do with his growing feelings for Brooke.

# Chapter 19

Breakfast was a very short affair for Brooke. She barely had time to eat five bites before her mother pulled her into a private drawing room.

"Brooke, are you all right?" Mama asked, looking around.

"Yes, Mama, I'm fine," Brooke lied.

"I know you heard some unsavory information about your suitor last night. But I wanted you to know that most of it isn't true. I spoke to Regina last evening, and Papa talked to your uncle," Mama said softly.

"It's not about what was said, exactly," Brooke protested. Why was it everyone thought she would throw him over because of a little gossip? Was it so difficult to understand she was more upset about the gossiping activity itself and not the content? Sure, most would end their courtship with a man many claimed was the product of an affair. But it really wasn't so important to her. Legally, he wasn't a bastard. He was born in wedlock. If he wasn't, then he wouldn't be an earl. That was all that mattered. As for the rest, the speculation about being too close to his mother for his own good as a child, well, that was just plain petty in her opinion.

Mama was motionlessly staring at her with worried eyes, so she forced her lips into a bright smile.

"If you're certain this will not cause you to lose interest in the man, then I'll say no more. I think he's quite a catch, and I believe you agree with me," she said with a knowing smile. "I should just hate for you to give up on him because of some old gossip that probably isn't true."

"No, Mama, I have not given up on him," Brooke assured her.

"Good," Mama said, getting up to leave the room. "Papa has promised to teach me this game called pall mall. I am positively thrilled at the idea of hitting a ball with a mallet! He is waiting for me, I must be off."

No sooner had Brooke gotten up to leave, than Mr. Grimes entered the room.

She sighed. Did he want to talk to her, too? She waited quietly by the door.

Mr. Grimes didn't speak though. He just walked into the room, smiled at her, and took a seat on a chair near the corner. He really was a handsome man. It was little wonder Liberty turned into a goose in his presence.

Brooke continued looking at him from where she was standing. He was definitely an odd one.

"I'll just be going now," she said more to herself than to him, since he wasn't paying her any attention anyway.

Brooke was walking back to the breakfast room to see if there was anything left to eat when Alex reached out and pulled her into the library.

"Brooke, I've given this a lot of thought," he said in a serious tone. "I'm not sure you should mention to Andrew what you heard last night. He doesn't take kindly to being talked about. I think it's best you don't mention it."

Brooke just stared at him, dumbfounded. She had no plans to mention what she'd heard or to ask him questions about it. If they were engaged or married, she might ask him a question, but now wasn't the time to dig into his past.

"I'll tell you what I know, if you'd like. That should be enough to satisfy your curiosity for now," Alex said uneasily.

"That will not be necessary," she said, waving her hand. "I have no desire to hear any more stories. I will ask him about it if it becomes necessary, but as for now, I have no interest."

The tension fled from Alex's face, then he bobbed his head up and down ecstatically. "Very well. I shall see you later."

Brooke took that as her dismissal and exited the library. This was turning into the most bizarre morning.

She made her way outside with only a quick wave and a chipper, "Good morning," to Papa.

Relaxing in the shade provided by a tall, leafy tree, Brooke was lost in a daydream. She dreamt of Andrew and his kisses. So far, he'd been the perfect gentleman. When he'd kissed her, he'd kept his hands in appropriate places. They might have rubbed her back a bit and tangled in her hair, but he hadn't tried to maul her chest or bottom like the others had.

The last gentleman she'd kissed prior to Andrew had been the Duke of Gateway. His kisses had been satisfactory, but paled in comparison to Andrew's. He hadn't tried to caress her before she ended their time together. However, that was the reason she'd ended things. She felt his hand straying from her shoulder, dropping lower. Just the idea of his hand on her breast made her cringe.

"Is that the face you always wear when thinking of Townson?" asked the object of her thoughts, coming to lean against her shade tree.

"No, not at all," she replied primly. "It's the one I wear when I think of you."

Gateway smiled a bit. "I'm flattered that I'm the subject of your thoughts. I do feel bad for Townson though. I believe he may be heartbroken to know the woman he's courting is entertaining thoughts of me."

"Don't flatter yourself, Your Grace. As you so kindly pointed out when you approached, they were not pleasant thoughts."

"Indeed," Gateway allowed. "But thoughts, all the same. Would you care to share those thoughts with me?"

"No."

"But if I'm part of them, then I think common courtesy would dictate you should share them with me." Gateway gave her an encouraging smile.

"Fine, I'll tell you, although they don't do you any favors. I was thinking of what an awful kisser you are. Have I satisfied your curiosity, now?" she asked, taking a small measure of delight in seeing his smile vanish and his eyes widen. Either his face changed because he was shocked she was so blunt, or he was shocked she thought he was a bad kisser. She wasn't sure which, and didn't care enough to ask.

"I'm sorry you feel that way. Would you like to give it another go?" Gateway asked, his smile fully recovered.

"No. I have suffered that tragedy once already. I have no wish for a repeat performance."

"Hmm, I'd think you'd like to kiss a man who's known to be skilled in that department." Gateway said easily.

Brooke snorted. "You're not *that* skilled."

"You would know," he quipped with a sly smile.

That stunned Brooke. Their conversation was already scandalous, not enough to ruin her reputation, but his last comment was. She looked around to make sure nobody had heard what he'd said.

After she was satisfied, she looked back to Gateway. "What do you want, anyway?" she asked tersely.

"To talk to you," he responded smoothly, taking a seat on the grass next to where she was sitting.

She groaned. "Why?" she asked, grinding her teeth. "You never have anything nice to say to me, so why seek me out?"

"I've come to talk to you about Townson."

"Don't. I don't want to hear another word about him. I don't care about the gossip. I don't care about his relationship with his mother, as a boy or now. And I don't wish to discuss my relationship with him, especially with you."

Gateway smiled at her. It was a rare smile that Brooke was sure she'd never seen before. She would even consider it to be a grin. Brooke was quite taken aback when she saw it. He had a very nice smile when it was genuine. And there was no mistake, this smile was genuine. She smiled in return.

"I think our discussion is complete," he said, regaining his feet.

"Good riddance," Brooke mumbled to his retreating back.

Briefly glimpsing the back of Gateway as he stopped for a moment to talk to Andrew, Brooke turned her eyes back to the yard to watch the different players at their various games.

Her eyes were presently on the pall mall players when Andrew took a seat on the ground right next to her. "Our horses are waiting when you're ready," he whispered in her ear.

Brooke couldn't stop the smile that took over her lips. "I'm ready now," she told him excitedly. She had been anxiously waiting to leave because she hadn't secured permission to do so. Instead, she'd given a note to the butler to deliver to her mother right before luncheon, telling her she had left to go on a picnic and would return shortly. The note had been vague about where she was going and when exactly she would be back, but Brooke didn't care.

Andrew helped her to her feet and led her to where the horses were saddled and waiting for them. "Miss Bluebell," Andrew said as they approached her mount.

"She's just as magnificent up close as she was across the field," Brooke whispered, stroking Bluebell's mane.

"Yes," Andrew agreed. "She is quite the beast."

Andrew helped her up onto her horse, then mounted his own.

Brooke watched in quiet awe as Andrew swung his leg over the back of his massive stallion. He sat up on his horse and adjusted himself in the saddle. Brooke was fascinated by the picture he made. It was like his massive body was part of the horse's. It just looked so natural that he would be on the back of a horse. She couldn't help it—she just sat there and stared at him.

It wasn't until she met his curious, blue eyes looking back at her that she jerked her eyes away. "I was just…ah…just making sure you mounted all right," she stammered.

Andrew's face formed an expression of pure amusement, but he didn't laugh. "I am quite capable of mounting my horse, among other things."

Brooke's face flushed. "That will be enough of that type of talk, my lord," she managed.

This time Andrew did laugh. "One day, you might enjoy such conversation."

"I assure you, I will never enjoy such a conversation," Brooke told him. Her voice had gained a sharp edge to it.

They rode their horses down a little tree-lined trail that led away from the house. "All right," Andrew allowed. "We shall talk of something else. How are you finding this party?"

Brooke was thankful for his change of conversation subjects. "It has been lovely so far. I have enjoyed meeting many new people, eating new dishes, and of course, having a break from London."

"A break from London?"

"Yes, a break. You know, time away from balls, pressure, and gossip," Brooke replied, trying desperately to forget about what gossip she'd witnessed yesterday. She was still determined not to ask him about it, but she also didn't want him to know she knew anything about it.

"Gossip," Andrew mused. "Are you telling me that you have heard not one jot of gossip since coming to this party?"

Brooke tried to keep her expression bland, but her face heated up nonetheless. "Well, I have heard some gossip, I confess," she stated. She couldn't lie and say she'd heard none. He wouldn't believe that for a second.

"Anything you find 'juicy', as they say?" he asked. His eyes were looking over at her instead of the path in front of them.

Brooke felt his probing eyes on her as if they were boring holes into the side of her face. She dared not turn her head and meet them, or she might unwittingly give herself away. "None that I have heard do I believe to be true," she said, her voice a little higher than usual.

"You've heard some, then?" Andrew asked quietly, still looking at her.

"Yes, I've already said that."

"And how do you know that what you've heard isn't true?"

"I just do not believe that the person who I heard such gossip about has the type of character to substantiate the veracity of the words," she said as smoothly as she could. For some reason he wanted to talk about this. What she couldn't comprehend was why? Why would a man wish to talk about gossip? He obviously knew what she had heard, and he was trying to get her to acknowledge it.

"That's a very admirable trait about you, Brooke," Andrew

said without a hint of his thoughts being betrayed in his voice.

Brooke moved her head slowly to look at him now. When she caught his eyes, they were full of disbelief. "Why do you look at me that way?" she inquired.

"Which way?"

"As if you do not believe what I say?" The man was looking at her as if he believed she was a liar, and that rankled her.

Andrew stopped his horse, which led to Brooke having to stop hers if she wanted to hear what he had to say, and she did. "It's not that I don't believe what you say. In fact, I do believe it. It's more that I don't believe you would so easily dismiss horrible gossip about my past with the little knowledge that you have of me." His words were even and smooth, but in his eyes, the truth was evident.

Brooke reached over to him, and for the first time she was the one to touch him first and without any warning, she slowly ran her hand up and down his forearm before giving him a light reassuring squeeze. "I suppose we're talking about the same thing. Yes, I heard gossip about you and your family last night," she acknowledged. "I don't believe it. I have no proof to support any of it. Therefore, like all gossip I hear, I don't hold it against the person until I find that it's true." She gave him a sweet, tilted smile.

Suddenly Andrew's bewildered face turned to one of pain, as if he'd been punched. "And if the gossip were true?" he choked out.

Brooke's eyes narrowed. Did he even know what she'd heard? How much of that gossip was he trying to own up to? Even if what she'd heard was true and he technically was a bastard, did any of it really matter to her? True, she had decided earlier she was going to stop at nothing (or nearly nothing, for the time being) to win a marriage proposal, and accept it, naturally—which would then lump her in with the gossip—but did any of these claims really change her true feelings for *him*?

In a split-second she had her answer. No, none of what she'd heard last night would change her opinion of him. She didn't care about his mother's activities. Whether she was a recluse or a woman of ill repute, it mattered naught to Brooke. She'd learned in her short time in England that a lot of women kept company with men who were not their husbands. Did it truly matter anymore how wild his father had been? He was dead now. As for Andrew's schooldays, they were of no account to her.

Brooke locked her eyes with Andrew's. "Even if what I heard last night were true, I have no reason to change my previous opinions."

Andrew looked relieved, but only momentarily. Then his face took on a grim look and white lines formed around his mouth. "Then you must not have heard it all," he said dully.

"I heard plenty of damning gossip," she snapped, trying not to smile at Andrew's look of surprise by her word choice.

He quickly recovered his features. "May I ask what you heard?"

"You may ask," Brooke said sweetly, "but I shan't tell you."

Andrew's face turned a fraction darker, which caused Brooke's smile to dim. Glancing at the watch pinned to her bodice, she said, "You have exactly one minute to clear up whatever you think you must. After that, I shall never speak of this again."

Before Brooke knew what was happening, Andrew started talking at breakneck speed. "My parents had a spat soon after their wedding. I don't know why. It ended up with him packing her away to a country estate he owned in Essex. Nine months later, I was born. Some question my parentage because of his absence, including, at times, my father. I don't believe there is a question. I look identical to him at this age.

"My parents never reunited, nor did my mother ever have any other children. My father was a drunkard and a gambler, who died in a duel eight years ago. My mother became a recluse. She comes to London rarely and our relationship is strained at best."

Andrew's face took on a contemplative look as if he didn't know what to say about his relationship with his mother. With a shake of his head, he muttered, "I guess you'll hear this at some point anyway. The reason for our strained relationship is my fault.

We had depended on each other greatly when I was young. However, when I started school and I was mocked because of her past and our close relationship, I decided to cut all ties with her in order to have an easier time."

Brooke nodded. She'd heard about all of this, but his explanations made sense. Every last one of them. "I heard those rumors last night, however, your detailed explanations, or at least the ones you were able to spew in sixty seconds, make the rumors pale in my mind."

"You don't care about any of it?" Andrew asked uncertainly.

"Not one whit," she said with a simple smile.

# Chapter 20

Andrew felt relieved and on edge at the same time upon hearing Brooke's words. She wasn't going to render their relationship void because of some trivial—and if he said so himself, irrelevant—gossip. Some London ladies would run screaming as fast as their slippers could carry them at just the hint of gossip, but not his Brooke. She didn't turn a hair.

At the same time, unease was quickly creeping in. She wasn't going to let gossip taint their relationship, but he was going to destroy it all by himself within the next few days.

After finding what he considered the perfect picnic spot, Andrew stopped his horse and dismounted. "I should think this spot will do for our purpose," he said, looking around.

The spot he'd chosen overlooked a small lake. Actually it was more of a large pond, but that wasn't important. A few surrounding trees offered both shade and seclusion. The area where the picnic blanket would be laid was made of a thick, green carpet of grass. It would be absolutely perfect for eating and maybe a few other activities…

His mind snapped back to present when Brooke cleared her throat. "Right," Andrew clipped. He walked over to where Brooke was still seated on her horse and reached his hand up to help her down.

"Thank you, my lord. I began to despair that I was going to have to sit upon Bluebell and eat oats with her while you enjoyed our picnic alone." Her voice was light and full of humor.

"I'm sorry," he murmured. "I was just scouting out the best place for our picnic and it slipped my mind that you were waiting." That sounded weak even to his ears.

"It's all right," Brooke assured him. "I just have a feeling that what's in there," she said, pointing to the picnic hamper that

Andrew had taken off his horse and was now holding, "is better than what's in there—" she pointed to the saddlebag where Bluebell's apples and oats resided.

"I assure you, what's in here is much better," Andrew said, giving the hamper a little swing. "Shall we?"

"Yes." Brooke placed her hand on his proffered arm.

Andrew laid out the blanket and made sure to position it the best he could so that it was hidden from view in case anyone happened by. He intended to ruin her, but he didn't want to do it today.

Once the blanket was in the perfect location, Andrew unpacked the hamper. He pulled out two cheese wheels, some bread, strawberries, a few pieces of chicken, a bottle of lemonade, and two glasses. Finally, the hamper was emptied and he looked to Brooke to take a seat, but she wasn't looking at him. She was looking around her surroundings.

He knew what she saw: a little area that had a wall of trees on three sides and only a little grassy stretch then the banks of the lake, pond, or whatever, on the fourth side. They were so secluded even their horses couldn't see them. Andrew thought she might panic. "If this won't do, we can move," he offered, hoping she would refuse.

"No," Brooke said breathlessly. "I have no objection to this location. I was just admiring the beauty of it." She waved her hand to indicate that she was taken with all her surroundings.

Relief flooded him. He didn't want to move an inch. This was the perfect spot to steal a few kisses, and he was looking forward to stealing as many as he could. He might even try to do more than just steal a few paltry kisses if she'd let him. He'd like to run his hands through her hair again or perhaps somewhere else, too.

Andrew forced his mind away from such lustful thoughts before his body gave him away. First, he needed to get her to sit down. "Would you like to take a seat," he invited, patting a spot on the blanket right next to him.

Brooke took a seat next to him, but not too close. That could be fixed. He smiled at her when she stiffened because he'd scooted so close to her their thighs were touching.

"Can I interest you in some chicken?" he asked, reaching behind them to grab two pieces of chicken.

"Thank you." She licked her lips, but didn't reach out to grab one of the offered pieces.

Andrew registered her reluctance. "It's just us. You don't have to be so formal as to cut it."

Her face lit up and he let out a little chuckle, accompanied by a wide grin. When Brooke grabbed the piece of chicken and bit a huge chunk out of it, Andrew let out a shout of laughter and shook his head. "You're something else."

"I have no idea if that is an insult or a compliment. Coming from you, I shall assume the worst," she managed in between bites of chicken. "But I forgive you,"

"Have no fear. It was not an insult in the least," Andrew said jovially. "I would be afraid to insult a woman who can tear apart a piece of chicken so savagely. It's no longer a mystery to me as to why the colonies won their independence. If the country is full of people like you, England never stood a chance."

Brooke laughed. "No, the real reason England lost is it was too hard for their soldiers to shoot straight with their vision impaired by their wig powder and spiky hats falling into their eyes."

Andrew laughed at her jest. He had never understood wearing a silly wig or even hair powder. He had never attempted to, and felt no shame in that. Thankfully, the trend was becoming less common by the time he'd reached his majority, however, there were still a few who felt the need to wear a wig or powder.

"You don't powder your hair—why is that?" Brooke asked curiously.

He shrugged, took the chicken bone from her, and put it by the basket. "I've never felt the need. Some feel that it allows them to be seen as older and wiser if their hair is white, whether naturally or because of powder. I personally do not put much stock in that idea. And on a personal note, I find the wigs and powders to be annoying and hideous, and they have a very foul odor."

Brooke giggled. "A foul odor?" she asked him while she

licked the chicken juice from her fingers.

"Yes, most of the powders used are held in place on the hair by fat—pig fat to be exact," Andrew stated and took satisfaction when she curled her pretty lip. "Let's not talk of this any longer. I hate to see how your lips react," he said in a husky voice. "I would much rather they be used for other purposes besides sneering and curling up in disgust."

"Oh," Brooke said in surprise.

Andrew leaned closer to her. His face was now less than an inch from hers. She swallowed as he reached up with his right hand and ran his fingers along her jawline. Brooke's lips parted and her eyes grew round with wonder as he continued to rub her jaw with his thumb while gently massaging her neck at the same time. "Does this feel good?" Andrew asked huskily.

"Yes," she gasped in reply.

He closed that last bit of space between them and his lips took hers. He kissed her slowly and gently, taking time to enjoy the feeling of her lips on his. His left hand took hold of the other side of her face and touched her jaw and neck the way his right hand had.

Slowly, Andrew sought to deepen their kiss and ran his tongue along her lips until she opened her mouth. When she let out a short gasp, Andrew let his hands fall from her face and onto her shoulders, where he rubbed them in small, circular motions with his thumbs.

"Is something wrong?" he panted, when she suddenly pulled away from his embrace.

Brooke's look of confusion did not change when she said, "No." Nor did her expression change when she looked down and noticed his hands on the front of her shoulders, with his thumbs tucked inside of the top of her gown.

"Do you want me to continue?" he asked hoarsely, praying she'd say yes.

Brooke didn't say yes, nor did she say no—she just gave a single nod.

Before she could change her mind, Andrew took charge of her

mouth again. This time it was not as gentle, it was more intense and demanding.

Her hands grabbed onto his shoulders and slid slowly up and down his arms, inspecting every bulge and plane as they went. Her action reminded Andrew of what he wanted to do. His hands left her shoulders and went to her side, taking pleasure in the way her soft body felt through her gown. He'd hoped she didn't wear a corset, and was pleased to learn she didn't. His hands slowly glided up and down her ribs several times before moving higher.

Brooke flinched and let out a little shriek. "It's all right," he assured her quietly. "I'll only do what you want me to, nothing more." The words were spoken, and he meant them now. He just hoped he could keep that promise in a few minutes.

Brooke needed no more convincing and pulled his head back down to hers. This time it was her turn to be in control of their kiss. Andrew groaned and he rolled her onto her back. He carefully ran his thumbs along the sides of her soft breasts. As she relaxed more under him, his caresses got bolder.

She let out an excited sigh when he ran his thumbs under and around the sides of her breasts. "Do you like that?" he asked between kisses.

"Yes, oh yes," she breathed.

He had certainly gotten lucky with Brooke. Not only did her body respond to his, but she openly admitted to enjoying his kisses and touches.

As his lips went back to kissing hers, his hands went to work on the front of her gown. The bodice of her gown was too high for him to be able to free her breasts just by tugging it down. If he did, it would rip. His hands roamed while his brain tried frantically to think of another way to expose her chest to his thirsty eyes. He reached up to her shoulders and found that her sleeves were not very tight. If he were able to slip them over her shoulders and pull them down a bit, he could free her breasts.

Brooke offered no resistance when Andrew grabbed her sleeves and pulled them down from her shoulders. She gasped when his lips left hers to kiss her cheeks, then her jaw, and finally down her neck and along her collarbone.

His hands were still working on getting the sleeves down and revealing her breasts, but her shoulders were bare and his lips ached to kiss them—then they did. He gave them slow, gentle, lingering, open-mouthed kisses.

Brooke let out a soft sigh, her head rolled back, and her eyes closed.

Andrew worked her gown down far enough that given only a little jerk; her breasts would be bared for him. He moved his lips from her shoulder up to the sweet hollow of her neck. He kissed her there with an open mouth, running his tongue in the depression. When she let out a gasp and arched her back from the sensation, he gave her gown that little jerk it needed.

Andrew was torn between feeling rather proud of his maneuverings and too lust-fogged to care. His eyes connected with her wonder-filled brown eyes before lowering. His gaze traveled from her eyes to her swollen, ruby lips, then descended farther down her body. When his gaze settled on her chest, he blinked.

# Chapter 21

Brooke had been lost in the moment, so taken with Andrew's kisses and caresses that she hardly registered he was trying to get her gown down. Not that she was completely unaware, mind you—she did know he had bared her shoulders. Maybe she didn't know at first, but when he started to kiss her there, she knew.

When he gave her gown a jerk though, her daze rapidly faded. But to be honest, his confused face complete with blinking eyes brought her all the way back to reality.

Trying her best to suppress a giggle, born equally of his confusion as much as her own mortification, she said, "I um…ah… as you can see…" She took a breath. How exactly does one say that they bind their breasts?

Andrew's face was one of complete bewilderment. "Why on earth did you bind your breasts?" he asked flatly, without regard that he had just asked her a question about a topic no gentleman should speak about with an unmarried lady.

He was so confused his brow didn't even arch.

Absolutely nothing on this Earth would make her tell him the real reason, which was because they were rather small, so small in fact, that even corsets that were meant to push them up did not help. At least if she bound them, she could add as much padding to them as she felt necessary with no chance of it being revealed that she stuffed or just how small they really were. Her mother and sisters knew she augmented her bosom, but she desperately hoped Papa didn't. She honestly doubted Mama and her sisters knew exactly how much of her bosom consisted of rolled up linen, though.

"Well, you see, in their natural state, my—" she gestured to her chest, not being as brave as he was to say the word— "do not quite fit this gown appropriately, so I had to bind them to make them fit." She'd let him draw his own conclusion, and if it were the wrong one—which was likely—that was his own fault.

Andrew nodded. Then his face took on a bright smile that Brooke would have bet her life meant he had assumed the wrong reason for the binding.

Their eyes locked and Andrew swallowed so loudly that it sounded more like a gulp. Then wordlessly, he ran his hands along the top of her bindings.

"What are you doing?" she asked shakily.

"Removing it of course," he said with a devilish smile.

He really meant to do it, too! The intense look in his eyes told her so. But now it seemed different and she didn't want him to. Had she not been wearing it when he tugged her gown down, she may not have cared. But now that her mind was no longer clouded by lust, she was nervous and rather embarrassed. "No," she said quietly. "I think it would be best if we headed back."

Andrew's face fell, but he nodded and said, "As you wish."

Together, they righted their clothes as best they could and packed up the picnic hamper in silence.

Andrew helped her onto her horse then mounted his own.

"I had a pleasant picnic," Brooke said after a few minutes, trying to eliminate the uncomfortable silence that was choking them.

"So did I."

The conversation had already run into a dead end. She'd hoped they could use that as a way to talk about ordinary things on the way home, but he'd not taken the bait.

After a few minutes of riding in silence, Andrew interrupted her thoughts. "How do my kisses rate?"

Brooke's head snapped in his direction. "What are you talking about?" she asked tersely, although she had a good idea. She'd seen Gateway and Andrew talking briefly before he came and sat next to her, but she would have never dreamed Gateway would tell Andrew about their conversation. She groaned. Of course he would —that was just Gateway's personality. He liked to stir up as much turmoil as possible without a second thought to how it would affect anyone else. He was such a jackanapes.

"I think you do," Andrew countered, not unkindly.

"All right, you had your moment of confession earlier, now shall be mine. I assume you spoke to Gateway about our conversation on the lawn. It's true that I kissed Gateway. I found our time together in the garden disgusting and nothing that I'd wish to repeat, not even in a nightmare, and I told him as much. As for other gentlemen I've kissed—" she gave a shrug— "there weren't so many. But there were a few. However, I feel no guilt about it. I know without a doubt that you've kissed more females than just me, and I expect no explanation about those kisses, therefore, I shall not give you one."

Her words brought him up short. Everyone knew boys past the age of fourteen had kissed a multitude of women, and it was impolite for women, even their wives, to ask them about it. Yet, women were only supposed to kiss their husbands, and maybe their fiancés. Brooke had always found that to be unfair.

"Is it fair to assume by your reaction to my kisses today that you do not feel an aversion to them?" Andrew asked, raising his brow.

She flushed. "Why would you ask that when it's so obvious?" she accused in a tight tone.

"Because I wanted to see you blush."

"I shan't give you that privilege in the future," she said sternly, hoping it was true.

Andrew waved his hand dismissively. "How unfortunate for you that you cannot control it."

"I can, too. I'll prove to you. Say whatever you wish, and I shall not give you the satisfaction of my face coloring." She was generally good at playing games with her sisters about not talking, laughing, or blinking, so how difficult could this actually be?

"How about I describe to you in explicit detail what I was going to do to you if you were not wearing that confounded binding," Andrew teased, his eyes alight with amusement.

Brooke held onto her determination. He had not said anything specific, but she had serious doubts that this would end like she'd hoped. His wolfish smile and mischievous eyes only confirmed that.

"Do you remember how I was kissing your shoulders and neck?" When Brooke nodded, his smile became wolfish. "I would have continued to kiss you like that on any part of your body that was bare. Which, had it not been for those confounded bindings, would have been your breasts," Andrew said in a husky voice. "I do believe, Miss Banks, you just lost."

Brooke just stared at him as her skin got hotter and probably colored just as he had predicted. Drat this man. How could he do this to her? His words brought her back to lying beneath him on the blanket as his hands and lips caressed her.

Brooke sniffed and inclined her head. "You, sir, are no gentleman," she proclaimed. Then she gave Bluebell a slight kick to increase her speed.

Behind her, Andrew snorted and laughingly said, "No gentleman, indeed."

Bluebell trotted toward the house at a moderate pace with Brooke atop, laughing as she thought of Andrew and their picnic together.

She hadn't noticed that Andrew hadn't caught up with her yet, when not far ahead of her on the path Liberty came careening toward her. Her sister's face was flushed and she was waving her hands wildly. She actually looked as if she were running away from a band of attackers who were bent on burning her at the stake.

"Liberty, what's the matter?" Brooke shouted to her sister.

"*Him!*" Liberty exclaimed hysterically. "That awful, dratted man is the matter. I swear, Brooke, I cannot abide him a moment longer. We must come up with a plan to send him back to whatever hole he crawled out of."

Brooke didn't need to ask who Liberty was talking about. She knew. She thought there was something a little bizarre about Mr. Grimes, but nothing that would lead any rational human being to have such an adverse reaction to him. "What happened now, Liberty?" she asked as she slowed her horse to a walk.

Liberty opened her mouth to tell her when Brooke put up a

hand and said, "This time, please do not leave any crucial parts out of the story."

Her sister's cheeks turned slightly pinker. "We were playing bowls—you know that game where you roll your wooden ball toward the target, which is called a jack."

"I do not think that I need a run-down on how the game is played," Brooke exclaimed, exasperated. "Just get on with what happened. I haven't got all day, and I am not particularly comfortable atop this beast."

Her sister nodded. "I wanted to play. When I asked to join, Mr. Grimes seemed to suddenly lose interest." She gave a little sniff. "I called him back and talked him into playing."

Brooke rolled her eyes. This did *not* have the makings for a good ending. For as much as she suspected Liberty might have formed a *tendre* for the man, it was probably best those two were kept as far apart as possible.

"We began to play, and everything was going well until someone suggested we bowl in teams. What I had not realized when I agreed was that I would have to partner Mr. Grimes. I tried to act gracious—even though he was snarling—and took my spot next to him. When his turn came, someone rolled him a bowl from the rack. He made no move to catch it, and it rolled right onto my toe."

Brooke tried not to laugh at what she knew was probably an accident. "What happened next?"

"He mumbled an incoherent, and insincere might I add, apology, took his bowl, and sent it toward the green. I was still upset about my toe, which seemed to be of no concern to him, so I might have…well, I may have overreacted a bit in retaliation. But that is no excuse for what he did afterward."

Brooke held up her hand again and gave Liberty her piercing stare before demanding, "What exactly did you do?"

Liberty's face turned redder and she said very quietly, "I may have elbowed him. But not as hard as he would have everyone believe." The look on her face made it clear she *had* meant to elbow him, but something had gone terribly wrong. "See, I pretended I needed his help, and when he came up behind me, I brought back my elbow…"

"What happened after you elbowed him?" Brooke asked, skewering Liberty with her gaze.

Liberty just stood still and stared over Brooke's shoulder. Brooke turned her head to see what Liberty was looking at. There, just a few feet away, was Andrew sitting on his horse and listening intently to Liberty's story.

"Miss Liberty, do you know where you hit the man?" Andrew asked carefully.

Brooke knit her eyebrows. Why should it matter where the man got hit? The fact remained, she'd hit him.

"I—I don't know," Liberty stammered. "In his midsection, I expect." Her brow furrowed in confusion and her mouth formed a thin line.

"You don't know?" echoed Brooke. "He didn't say?"

"No, because a gentleman does not discuss body parts in mixed company," Liberty said weakly, inclining her head just a little, as if to say she was starting to regain some of her dignity.

Brooke flushed. Liberty's comment reminded her of her earlier conversation with Andrew about her breasts.

Andrew coughed. "What happened next, Miss Liberty?"

"Well, he let out this high-pitched yelp, and then leaned over for a minute before hobbling away. A little later, Papa summoned me and said I must make amends." Liberty's tone started to change again from normal to mildly hysterical. "I saw that Mr. Grimes was in the room, and that beast had the nerve to say, 'I would prefer that she just stay away from me from this point forward. That's the best way for her to make amends.'

"I felt like elbowing him again for that comment." She shook her head and pursed her lips. "But then Papa said that was not good enough, since we are going to have to be in one another's company for as long as we remain in England, and we cannot have a rift or some such nonsense." Taking a deep breath, she finished her drama. "Papa kept saying how I was to make amends by doing anything Mr. Grimes demanded, and then he left. I was in that room alone with Mr. Grimes for no more than two minutes before he started to unbutton his clothes!

"Oh, Brooke, I didn't know what to do and I p-panicked, and I m-may h-have ov-overacted again."

"Just what did you do?"

"I grabbed the nearest book and threw it at him," she cried, burying her head in her hands. "That man wants my virtue!" Liberty sobbed hysterically, her body shaking uncontrollably. Her lower lip quivered as she tried to firmly declare, "I shall not give it!" She swiped at the tears that had snaked down her cheeks. "Please, Brooke, hide me and go talk to Papa. Tell him that… that...creature wants to take away from me the only thing I truly own." She fell to the ground and curled up into a small ball.

Brooke looked to Andrew, hoping that he would help her down from her mount without her having to ask.

As if he read her thoughts, he dismounted and helped her down as quickly as he could, then led the horses back to the stables while Brooke comforted her sister.

"Liberty," Brooke said softly, "have you told me everything?"

When Liberty's wet eyes, spilling tears, met Brooke's, she knew Liberty had not left out any details this time.

Why did she always miss these situations between Liberty and Mr. Grimes? More importantly, what was she going to do now?

# Chapter 22

In the blue salon, Mr. Paul Grimes was lying unconscious on a settee, dreaming of what his life might have been like had he decided to join the military rather than the ministry.

He dreamed of horses, swords, guns, and the smell of gunpowder. Oh, that smell seemed so sweet right now. He'd trade almost everything he had to be in the military and be smelling gunpowder. He took another deep whiff, trying to sniff up as much as he could before he woke up to his hellish reality.

"That's it, take another deep breath," he heard a familiar voice coax.

Who was he to argue? He inhaled as deeply as he could, then coughed. That was not the smell of gunpowder. It was a very nasty smell that he recognized as smelling salts. He snapped his eyes snapped open. He was expecting to see Mrs. Baker, an older woman from his church who carried those nasty salts with her everywhere, but instead he was greeted by John and Carolina Banks.

Carolina was sitting right next to him on the settee holding a bag of salts; her husband was sitting in a chair right next to her. His face looked worried, as if he'd been given bad news about someone and he was about to be the one to tell them.

"Mr. Grimes," John said solemnly.

"Please, call me Paul."

"Paul," John started again. "Do you know why you were unconscious?"

Unconscious, thought Paul. He knew he was sleeping, but not unconscious. "I was unaware that I was unconscious," he replied and tried to force himself to sit up, but his head throbbed when he moved, so he lay back down as quickly as he could.

With his hand, he reached up to rub his face and felt a huge bump the size of an egg on his forehead. Then it all came back to him. The game of bowls, getting hit in the unmentionables, John seeking him out after the baron told him what had happened, the Banks family meeting, and he and Liberty being alone for a few minutes.

That last event is what led to his current headache. He had been so angry with her he felt like he was choking. That's when the devil in disguise, also known as Liberty, threw a heavy tome at his head. Once again, her aim had been surprisingly accurate and he now sported the bump to prove it.

"On second thought, I do know why I was unconscious," he corrected.

Mrs. Banks looked relieved that he had figured it out. Clearly she had no idea that it could have been caused by Liberty.

John, on the other hand, looked almost sick. He measured his words carefully before he finally spoke. "How did it come to pass?"

"A flying book," Paul bit off.

Mrs. Banks let out a little peal of laughter. "A flying book?" she asked, her lips curving up.

"Yes, a flying book," Paul confirmed flatly.

Carolina must have really thought he was delusional because she pressed him, "How did this book take flight? Did it have wings?" She giggled again at her own joke until John placed a hand on her shoulder.

Paul had had enough. At present, Carolina was quickly becoming just as irritating to him as Liberty was. "Actually, the book did not have a pair of wings. It did not need them. It would seem that your demon…er…I mean daughter, gave the book enough of a heave that wings weren't necessary to carry the book all the way across the room to meet its target: my forehead."

Carolina gasped. "I am so sorry. I'm also sorry for my jest, and I am even sorrier for my daughter's actions. I shall speak to her immediately."

"Why did she throw the book?" John asked gravely, ignoring his wife's words, but holding her arm.

Paul shrugged. "I haven't a clue." He really didn't. He tried to think back to what had happened. She had been furious ever since that bowl accidentally hit her foot. He had tried to stop it, but had not gotten a good hold on it and it kept rolling. But that was why she had elbowed him, not why she threw the book. His mind raced forward to the conversation in the salon. He remembered asking that her parents keep her away. He remembered they wouldn't agree to that. Then they left.

What happened after they left? Nothing. He couldn't remember anything happening at all. He and Liberty stared at each other for a moment before he jerked his gaze away. He was so mad he didn't even want to see her. He may be a man of God, but he was still a man, and anger was something he couldn't always control.

Paul was trying to think hard about the earlier events and rubbed his chin. Then his fingers brushed something. It was his cravat. Why wasn't that lying flat on his chest? Then he remembered exactly what happened.

"I do believe I may remember what transpired." His face pinched up in confusion. "Though I remember it, I have no idea why it caused Miss Liberty to throw a book at me."

"That's all right, Paul, just tell us what happened," John said as smoothly as he could. His body looked like it was tensing up and his hand tightened on his wife's arm. His face looked especially hard and tortured.

"I was sitting here, wishing she would just go away, when I started feeling overly warm. I felt like I was about to choke to death on my own cravat, so I undid it, and the top button of my shirt in order to get a little air. Less than a second later, this giant brick of a book came flying at my head. The next thing I knew, I was dreaming of being a soldier and sniffing gunpowder, which turned out to be Mrs. Banks's smelling salts."

John's face was blank, except for a puckered brow. "I shall speak to my daughter immediately," he stated with a harsh voice that startled Carolina and Paul so much, they both jumped in unison. John abruptly let go of his wife, shot up out of his chair, and started for the door.

"That will not be necessary…" Paul started.

John quickly turned back and leveled an icy glare at Paul. "It is necessary. You stated earlier you wanted to avoid her presence. Now, you shall have your wish." John strode back toward the door then turned back around again to speak to his wife. "Carolina, after I am finished talking with her, she may need some consoling. That will be your job—be forewarned."

As if he were going off to war, John stomped out the door and down the hall in what Paul could only presume was the beginning of his search for Liberty.

Mrs. Banks stayed behind with Paul and waved her salts in front of her own face, repeatedly saying, "Oh dear."

***

By the time John found his daughter, who had been hiding from him for several hours, his temper was beyond his control. He had long ago decided he was not going to demand a reason for her actions, nor did he even care what reason she did or didn't have for her behavior. He just walked into the room where she was sitting all curled up on a settee by the window. She had tears on her cheeks and her face was whiter than a lily, making the little blotches of red on her cheeks more prominent. He took one look at her and thundered, "Liberty, your recent behavior toward Mr. Grimes is unacceptable. From this point forward, you are not allowed out of your mother's sight. Is that understood?" John looked over at his daughter who had not spoken, nor made any move to agree or disagree with his words. "You will not attend any balls, soirées, or any other social event until I say that you may. You, young lady, may very well be a spinster before I let you out into society again!"

"But…but…" Liberty tried to speak between sobs.

John understood she only wanted to tell her side of the tale, but he didn't want to hear a word of it. "That's enough," he barked. "I have made my decision, and it's final. You have five minutes to go find your mother. If I see you more than five paces away from her at any given time, I will personally load you onto the next ship bound for America and you shall go back to New York alone and wait for us to return."

Feeling a little stab of guilt at his threat, John decided to duck out quickly before adding more heartbreaking words. Until today, he'd never spoken so harshly to any of his family, but Liberty was determined to bring out the worst in him.

# Chapter 23

Andrew lay in his bed that night thinking of Brooke. Her soft skin. Her flowing hair. Her bright smile. Her delectable body. He even smiled thinking of her bound breasts.

In his mind, she was the perfect woman. It was too bad that she couldn't be *his* perfect woman. That thought made his smile disappear.

She could never be his woman. He could not offer for her, and if he did, she would never accept him after what was about to happen tomorrow night.

Earlier in the evening he'd planned it all out. He was going to take her out to the woods promptly after dinner. He'd suggested to a few of the gentlemen tonight that they should go out and see Alex's telescope tomorrow night. Andrew wasn't into astronomy much, but he did know a little. He casually mentioned that some planets could be easily seen tomorrow night. Whether true or not, he didn't know, nor did he care. All he needed was for a few people to see that Brooke had been compromised.

The extra benefit to doing it this way was only the truly scientifically interested would be coming out. Which would be enough for Brooke to be shamed, but this group was not a bunch of gossips, so the tale was unlikely to spread so quickly it would cause her undue stress. It would spread of course, but not so quickly that her whole family would be forced to steal away in the dead of night.

The whole idea made his stomach turn sour. How could he have ever agreed to such a stupid scheme? What on earth had possessed him to do so? Until a day or two ago, he'd kept reminding himself of the money he would be able to earn after he got the estate back. Not a lot, but enough to get him out of debt and get on with his life. Then, the money problem seemed to fade when

Willis mentioned the mines. Not that he wanted the mines, but if there was no other choice, he would drill. The problem was he would still have to come up with the blunt to put the mines in, but that was minor compared to what he was about to do.

Then he'd tried to use his guilt over his past relationship with his mother as a reason to go through with it. The dowager house at Rockhurst had burned down fifty years ago and the impoverished earl at that time could not afford to rebuild it. No one since then had bothered to, either. His guilt consumed him. He had wronged his mother so many years ago by sending her back into that isolation in Essex, all because he couldn't handle the taunts and rumors about them.

The problem of his mother's residence could also be solved by the mines. If they made enough money, he would be able to build a house wherever she wanted.

So why was he still going to go through with it?

Then he remembered the written agreement he had with Gateway. There was nothing written about consequences Andrew or Brooke would face if he didn't go through with it, but he knew there would be. There always were.

More than ten years ago, he'd learned that lesson for himself when he'd refused to lie for Gateway. Gateway had gone out drinking one night and had missed a mathematics examination the next morning because he'd overslept. Not only had he not lied about Gateway's whereabouts, but he'd refused to tell him what was on the examination. Later, when Andrew was riding to London, he was attacked by a band of highwaymen who had stolen all of his valuables, including his horse. Then when he was walking down the road to find a new mount, Gateway came up behind him and jumped him. They each threw a few good punches, but because Gateway had the advantage of catching Andrew unawares, he came out the victor of the fight, if one could call it that. That's when his nose had been broken and he decided to never deal with Gateway again. He'd held to that well enough for ten years. Now he wished he'd held to it longer.

Shaking his head, Andrew rolled over, stuffed a pillow under his stomach, and tried to sleep.

But sleep wouldn't come.

The next day passed in waves of boredom and tension. Tonight was *the night*, he kept reminding himself. Both of their futures would drastically change after tonight—one for good, one for bad. Knowing this led to Andrew's inability to pay attention to anything anyone was saying.

Andrew was still trying to get past his guilt and unease when he met Brooke outside the servants' entrance. They'd arranged to meet there to sneak out to the telescope to look at the stars.

They walked in silence to the gazebo where Alex kept his telescope. Andrew occasionally looked over at her. She was beautiful. She walked with such grace and she had good posture, especially for an American. Her body was so straight and lean, and when she walked, she looked like she was floating. She never stumbled or misstepped. She was perfect. Too bad this would be the last time he'd get to look at her thus.

When she looked over and almost blinded him with her smile, a knot formed in his gut. He tried to chase it away by thinking of the wrong he was going to be able to correct by pulling this off. He was going to make amends to his mother, and Brooke was going to be safe from Gateway back in America. However, with as much rationalizing as his mind was doing, his heart still felt heavy and for some reason hurt. Was there really any greater good after such a vile action? Andrew gave a harsh laugh at the thought.

"Is something funny?" Brooke asked innocently.

Andrew started when Brooke's voice interrupted his thoughts. "No," he answered smoothly.

Brooke nodded, but looked like she didn't understand at all.

They continued to walk in silence. "I must say that I didn't pin you as one who was interested in stargazing," Brooke said lightly.

Andrew flashed a smile. "No? I may not be very knowledgeable, but when I go to Rockhurst, sometimes I look up at the sky." That wasn't entirely a lie; he did look at the stars at Rockhurst, just not from a telescope.

"I've noticed it's nearly impossible to see anything through the thick fog in London."

"Is it easy to see the stars in New York?" Andrew asked casually, fighting for calm from the storm that was brewing in his body.

"Yes. Well, most times. To be truthful though, I have no earthly idea what anything up there is besides the sun, moon, and stars."

Andrew put his arm down and grabbed Brooke's hand. With her hand in his, he intertwined their fingers. "You mean you have no idea about the constellations?" he asked in mock horror. At his words, her brow puckered. "Is that not a term you are familiar with?"

"No," she admitted. "I assume it has something to do with the stars. Beyond that I fear I am uninformed."

"We're even then. I haven't a clue about them, either. Alex has a telescope out here that we can look through, but I have no idea what we'll be looking at," he confessed with a small smile.

Brooke smiled at his open acknowledgment of his ignorance. "Most men I know would never admit such a thing. Instead, they would try to pretend they knew everything about the subject until they were proven wrong. Even then, they would still be reluctant to admit they were without knowledge all along. That's what I like best about you, Andrew. You're so honest with me."

His heart felt every word of her statement. If only she knew just how dishonest he'd been with her since the day they'd met.

They walked together in companionable silence a little farther before Brooke stopped walking and turned to face him. "We're not just here to look at stars, are we?" she asked. Her voice had a hint of excitement.

"Perhaps. But then again, we might do something else," Andrew allowed. Was he really that transparent? He hoped the excitement in her voice was not nervous excitement.

They walked a few more steps before finding a little gazebo-type structure that was tall and thin. Up at the top of the gazebo was a long tube hanging out one of the top windows.

"This is it," Andrew said, gesturing to the gazebo. "I believe we must climb up a few stairs in order to get to the eyepiece." He walked over to the entrance and waited for her to step inside.

Brooke stepped inside and looked around. "It's rather dark," she mused after a minute.

"Good thing I brought these, then," Andrew said as he pulled two candles and small holders out of his pocket. "I wasn't sure if there were candles already in here, so I took the liberty of swiping some on the way out."

Andrew lit the two candles and handed one to Brooke, who took it and walked a whole three steps to the other side of the gazebo.

"Not very big is it?"

Andrew stifled a small laugh. "No, I'm afraid not. Alex probably doesn't make a regular practice of bringing guests here. We're probably the only people besides Alex to ever step foot in here."

Brooke walked back to his side and together they looked at the makeshift ladder. "I hope this can hold us both," Andrew said, giving it a shake to test its durability.

Brooke let out an unfeminine laugh.

Andrew's gaze shot to her. "Is something funny?" he asked, repeating her own words back to her.

"Yes. No. Well, a little." Andrew's arched brow prompted her to say, "It's merely that you are just like other gentlemen. Instead of inspecting the wood to make sure there are no major cracks or broken steps, you jiggle the ladder to see if it gives way." She shrugged. "It's just funny the way you're testing the ladder, that's all."

"Why?"

"It doesn't seem to fit your personality. I thought you'd just walk right on up," she said flippantly.

"And find out the ladder is unstable that way?" Andrew asked, stepping away from the ladder. If she thought he looked ridiculous by jiggling the ladder, he'd just let her test it herself. "All right, the ladder is all yours. You may check it however you see fit."

Brooke put her candle down on a nearby ledge, marched right

up to the ladder and began to climb.

Immediately Andrew's hands went to her waist and tried to pull her off. "What do you think you're doing?" he demanded.

"What does it look like?" she responded defiantly.

"It looks like you are about to break your silly little neck."

"Do try not to act so worried. If Alex climbs up this ladder, there is no reason that it would not be able to hold me." She looked over her shoulder, and cast him a skeptical look. "Do you see a reason it would not?"

"No," Andrew said hastily.

"Good, because if you were going to imply otherwise, I was going to have to brain you with the telescope," she said with a smile.

Brooke climbed up a few steps to the telescope and looked out. "Oh, it's wonderful! It is like the stars are so close I could touch them."

Andrew put his candle down next to hers and came up behind her. "Are they?" he murmured in her ear as his hands moved to clasp her waist.

Brooke jumped slightly at his touch.

Andrew steadied her. "It's all right. Just relax. What do you see?"

Brooke put her eye back up to the telescope and looked out again. "Stars. Lots of stars."

"Anything else?"

She gave a little shrug. "The moon."

"Tell me about the stars you see," Andrew whispered in her ear, his fingers rubbing slow circles on her waist and hips.

Breathlessly, Brooke went into detail about every star she saw until she was rambling about absolutely nothing.

Andrew took Brooke's inability to form a proper sentence as a good sign. His hands moved from her hips and he was massaging her lower back with his thumbs while his fingers were splayed over her ribs.

"No corset tonight?" he murmured against her ear.

"No," she breathed.

He lowered his head and feathered kisses along the back of her neck and in between her shoulder blades. Slowly he took his hands from her sides and brought them up to where the buttons started at the back of her gown.

Resisting his primal urge to rip that row of buttons apart with no regard to her gown, he traced slow patterns on her neck and upper back where it was exposed. He took delight in the shiver that ran through her body.

He bent his head close and reverently kissed her soft, warm skin again. Her skin was so perfect against his lips, and her sighs so sweet to his ears, he had to resist his own urge to sigh.

He kissed her with open-mouthed kisses on her back while undoing the first button of her gown. He undid two more and pressed his lips to each of the points of her spine he'd just exposed, giving each a warm, wet kiss.

Her whole body relaxed against his. "We should probably get off this ladder," he whispered in her ear.

Brooke let out a little gasp as he undid a few more of her buttons, but did not resist when he stepped down from the ladder, taking her with him.

Once she was off the ladder, he snuffed their two candles and tucked them back into his pocket. Taking Brooke by the hand, he led her outside.

They had walked about twenty feet in the direction of the house when he tugged on her hand and walked over to a little area of trees he had seen earlier. This area afforded them some privacy, but was still close enough that anyone who came walking by would notice something going on and would be likely to stop and inquire—which would in effect lead to the demise of Brooke's reputation.

Shaking off his guilt as best he could, Andrew dropped to his knees and pulled Brooke down with him.

Brooke's hands went to his face and she ran her fingers along his hard cheek and jaw bones while his hands found her hair and began to remove the pins. "I've wondered what it looks like when it's all down," he murmured before taking her mouth in a consuming kiss.

Brooke's lips relaxed and relinquished control. Andrew's lips took the control that was offered and he kissed her with the stark hunger of a starving man who could only survive if he consumed what Brooke's lips alone could offer.

Her hands left his face and she wound her arms around his neck. Andrew gently pushed her backward until she was lying on the ground. She ran her fingers through the curls that rested on his neck before she moved them to explore his hard shoulders.

He sought to deepen their kiss, and she willingly responded by opening her mouth to his. His fogged brain remembered this. He remembered how sweetly she tasted the other day in the orangery and again when they kissed on their picnic. His hands finally freed all of her hair and he broke away to look at it.

"Your hair is so beautiful," he panted, running his fingers through her long, silky brown locks.

"So is yours," she said.

Andrew smiled. "As much as I admire my hair, it pales in comparison to yours." Then before she could argue or say another inane comment, he took her mouth again.

Gently, he came to settle his upper body directly on top of hers, his legs on the ground next to hers. His hands left her hair and went to her sides where they skated up and down her ribs.

Brooke's hands squeezed and kneaded his shoulders before they moved down to explore his muscled chest. After a minute she moved them inside his coat, and ran her fingers along the top of his shirt and waistcoat. The warmth of her fingertips radiated through the layers of his clothes.

He pulled away from their kiss and looked down at Brooke. She was staring at his face as it hovered above hers. Her eyes were wide with wonder; it was a sight he could look at forever.

It took only a matter of seconds for him to remove his coat and waistcoat then toss them in a pile beside them.

Taking hold of Brooke's hands he brought them up to his chest and leaned back in to kiss her again. "Touch me again," he said, breaking their kiss for a second.

Instantly, she resumed touching his muscled chest through his shirt. When she reached a finger in between his buttons and touched his bare chest, Andrew groaned. When she started to undo his shirt, he groaned again. "You're too much for me, sweetheart," he panted, rethinking his decision to leave his shirt on. He had only left it on so she wouldn't think he was pushing her.

Brooke's fingers worked the best they could at getting the buttons at the top of his shirt undone. When she had three unfastened, she ran both hands up and down his chest. Her fingers set out to explore his chest, searing his skin with each and every touch.

Taking advantage of Brooke's interest in his chest, he moved his lips from hers and kissed her jaw, then moved onto her neck. When his kisses drifted to the top of her chest, her fingers stopped moving and her head lolled to the side. His hands slid down the front of her body, caressing every part of her they could. She was so soft and curvy in all the right places.

His hands traveled down to her skirt and, grabbing handfuls of the thick masses, he pulled it up, baring her delicate stocking-clad legs, inch by delicious inch. Moving his body lower, he kissed the plane of her chest while reaching for the leg he'd just uncovered.

He put his hand on her slim ankle and used his thumb to gently massage above it before sliding his hand up the delicate curve of her calf. Her flesh was smooth and pliable, just like a woman ought to be. His hand found her knee and he lightly ran a finger along the back of it.

Brooke released a gasp when Andrew's fingers touched her thigh and massaged the soft flesh around her garter.

Andrew took her gasp as encouragement, and he hooked his fingers around her garter and undid the tapes. Her body tensed and he moved his hands lower to caress her knee and calf again.

"Are you all right?" he asked.

Brooke bit her lower lip, but didn't answer.

Seeing her hesitation, Andrew removed his hand from her leg. He resettled his body with one of his legs settling in between hers, then came up on his elbows to look into her beautiful brown eyes.

"Brooke, I'll stop if you ask it of me." His lust-riddled mind hoped she would not ask, but he needed her to know he would never force her.

Her body relaxed once again, and she moved her hands to his neck and pulled him down to her. Their mouths met and they were kissing again. Brooke's hold on his neck loosened and she ran her hands back down to his chest and slipped them inside his shirt, but this time she moved her hands to feel the broad expanse of his shoulders.

Slowly breaking their kiss again, Andrew's lips kissed her chin and jaw while his hands went to her chest to gently trace the curves of her breasts, going under and to the sides of them without actually touching them, the same way he'd done yesterday. He remembered how much she had liked it before and how relaxed she had been when he'd done it. Once her fingers loosened on his shoulders and her eyes shut, he moved lower.

She was enjoying this, he was sure of it—and he was, too. He was so caught up in the present, all thoughts apart from their immediate actions were forgotten. He forgot about everything and everyone except this moment with Brooke.

He moved one hand to her thigh and tenderly massaged her supple flesh. Slowly, he moved his caresses higher. She offered no protest when he reached the bottom of her drawers and slipped his fingers inside to run them along the bottom of the fabric.

While his bold fingers moved higher to do a slow and thorough exploration of her thigh, his mouth kissed her upper chest and around the bodice of her dress. He wished now he'd taken time to lower it, but at this moment nothing could make him move his hand from where it was.

He moved his lips back to hers and his hand glided higher inside her drawers until it was at the juncture where her leg joined her body, his fingers resting near the slope of her leg and the dip that led to her most secret area. Cautiously, he brushed his fingertips back and forth, delighting in the way her body arched in response to his touch.

He shifted his hand just a fraction and silently rejoiced when she didn't stop him. He could now feel her springy curls and knew he was within inches of touching the core of what made her a woman. He was shocked to discover just how much he wanted to touch her, and only her, there. He would have never known the truth himself if he were not currently so close to doing so.

He reached his fingers closer to where he longed for them to be: tangled in her nest of curls, when abruptly Brooke was no longer kissing him and her whole body went stiff. Her legs violently clamped together and her hands suddenly shoved at his chest. "Stop! Stop! I cannot do this," she exclaimed.

Andrew took his hand out from under her skirt and pulled her skirt down the best he could to cover up her legs. "I didn't mean to go so far," he lied in a voice that sounded uneven to his own ears.

Brooke looked at him blankly like she was still trying to comprehend everything herself. "I'm sorry, Andrew, I just cannot do this," she said fiercely.

***

Brooke could read the disappointment that was stamped on Andrew's face. But as disappointed as both of them were, she had to be true to herself.

Long ago she had made her mind up that she'd never let a man who wasn't her husband seduce her. Fortunately, she hadn't learned this hard lesson for herself, but she had seen more than one of her intimates fall victim to men who would seduce them and then discard them quickly thereafter.

One of the most drastic situations she had been privy to had resulted in the girl getting with child, and after telling the father, he had denied involvement with her and abandoned her. Brooke shivered just thinking of it, but the memory helped her to hold onto her resolve.

"Thank you for keeping your word," Brooke said, gaining more control of her voice.

"It's all right. I respect your wishes. I told you I'd stop if you wished it," Andrew assured her with a faint smile, then moved away to go sit with his back against a tree.

Brooke sat up and looked at him. He was taking this rather

well for being denied what men wanted above all else—or at least that's what she'd been told.

Where they were sitting was very dim, but there was enough moonlight shining on them that she could make out his features, which did not look as calm as he was pretending. His jaw was tense, his face looked as dark as a thunder cloud, and his chest was rising and lowering considerably with each breath he took.

"I—I um, well, thank you, I just can't…" she trailed off and waved her hand as if that would state what her voice could not.

"It's quite all right," Andrew said in a measured voice. "You owe me no explanation. A lady is allowed to change her mind."

"I didn't change my mind," Brooke snapped. "I never said that I wanted to do…to do…that. You just took my lack of protest as confirmation that I would allow further advances."

"Once again, you are correct." Andrew reached for her and pulled her to his lap.

"I shouldn't," she protested weakly.

"I promise not to do anything other than hold you," Andrew assured her.

Brooke trusted him to keep his word and clumsily allowed herself to be pulled onto his lap.

She wiggled to get settled and Andrew groaned. She felt a hard ridge below her bottom. She cast a questioning eye to Andrew who just looked at her and said, "Not to worry, it will go away shortly." When she relaxed a little, she could have sworn he muttered, "I hope."

She wanted to ask what he had in his pants that was hard and prodding her, and then ask him to move it because it was rather uncomfortable. But then she remembered the day at the museum and the statue she'd seen and decided not to mention it. She knew what it was, and there wasn't anywhere he could move it. It was attached. Her face flamed and she was glad it was dark outside so he couldn't see it.

"Andrew, I'm sorry for my reaction. It's just that I shouldn't have allowed you to go so far. I shouldn't allow anyone to go that far."

"I see."

"No, I don't think you do. I have convictions."

"Convictions?" he echoed.

"Yes. I cannot give my virtue to the first man who comes along," she said before giving any consideration to how that sounded.

"Of course not," he agreed.

Brooke's body shook on its own accord and her mind went to war over all the reasons this was right against all the reasons it was wrong.

She had come to realize she did indeed love Andrew, but did he love her? That was what it all came down to. If he truly loved her, he wouldn't rush her, right? But he hadn't rushed her, not yesterday and not today. He'd stopped both times without complaint. She was so confused. The feelings she had just minutes before came flooding back to war with her decision.

She had felt so safe and comfortable with his caresses, but once he touched her as no man ever had before, she panicked. What if he took what she offered and abandoned her? What if her feelings for him outweighed his feelings for her and she ended up alone and stripped of the only valuable thing that a woman had? Her virtue. That realization shook her to the core. She had been so close to throwing it away, all for a man whom she loved, but had no idea if he felt the same.

After a few minutes of them both sitting there consumed with their own thoughts, Andrew wrapped his arms around her and pulled her as close to him as he could. "Are you all right?" he asked soothingly.

With his strong arms wrapped around her, she felt safe, like nothing bad could ever happen to her. "Yes. I was just thinking of something," she answered, looking up to meet his eyes.

"What are you thinking about?"

"It's nothing." Brooke tried to keep her voice firm, but it cracked anyway.

"You can tell me anything," Andrew said with a tender smile.

"I feel that I've ruined everything. That you won't feel the same about me now that I've ended…" she trailed off and lowered her gaze.

Andrew gave her a reassuring squeeze. "I can assure you my feelings for you are the same as they were half an hour ago, and if they have changed, they're stronger. Why would you think that my feelings would change?"

Brooke turned her gaze back up to his and said, "Most men change their minds when they're denied."

"Not this one," he said softly. His embraced tightened slightly. "How would you know that? How many men have you gotten to know in the dark?" he asked in a rough voice.

"No need to be jealous," she teased. "I have never been this far with any man. Anytime I've let a man kiss me and then have stopped him from advancing it seems to have ended up with him never speaking to me again, or not kindly at least."

Andrew laughed softly; the rumble of his chest tickled her cheek. "Their loss, I'd say," he told her, placing a tender kiss on the top of her hair.

"I'm fairly certain they don't think so," Brooke said laughingly.

"They're just angry you didn't allow them to hold you like this," he said, giving her another tight squeeze.

"You're too kind, but I do not think holding is what Gateway had in mind when he took me into the bushes, nor did he feel at a loss when I ended it and he called me a tease." Brooke brought her hand up to his face and pushed some of his hair away from his eyes.

"Gateway?" Andrew thundered.

"Yes, Townson," came a reply from ten feet away in the dark bushes.

# Chapter 24

Brooke jumped nearly a foot in the air, knocking Andrew squarely in the nose, when Gateway's voice floated to her ears.

Andrew's reaction was slightly different from Brooke's. Instead of jumping, he went still as a portrait, his big arms squeezing tightly around Brooke's midsection.

When it was clear Andrew wasn't going to speak, Gateway stepped closer and looked them over.

The blood rushed to Andrew's head. This was what he had planned, wasn't it? He wanted someone to discover the two of them in an inappropriate situation that would result in her shame and his success. However, now that it had happened, it all felt different, wrong even.

"What are you two about?" Gateway inquired, cocking his head to get a better view.

In his arms, Brooke's body stiffened and she buried her face against his chest. His bare chest. In less than a second, he comprehended just how bad the situation really was. He was without a coat and waistcoat; his shirt was for the most part undone. Brooke's hair was down, her gown half unbuttoned in the back and she was sitting on his lap.

"Just out enjoying the night," Andrew replied smoothly.

"Enjoying each other seems to be a more accurate description," Gateway said with a chuckle.

Something wet touched his chest. He tensed. It was Brooke's tears. He had hoped he could help her avoid complete mortification, but he had failed. Andrew relaxed his right arm and brought his hand to her back where he rubbed small, comforting circles, trying to calm her shaking body.

"Now, now, Miss Banks, was his performance so bad you have to cry about it?" Gateway asked with a grin.

"Better than yours would have been, I'm sure," Brooke retorted hotly as she twisted around to face him and swiped the tears off her cheeks.

Andrew couldn't see her face, but he imagined rage was visible in those expressive eyes of hers, because Gateway did not immediately respond to her taunt.

Their good luck did not hold out for long though. "You'll never have the privilege to find out what it's like to have a real man. It seems to me that you have made your selection."

Brooke's body stiffened again at the duke's implication that if —no, when—someone found out what they'd been doing, or how they were found, they'd be forced to marry. Her body's reaction to that knowledge hit Andrew like a punch to the gut. He wasn't the man Brooke wanted.

He should feel relieved, but instead he felt agitated. Why was she so affronted by the idea of marriage to him? Not that he was going to offer it, but to know she was so opposed hurt.

Brooke settled Gateway with a stern look. "You would not be so much a cad as to spread this story, would you?"

"No," Gateway allowed. "I have nothing to gain from your circumstances, unlike your companion." The duke glanced pointedly to Andrew.

Andrew seethed. Was Gateway about to expose him to Brooke and ruin everything? What purpose would it serve for him to do so? And what did he mean he had nothing to gain from her circumstances? He had everything to gain. This whole thing was his idea. He was the one who wanted them to go back to America, for whatever reason.

As if hit by lightning, Andrew had a revelation. He still didn't know why Gateway wanted them to be sent all the way back to their homeland, but he now understood why he wanted the family shamed: Brooke had rejected him.

Andrew let out a loud, harsh laugh. Brooke had told him as much just before they had been discovered. And if he had been able to think about it for a minute before they were interrupted, he would have solved that piece of the puzzle already.

Brooke turned a quizzical eye on Andrew. "How can you laugh at a time like this?" she demanded.

His amusement ended instantly. He turned his eyes back to Gateway. "As delightful as this conversation has been, I think it's time I return Miss Banks to her parents."

Neither Brooke nor Andrew made a move to stand up. They both waited for Gateway to leave, so they could repair their clothing.

Gateway's eyes met Brooke's and he said in an earnest tone, "I will not mention this to anyone."

Brooke gave a relieved sigh.

Andrew gave him a questioning look, which Gateway didn't respond to before he walked away.

They stood and were fixing their clothing when Brooke whispered, "Do you believe he'll hold his tongue?"

Andrew stopped buttoning her gown. "Truthfully, I have no idea. He said he would, and for all his faults, I've never known him to go back on his word."

Brooke released another sigh of relief. "Good. I have no idea how I could ever be accepted around here again, if he were to tell anyone about my disgrace."

Andrew bristled next to her. "Would it be that bad?" he asked bitterly. Not that he planned to marry her, but once again she was pricking his pride by declaring she didn't want to marry him.

"Yes," she exclaimed. "If it were known I was found in the woods on a man's lap with my hair all disheveled and my gown in disarray, it would be dreadful. My reputation would be ruined, my family would have to bear the shame, it would cause my sisters' marriage prospects to dwindle, and I cannot imagine what would happen to Papa if people thought his daughter a trollop!" Her tone was laced with real horror.

He decided not to press her any further and his fingers resumed their work on the back of her gown. He was so busy fastening the buttons that he didn't hear anyone approach, until he heard Lady Algen's voice say, "Good evening, Townson. To whom are you playing lady's maid?"

Andrew spun around as quickly as he could and realized Lady Algen's position allowed her to see his face and hands, but blocked Brooke's turned face. He gave Brooke a light push and turned to step in behind Brooke's back, doing his best to shield Lady Algen's view of Brooke's face.

"Yes, it is a good evening, Lady Algen. What brings you out?"

"I was told that there were some sights to see up in the sky. I didn't know there would also be some sights to be seen on the path. Who is the young lady?" she inquired again.

They had just made a narrow escape by getting Gateway to agree not to say anything. But if Lady Algen knew Brooke was with him, there would be no chance to save her reputation. Which is what he wanted, wasn't it? To ruin her reputation? He glanced over his shoulder. She was dressed for the most part, only a button or two remained undone on her gown, though her hair was still down with a few twigs in it. It would be easy to move aside, let Lady Algen see her and get the gossip started. At least he had saved Brooke the embarrassment of actually being caught in the act.

No, he was not going to shame her that way. He'd have to think of something else. Lady Algen was a gossip-hungry harpy, and she'd be all too happy to spread this tale and probably spice it up a little. There was no way he'd let Brooke suffer that.

Just as Andrew reached forward to grab Lady Algen's arm to escort her somewhere else, Alex walked up. "Andrew, have you seen Brooke? We've been looking for her for over an hour, and nobody has been able to find her." His voice was filled with serious concern.

Lady Algen's eyes lit right up. "I think the lost has been found," she said smugly.

Alex looked around owlishly, but when he looked past Andrew, his eyes almost popped out of their sockets before he stepped forward and grabbed Brooke's arm. "What is going on?" he demanded.

Brooke slowly turned to face Alex. Her face was whiter than a cloud and she was panicking. His heart dropped to his stomach.

How could he ever have thought he could go through with this?

"Nothing is going on," Andrew answered curtly.

Lady Algen snorted. "It doesn't look like nothing to me."

"Madam, your opinion does not concern me," Alex snapped at Lady Algen. Turning back to face Andrew and Brooke, Alex said, "I will have the meaning of this. Now!" His last word came out as almost a roar.

Andrew didn't know what to say. Nothing he could say would resolve the situation. It would likely only make it worse. He just stared back at Alex and adopted a defensive stance.

"Brooke, I'll ask you once and only once—did he force you into this?" Alex's eyes shifted between Andrew and Brooke as he waited for her answer.

Brooke looked like she was about to crumble, and all Andrew could think was that he wanted to wrap his arms around her and protect her the way he should have from the beginning. Now it was too late, and it was entirely his fault.

"You're hurting me, Alex," was all Brooke said.

Alex let go of her arm and stepped away. "All right, now that I'm not hurting you, please answer my question. Did he force himself on you?"

Andrew thought she was going to say yes. Considering what he'd put her through, he wouldn't have blamed her for doing so, but she just shook her head, and quietly said, "No."

"Alex, I think we should take this conversation somewhere a bit more private," Andrew said with a glance at Lady Algen.

For the first time, Alex looked at exactly who was outside with them. With a sharp inhalation of breath, he nodded tersely in agreement with Andrew. "Let's go inside."

The small group made their way to the library. Alex positioned himself to walk between Andrew and Brooke, and Lady Algen followed with a bright and devious smile, probably thinking of what she'd say when she went back inside and how she'd write her article for her weekly newspaper column, *Tattle and Prattle*.

When the library doors opened, Brooke marched in and took a seat upon the closest settee. Alex went to a chair and Andrew spun around to face Lady Algen. "Your presence here is not needed," he declared loudly.

"I think the young lady is in need of a chaperone," she retorted as she tried to wedge herself through the library doorway.

"I don't think that's necessary," Andrew said in a steely tone. "Her cousin is here and he is able to act as her chaperon." Before allowing her another second to argue, he slammed the door as hard as he could right in front of her squinty face. Knowing Lady Algen wouldn't let that deter her, he locked the door and tossed the key on the floor across the room for good measure.

"Nice display there," Alex said with a sneer. "Are you upset you've been caught by the biggest gossip, or are you genuinely concerned about how this will affect Brooke?"

Andrew swallowed. "I'm genuinely concerned for Brooke's welfare," he conceded.

"Very well, you shall marry," Alex stated matter-of-factly.

"What?" Brooke cried.

"No," Andrew said sternly.

"No?" Alex echoed. "How dare you say no? You know as well as I do that in the next fifteen minutes the entire house will have heard this tale, and her reputation will be completely destroyed. If you're any type of a gentleman, you'll do the right thing and marry her."

"I cannot," Andrew replied solemnly.

"And why not?" Alex burst out.

Andrew scanned Alex's face. In all the years they had known each other, the only time he had seen Alex angry was the other night, but that didn't hold a candle to how angry he was now.

"I just cannot," Andrew replied baldly, wishing against all odds he actually *could* marry her.

Alex sprang out of his chair and stalked over to where Andrew was, pulled his fist back and punched Andrew in the right eye. Andrew briefly lost balance, but quickly regained it. "I'm going to ask you again." Alex's voice was a low, angry hiss. "Why are you refusing to do right by Brooke?"

"I'm in no position to take a wife," he answered calmly,

belying the storm raging in his eyes.

"If you refer to your lack of funds, that's of no account," Alex replied with his normal, nonchalant tone, coupled with a dismissive wave of his hand. "I'm certain Brooke comes with a sizable dowry."

"I do not," Brooke countered stiffly, as she came up off her settee and joined the men in their argument. "Nor do I appreciate you two fighting about Andrew having to marry me. He clearly has no desire to do so." She shot an accusing look at Andrew then shifted her gaze to Alex. "Furthermore, I'm not a possession to be bartered or traded. You have no business trying to marry me off. I'm not your daughter. You have no authority over me," she snapped.

Andrew had to admire her nerve. She had every right to be angry with both of them. They were essentially planning her life for her without considering her feelings.

"You're correct," Alex allowed. "I'm in no position to tell you what to do. Perhaps we should wait for your parents."

Brooke's face went pale as she resumed her seat on the settee. It must have just occurred to her that Lady Algen was running the rumor mill in the drawing room and her parents would shortly join their small party in the library. She sat back and stared straight ahead with a blank look on her face.

Andrew felt lower than he ever remembered feeling. How could he have let this go on so long? How was he ever going to be able to finish it? The look of hurt on Brooke's face was enough to almost make him crack. But suddenly he remembered how she reacted when they were found by Gateway outside and her relief when he said he wouldn't tell anyone, thus eliminating Brooke's ruined reputation and hasty marriage to him.

Lost in his own thoughts, Andrew didn't register the shaking of the door handles, but was broken from his thoughts when Alex said, "I believe that should be Brooke's parents."

No one spoke as Alex grabbed the key from the floor and unlocked the door.

In stormed Brooke's parents with Lady Algen right on their

heels. Nothing on earth would make Andrew allow that woman in the library, and without preamble, he slammed the door in her face again.

"You're nothing but a no-good scoundrel!" Mr. Banks blustered as soon as the library door was shut.

Mrs. Banks took a seat next to Brooke on the settee and tried to comfort her, casting a scathing eye at Andrew. "Are you all right, darling?" she cooed in Brooke's ear.

"Yes, Mama," Brooke said brokenly.

Andrew's heart twisted yet again. Her eyes were full of tears, but she looked determined not to let them fall. She was being so brave in the face of ruination. All of which had befallen her at his hands.

"When is the wedding?" Mrs. Banks demanded of Andrew.

All eyes turned to him, Mrs. Banks' full of concern, Mr. Banks' were angry, Alex's taunting as if to say, "I told you so". He could handle all of those, but the ones that tormented him the most were Brooke's. Her eyes that were normally full of laughter and amusement, looked shuttered and sad.

"There will not be a wedding," Andrew declared in his most superior voice.

There was a moment of silence before Brooke said, "You see, Lord Townson has no desire to marry me, and I share the feeling." Her voice was steady and smooth. She lifted her chin a notch, no doubt attempting to show everyone she was satisfied with that conclusion.

"I will not accept that," Mr. Banks burst out. He marched right up to Andrew. "How dare you? Do you think she is not good enough for you, is that it? She's only good enough to provide you with an evening's entertainment in the bushes, but not to be your wife?"

"Papa, please," Brooke begged, her face flaming red.

Mr. Banks whirled around. "Brooklyn, if you know what's best for you, you will not interfere in this. This man," he shouted, pointing an accusing finger toward Andrew, "has ruined your reputation and you're asking me to pretend it hasn't happened?

Think again, Brooklyn. I am not leaving this room until there is a wedding date."

"I cannot do that, sir," Andrew said politely.

"Why the blazes not?" Mr. Banks demanded.

"Currently, I cannot afford to give Brooke the life she deserves," Andrew admitted, though it killed his pride to do so. What else could he say? *I'm sorry, sir, I cannot marry your daughter because I made an agreement with a duke that I'd ruin her and drive your family away in order to get my estate back.* That answer would not go over well.

"Poppycock," Mrs. Banks said. Her face had taken on a more relaxed, almost excited look. "Brooke comes with a five thousand pound dowry."

Andrew ground his teeth. How could they dismiss his lack of money so easily? Was this just their way of keeping scandal at bay, or was it his title?

"Just think, you will be a countess. My daughter, a countess," Mrs. Banks exclaimed with a happy clap of her hands.

Her words felt like another punch in the gut. Earlier, Brooke seemed reluctant to marry him at all and now her family was pressing her to do so for the title of countess. It always amazed him what his title could gain him, and in this case, an heiress was his prize for being born heir to an earldom.

Fighting to keep the bile from rising up his throat, he said, "Madam, my title is not for sale. A title neither makes a man nor a husband."

"You've already demonstrated that this evening," Mr. Banks growled. "You have no integrity or morals that a gentleman of your rank should possess. If you had, you would not resort to seducing an innocent girl in the woods. Instead, you would ask for her hand in marriage and keep your pants buttoned up in the meantime."

"John!" Mrs. Banks exclaimed in horror. "That is a vulgar thing to say."

Shame washed over Andrew. It was nothing less than he deserved to be accused of being a blackguard and a cad, but to embarrass Brooke that way was unfair to her, and he wasn't going to have it. "Sir, I demand you apologize to your daughter for that unkind and unfair statement."

"Demand? Apologize? You?" Mr. Banks said with a harsh laugh.

"Your words were unwarranted. I understand your anger toward me. You can say those things to me alone. You do not need to be so crude in her presence."

"Indeed? Are you telling me my daughter has not been exposed to anything crude this evening?" Mr. Banks snapped.

"No. She has not."

"No?" he echoed. "I don't believe that. I don't believe you even care what is said or done in front of her. She was nothing but a dalliance for you."

"Enough!" Brooke screamed, jumping to her feet. Determination changed her features, making them stronger, as if she were her composed self again and ready to conquer the world. "I don't appreciate being referred to as nothing more than a dalliance. I would appreciate it if you two would stop arguing and accept there will be no match between us."

"Yes, there will be, young lady," her father countered. "If you think you will just go to sleep tonight and wake up in the morning with this all behind you, you are mistaken. As we speak, the whole house is talking about you as if you are a common lightskirt." John turned his eyes back to Andrew. "I will not ask you again. When is the wedding?"

"There's not going to be a wedding," Andrew replied firmly.

As soon as the words had left his lips, there was a shout. "I challenge you to a duel. Tomorrow. Dawn. Name your weapon and second."

Everyone's head snapped around to where Alex was standing by a bookcase and a rolling ladder. Andrew wasn't sure about anyone else, but he'd been so caught up in the conversation, he'd completely forgotten Alex's presence until he issued the challenge.

Andrew's head spun. A duel? Was he serious? Andrew knew it was a possibility this might happen, but he didn't figure Alex would be the one to challenge him. Besides their long friendship, which he knew this whole situation was about to demolish, Alex was an abominable shot. If he picked pistols, there was no telling how it would all end. He could aim high and miss Alex. But whether Alex meant to or not, there was a very real possibility of Andrew actually being injured, although it would likely be an accident. He wasn't concerned so much about being killed, but who knew where Alex would unintentionally hit him with that bullet.

That left swords. But once again, Alex was not skilled in that department, either—probably less so than with pistols. Why did he make a challenge he didn't have a chance to win? Was he trying to get himself killed, or was his mouth working without consulting his brain first? There was only one way to find out. "Swords, and I don't need a second. You won't require one, either."

Alex paled, but nodded.

"Stop it, you two," Brooke said impatiently. "There will be no duel. First, it's illegal. Isn't it?" She stopped and waited for her father's nod of confirmation. "Second, Alex, let's be honest. You have no sword skills." She raised her hand to stop him from interrupting. "I know you have your pride and honor and all that, but I saw you fighting with the gamekeeper's son with wooden swords yesterday and you lost, badly. Oh, and do not tell me you let him win. You were trying harder than he was, and you still lost."

Alex's mouth snapped shut, and his face turned a bright shade of red.

"There's still one other option left. I can return to New York," she said, her voice went high and cracked mid-sentence.

"No." Andrew said. Now it was his turn for his mouth to run independent of his brain's influence. He didn't know why he spoke. This was exactly what he'd wanted. What he needed. If they packed their bags and left for New York, everything would work out according to plan. She'd be gone and able to start over in America without this tainting her reputation, and he'd get his estate back and be free of Gateway.

"No?" Brooke questioned. She looked to Andrew to explain

what he meant, but he said nothing. "It's the only course left open to our family. Nobody over there would know what happened here. My sisters will not be marred by my mistakes," she said with a sob. "You win, too. You will not have the death of my cousin on your hands."

Everyone looked back at Alex, who looked angry and relieved at the same time.

"We all know he could never survive a duel. Sorry, Alex, but it's true." Then she turned back to face Andrew. "Men don't bear the same shame with a scandal such as this. In a few weeks' time, you'll be accepted in places I would not be if I were to stay."

Andrew watched her face as she said her speech; it changed from composed, to sad, to angry, and then to resigned.

With as much dignity as a young lady could have in her situation, she swept out of the library, leaving them all in her wake.

"Wait! Brooke, come back," Andrew said, trying to grab her arm and pull her back toward him.

Brooke shook off his grasp and met his eyes. "You don't want to marry me, and quite frankly, I don't want to marry someone who does not want me. I will return home in the morning and put this all behind me."

Andrew let go of her and watched her walk down the hall, taking his heart along with her. Andrew started at the thought. Did she have his heart? She must or else he wouldn't have this empty ache in his chest where his heart used to reside.

He looked back to see Alex, John, and Carolina all standing in a line with identical looks of contempt on their faces.

Not wanting to speak to any of them at the moment, he turned and walked away.

There was someone he did need to see at the moment, and now it was time to find him.

# Chapter 25

Brooke would always wonder how she made it back to her room. Her eyes were filled with tears that threatened to spill, but somehow didn't flow until she reached her bedchamber and closed the door tightly behind her.

She wearily made her way to the bed and threw herself down on top of the counterpane. How had her life come to this? One minute she was being held and caressed by a gentle and loving Andrew, then not ten minutes later, he was rejecting her as his wife. All the while, everyone in the house thought she was a fallen woman.

Going back home seemed the only option she had left. She could start over without this hanging over her head. It was clear that if she stayed, Andrew had no intention of marrying her. And nobody else would want to marry her, if they knew about this, which, of course, they would. Oh, why did that dreadful woman have to show up? Why could she not have come five minutes later, when Brooke's gown was buttoned and hair was up? And why on earth did Lady Algen of all people have an interest in astronomy?

How would she explain this to her sisters? How would she face Papa and Mama tomorrow, bearing the humiliation of them thinking her a shameless wanton? Would they ever forgive her this, or would they hold her in contempt?

Way too many thoughts and questions flooded her head before she fell into a dreamless slumber.

Brooke awoke the following morning to a loud voice outside her door.

"Move out of my way," a voice that sounded like Andrew's boomed.

"No." That voice she recognized as Mama's.

"You've done enough. If you think I'm going let you in there for one final romp, you are greatly mistaken, young man," Papa yelled.

"Have a care for your daughter and keep your voice down," Andrew said tightly.

"Why, all of a sudden, do you have such interest in our daughter?" Papa demanded.

"Because she is to be my countess, and I will not allow any gossip spread about her," Andrew stated as if he were reciting a well-known fact.

Mama squealed with delight and Papa mumbled something inaudible—knowing Papa, it probably was one of his ridiculous curse-like phrases he'd coined to say in times of great frustration. Brooke had little doubt this was one of those moments.

"Now that you know my intentions, please step aside," Andrew said.

Brooke froze. Was he going to come into her room now? She was still wearing her gown from last night. Her hair was a rat's nest. She wouldn't be surprised in the least if there really were a rodent in it at this point. She was sure without having to look in a mirror that her face was not a picture of beauty, with her skin all red and eyes puffy from crying. She was not presentable, especially for her potential groom.

Her heart skipped a beat. Her potential groom. Just last night he didn't want to marry her and now he did. Why? What had changed?

That thought brought her back from her musings. Why was he really here?

Heedless of her scary appearance, she walked to the door and swung it open. "What's the meaning of this?" she demanded.

Four sets of eyes locked onto her disheveled form. Mama gasped when she saw her and quickly tried to cover it up with a cough. Papa's mouth dropped open, then he closed it with an audible snap as his teeth met. Her eyes met Andrew's. His eyes held a hint of humor, but he merely raised an eyebrow at her. Then she heard a slight cough and jerked her gaze over to the right, where she was greeted by the sight of Mr. Grimes. "Perhaps this conversation should wait? Will you be….er…presentable within a half hour?" he asked quietly, not meeting her eyes.

"Yes," Brooke answered shyly, then closed her door.

After she shut the door, she attempted to take her gown off as quickly as she could. She thought to ring for a bath, but quickly dismissed the idea because she had only a half hour in which to be dressed and downstairs. That only gave her time to change gowns and try to pick out as many twigs from her hair as she possibly could in order to get it up into her coiffure again.

She had successfully removed her gown and was looking for another when Mama let herself in.

"You'll need to wear something very special for your engagement," she exclaimed.

Peeking around the corner of her wardrobe, Brooke took in her Mama's face. She looked so happy. "Why are you so happy?" she asked.

"Because my daughter is going to be married, without delay I expect, to a gentleman of rank. And you must admit he's rather good looking."

Brooke shrugged. Andrew wasn't *that* good looking. By no means was he ugly, but she still stuck to her original opinion. He was not the dashing knight that young girls dreamed of, but to some women he would be considered handsome. She fell firmly into the latter category.

"Who cares about his rank? He's only marrying me because he feels it's his duty. He doesn't want to marry me," she said dully.

"That's not true," Mama protested. "I've seen the way you two are together. Don't think I haven't noticed those secret smiles and looks exchanged between the two of you."

Brooke blushed. Was she so obvious? "All right, I admit it. I have feelings for him. But I don't think he returns them."

"They'll come," Mama assured her. "Does it matter so much if he doesn't feel as strongly for you as you do for him? He will, and in the meantime, think of the wonderful life you will live. You will have one of the top positions in society and will be invited everywhere. The scandal surrounding your wedding will pass in time. I know some harsh things were said and done last night, but the truth is, returning home isn't really an option. You know that. "

"I suppose you're right," Brooke conceded, taking out an ice blue gown from her wardrobe.

"That is truly beautiful," Mama said, helping her put it on. Mama quickly took charge of fastening the buttons on the back. "Brooke, I don't know how to approach this, but we may not have any other time alone."

"Yes?"

"Last night, did you…did the earl…umm…do you need me to explain anything?" Mama stammered in an uneasy voice.

"No, I don't think so," Brooke replied, absolutely mystified by what on earth Mama was speaking of. Looking in her mirror, Brooke caught sight of a strange look passing over Mama's face. Before she could determine what it meant, it was gone.

"In that case, I guess my day just got a little easier." She flashed a bright smile. "Now about this mess," she said, trying to bring a brush through Brooke's tangled hair.

It took a quarter of an hour longer than anticipated for Brooke to become presentable. Walking to where the men waited in the library, Brooke was a bundle of nerves. She wanted to marry Andrew. She'd decided several days ago that if he were to propose, she would accept. But under the circumstances, she wanted to ask a few questions first. The first of which would be why he wanted to marry her. Was it duty? Honor? Had he been pressured into it? Or did he truly care for her?

Upon entering the library, Brooke took in Andrew's state of disarray. He was wet. Soaked to be exact. And where he was standing, a puddle had formed on the carpet. A quick glance out the window behind him confirmed it was storming outside. When had he gone outside? Not only was he wet, his hair looked like a windstorm had blown it about. His clothes were dirty, and ironically were the same ones he'd worn the night before. A little giggle escaped her at that thought.

In response to her giggle, Andrew raised an eyebrow.

"I'm sorry, it's just that everyone was so horrified over my splendid ensemble earlier but no one, myself included, noticed yours," she said, gesturing to his torn clothes, messy hair, and wet body.

"Indeed, you are correct. They were so intent to stop me from seeing you that they said naught about how I was dressed. I would have changed when you did, but I find my belongings have mysteriously disappeared from my room."

Papa let out an uncomfortable cough and patted his chest. "Excuse me."

"Shall I translate that for you?" Brooke asked Andrew. "That's what Papa does when he gets uncomfortable, typically because he's just been caught after doing something wrong. I would wager, if I were the kind of woman who wagers, that your belongings have probably been burned."

"Burned?" Andrew said hollowly. The look on his face indicated he sorely hoped she was jesting.

"No, not burned," Papa interrupted. "You will find all of your things when you get back to London. I exercised what little power I have in England and I asked my brother, the baron and your host, to please have your things removed post haste."

"I see," Andrew said, though he looked like he didn't see at all.

"That's immaterial. What do you have to say to Brooke?" Papa said harshly.

Andrew came forward and dropped to one knee right there before everyone in the room. "Brooke, will you do me the honor of becoming my wife?"

Brooke looked into his eyes. During their brief association, she'd come to be able to read him just by looking in his eyes. He didn't laugh or smile as much as she did, but his eyes changed colors and looked brighter when he was amused or thought something humorous. She had seen them darken on a few occasions, indicating what she thought to be desire. She'd also seen them look hard as steel when he was upset or determined, like last night. How they looked currently was the only mood she couldn't read. They were impassive, showing neither happiness nor sadness, neither desire nor determination. Nothing. She had seen this look but a handful of times, like when they first met and when they first arrived at the museum.

"Why?"

"I think it should be obvious. I have a need for a wife and you have a need for a husband. Certain circumstances have arisen which make a match between us expedient."

Those weren't the words of love she so dearly longed to hear, but what he said was true. They both required a spouse, and after this, she would be very unlikely to find one. She sighed. At least he had only said, "circumstances which make it expedient" rather than coming out and saying he felt honor bound, or it was his duty, either for causing her ruination, or for him to produce an heir.

"All right, I'll be your wife," Brooke said with a tight smile.

Andrew quickly rose to his feet and waved to Mr. Grimes in the corner. "Paul, are you ready?"

"Indeed, my lord." Mr. Grimes walked over to where Brooke and Andrew stood in the drawing room.

"What's going on?" Brooke asked Andrew.

"Our wedding," he said, then reached into his breast pocket and removed a wet special license.

"Right now?" she asked, shocked. "But why here? Why now?"

"I thought it would be best to marry quietly and depart the house party this morning, in order to put a stop to the gossip."

He was right of course. "Can we ask my sisters to join us?" she asked nervously.

"You're quite right," Papa said before anyone else could speak.

Within moments Madison, Liberty, Alex, Edward, and Regina were summoned to bear witness to their ceremony.

All too quickly it was over—she was married and being hastily escorted out of the room by her husband.

On their way out the door, they were almost run over by Mr. Grimes, who was walking as fast as his legs could carry him—probably trying to get away from Liberty, Brooke thought with a wry smile. A lot of people didn't understand Liberty, that was for sure, but she had never seen anyone with such a strong dislike for her. It almost rivaled Liberty's own dislike for him. Almost, but not quite.

Outside, Andrew's carriage was waiting to take them away. Brooke climbed inside and waved goodbye to her family as they rolled down the road.

"Where are we going?" Brooke asked after a while.

"Rockhurst," Andrew said simply.

Judging by how Andrew was sitting, Brooke assumed he was in no mood for conversation. She wondered why that was. They had just gotten married, and prior to that he was in a good mood. What had changed?

She looked into his eyes. They looked distant, lost, almost cold even. Did he regret marrying her only fifteen minutes after they'd said their vows? Did this mean he had only gone through with it because of honor?

Right then and there, Brooke decided she was going to make him happy and come to love her. No matter what she had to do to change his feelings for her, she would do it.

It took an hour to get to Rockhurst. When they rolled up, her eyes grew wide and her jaw dropped a little. "It's beautiful," she breathed.

"Yes, I suppose it is. It's the seat of the earldom, so of course it has to be well kept and attended to properly," he said bitterly.

Paying him no mind, Brooke continued to ogle the estate. It was huge. In the middle was a large house that was three stories tall. It was made of a heavily textured, dark brown brick. The windows on the upper two floors were tall and slim, the ones on the bottom floor were huge, but there were only a few. "It looks medieval, like a castle," she said without thinking.

"At one time it was. There have been many renovations over the generations, but part of the original castle still stands. That's why the windows on the upper floors are tall and slim. Archers would stand there and fire out." He offered no further information.

Brooke looked out in amazement. It must have been a great adventure to grow up here.

The carriage came to an abrupt halt and Brooke was nearly thrown from her seat. Andrew's hand gripped her shoulder. "Are you all right?" he asked, helping her regain her seat.

"Yes."

As soon as she readjusted herself, the carriage door swung open and a footman let the stairs down for them.

Andrew climbed down and reached up to help Brooke descend from the carriage. She took his arm and together they walked toward the house where two servants were assembled to greet them.

"This is my wife, the new countess, your new mistress," he said unceremoniously and gestured to Brooke. "These are my servants," he said with an equal amount of enthusiasm. Then he led her to his housekeeper. "Mrs. Cleansweep, I trust you can show her around. I'm off to bed. When you're done, you can escort her to the countess' rooms." He shifted his gaze to Brooke. "I'll join you for dinner."

On his way inside the house, a tall manservant dressed impeccably in solid black, whispered something to Andrew. Brooke strained to hear what he said, but the only word she picked up was: friend. Andrew's face grew dark during the conversation. Whoever they were speaking about was not just a casual friend such as Alex, but probably his mistress.

She felt like she was going to faint. Of course he had a mistress; all men save Papa had one. She tried to strengthen her resolve and gave the housekeeper a tight smile, hoping it would not be too transparent, while in the back of her mind she vowed she would get rid of this mistress—immediately. She couldn't demand it of him, but she could beguile him enough that he'd dismiss her on his own.

"Mrs. Cleansweep, I would like very much for you to show me around. I fear I'd get lost if I had to navigate it on my own."

Mrs. Cleansweep quickly introduced her to the other servants. There was Rawlings, who worked as the coachman and did outside footman duties. Next was Stevens, who acted as the butler and did inside footman duties. Mrs. Cleansweep explained that she was the housekeeper and cook.

They took a tour of the house, stopping in all the common rooms to look around. The house was amazing. When at last they had reached the far end of the eastern wing of the second floor Mrs. Cleansweep opened the door. "This is your room. I do apologize it has not been aired for some time. I was not expecting his lordship to marry, and it has been a while since the dowager countess used this room."

Brooke walked in and looked around. The room was a little stuffy, just as she had expected. She noticed it had recently been dusted, probably this morning, and the windows were opened to allow the room to ventilate.

In the middle there was a large four-poster bed. Brooke ran her hand up one of the posts and sat on the feather mattress. On one side of the bed there was a small night table that held a lamp stand with three candles in it. There was a little drawer in the side of table. Brooke pulled it open to reveal two books that must have belonged to the dowager countess. She coughed from the dust and slid the drawer back into place.

In the corner was a large wardrobe made of a beautiful, dark wood that matched the bed. Next to it was a vanity table that had a water basin and pitcher. The vanity was large enough to display her brushes and combs, and toward the back of it was a small, round mirror. To the side of the vanity table was a full-sized standing mirror with a hairline crack going down the length of the glass.

She glanced to the other side of bed. A small writing desk was positioned beneath one of the windows. She walked away from the mirror and went to the door in the middle of the wall.

When she put her hand on the doorknob, Mrs. Cleansweep cleared her throat. Brooke's gaze shot to hers and Mrs. Cleansweep said bluntly, "That's the connecting door to the master's room. I imagine he'll come through it soon enough."

Brooke blushed before removing her hand from the door.

"If there is nothing else, my lady, I need to be about my duties," Mrs. Cleansweep said.

"Just one question." Brooke walked to the desk across the

room. When she reached the desk, she pulled out a stack of yellowed paper and eyed it curiously. "How long has it been since this room was last occupied?"

"Nearly thirty years ago, but for only one night. Before that, maybe twenty," Mrs. Cleansweep said in a low tone.

It had been nearly fifty years since this room had a regular inhabitant. Why? Wasn't Andrew's mother still living? "One night?" she asked the housekeeper who had not left yet.

"Yes. The late earl brought his bride here after their wedding, and the next afternoon he sent her away to Essex. She lived there until a few months ago."

Brooke nodded. Andrew had told her that much the day of their picnic. He'd told her something had caused his parents to live separate lives, but even he didn't know what it was. "What happened a few months ago?" Brooke asked, knowing she had told the housekeeper she was only going to ask one question.

"The estate in Essex had to be sold. For lack of anywhere else to live, she now lives here. Not to worry, she stays on the third floor. I can't imagine this place has any happy memories for either her or Lord Townson."

"I see. Thank you, you may go now." Brooke took a seat on the chair by the desk and started to think about what the housekeeper had told her. Was that why he had such a distant look on his face on the way over? Did it have nothing to do with her, but rather where they were going? If that was the reason, that could easily be fixed.

Brooke walked around the room again. This time she looked out one of the windows to scrutinize the view. Directly outside was a large pond. She walked to the other window and smiled when her eyes discovered the stable a few hundred yards away. Maybe they could go for a ride tomorrow. A wistful smile transformed her lips as she remembered their ride and picnic earlier in the week.

Walking back to the bed, she laid down in hopes of taking a quick nap. She'd had a long night last night and a very eventful day so far.

Sometime later there was a swift rap on her door.

Rolling over, she glanced at the clock on the shelf in the corner. Was it possible she had been asleep for more than four hours?

She stood and resisted the urge to look in the mirror on her way to the door to see whether or not her hair was a mess.

Stevens greeted her with a low bow when she opened the door. "Dinner will be served in quarter of an hour, my lady. I was instructed to invite you to the drawing room until dinner is announced."

Brooke nodded and followed him down the hall, all thoughts about the state of her hair and gown forgotten. Her thoughts were now occupied with Andrew. What would he wear? Would he be glad to see her at the table? Obviously he desired her presence or he wouldn't have sent for her. What would they talk about at dinner? What would they do after dinner? Would he visit her room tonight? A shiver ran through her just thinking about it.

She was not disappointed when she reached the drawing room. Andrew was waiting for her by the fireplace. He was dressed in some of the finest clothes she'd seen him wear. He wore solid black except for a white shirt and an emerald pin in his white cravat. With his dark hair slicked back, he looked magnificent.

"Join me." He gestured toward a settee next to where he stood.

"Thank you," she murmured, looking around the room. "Is your mother going to join us tonight?"

Andrew's head snapped in her direction at the mention of his mother. Was she not supposed to know his mother lived there? His eyes flickered with some emotion she didn't recognize. Then he shook his head. "No, she takes her meals in her room. Have you met her?"

"No. I thought it would be best if you introduced us."

Andrew nodded. "I'll introduce you tomorrow. Tonight, you're all mine." His eyes held a wicked gleam.

Brooke blushed and wondered if that meant he would indeed be visiting her room tonight. She remembered his kisses and caresses from the night before and hoped he would do that again tonight. This time she wouldn't stop him.

Andrew must have read her thoughts because he chuckled. “Like the idea of that, do you?”

Her face heated. Not knowing what else to do, she restlessly looked around the room.

They sat for only a few minutes before Stevens walked in. “Dinner is ready, my lord.”

Andrew offered Brooke his arm and together they walked into the dining room.

“For the lovely bride and her groom, only the best food in the house,” Stevens said, gesturing to the sideboard where the food was waiting for him to serve it.

Brooke had never seen such a shabby meal. Only four bland and paltry courses were served. The first was a salad made with slightly brown lettuce and soggy tomatoes, nothing else. The second course was stewed cabbage. It smelled awful and tasted worse, but seeing the size of the portions and the way Andrew was eating, she ate every bite. The third, and largest, was a potato, just a little baked potato with a small pat of butter. Dessert was the final course. It was nothing more than just a couple of spoonfuls of custard.

“You weren’t jesting when you said you couldn’t afford a wife,” Brooke teased without thinking it insulting or vulgar to discuss a man’s money with him, at the dining table in his house no less.

“I tried to warn you,” Andrew said with a wry smile. “It's too late to cry off now.”

“What of an annulment?” she asked with a teasing smile.

“That’s not a possibility, I’m afraid,” he informed her. “Aside from the fact that I wouldn’t agree to one, you’d never be able to prove me incapable. Actually, I’m more than content to prove to you just how capable I am within the hour.”

His innuendo and wolfish smile made Brooke flush. Did he mean what she thought he did? They were going to have marital relations, whatever those were, in less than hour? How could that be? She had no idea what she was to do. Her mother never had the talk with her that she was supposed to before her wedding.

A nervous giggle ripped through her as she suddenly understood what Mama had tried to ask her earlier.

"I assure you, it's no laughing matter," Andrew said with a sweet smile on his lips. He scooted his chair back and came to Brooke's side. "Lady Townson, would you like me to escort you to your room?"

Brooke understood his question held a dual meaning. There was the obvious meaning, Andrew asking to escort her upstairs. But there was a hidden meaning as well. He was also asking her permission to share her bed.

"Yes," she said nervously, biting her lip.

Andrew reached out with his thumb and ran it along her lip, causing her to release it from her teeth. "No need to be so nervous," he murmured, then helped her out of her seat.

As they walked up the stairs, Brooke could not help but peek up at him from beneath her eyelashes. Was this how all brides felt on their wedding night? Nervous with a hint of excitement?

As they reached the end of the hall and drew closer to her door, she slowed her steps, causing Andrew to slow his to match. "I know this all seems rather sudden, so if you're not ready, we can wait," he whispered quietly.

"I'm just nervous, that's all."

Andrew stopped walking and brought his hands up to her face. Cupping her chin, he bent down so his lips were so close to touching hers, she could almost feel them. "I'll be gentle. I promise."

Then he pressed his lips to hers in such a reverent way she knew he meant to keep his promise.

His hands caressed her face, while his lips caressed her lips. "I love kissing you," he said against her lips.

Brooke soared on hearing those words. They may not have been, "I love you," but they were close enough. If he loved something about her, such as kissing, it was a step in the right direction to winning his love and getting him to abandon his mistress.

Brooke gasped against his mouth, after his hands slid down

her body and settled against her ribs right below her breasts. She loved it when he touched her there. She couldn't explain why, but when Andrew touched her there it felt like sparks were flying through her body.

He moved his hands from her ribs to the top of her bodice and gently pulled it down, exposing the very tops of her breasts.

Andrew ceased kissing her and took hold of her hand. With a small squeeze and a gentle tug, he led her to her room. When they were both inside, he shut the door with a loud thud then took her mouth again as they stumbled together to the bed.

He broke their kiss and looked at her with a consuming gaze. "You're so beautiful, Brooke," he rasped before he reached for her gown again and unfastened the buttons that ran down the back. With only half of the buttons undone, he moved his hands to grip the sleeves and in one swift tug, he pulled her gown down, causing it to fall in a pile on the floor.

Brooke looked down at what clothes remained. Only a few scraps of clothing now stood in the way of her being completely exposed to his hungry gaze.

Stepping closer, Andrew grabbed the straps of her chemise and went to pull them down over her shoulders, but Brooke grabbed his wrist to stay him. "You first," she said shakily. When he didn't make a move to remove his hand or step back from her, she gave his chest a gentle push.

Andrew took a step back and grunted. His hands flew to his front and he quickly removed his coat, cravat, waistcoat, and shirt.

Brooke let out a gasp. She'd felt his chest before and knew he had muscles and hair all over it, but to actually see it was something altogether different. She resisted the urge to reach out and touch him. But her resistance wasn't very strong and soon she found herself running her hands along the hard planes of his chest and stomach, twirling her fingers into the mat of black hair that covered his chest.

Andrew groaned. "Is this good enough?" he asked in a husky voice.

"No."

Andrew grunted again. "You're trying to torture me. Is it because of our pitiful dinner?"

"No. I just want to see you, too."

Andrew arched an eyebrow.

"Keep going," she said breathlessly.

He removed his boots and reached for the buttons on the fall of his pants. In seconds, he had them undone and let them drop. He stepped out of them, peeling off his stockings as he went, leaving him clad only in his drawers. "Is this good enough now? Or do you require that I remove my smalls as well?"

Brooke didn't answer. She couldn't answer. She just stared at him, her mouth slightly agape.

Andrew needed no further invitation. He stepped closer to her and ran his fingers along the crest of her collarbone and over to the straps of her chemise. Not allowing her time to protest or try to stop him, he tugged the straps so hard and fast, the stitches attaching the straps to the rest of the garment ripped, leading to her chemise joining her gown on the floor.

Andrew took another step back and raked her from head to toe with his intent gaze. There was much more of her visible now. Her stomach was bare and so was the top of her chest. She still had on her drawers, stockings, and the bands she wore wound around her chest.

Without another word, he grabbed the top piece of cotton that was tucked into the top of her binding and unwound the first round of linen.

"Please don't," she said suddenly, panic creeping into her voice.

His hands froze. "Why?"

Brooke shook her head. She couldn't say, "*My breasts are actually much smaller than what they appear because I have two folded up pillow linens stuffed under these bands.*" But she was going to have to say something. He was going to see them eventually, and it appeared it would be relatively soon.

"My size is not what it appears," she said stiffly, not meeting his eyes.

"Yes, you explained that before. They're too big for your bodices."

"I did not say they were too big," she corrected. "You just assumed that. Because like all other men, you like to ogle ladies bosoms and the bigger the bosom, the more you ogle."

Andrew gave her a curious look. "Then why do you bind them?"

"Because I have quite the opposite problem, thank you."

"You think they're too small?" he asked bluntly.

"Yes," she conceded flatly.

"Let me be the judge of that." Grabbing hold of the offending linen, Andrew unwound it so quickly that, try as she might, she couldn't stop him. After two times around, there were twin thuds on the floor. Andrew reached down and picked up one of the wadded up pillow shams before tossing it down and shooting Brooke an amused glance.

Brooke felt a little relieved that at least he found some amusement in the situation. She, on the other hand, was not amused at all and her lower lip trembled. Standing in front of him thus, she honestly thought at any minute she was going to swoon, which she had never done before, but there was always a first time.

The last round of linen came off and Brooke felt the cool air hit her bare breasts in one big whoosh. The cool air was quickly replaced by Andrew's warm hands that came up to cup and shape her swollen breasts.

Her eyes flew to his face. She watched him as he swallowed and his eyes grew darker with desire.

"They're perfect," he rasped unevenly, giving them a gentle squeeze.

Brooke looked down and saw how wonderfully they filled his hands. They fit perfectly into his palm, slightly spilling over each time he massaged them with his fingers. She thought he would have been disappointed they weren't bigger, but his reaction to seeing them had disproved the notion and sent a flood of relief through her. She couldn't help but smile up at him.

"Who told you something was wrong with your body?" he

growled as he brushed both of her nipples with his thumbs.

"Why?" she asked tentatively. Nobody had told her there was anything wrong with her. She had eyes. She could see that most other women spilled out the top of their gowns, and she didn't.

"Because I'm going to string him up from the nearest tree, that's why. Your body is absolutely perfect," he repeated. Then he dropped down to his knees and showered kisses across the tops of her breasts and the valley between them.

Brooke let go of any restraint she had left. He thought her body perfect. Who was she to argue? It would make life a lot easier not having to bind them each day.

Andrew wrapped his arm around the back of her knees and the other around her waist, then with one quick movement, he picked her up and placed her on the bed. It was only a second later that his hands were caressing her all over her body, leaving nothing that was bared untouched.

He lowered his head and drew her tender nipple into his mouth. She gasped at the warm sensation. Nothing they had done so far could have prepared her for what she was feeling now. Just when she felt it couldn't get any better, he circled it with his tongue then gently nipped the tip.

Her body relaxed into a boneless mass and she closed her eyes to better savor the sweet sensations Andrew's hands and mouth were sending through her body. She let out a nervous sigh when his fingers reached into the slit in her drawers and ran along the crease between her leg and her most intimate area.

"Just relax," Andrew whispered as his fingers moved to lightly dance through her curls.

His mouth left her chest, where he had been kissing a slow trail down her sternum, and met her mouth. Stilling his fingers, he pressed his mouth to hers and took full control of her lips. She let out a soft moan when his lips left her mouth and kissed a hot path down to her jaw. He ran his tongue along the ridge then moved down to kiss her neck, causing Brooke to shiver in excitement.

Descending down her body, his mouth reached her nipple and he took it into his mouth, gently suckling while his fingers left her curls and trailed along her soft stomach, circling her navel and leaving a hot, searing sensation in their wake.

Dipping lower, his fingers lightly skimmed over her mound and found their way to her swollen, aching flesh. He massaged her there, causing her ache to grow into an intense throb. Finding her wet, silky opening, they both groaned when he slipped his finger inside, filling the part of her that ached with need for something more. She didn't know exactly what it was aching for, but Andrew did.

Rhythmically, he moved deeply in and out, building something deep inside her she couldn't describe.

His pace increased, as did her pleasure. She let out another groan when he added a second finger.

Suddenly, Brooke's legs felt like they were being licked by fire and her mind was spiraling away from reality. Then her whole world exploded. All the pressure that had built up released in a flood, and her whole body tensed then completely relaxed, leaving her with a very content feeling.

A few moments passed before she was able to bring herself to meet Andrew's gaze. "Did you intend to do that?" she asked.

"Yes, it was my intention," he said honestly with a self-satisfied smile.

"If I had known that was the result of you reaching into my drawers, I might have let you last night"

"I doubt it would have been nearly as enjoyable if either Gateway or Lady Algen happened upon us doing that."

Brooke scrunched her nose up and giggled. "No, I don't suppose it would have." Brooke met his eyes again. "Is that all? Was that the marital act?"

Andrew gave her a puzzled look. "No. Didn't your mother explain it to you?"

"No," Brooke said shyly. Oh, how she wished she had known what Mama was talking about earlier this afternoon. Then she wouldn't be such a ninny now.

"There's more," he said raggedly, tracing a lazy pattern across her thighs.

Brooke reached out and touched his face tenderly then grinned. "Well, what are you waiting for? I'm ready."

Andrew threw his head back and let out a bark of laughter. "That's good, because if you weren't, I was going to have to excuse myself to go bathe in that pond out there."

Brooke had no idea what he was talking about and was about to ask when he rendered her speechless by laying her back down and literally ripping off her drawers and stockings.

Her hands refused to be idle and freely roamed his body. She dug her fingers into the hair on his chest, twisting and twirling it. Then she moved them to feel the corded muscles in his shoulders and neck. Except for that statue at the museum, she had never seen or felt a man's body before, and this was an experience she thought she could enjoy doing for the rest of her life. But then he pulled away from her touch and stood up.

Her eyes traveled down his body, stopping where his hands were working at the strings of his tented drawers. Then the drawers dropped.

Her eyes were fixed on that part of Andrew that had just been revealed like it was a novelty in a curiosity shop.

Andrew's mind must have been on something else because he didn't comment on her scrutiny and joined her in the bed.

"What exactly are you planning to do with that?" she squeaked and pointed toward his waist as he positioned himself over her.

"You'll see," was all he said before his mouth was kissing hers again. His kisses were not as gentle and tender as they had been earlier. Instead, they were intense and with purpose.

Brooke became mindless again and surrendered to his kisses. She only noticed something was between her thighs when he pulled back from their kiss and whispered in her ear, "I'm sorry, sweetheart, this will hurt a little."

Her mind tried to put together what he was saying but didn't have enough time before she felt something prodding her where his fingers had been only a short while ago. He pushed forward very slowly. She focused on his face and thought he looked like he was the one in pain. His face was grim. His lips were clamped shut in a flat, tight line, causing white lines to form around them. His blue eyes looked hard as they stared intently at her. Finally, he gave one last push and she let out a cry of surprise.

His body stilled on top of her. "Are you all right?"

She nodded and tightened her grip on his shoulders, slightly digging her nails into his skin.

Andrew leaned down and sweetly placed a kiss on her forehead. "Please know that I didn't want to hurt you. If I could have avoided it, I would have."

"I know," Brooke told him, wiggling her hips a little to get more comfortable.

He groaned. Then he started moving on top of her with slow, even strokes, moving as deep as she could take him then almost completely withdrawing.

It felt rather uncomfortable at first, but once her body adjusted to his size, she relaxed and started to move with him until, together, they found a steady rhythm.

The pressure she'd felt earlier quickly built up again, pushing her higher and higher with each stroke. This time it only took a few minutes for her to find a release that was even more intense than the one earlier.

Then, Andrew pushed in once more and with a harsh groan, reached his climax before collapsing.

Minutes later when Brooke was losing the battle to stay awake, Andrew's lips moved against her hair as he whispered, "*That* was the marital act."

# Chapter 26

Andrew was awakened in the morning by the sun shining through the thin little windows, lighting up the room where he and Brooke lay together, tangled and naked.

Brooke was sleeping. Next to her, he kept as still as he could so not to wake her. They'd made love a second time the night before. She had to be tired and sore; there was no need to rouse her yet.

Lying in bed gave him some time to think about what he'd do next. When Willis suggested he mine his land, he'd refused. But now that he had lost his estate, he saw no other option, unless they were to continue to live like paupers for two years until the rest of the debt was paid. But even after his father's debt was paid, they'd still have to live meagerly.

He would just have to borrow the money and build the mines, but from where? Who would lend him any money? No banker in his right mind would be willing to lend him money. He had no friends or acquaintances who would lend him the money, except Alex. Alex was the only one he knew who had the money and would lend it to him despite his lack of collateral. But Alex may not want to lend the money after what Andrew had done to Brooke. Even though Andrew had married her, Alex might be upset Andrew took liberties before marriage and refused to do the right thing, at first.

The only other person he knew who would have access to that sort of money was Brooke. Her dowry was five thousand pounds, which was enough money to not only get the mines up and running, but also let them start living the lifestyle to which Brooke was accustomed. But he'd told her father he would not use one shilling from her dowry. He was not one to live off his wife's generosity. Her money would be set up in a trust for their children or given to her as pin money. Anyway, the idea of borrowing money from one's wife was laughable.

He hadn't realized he'd actually laughed until his wife's sleepy face turned up to look at his.

She didn't say anything, but raised her eyebrow the way he did. Married only one day and she had already picked up some of his habits.

"I was just thinking about some things you don't need to worry about," he said, pushing some of her thick hair away from her face.

"I'm not a featherbrain, Andrew," she countered and leaned over to kiss him. "What were you thinking about?"

She was right, she wasn't a featherbrain, but he didn't want to burden her with this. "Just thinking about our future, and what we're going to eat and wear," he said lightly, hoping she'd think he meant the present.

"I'm certain Mrs. Cleansweep will bring us breakfast if you ring," she said. Then her face went white, and she looked at the ground. "Oh no, what am I to wear?" she exclaimed.

"What you're wearing now seems to fit you well," Andrew said honestly.

She made her best attempt at a sharp look. "As much as you'd like it, I cannot spend the whole day naked. The only clothes I brought here are destroyed," she said, pointing to the floor.

His eyes followed her pointing finger. Next to the bed was a pile of discarded clothes. Her gown lay at the bottom in a crushed and wrinkled mess. Her chemise was on top, with both straps broken. Andrew cast her an apologetic look. Next to that was her linen binding and pillow shams. Surely there was something down there she could put on for a while.

"Don't you dare suggest I put on that crumpled gown. And I'm not going to try to fashion some sort of outfit out of the other clothes, so don't even suggest it."

Andrew raised his hands in mock innocence. "I would never even think such a thought," he said with a wry smile.

He rose from the bed and covered her with the sheet. "Wait

here, I have something." He came back a few minutes later wearing trousers and a shirt, holding a red dressing robe. "You can wear this. I'll run downstairs to order breakfast and dash a note off to Alex asking him to have your clothes sent right away. Well, maybe not right away," he amended with a wink.

He tossed the dressing robe on her bed beside her and left the room.

Walking down the hall, he spotted Mrs. Cleansweep dusting a wall sconce. "Can you bring breakfast to my wife's room right away?"

"Yes, my lord," she answered and scurried off to complete her task.

Andrew went down the staircase and proceeded in the direction of his study, not bothering to talk to Stevens who was trying to no avail to get Andrew's attention. "Whatever it is, Stevens, I trust you can manage it. I need to send a quick note then I am back upstairs to spend the day with my wife," he said in the superior tone that he used to dismiss his servants when they were being bothersome.

As soon as he entered his study he wished that for once Stevens had been an insolent servant who insisted on arguing with his employer. What awaited him in his study was not what he'd expected to find, but was probably what Stevens meant when he kept claiming there was a "sticky situation" afoot. His mother was on the settee by the fireplace, and not ten feet away, sitting behind his desk, was the Duke of Gateway.

"Good morning, Mother," he said stiffly, ignoring Gateway altogether.

"Good morning, Andrew. Where is your bride?" she asked crisply, hurt marring her normally gentle features.

Andrew supposed she was upset because he had not introduced them sooner. But, she could also be unhappy that he had married without telling her about it. There hadn't exactly been time the day before to introduce them, and he hadn't sent word for her to join the wedding party, because he didn't want her to undergo any unfair scrutiny.

"Yes, where is your bride?" Gateway drawled. "I'm rather surprised to see you so early, or has she already proven to be uninteresting."

The dowager countess shot the duke a reproachful look, but that was nothing compared to Andrew's reaction. Andrew leapt across his desk to where Gateway was sitting, grabbed him by the lapels and with more force than necessary, threw him to the floor. "Don't you ever speak of her in such a way again," he thundered.

Gateway's face went red, but his hands came up and grabbed Andrew's arms and brought him down to the floor with him. "I broke your nose once, Townson. Don't think I won't do it again," he roared.

"That was many years ago, and it wasn't a fair fight. You caught me unawares, the coward's way," Andrew spat.

They both rolled around on the floor of Andrew's study, punching and trying to strangle each other. One second, one would have the advantage and be on top, and then a second later the positions were reversed.

"Stop! Both of you behave yourselves," Mother yelled. "This is ridiculous. You are two grown men and you're acting like petulant children. What's worse is that there is no reason for it. Benjamin, apologize for insulting his wife."

"I will not apologize. I have no reason to. The remarks I made were fair. Everyone knows his wife is a lightskirt." A satisfied look came over Gateway's face when Andrew's face turned murderous.

"You only have a grudge against her because she rejected you," Andrew said sourly as he punched Gateway square in the jaw.

"Is that what she told you?" Gateway rubbed his jaw. "I'll have you know I wouldn't have her if she served herself to me naked on a platter."

Andrew rose off the ground while Gateway rubbed his jaw. "I want you out. Now!"

"No," Gateway said, as he rose to his feet and held up his fists, preparing for round two. "We made a bargain and you didn't hold up your end. I demand satisfaction."

"Bargain? Satisfaction?" Mother repeated, her brow furrowing in confusion. "What is he talking about, Andrew?"

"Nothing, Mother," Andrew said tersely.

"It's not nothing," Gateway snapped. "We had a bargain and, if I remember correctly, the bargain did not involve you marrying her. In fact, you were specifically not to marry her. Or did you forget that part of the agreement?" he asked accusingly.

"No, I didn't forget," Andrew replied flatly. "However, there was nothing in the agreement that said you would demand satisfaction if I failed to see it through. If I remember correctly, you're the one who wanted to end the agreement a few days ago when you thought she would throw me over due to some old gossip. Why is it fine for you to end the agreement, but not me?" Andrew asked with a sneer.

"Because I was going to call it off and find someone who could handle it. As it turns out, that is exactly what I should have done," Gateway shot back.

"What agreement?" the dowager demanded in a voice that was so loud it shook the wall hangings. "I want to know exactly what's going on right this instant."

Andrew and Gateway exchanged looks so sharp that if they had been daggers, they'd both be dead. Andrew thought he should be the one to tell his mother what was going on. He couldn't trust Gateway to tell the truth, and why should he? She wasn't his mother, or any relation for that matter.

"Now, Andrew. Tell all of us about this agreement," said a voice behind him, cutting him off before he could speak.

He turned around very slowly, hoping his mind was playing tricks on him, but it wasn't and his heart dipped to his toes. Behind him, standing in the doorway of his study, was his wife. She wore only his red dressing robe and stood still as a statue.

Everyone was looking at her, but Brooke didn't act like she knew or cared she was now the focus of everyone's attention.

"Brooke," he said, coming to her side.

She wrenched her arm away from him. "What agreement, Andrew?" Her voice was so icy it could freeze a pot of boiling water on the spot.

"Tell her, Townson," Gateway urged. "Tell her all about your plan to have her shamed right out of England and sent back to America on the fastest vessel."

Andrew ignored Gateway. He'd take care of him later. Right now he needed to talk to Brooke. "Brooke," Andrew started again.

"It all makes sense now," she snapped, halting his words. She pulled further away from him. She was clutching his dressing robe so tightly her knuckles turned white and he thought the seams around the sleeves were going to pop. "Why you showed up at my house not knowing me or my sisters. When we caught you, you made up some lie about seeing us across the room at some ball you probably didn't even attend."

"That's not true," Andrew interrupted defensively. "I was at that ball."

"What was I wearing?" she countered tartly. She shook her head at his lack of response. "I thought so. You were always trying to get me alone, and when you did, I fell right into your trap. I believed your words about having feelings for me and how much you cared for me. But now I know the real reason you were reluctant to marry me, even after Alex challenged you to a duel."

"Indeed, a duel?" Gateway chimed in when she paused.

Brooke's eyes left Andrew and darted to Gateway. "What I don't understand is your part in this," she said stiffly.

"My part was simple, really. I had something your husband wanted more than you," he said, shrugging. "Something he wanted badly enough that he planned to bring on your ruin and send you back to America on the earliest departing vessel." He flashed her a cruel smile that made her go pale.

Andrew's mother let out a gasp, but wisely closed her mouth when Andrew gave her a quelling look.

"You can give him whatever he would have gained," Brooke said with a sob in her throat. "I shall return to my family and convince them to leave England without delay." She turned and fled the room.

Andrew ran after her. When he reached her, hc tried to pull her back to him. "Stop, Brooke, let me explain."

"There's no need," she assured him, the tears rolling down her cheeks betraying her words.

Andrew moved to stand in front of her, trying to block her way. "There is a need," he said softly.

She pushed his chest. Hard.

He didn't budge.

She placed both hands squarely on his chest, not caring that the dressing robe she wore fell open in the front and revealed her naked form to his eyes. This time, she shoved him with all her might.

Andrew was rather shocked when his body fell backward and crashed into the banister, breaking it as it broke his direct fall to the edge of the stairs. She had some muscles. For being a girl, that is. He would have smiled at the discovery, if he wasn't in so much pain.

She took advantage of his misfortune by grabbing her robe together and running toward the servant's stairs. She had almost made it when he grabbed her waist from behind. "Would you please just stop for a moment. I can explain everything," he ground out.

She faced him, her eyes still filled with fury. "For fear of having to repeat myself again, please listen well, Lord Townson. There is no need. I understand everything. I was present for most of that enlightening conversation."

"What did you hear?" he growled.

"Enough" she snapped. Her body trembled from sobs wracking through her. "Now, would you for once in your misbegotten life be a gentleman and release me?"

Andrew relaxed his hold on her and she scurried to the top of the stairs, leaving him at the bottom. "Where are you going?" he demanded softly when she reached the top.

"I already told you," she snapped. "Right now, I'm going back to my family, then back to America."

"No," he said coolly.

"No?" she echoed.

"No. I forbid it," he said in a steely tone.

"You forbid it?" She crossed her arms.

He crossed his arms in the same manner. "As your husband, I forbid you to leave this house." His voice would have made most people cower to his demands, but not Brooke.

"You are powerless over me," she huffed defiantly. "I will leave this house if I choose to. I will go where I want and do what I want. You don't own me." She ran down the hall faster than he'd ever seen her move.

Andrew took the stairs two at a time and ran down the hall after her only to find by the time he reached her room, she was already safely inside and slammed the door right in his face.

Moving his hand to the knob, he tried to turn it but it was locked. He made a fist and banged it on the outside of her door. "Open this door right now!" he called.

He didn't hear any response and almost kicked himself when he remembered how easily he could get inside her room. With a shake of his head, he strolled to his room. He walked over to the connecting door and turned the handle.

It wouldn't turn.

Not so easily put off, Andrew looked around for the key. It was in here somewhere. He shuffled some papers on his writing desk. Not there. He looked around his vanity. Not there. Finding a cup-like object that held quills and other miscellaneous objects, he turned it over, dumping the quills and other odds and ends out, but the key was not there, either. The key had to be there somewhere, he just knew it. That room had not been used in so long, there was no need to lock it, but surely the old earl had kept the key around here somewhere.

He finally resigned himself to the idea that the key was not close at hand and walked over to the connecting door. "Brooke, unlock the door this instant or I will break it down," he yelled through the door. He wasn't sure if that were even possible, but she didn't need to know that.

He waited silently for a minute, listening for her response. He heard none. "Brooke, I'm serious. If you don't open up, I'm coming in."

He stood quietly again, listening once more for any noise, her moving, unlocking the door, crying, anything. But he heard nothing. "All right, I'm coming in, you had better move back."

He walked across his room, and with as much speed as he could gain, he ran straight toward the door, hitting it directly with his shoulder. A faint cracking noise resulted, but the door was still firmly in place. Stepping away from the door, he ran his fingers over his now smarting shoulder that matched his equally sore back and face.

Andrew decided this was not the best method to enter the countess's chambers, and later today that door would be taken off its hinges and burned. Looking around, Andrew spotted his penknife lying on the vanity.

Fighting his irritation with himself for not thinking to use it sooner, he pulled out the blade and stalked over to the door.

In less than fifteen seconds he had the lock picked and was pushing open the door. He was expecting Brooke to scream in surprise. He was expecting her to rage at him. He was even expecting flying objects to be hurled at his head.

He was not expecting the room to be empty.

He looked behind the wardrobe and dressing screen. He peeked under the bed. She wasn't anywhere. There was nothing out of place and no sign of her. He turned in a half-circle and smiled grimly. The door leading to the hallway was slightly ajar. He walked over and opened it, then looked up and down the hallway, but it was empty.

He stormed back into her room in time to see movement out the window. Wanting to get a closer look, he walked to the window just in time to see Brooke tearing across the lawn toward the duke's carriage, clad in nothing more than his red dressing robe.

# *Chapter 27*

Andrew ran down the stairs to the front door as fast as his feet could carry him, all the while wondering what had possessed her to accept a ride from the duke.

He couldn't overtake the carriage on foot; he'd have to saddle his horse and run into her on the road. He was almost certain she was going back to Alex's, where she could convince her family he was an awful monster—which he was—then they'd leave and he'd never get another chance to see her again. He had to catch up to her.

He reached out to open the front door and froze at the sight of the duke's shadow. A wave of relief rushed through him knowing the duke had not been in that carriage with her. Call it whatever you want: jealousy, possession, or love, it made no difference; something in him did not like the idea of Gateway spending time alone with her, especially when she was only wearing that little scrap of fabric.

"It looks like your luck just improved," Gateway drawled from behind Andrew's back. "She's gone. Now that you're free of her, I'll give you your deed. A house is so much better than a trollop for a wife, anyway. They both require a bit of money, but at least with the house, you know who inhabits it while you're away." He cackled at his insinuation.

Andrew's blood was thundering so loudly in his ears, he did not hear his mother shriek, "Benjamin Archer Leopold Charles Robert Collins!"

All thoughts of rushing after Brooke fled his mind and he took his hand off the door handle, spun around, and without hesitation, brought his fist up to connect with the center of Gateway's face, creating a sharp cracking noise, followed by a loud thud.

He took a measure of satisfaction when Gateway dropped to

the floor like a lead weight and lay there in a tangled pile of limbs, groaning in pain.

Andrew's mother ran over to where Gateway's still form lay groaning on the floor. She bent over him to smooth his hair back when she made a cry of distress.

"Why are you crying over *him*?" Andrew growled, hauling her up off the floor.

She didn't answer. She just glanced at Gateway on the floor then to Andrew, her eyes full of unshed tears. "Why can't you two get along?" she cried, fighting Andrew's grip on her arm.

"Why should we?" Andrew countered, tightening his grip. Then it dawned on him, his mother had said something before he punched Gateway. He could have sworn it was Gateway's full name, but why would she say that? And how would she know it? She was a recluse, after all. He released his hold on her arm and crossed his arms in front of his chest. "Why did you call him by his full name? How did you even know it? Since when have you two become fast friends?" He bombarded her with questions, taking a step closer to her with each one, thus causing her to back up until she backed straight into a wall.

When she didn't answer him, he wondered what he was missing. What had she called him? Benjamin Archer Leopold Charles Robert Collins. Then it fit. *Archer.* That was the name of his playmate in Essex.

"Who is he to you?" Andrew bellowed, making her go pale. "Don't deny that you know him on a personal level. I remember playing with a little boy named Archer until I was about five and he suddenly disappeared. There's no reason for you, a recluse, to know his full name unless he is the same Archer I played with. Now tell me what's going on."

"I need to sit down," she choked out, holding onto the corner of the table beside her for balance.

Andrew backed away a step to give her some breathing room. Then taking her elbow in a firm grasp, he led her over to the settee.

"May I have some water?" she asked meekly, her hand patting the top of her chest.

Andrew stalked over to the carafe on his desk, picked it up, grabbed a glass from a nearby shelf, slammed it down, and carelessly dumped some water inside. When it was half full, he snatched it up and thrust it in his mother's face. "Here," he growled. "Will that be all? Or do you require anything else before your grand revelations? Perhaps I should stoke the fire, or get on my knees and rub your feet?"

"Your tone and sarcasm are quite unbecoming," his mother criticized.

Andrew ground his teeth. "Begin your tale, madam."

She tried to hold onto that glass of water with all her might, but she could hardly grip it. Her hands were shaking, and her fingers were slipping off the sides. She held the glass in one hand, while wiping her free hand on her skirt to dry off her sweaty palm, then transferred it to the other hand and did the same thing. Her skin was still whiter than any table linen he'd ever seen and the tears that were brimming in her eyes earlier were now on the brink of spilling out.

Taking pity on her, Andrew walked over and carefully took the glass from her hands. He gently placed it on the table and took a seat next to her.

"Leave her alone," Gateway interrupted from the doorway, looking resolved and considerably worse for the wear. "I'll tell you what you want to know, just leave Lizzie alone."

"Lizzie?" Andrew repeated hollowly. His mother's name was Elizabeth, but he'd never heard anyone call her Lizzie.

"No," Elizabeth spoke up, rubbing her hands up and down on her skirt. "Andrew is my son. I shall tell him." Fixing her gaze on Andrew's chest, she said, "Benjamin, Archer, Channing, Gateway or whatever you want to call him, is a relation of mine."

"A relation?" Andrew echoed. "What kind?" His tone was full of disbelief.

"It's complicated," Elizabeth said with a small smile. "Can we just leave it at that?"

Andrew looked at her as if she had just grown an extra head. "No." If Gateway was a "relation" to his mother, that would make him one of Andrew's relations, too. Just the thought made him spring to his feet faster than sitting on a metal spike would have. "No, we cannot leave it at that. If that scoundrel is your relation," he yelled, pointing an accusing finger at Gateway, "that means he is also a relation of *mine*! I demand to know. Now!"

"We're siblings. Of a sort," Gateway said uneasily.

"Siblings? Of a sort? How can that be? You either are or you're not. Which is it?" Andrew asked, his head snapping back and forth from his mother to Gateway, who he just noticed was holding a bloody handkerchief around his swollen nose.

"If one digs deep enough, they can find a connection through our father, Robert Collins, the previous Duke of Gateway," his mother said without much emotion.

Andrew's brow shot up so far it was almost lost in his hairline.

"When Robert was younger, he seduced a young woman," Elizabeth said uneasily, before Gateway jumped up and cut her off.

"Lizzie, stop," Gateway cut in irritably, putting a swift end to Elizabeth's evasive story. "He's a man, or at least he'd like us to think so, just get on with it."

Andrew scowled at Gateway, but didn't bother to give his meaningless dig a response. Life was too short to spend it in Gateway's presence.

Elizabeth shot Gateway a questioning gaze, then cleared her throat and nodded. "All right," she said in a normal, if not somewhat clipped tone. "The previous duke was a randy lad when he was eighteen and seduced his mother's lady's maid. Not wanting to lose her highly coveted lady's maid, the duchess chose to ignore the fact she was increasing and the maid kept her position. A few months later the maid died in childbirth.

"For some reason, Charles, Robert's father and the duke at the time, had sympathy for the motherless, and essentially fatherless, child and he decided to keep me as his ward, even though this infuriated Robert."

Andrew just stared at her, stunned. He'd always heard rumors and speculation about his mother's family, but he'd never had the heart—or desire—to bring it up with her. But to know she was a by-blow from the old Gateway was enough to shock anybody into a state of horrified silence.

"My grandfather was the sweetest man, and much to Robert's dismay, he spoiled me beyond belief. When I came of age, he decided I should have a come out. However, just weeks before I was to be presented to court, Grandfather died," Elizabeth said sadly, then swallowed a couple of times and looked across the room with a sad expression on her face.

"Mother," Andrew said abruptly, startling her out of her daze. "You've just told me how you're related, but how did you two become so close? You're nearly twenty years older than he is."

"If you'd let me finish, you'd know," Elizabeth said with a sniff.

"Well, excuse me for hurrying you along. This isn't exactly one of those charming family stories one sits in front of a cozy fire all bundled up in blankets, drinking chocolate and begging one's parents to repeat for the hundredth time. Now could you tell me the rest, so I can punch Gateway once more for good measure and go after my wife?"

Elizabeth shot him a sharp look. "There will be no more hitting. It's barbaric and I raised you both better than that, or so I thought."

"'Fraid not," Gateway said jovially. "And there will certainly be more hitting if he goes after her."

"No, there won't," Elizabeth snapped, jerking her gaze back and forth between Andrew and Gateway. "I don't know what's going on between the two of you, but it's obvious that beautiful young woman who came in here earlier has had her heart broken, and Andrew will be going after her even if I have to drag him."

"Not to worry. I'll be on my way to fetch my bride as soon as you tell me how the two of you became bosom friends," Andrew said irritably, meeting his mother's stare with one of his own. "Could we please get on with it? I've never heard you ramble so much. You're starting to sound like Liberty."

Gateway snorted. "Nobody could talk that much," he muttered, shaking his head.

Elizabeth eyed them both curiously, but didn't ask. "Robert had just married my closest friend and didn't want to spend the time or money on presenting me to court. But his father's will said he'd be disinherited if he didn't make a match for me. So in less than a week, he managed to match me with the biggest reprobate of the season, Lord Townson.

"I don't know what he told Thomas to get him to marry me, but whatever it was, it didn't include the actual amount of my dowry, nor my parentage," she said dryly, rolling her eyes. "The day after our wedding, Thomas and Robert were in the Rockhurst library fighting over my dowry. My friend thought she was helping and stepped in to convince the duke to give Thomas the rest of the money. He refused, and that's when she accidentally let slip it was only hurting his daughter more by withholding the money."

"That's why he packed you off to Essex?" Andrew asked softly.

Elizabeth gave a stiff nod, her body was rigid and her eyes were fixed on an empty vase across the room. Andrew sat back down and wrapped his arm around her. Pulling her to him, he brushed a kiss on her forehead and murmured, "I'm sorry."

"No need to apologize," she assured him with a stiff smile. "It's not your fault. It was for the best. I couldn't imagine having to live with that despicable man the rest of his life."

"That explains the estrangement, but I fail to see how Benjamin fits into all this," Andrew said curiously.

"Well, see that's where the story gets stickier," Elizabeth said cautiously.

"Lizzie, you're beating around the bush again," Gateway declared, sounding agitated. "The duke wasn't the only randy rascal around. His wife cuckolded him, and when I was born it was undeniable proof she'd been shaking the sheets with the second footman. They ran away together and the duke packed me off to Essex with a nurse."

Andrew's jaw went slack and his mouth hung open, but no matter how hard he tried, he just couldn't get it to close. The irony of it was too much. Gateway was a bastard through and through, in action *and* deed. "That's what you meant by being siblings 'of a sort', one of you is actually the duke's child by blood and not paper, and the other is the duke's child on paper but not by blood," he mused, trying not to let his fascination show. Truly this was the stuff for novels.

"Yes, well, I'm glad you find it entertaining, Andrew," his mother said shortly. "After Ben was moved to Essex, the duke wrote and told me he would send me what my grandfather had set up for my dowry, if I would watch out for Ben until it was time for him to go to Eton. I was penniless, so I agreed. Naturally, I let the two of you play together, and would have continued to, had your father not gotten wind of it.

"When you were five, Thomas found out about the situation and demanded you go live with him in London. I wrote letters every day begging him to let you come back, but it was only after I agreed to give him half the money that he let you come home. While you were gone, the duke wrote and demanded you two not have any more interaction because he didn't want you to recognize each other at school, start asking questions, and cause a scandal. Realizing he was right, I reluctantly agreed and when you came back, I told you he'd moved. That's when you started spending the afternoons with the nurse, and I'd go see Ben."

Every muscle in Andrew's body tightened. The feeling of sympathy for his mother's plight was swiftly changing into rage. She had told him it was countess duties, but all along she'd been stealing away every afternoon to go see Benjamin. He was her *son*, he had needed her. "You left me, your son, to go spend time with someone who isn't even really your brother?" he questioned, piercing her with his stare.

Elizabeth stiffened and pursed her lips. "How dare you?" she demanded, her voice telling how offended she was. "I had to. I'd agreed to look after him. That was how I made my way in this world. You should be grateful I went. How do you think we survived? If it had been up to your father, we would've starved to death out in the country," she snapped.

"Did you have to check on him every day?" Andrew

countered. "Wasn't once a week enough?"

"He was lonely!" she burst out. "All he wanted was a little human interaction. Other than me, the only person he saw was his nurse. You at least got to see your father, even if the visits were miserable. He had no one. On the two occasions the duke did come to see him, all he did was condemn him for his mother's transgressions." She jumped up and wagged her finger at him. "If you'd been listening at all to what I just told you, you'd know that I was the object of the duke's scorn for years. Whether Ben is really my brother or not doesn't change that I love him the same way I love you. He and I share a tie similar to the one you and I share. You and I were hated and the objects of scorn by your father, and Ben and I were the objects of the duke's scorn." With a huff, she plopped back down on the settee and crossed her arms defensively.

Shame washed over Andrew. She was right. She had to go see Benjamin; not only for the money, her other reasons were valid as well. He had no right to be angry with her for loving and being loved by someone else. "I'm sorry for what I said," he said softly, squeezing her hand. "It wasn't fair of me to say those things to you. You did the best you could, and I appreciate all you did for me."

Mother didn't say anything. She just wiped away a tear that was rolling down her cheek and squeezed his hand back.

Coming to his feet, Andrew silently walked out of the room. This was all too much. In the last two days, he had ruined an innocent girl's reputation, been challenged to a duel, gotten married, been in a fist fight, found out his mother was illegitimate, learned in a twisted way he had a bizarre connection to the depraved Duke of Gateway, and worst of all, he'd lost his wife.

"Where are you going?" Gateway shouted to Andrew's back.

"Out," Andrew answered simply in a clipped tone.

"Out? Not to the baron's house party, I hope?"

Andrew whipped around to face Gateway. "It's none of your business where I go or what I do," he said in a steely tone. "You might have some strange connection to my mother, but that doesn't improve my opinion of you."

"I'm warning you, Townson, if you bring her back, I'll never return that estate," Gateway thundered.

"I don't want it," Andrew said, realizing it was the truth. "I thought I did. I thought that if I could get that estate back, it would solve all of my problems." He looked at his mother. "I thought if I could get that estate back, I would be able to have the income that I currently lack and could give the house to my mother to heal the pain I caused when I rejected her. But ruining someone else's life is not the way to go about fixing things. I don't know why I let myself believe it was." He met his mother's eyes. "I'm sorry for what I did and said back then, but I was just a boy and didn't realize the pain I was causing. I do hope you'll forgive me."

"You ruined a girl's reputation to get back that musty, crumbling estate, because you thought it would mend our rift?" Elizabeth shrieked, leaping off the settee and putting her hands on her hips. "You, my son, are a coxcomb. I hated that estate. I only went there because I didn't have anywhere else to go. As for our separation, well, that was your father's doing. I did send you letters, but per Thomas's request, they were returned by the school master. During breaks, he demanded you go stay with him. He did it to torture me and it worked, but I never held that against you."

Andrew swallowed, closed his eyes, and sank into an empty chair. Everything he believed about the rift in their relationship had been wrong. For years he'd felt guilty about what he'd done. And now he found out it had nothing to do with him at all. He was a coxcomb.

His whole body felt numb. Everything he'd done concerning Brooke was all for naught except a lot of grief for both of them. If he'd ever bothered to talk to his mother, he'd have known all of this earlier—much earlier. More importantly, he wouldn't have tried to ruin Brooke in an effort to mend their rift. His blood chilled at the thought. If this hadn't all worked out this way, he might have never met Brooke. She was what was important now.

"Andrew," Elizabeth said abruptly, snapping her fingers in front of his face and breaking Andrew from his trance. "I know all these revelations are shocking, but what are you waiting for? Get off your arse, go get your bride, and bring her back for a proper introduction."

Andrew's eyes popped open and he shook his head at his mother's blunt words. "I suppose that wasn't the finest first meeting," he said dryly.

"No, and as fetching as she looked in that dressing robe, I imagine she's quite a beauty when properly attired," she said with a simple smile.

"That she is," he agreed. Although, he was rather convinced she looked even better without it. Andrew rose from his chair and turned to face Gateway. "Thank you. If not for you and your idiotic scheme, I would never have met the love of my life."

Andrew smiled at Gateway's unhinged jaw before running out the door and saddling his horse.

# Chapter 28

Brooke could hear Andrew rifling through his things. He was looking for the key to the connecting door, she supposed. Too bad for him, she'd swiped it while he was still in the hallway banging on her door like a madman.

Leaning down to where her clothes were in a heap on the floor, she scooped them up and quietly padded over to the door. She slowly opened it so as not to let it creak. She got it opened far enough to slip out and stood quietly to make sure Andrew was still digging around. He grunted and dumped over what sounded to be a container meant to hold ink pots and quills. Taking a breath, she darted out the door and headed to the main staircase. She was afraid if she tried to go down the servants' stairs, she'd have to walk past his room, and if he'd left the door open, he might see her.

Running down the hall, she was glad she had chosen to carry her slippers rather than wear them, because their heels would have made too much noise on the uncarpeted stairs. She walked down the stairs as fast as she dared, trying to go quickly but not make noise. When she got near the bottom, she heard the duke and Andrew's mother talking about something. She almost wanted to stop and listen in order to try to understand why they were calling each other by their first names, but she dared not.

She walked quickly to the servants' entrance and ran to the duke's carriage. His coachman, who looked older than Methuselah, was standing close by and she bribed him to take her to her uncle's house party.

When she climbed into the carriage, she couldn't help but snicker at the lack of loyalty he must have for his employer if he were willing to take a bribe to use his employer's carriage. That's when she remembered whose carriage it was, and her humor dissolved.

She was angry with both of them, but her anger for Andrew far surpassed her anger toward Gateway. She knew Gateway was a snake. She'd heard the rumors about him and knew from just the handful of conversations they'd had that he was capable of just about anything. But she would have never believed Andrew capable of this. How could she have been so blind?

She leaned her head down and clutched her garments to her as best she could, and the tears flowed. Not just one or two, but a steady stream. Her life really was over now. Had she left without marrying Andrew, she still could have married, but not now. Now, she was damaged beyond redemption. The worst part was that in her mind, it was all worth it. It was worth facing the future she would have as a spinster for the few passionate interludes she had experienced with Andrew. He'd been so sweet and tender. Nothing could take that away. Even if he ended up being a cad, she could cling to those memories she had of him when she thought he was her Prince Charming.

It felt like only minutes in the carriage before they were pulling up to her uncle's house. The coachman came to open the door to let her down. His eyes went wide, reminding her she was only wearing a flimsy dressing robe, which would cause a scandal if she were to be seen wearing it. She had a quick thought to what Liberty's expression would be if she saw her wearing the dressing robe, and only the dressing robe. The image brought a smile to her face, but did not solve her problem.

"Could you do me another favor?" she asked the coachman. "I promise it will be worth your while."

"Aye, miss," the scraggly coachman replied as he ran his fingers through his wind-whipped hair.

She asked him to move the coach to where the other coaches were parked, then go in and request that Mama meet her in the family coach.

After the man moved the coach and was on his way, Brooke peeked out and saw that nobody was about. Then she quickly climbed out of the duke's coach and into the Banks' coach. Once she got settled, she made a mental note that stairs were the preferred way to get in and out of a coach and vowed to always use them in the future.

She waited mere minutes before Mama showed up with Madison in tow. She felt a pang of relief that Liberty wasn't with them, but it was all forgotten when Mama wrapped her arms around her and the floodgates surrounding Brooke's eyes opened once again.

Brooke looked up and met Mama's eyes. "Take me away, please."

Under normal circumstances, Mama would have probably told her she needed to make the best of things and insist she would have to just brazen out her troubles, but she must have read more into Brooke's words because she turned to Madison, and said, "Go get our coachman, and please bring her a new gown."

Madison dashed away and returned so quickly Brooke thought she must be dreaming, but she wasn't. Mama gave Madison more directions but had no idea what they were.

Brooke barely had her new gown on before the carriage was hitched and lurched forward to start their journey to London.

Long before they reached their townhouse in London, the whole story had come out. All about how he'd set everything up to shame her and had made an agreement that involved her losing her virtue and him gaining something, but she didn't know what. She told Mama how she'd snuck out when he'd been busy and had bribed the coachman, who, she realized, she hadn't even payed, to bring her back.

Brooke didn't mention that she secretly feared, and if she were being honest, hoped, Andrew would follow them back to London. She wasn't sure what she'd do if he showed up, nor did she trust herself to find out. As mad as she was with him about what he had done, she still knew he could be persuasive. A handful of sweet words and skillful kisses could send her back into his trap.

She walked up the stairs and through the front door of their London residence. She had no idea she would ever be happy to see the wretched inside of that townhouse, but she was.

She went upstairs, took a bath, and crawled into bed without bothering to eat dinner. She was almost asleep when there was a gentle knock at her door, followed by Mama's skirts swishing as she entered.

Mama didn't speak. She just sat down on the bed next to her and ran her fingers through Brooke's hair, the way she had done when the girls were young and needed to be soothed.

Brooke fell asleep and didn't wake until a little before noon the next day. It wasn't normal for Brooke to sleep so late, but given the circumstances, it didn't come as a great surprise.

She dressed quickly before sitting down to do her hair. While brushing her hair, she decided she was going to face the day with renewed vigor. Her anger with Andrew was firmly in place.

Yesterday, Brooke had told him that she was going to go back to New York as soon as she could. When she told Mama about the conversation, Mama hadn't acted very accepting of the prospect. Not to say that she dismissed it, but she acted reluctant about Brooke returning to New York, which Brooke knew Mama would be.

Brooke walked down the stairs and headed to the parlor, where they ordinarily ate their meals. She walked with her head down, watching her slippers peek out from under her gown with each step she took. She was so lost in her own thoughts that she did not notice someone walking toward her until she collided with a male figure. Looking up, she gasped. "Papa."

Papa wrapped his arms around her in a tight embrace. "We came as soon as we could get everything packed."

"You didn't have to," Brooke protested.

"Yes, I did," he told her firmly, giving her another reassuring squeeze. "You are my daughter, even if you are married. I will take care of you. Always."

"Oh, Papa," she cried and leaned into him.

He reached up and wiped a tear off her cheek she wasn't even aware had slipped out. "Mama told me everything. We'll work something out."

She knew there was nothing Papa or anyone could do to make

this better, but she smiled at him just the same.

He offered her his arm and together they walked to the parlor to enjoy a late breakfast together. They filled their plates and sat down in comfortable silence. Halfway through the meal, Mama came in and asked to speak to Papa in the hall for a moment. A minute later Mama came back and joined Brooke, saying that Papa had to take care of something right away.

Mama just watched her from across the table. Her face was full of concern, but she wisely held her tongue. Papa returned shortly, looking a little distracted, but he smiled at her when he entered, then resumed his meal.

Brooke made her way through the meal and the rest of the afternoon without saying anything that didn't need to be said. She enjoyed being able to be quiet with her thoughts without anyone pressing her to respond or getting agitated when she didn't.

The following two days were much the same. She got up, dressed, ate, embroidered, ate, sat in the drawing room, ate dinner, then went to bed. She moved about as if she were in a trance.

With each passing day, her anger toward Andrew intensified. He had not one time come to see her and that made her heart ache. In the end, he had used her the way he had set out to from the start.

She didn't know why that hurt her so much, but it did. She'd told him to leave her alone and that she was leaving England, but she didn't really mean it. She'd been upset at the time and it seemed like the easiest choice. Apparently, he'd believed her and it had been easier for him to forget her and move on with his life than it was for her.

That night at dinner she announced she'd like to go back to New York on the passenger ship that was scheduled to depart the next day. At first everyone was quiet, then Mama put her fork down and asked, "Are you sure?"

Brooke nodded. There was no use remaining here and hoping Andrew would come to see her. If he hadn't already, then he probably wasn't going to. That was the kind of man he was. Just look how he'd conducted his courtship with her. They'd barely even known each other a fortnight and he had snared, ruined, married, and rejected her already. If he had wanted her back, he would have done something by now. It wasn't a great mystery as to where she was. She had as much as told him her plans.

"Do you not want to wait another week?" Mama suggested.

Brooke shook her head. Her decision was already made, and she was going to stick by it. "I know you're disappointed your daughter will not be the great countess you'd hoped, but I cannot go on this way."

Mama started. "Brooke, I don't care more for your status as countess than I do for your happiness. If you'd wanted to marry a chimney sweep, I would have allowed it." Taking note of the dubious gaze that Brooke leveled on her, she changed tactics. "All right, I admit I reveled in the idea. But the title means nothing, if you're not happy. If he had a brain in his skull, I think you two could have been happy together, but since he clearly does not, I don't blame you. I just don't want you to make a hasty decision."

Brooke understood what Mama meant, but she also understood things would never be the same. In her mind, the sooner she returned to New York, the sooner she could start forgetting this whole mess.

"Tomorrow is too soon to go back," Papa stated. "We cannot all be packed and ready to board tomorrow afternoon. It just cannot be done."

He had a point. "I can go alone," she said quietly.

"Absolutely not," Papa said sternly. "I will not have my daughter sailing across the Atlantic Ocean by herself."

"I wouldn't be alone," Brooke pointed out cheekily, smiling her first genuine smile in days. "There will be plenty of other passengers on board."

"Don't get smart with me, young lady. You would require a lady's companion just to cross. Then, when you got there, you could not live in that house alone. It's not done."

"The Whitakers will still be there. As for a companion, we could hire one tomorrow. I've heard there are women around the docks who would be willing to take jobs like that," Brooke said hopefully.

"Absolutely not," Mama chimed in archly. "I know you are a married woman and know about certain things, but those women are not fit company."

Brooke sat back in her chair and looked around the room. Then an idea occurred to her. "I could take Liberty with me." Everyone's eyes, including Liberty's, impaled her and she added hastily, "Didn't you tell Liberty if she couldn't behave herself, she'd be boarded on the next vessel? Well, if she goes with me, she won't have to worry about behaving herself around Mr. Grimes." Brooke thought it was an excellent solution.

Liberty's face made it clear she did not agree, which was fortunate for her, because neither did Mama and Papa. "No," Papa said, wiping his mouth and resting his napkin on the table. "It's true I told her that, but she's behaved herself so far. I see no reason to send her back. Unless you want to go," he said, looking to Liberty for an answer. When she shook her head, he sighed. "Brooke, if you want to go back, you may. I shall book your passage in the morning."

"What of a companion or chaperone?" Mama asked, tension creeping into her voice.

Papa's face turned a little red and he cleared his throat. "As you pointed out earlier, Carolina, she is a married woman. Therefore, she requires neither. I would prefer she have one, but given the choice between going alone and sharing the room with a woman from the docks, I would prefer she travel alone."

Brooke went upstairs after dinner to pack. She was taking out her trunks when Madison came in. "Do you truly mean to go?" she asked bluntly.

"Yes," Brooke replied, taking her last ball gown and matching slippers from her wardrobe. "I cannot stay here. He has no interest in me, and you know it is only a matter of time before the scandal gets out. I'm honestly surprised it hasn't already."

Madison walked over to Brooke's vanity and began to help her put things into her trunk.

"You do realize once news of this gets out that you'll probably be returning home as well," Brooke continued as she picked out the traveling costume she'd wear on the ship tomorrow. "I predict you'll be only a week behind me."

"That may be so," Madison allowed. "But you don't have to go, you know."

Brooke went to her sister and wrapped her arms around her. "Yes, I do. You know I cannot stay here. I am living separate from my husband of one day. I will be publicly humiliated and ridiculed when the story breaks. Tomorrow everyone will be coming home from that house party. A day, maybe two, later everyone will be coming here trying to learn why we're living separately. I cannot bear it."

"Why don't you go after him?" Madison asked quietly, trying, and failing miserably, to hide the tears in her eyes.

Brooke let go of her sister, sat on the bed, and stared at the wall. "I can't."

"Why not?"

Letting out a resigned sigh, she told her sister everything. Mama had assured her she hadn't told anyone except Papa about her disaster, so she knew that Madison didn't truly understand just how bad it was.

When she was finished, Madison slipped her arm around Brooke and pulled her into a comforting hug. "What I still don't understand is why you cannot go to him. I mean, he did marry you, didn't he?"

Brooke nodded. She couldn't deny that.

"It sounds to me as though he tried rather hard to get you to listen to whatever foolish explanation he had, but you were too stubborn and upset to listen. Why not go tell him you're ready to hear it now?"

Brooke's eyes snapped up to her sister. "Go? Go where? To Rockhurst? His townhouse in London? I have no idea where he is."

"That's a feeble excuse, Brooke," Madison said firmly, but not unkindly.

Brooke took a deep breath, but it did little to help her get through her next words. "I'm afraid," she said quietly.

"Of what?" Madison asked, giving Brooke's hand an

encouraging squeeze.

"I'm afraid of rejection. He's already rejected me once. I don't think I can bear him doing it again."

"Why do you think he will reject you?" Madison asked softly.

"Why wouldn't he? He's never professed any type of true feeling for me. He's never said he loves me," she said with a sniff. "If he doesn't feel that way for me, why would he do anything but reject me? He wants whatever the duke has, not me. And I will not seek him out only to be rejected again. It hurts too much."

"I know," Madison cooed to her sister, trying to soothe her.

Madison did understand rejection better than most. She had fancied herself in love with Robbie Swift, a local banker's son, since she was thirteen. When Madison came of age, she did everything she could to get his attention, then one day he started courting her. They courted for an unusually long time—five years. The promise of a proposal always seemed to hang in the air, but nothing more than a promise. However, it seemed to be enough for Madison not to look elsewhere. In the end, he decided Madison wasn't up to his high standards for a wife and he cast her aside for Laura Small, who he had married after only courting her for a matter of days. This hurt Madison deeply and she had felt rejected, but it actually was for the best and Madison realized it now. However, Brooke wasn't going to be cruel and point that out.

"I have an idea," Madison burst out excitedly, bringing Brooke back to the present where she belonged. "Your ship doesn't board until three tomorrow afternoon. That means we still have some time in London together. Why don't we do something fun in the morning?"

"What do you have in mind?"

"I don't know," Madison admitted. "What's something you wanted to do while we were here that we never did?"

Brooke had to think about that. They'd gone to balls, musicales, soirees, breakfasts, operas, plays, and even the British Museum. It seemed they'd done everything already. Then an idea struck her and she couldn't suppress the burble of laughter that passed through her lips. "You cannot laugh," she told her sister, who looked at her like she wanted to point out that Brooke was already laughing, but she didn't say a word. "I should like to go to Covent Garden and see the street performers."

Madison tried to keep a straight face. Brooke could see she was trying to restrain herself from laughing, but in the end she couldn't hold it and she let out a tiny giggle. "Very well then, if you want vendors to hassle you to buy their vegetables while you're trying to strain your neck to watch a man on stilts juggle six knives during your last day in London, then I shall be right there with you."

# *Chapter 29*

Andrew's past few days had not been any better than Brooke's. He'd left Rockhurst and ridden his horse as fast as he could to the Watson estate.

He looked around the estate and saw no sign of Gateway's carriage, and his heart sank. He wondered if she went straight to London instead of coming here first, but he needed to be sure of that before he left.

He left his horse with a groom and headed for the house. He had a feeling he wasn't going to be well received when he arrived. But he had no choice. He had to find out if she was there and try to explain everything to her.

Before he'd even reached the house, he encountered Alex. "I didn't expect to see you so soon, old chap," Alex said, clapping him on the back.

"I didn't expect to be back here so soon, to tell the truth," Andrew replied solemnly. Judging by Alex's tone and manner, he guessed his friend knew nothing and didn't even suspect anything was amiss. Did that mean she hadn't come here? Or did it mean that in typical Alex fashion, he was oblivious about the whole situation?

Quickly concluding that he'd have to seek out another source to obtain information about Brooke's whereabouts, he made his excuses and went in search of someone who would know where Brooke was.

He walked about the house and found the chamber Brooke had occupied during her stay. He knocked on the door and waited for an answer. None came. After surveying the hallway, he opened the door. He stepped inside and quickly looked around, only to find an empty room for the second time that day.

He left her room and decided his best course of action would be to locate her father. When he found Mr. Banks, he was in the baron's study speaking with his brother. It was rude to interrupt, but he did it anyway.

John turned a stiff smile to him and invited him to sit down. Andrew took a seat and inquired about Brooke's whereabouts. "Lost your wife, have you?" Watson asked jovially.

Andrew nodded and waited for John to tell him something useful.

John didn't speak right away. He just sat there looking at Andrew as if he were enjoying his distress.

"To be honest, I have no idea what's going on, nor do I know her whereabouts," John said at last. "But, if you would like to wait here with my brother—" he shot a glance to Watson, who nodded in return— "I would be happy to go speak to her sisters and see what I can find out."

"Thank you," Andrew said stiffly. He would rather have been the one to go track down Brooke's sisters and find out where she was. Reluctantly, he agreed to wait while John talked to his own daughters. They were more likely to tell their father Brooke's whereabouts than him anyway.

Andrew and the baron didn't have much to say to each other. They just stared at one another for a few minutes then looked around the room. Every so often, they'd share a couple of words about who was hosting a hunt this fall or other such nonsense. Andrew resisted the urge to look around at the clock several times. It felt like time was crawling by, but he convinced himself it was only his imagination.

He put his elbows on his knees and leaned his head down, cradling it with his hands. He threaded his fingers through his hair. All he could do was sit and wait.

Keeping the same position, he studied the floor. The patterns made from the lines in the wood were not very interesting, but at least it kept his mind off the time. His gut was in knots from anticipation, when the door finally opened.

His head shot up and disappointment washed over him when he looked up to see it was just the butler.

"Dinner is served, my lord," the butler told Watson.

At those words, Andrew twisted his neck around to see the clock that hung right behind him. "You tricked me!" he burst out at Watson.

"I did no such thing," Watson countered, his lips twitching. "My brother did. He thought you'd come here before going to London. While he and I were talking, a carriage was being loaded. Sorry, but they left—" he looked at his watch— "more than three hours ago. I'm actually surprised you lasted so long."

Fighting the impulse to strangle Watson, Andrew dashed out of the room. He was trying to be polite by not checking the time, convincing himself it was just his imagination, and all the while he was being made a fool.

He rode as fast as he could to London, but didn't arrive fast enough for it to be an acceptable hour to make calls. He considered doing it anyway, then dismissed the idea because he didn't want to cause more trouble by going over there so late, even if it was his right as a husband to collect his wayward bride.

The next morning he left his house at noon and arrived at the Watson townhouse in less than twenty minutes. He knocked on the door and demanded the butler allow him to see his wife. Turner, not the most professional butler in England, gasped at the idea of a countess in residence. Then he gathered his wits the best he could, told Andrew the Bankses were not home, and extended a hand to take Andrew's card.

Andrew wasn't about to be deterred. "I know the way," he told the butler tersely, leaving Turner in the entryway with his mouth agape.

He'd only walked about three steps when Mrs. Banks appeared. "Out!" she ordered, making a rigid shooing motion toward the door.

"I have come to collect my wife," Andrew said, hoping it sounded nicer to her than it did to him.

Mrs. Banks eyed him skeptically and looked like she wanted to blister his ears. "Wait here. I'll be right back," she said coolly.

Andrew shot her an icy glare. "If you think I'm going to fall for that again, you've got a lot to learn."

Mrs. Banks looked at him with a confused look on her face but didn't ask him anything. "Young man, you may be a peer of the realm and, as much as it pains me to say it, my daughter's husband, but you are still a guest in this house and will act accordingly or be removed," she scolded.

"Fine," he ground out. Then he stood and watched her leave.

In no time at all, two pairs of footsteps could be heard coming in his direction and his heart almost burst out of his chest knowing she was going to speak to him. But when those feet rounded the corner, Andrew's heart nearly stopped. The owner of the pair that didn't belong to Mrs. Banks wasn't Brooke as he'd expected, but Mr. Banks.

The following conversation was very one-sided in which Mr. Banks told Andrew in no uncertain terms that he was not allowed back in their house or anywhere near it. Mr. Banks took a minute to recount Andrew's many sins involving Brooke and told Andrew it would take his witnessing a miracle before Andrew would be allowed to speak to Brooke again. Quite simply, he was being permanently dismissed.

The next two days had been just as fruitless. Both days, he'd knocked on the door to Brooke's townhouse. Both times, he'd been denied entry. After each time, he'd sat on a bench across the street holding up a newspaper and waited for her to come out so he could speak to her. Unfortunately, luck had not been on his side.

At the end of the second day, he decided he would try this method one more time. After that, he'd make sure to maneuver his way inside. If not in the traditional way, by using the front door like normal, civilized society members did, then he'd scale the wall and go in through the window the following night.

The only problem was that he had no idea which window was Brooke's and he wasn't keen on the idea of entering the wrong room. It would not do for him to creep into John and Carolina's bedchamber, or even worse, Liberty's. He would just deal with whatever happened when the time came. He couldn't stand to go any longer without talking to her.

He rose from his chair and walked to his bedroom, resigned to spend another sleepless night lying in his bed and staring at the ceiling, thinking of how much he missed his wife. He'd hardly slept in the past few nights. Tonight would be no different.

Just when he'd finally passed out from sheer exhaustion, there was a knock on his door. Ignoring it didn't make it go away, like he'd hoped; instead, the knock just got louder and more adamant.

Andrew crawled out of bed and threw on his dressing robe to cover his naked body before yanking open the door.

"Yes," he barked irritably at a very tired Addams who wore a slightly askew night cap, but otherwise resembled his usual stiff-rumped footman who doubled as his butler.

"My lord, you have a guest," Addams told him.

"A guest?" Andrew repeated. He wasn't expecting any guests. The only person who ever came to see him was Alex. It wasn't likely Alex would come this time of night. Why would he? Unless he'd found out about what happened with Brooke and was coming to rescind his offer for a loan. Andrew hoped that wasn't the case. He had run into Alex earlier in the evening and explained his situation with the mines, and even though it killed his pride to do so, he had asked his friend for a loan. Alex was in an excellent mood and readily agreed. Maybe now that he'd had time to think about it he'd changed his mind. Andrew groaned. "Is it Alex?"

"No, my lord," Addams said, turning a little pink. "Your guest is a not a man."

Andrew's heart skipped a beat. "Is it Lady Townson?" he asked hoarsely, not remembering that Addams had never seen Brooke before.

"I do not believe so, my lord. Though your guest is female, I do not believe she is a lady. She is more of the hooded female variety," Addams said with a slight cough.

Andrew gave a sour look. "Tell her I have a wife and send her away. I'm not in the mood to deal with this now."

"I tried, my lord. But she is most persistent. She said it is most urgent she speak to you immediately. She is waiting in your study."

Andrew glanced longingly at the bed, but walked to the door.

He didn't bother to dress. There was no need. He was going to go speak to a woman of ill repute. She was used to men in their dressing robes, and less.

His study was almost completely dark. Only one candle illuminated the middle of his desk. "Hello," he hollered, hoping the woman had already left. When he heard a delicate cough from the shadows, he stopped walking. He couldn't see anyone and his hands flew to the sash around his robe to make sure it was tight. There wasn't anything he could do about the middle of his chest showing where the robe came together, nor could he help that his legs below the knee were exposed, but he could do his best to cover up the rest from this mystery woman's gaze. He was now wishing he had taken the time to dress. It felt awkward to be almost naked in front of another woman after he'd been intimate with Brooke. Nor did he want this woman to take his state of undress as an invitation. "Madam, I have no need of your favors. If you would be so kind as to remove yourself from my study so I can return to bed, I would be most appreciative," he said icily.

"I object. I think you're in need of my favors," a female voice whispered.

"I assure you, I do not." Andrew said, stepping closer to the shadows to determine who this woman was. It was hard to recognize voices when they were whispering, but he knew when she first spoke that she wasn't Brooke.

"Do not come any closer or I will not help you," the voice hissed.

Andrew thought he heard a hint of panic in her voice and he stopped walking.

"Step back, please," she whispered again.

With an irritated sigh, Andrew stepped back and sat in his chair.

"I have some information about your wife, Lady Townson," she whispered at last. "She is leaving for America tomorrow."

Andrew's throat convulsed. Was she telling him this to torture him or spur him into action? His throat was too thick to push words out, and he made some sort of grunt that the woman must have taken as a response.

"I may have heard she and her sister are going on an outing tomorrow morning, if you'd like to catch her."

"Catch her?" he choked. Had people taken notice of him sitting on the bench across the street from her house? "Where are they going?" he asked when she didn't elaborate.

"Covent Garden, I believe. Lady Townson and Miss Madison were heard speaking of it to Mr. and Mrs. Banks. I do not know the time."

"Will the whole Banks family be present?" he asked, hoping she'd say no.

"No."

"Just Brooke and Madison, no maids or anyone else?" he asked skeptically.

"Correct."

The pressure lifted from his heart. Madison wasn't a bad sort at all. In fact, she probably wouldn't try to stop him from speaking to Brooke. Rising from his seat, he kept his gaze fixed on the dark corner she was in. "Thank you for the information, miss. Is there anything I can do for you in return?"

"Yes, there is one thing."

"What?"

"Dismiss your mistress."

Andrew's jaw dropped. Where had that come from? "Excuse me. If I had realized that would be your price for this information, I might have taken my chances sitting on the bench," he said irritably.

"I'm not vying for the job. I am quite satisfied with my current position," she whispered, sounding annoyed. "I just think Lady Townson deserves to have you—all of you. That is if she decides to take you back."

Andrew nodded. This was obviously a woman who cared a great deal for Brooke, and she was only looking out for her happiness. Realizing this, he said, "I do not make a habit of talking about my personal life, but, I do not now, nor do I plan to, have a mistress. Ever."

"Excellent choice," she whispered.

Andrew took that as a dismissal and started to go. But when he reached the doorframe, he turned around. He'd reached the conclusion this was a servant from the Watson townhouse. Servants always knew everything. He didn't know why she would want to help him and he wasn't going to question it. She'd offered him invaluable information; he needed to repay her in some way. "Your information has been invaluable to me. I thank you very much. If you ever need anything in the future, please do not hesitate to come to me."

"Thank you," she whispered softly.

He walked back up to his room and went to the window. He watched the cloaked woman climb into a hired hack and drive away before going back to his study where he stayed until morning.

Andrew decided his best tactic would be to intercept Brooke at the main entrance. There was still a chance of missing her, but he had a better chance of being allowed to speak to her if he waited for her there rather than outside her residence.

He waited at the entrance all morning. He sat. He stood. He paced. He leaned on a post. All the while tamping down his nerves and thinking of what he would say to her when she finally arrived.

He started to fear he'd missed her and would have to go in search of her. He took out his pocket watch once again and frowned. With a snap, he closed his watch, pushed off the post he was leaning against, and looked up. That's when he saw her and his heart raced like a horse at Ascot.

# Chapter 30

Brooke tried to put on a happy face, but her smile just wouldn't stick. Madison only wanted to spend time with her before she set sail for New York, she reminded herself every time she opened her mouth to suggest they go back. Unfortunately, her tangled mess of emotions regarding Andrew got in the way of her enjoying their day together.

Madison had convinced her to go to Andrew's townhouse, demand an explanation, and see if they could work it out. But when they arrived, the snobbish man who answered the door informed them stiffly that ladies do not call on gentlemen under any circumstances, besides which, his lordship was not in.

Willing herself not to lose her composure, Brooke smiled and walked away. She decided to continue with their original plan and go to the garden to be harassed by vendors and watch men on stilts juggle dangerous objects.

They were just about to the entrance when Madison stopped walking and looked straight ahead. Brooke followed her gaze. Next to the entrance, leaning on a post and looking at his pocket watch, stood Andrew.

Now that the moment had arrived, she briefly entertained the idea of running away. However, that idea was soon dismissed when Madison softly touched her elbow. "You wanted to know. Now is your chance."

Brooke nodded. "What's he doing here?" she asked numbly.

"I don't know," Madison replied. "But since he's here, you can get your answers. Let's go," she prodded, "he's looking in our direction. If he hasn't noticed you already, he soon will."

Brooke attached a bright smile on her face and started walking in his direction. Andrew had also started walking, or running if one wanted to be precise, toward her.

He closed the distance between them within seconds. "Brooke," he said unevenly.

"Andrew," she said in a stilted tone.

Andrew turned to look at Madison and bowed. "Good morning, Madison."

"How did you know we were coming here?" Brooke demanded.

Andrew gave her a little smile. "That's my little secret."

"You seem to have a lot of those, don't you?" Brooke shot back. Her anger with him was quickly returning.

Andrew sobered.

"Well, I can see my presence here isn't needed," Madison said airily, then pointed to an empty bench. "I'll be right over there."

"Thank you," Andrew said with a surprisingly grateful look on his face. He waited for her to leave, before he met Brooke's eyes again. "I don't know what to say," he admitted.

"Starting from the beginning would be my strategy," she replied tartly.

Andrew's jaw clenched. Then with a nod, he released a pent up breath and words started tumbling out of his mouth. "I borrowed money from Gateway. I couldn't pay and he repossessed my estate. In order to get it back, I was asked to bring shame on your family. I refused at first, but then he twisted the words around and I got defensive. Then, before I knew what I was saying, I'd agreed to do it. That was the night before we met."

"Wait," she interrupted, putting up a hand to stop his rambling. "You just said you were to bring shame on my family. Why?"

"I don't know," he admitted. "I asked, but he wouldn't say. All I know is he wanted your family on the next ship bound for America."

"So you're saying it wasn't me specifically?" she asked skeptically, her brow furrowing in confusion. What would anyone, especially Gateway, have to gain from her family returning home?

"No."

"All right," she said cautiously. "I don't quite understand, but pray continue." Maybe she'd understand better if she just let him keep talking.

"Gateway just wanted enough shame to fall on the family that you would all go home. He didn't care who it fell on, just that it happened and your family left. I don't know about in America, but here, a lady's reputation is everything, so I assumed it would be the easiest avenue to pursue. Gateway knew that, too, and when he first approached me, he even suggested it."

"From the day we met, you'd set out to ruin me?" she asked quietly.

"Yes. No. Not exactly. At first, I wanted to try to find out some sort of family secret, expose that and be done with it, but there wasn't one. Once I realized that, I had to rely on ruining your reputation."

"Why me?" she cried. "Is it so well known I've been in the garden with a few gentlemen that you thought I'd be the easiest to ruin? Is that it?" Tears formed in her eyes and her throat constricted.

"No," he said fiercely. "I didn't even know your penchant for kissing in the shrubs until later. I picked you because I liked you. From the moment you entered the room, I liked you. Nobody had ever had the nerve to just stare at me that way. Nobody had played such a prank on me before. I truly believed for the better part of a day, you had indeed decorated that atrocious room. It wasn't until I saw the initials on that mind-numbing painting that I realized you were having me on. I liked it. I liked you. That's why I chose you."

Andrew ran a hand through his hair. "Then we went on our ride in the park. I enjoyed teasing you that day. I also enjoyed taking you to the museum. I had never enjoyed a kiss as much as I did that day. Before I knew what was happening, I was looking forward to our next meeting and being with you."

"If that's true, then why didn't you just tell Gateway you could not go through with it?" she interrupted.

"Because he would have just found someone else to do it. I knew that if I just carried it out, I could keep you protected. Someone else would have been completely heartless about the whole thing and would have caused you, or possibly one of your sisters, more pain and embarrassment than necessary."

"Whereas you were just doing enough to send us away, is that it?" she asked flatly, belying the rage that was coursing through her.

"Yes," he said solemnly, then he grabbed her hand and pulled her over to a bench in a somewhat secluded area. "This all sounds really bad. Believe me, I know. But the truth is, the more I got to know you, the more I didn't want to hurt you. I honestly thought once we married, this would be taken care of without you ever finding out. I knew Gateway would confront me. I just didn't know he would do it so soon, or in such a way. You were never supposed to know about this. I didn't know how I was going to handle Gateway, but when I saw you walk out of that library that night at Alex's, I realized you were more important to me than anything else."

"Even the estate he held?" she asked shyly.

"Even the estate." Andrew confirmed, interlacing their fingers. "When I saw you walk away from Alex's library, I realized what I'd known all along: I couldn't live without you. I didn't want you to go back to America, nor could I stand it if you came back to London and I wasn't allowed to see you. The only way to keep you in my life was to make you my wife. I wanted to marry you enough that I didn't give a second thought to enduring whatever Gateway might do to try to destroy me. Having you is worth more than anything else."

"If I understand correctly, you're telling me that you realized that night that you enjoyed my company?" she asked uncertainly.

Andrew gave a harsh laugh. "Yes, I do enjoy your company. But what I mean to say is that I love you. I realized that night that I loved you enough not to care about making an enemy of Gateway or losing the estate because I failed to follow through with our deal. I rode through the rain for six hours to get my hands on that special license. I couldn't wait another day to have you—all of you."

"You love me," she whispered, wondering if she had heard him correctly.

"Yes. I may not have been very good about showing it so far, but I will get better, I promise. How could I possibly get any worse?" he teased, coming to his knees in front of her. He leaned over, reached into a bag she hadn't noticed he had with him, and removed what looked like a yellow object resembling a rose. Handing it to her, he said sheepishly, "Because I'm sorry for what I've done." He reached in again and withdrew a pink one. "Because I adore you," he said, replacing the yellow one he had just given her with the pink. He reached down again and this time he pulled out a red one. "Because you're my true love," he said, handing her the paper rose. Then he moved his hands up to frame her face. Cupping her chin and tipping it down toward him, he said solemnly, "Brooke, you know I'm not a man of great means, so please know if I could afford to shower you with dozens of the real things, I would have bought every stem in every hothouse between my house and the Garden this morning rather than staying up all night trying to fold colored squares of paper to resemble roses."

"Surely you're not so poor you couldn't have afforded three," she teased, remembering their pitiful dinner at Rockhurst. But in her mind, it was better this way. She was glad he hadn't bought them. Money could be earned and spent, but time could only be spent. Him spending time folding silly little scraps of paper meant far more to her than one hundred bouquets of the real thing would have.

Andrew cracked a small smile. "I said I'd shower you with dozens if I could." He tipped the bag so she could see inside where dozens of paper roses were resting. "I didn't think you'd really appreciate it if I poured these out on you right here, but if you want…" he trailed off, his eyes dancing with amusement, letting her know just how much he'd enjoy dumping the bag over her head. "If you must know I had to fold all of these—" he looked down at the bag— "just to remember how to do it." He gave her a self-deprecating smile.

Setting the bag of paper roses aside, he came back to his knees in front of her. He cupped her face with his hands again, and tilted her head to look straight into his eyes that were full of concern, but she also recognized a glint of hope in them, too. "I know nothing changes what I've done. But I'm asking you to stay. Stay with me. Give me the chance to prove to you how much I love you, and perhaps earn your love in return."

Brooke met his eyes and brought her hands up to where his hands were holding her chin. "You cannot earn my love, Andrew," she said, her voice so quiet, it was barely more than a whisper.

"Oh," he said solemnly, clamping his mouth into a tight line. He nodded once and his hands loosened their grip on her face, but they didn't move. He swallowed visibly, his face looked shuttered and his eyes looked watery.

Brooke let go of his hands and reached out, grabbing his face the way he was touching hers. Pulling him closer to her, she smiled sweetly and said, "The reason you cannot earn my love, is because you already have it."

Andrew's grip on her face tightened again, and a broad grin split his handsome face before he closed the gap between them. Then, right there on a bench outside of Covent Garden in front of anyone who happened to be walking by, the Earl and Countess of Townson engaged in a scandalous kiss.

If you enjoyed *Intentions of the Earl*, I would appreciate it if you would help others enjoy this book, too.

**Lend it.** This e-book is lending-enabled, so please, share it with a friend.

**Recommend it.** Please help other readers find this book by recommending it to friends, readers' groups and discussion boards.

**Review it.** Please tell other readers why you liked this book by reviewing it at one of the following websites: Amazon or Goodreads.

*Other Books by Rose Gordon*

*BANKS BROTHERS' BRIDES*

***His Contract Bride***—Lord Watson has always known that one day he'd marry Regina Harris. Unfortunately nobody thought to inform her of this; and when she finds that her "love match" was actually arranged by her father long ago in an effort to further his social standing, it falls to a science-loving, blunt-speaking baron to win her trust.

***His Yankee Bride***—John Banks has no idea what—or who—waits for him on the other side of the ocean... Carolina Ellis has longed to meet a man whom she can love, so when she glimpses such a man, she's determined to do whatever it takes to have him—Southern aristocracy be damned.

***His Jilted Bride***—Elijah Banks *cannot* sit still a moment longer as the gossip continues to fly about one of his childhood playmates, who just so happens to still be in her bridal chamber, waiting for her groom to arrive. Thinking to save her the public humiliation of being jilted at the altar, Elijah convinces her to run away with him, replacing one scandal with one far more forgiving. But when a secret she keeps is threatened to be exposed, it falls to Elijah to save her again by revealing a few of his own...

***His Brother's Bride*** —Henry Banks had no idea his brother agreed to marry a fetching young lady until the day she shows up on his doorstep and presents the proof. To protect the Banks name and his new sister-in-law's feelings, Henry agrees to marry her only to discover this young lady's intentions were not so honorable and it wasn't really marriage she sought, but revenge on a member of the Banks family...

*Coming July 2013*
*Celebrate America's independence with the:*
*FORT GIBSON OFFICER SERIES*

(American Historicals based in Indian Territory mid-1800s)

***The Officer and the Bostoner*** —A well-to-do lady traveling by stagecoach from her home in Boston to meet her fiance in Santa Fe finds herself stranded in a military fort when her stagecoach leaves without her. Given the choice to either temporarily marry an officer until her fiance can come rescue her or take her chances with the Indians, she marries the glib Captain Wes Tucker, who, unbeknownst to her, grew up in a wealthy Charleston family and despises everything she represents. But when it's time for her fiance to reclaim her and annul their marriage, will she still want to go with him, and more importantly, will Wes let her?

***The Officer and the Southerner***—Second Lt. Jack Walker doesn't always think ahead and when he decides to defy logic and send off for a mail-order bride, he might have left out only a few details about his life. When she arrives and realizes she's been fooled (again), this woman who's never really belonged, sees no other choice but to marry him anyway—however, she makes it perfectly clear: she'll be his lawfully wed, but she will *not* share his bed. Now Jack has to find a way to show his always skeptical bride that he is indeed trustworthy and that she does belong somewhere in the world: right here, with him.

***The Officer and the Traveler***—Captain Grayson Montgomery's mouth has landed him in trouble again! And this time it's not something a cleverly worded sentence and a handsome smile can fix. Having been informed he'll either have to marry or be demoted and sentenced to hard labor for the remainder of his tour, he proposes, only to discover those years of hard labor may have been the easier choice for his heart.

If you never want to miss a new release visit Rose’s website at www.rosegordon.net to subscribe and you'll be notified each time a new book becomes available.

*Also Already Available*

*GROOM SERIES*

Four men are about to have their bachelor freedom snatched away as they become grooms...but finding the perfect woman may prove a bit more difficult than they originally thought.

***Her Sudden Groom***—The overly scientific, always respectable and socially awkward Alexander Banks has just been informed his name resides on a betrothal agreement right above the name of the worst chit in all of England. With a loophole that allows him to marry another without consequence before the thirtieth anniversary of his birth, he has only four weeks to find another woman and make her his wife.

***Her Reluctant Groom***—For the past thirteen years Marcus Sinclair, Earl Sinclair, has lived his life as a heavily scarred recluse, never dreaming the only woman he's ever wanted would love him back. But when it slips out that she does, he doubts her love for his scarred body and past can be real. For truly, how can a woman love a man whose injuries were caused when he once tried to declare himself to her sister?

***Her Secondhand Groom***—Widower Patrick Ramsey, Viscount Drakely, fell in love and married at eighteen only to be devastated by losing her as she bore his third daughter. Now, as his girls are getting older he realizes they need a mother—and a governess. Not able to decide between the two which they need more, he marries an ordinary young lady from the local village in hopes she can suit both roles. But this ordinary young lady isn't so ordinary after all, and he'll either have to take a chance and risk his heart once more or wind up alone forever.

***Her Imperfect Groom*** —Sir Wallace Benedict has never been good with the fairer sex and in the bottom drawer of his bureau he has the scandal sheet clippings to prove it. But this thrice-jilted baronet has just discovered the right lady for him was well-worth waiting for. The only trouble is, with multiple former love interests plaguing him at every chance possible, he must find clever ways to avoid them and simultaneously steal the attention—and affections—of the the one lady he's sure is a perfect match for him and his imperfections.

**Already Available--SCANDALOUS SISTERS SERIES**

***Intentions of the Earl***—A penniless earl makes a pact to ruin an American hoyden, never suspecting for a moment he'll lose his heart along the way.

***Liberty for Paul***—A vicar's daughter who loves propriety almost as much as she hates the man her father is mentoring will go to any length she sees fit to see that improper man out the door and out of her life. But when she's forced to marry him, she'll learn there's a lot more to life, love and this man than she originally thought.

***To Win His Wayward Wife*** —A gentleman who's spent the last five years pining for the love of his life will get his second chance. The only problem? She has no interest in him.

# About the Author

*USA Today* Bestselling and Award Winning Author Rose Gordon writes unusually unusual historical romances that have been known to include scarred heroes, feisty heroines, marriage-producing scandals, far too much scheming, naughty literature and always a sweet happily-ever-after. When not escaping to another world via reading or writing a book, she spends her time chasing two young boys around the house, being hunted by wild animals, or sitting on the swing in the backyard where she has to use her arms as shields to deflect projectiles AKA: balls, water balloons, sticks, pinecones, and anything else one of her boys picks up to hurl at his brother who just happens to be hiding behind her.

She can be found on somewhere in cyberspace at:

http://www.rosegordon.net

or blogging about *something* inappropriate at:

http://rosesromanceramblings.wordpress.com

Rose would love to hear from her readers and you can e-mail her at rose.gordon@hotmail.com

You can also find her on Facebook, Goodreads, and Twitter.

If you never want to miss a new release visit her website to subscribe and you'll be notified each time a new book becomes available.

8101827R00157

Made in the USA
San Bernardino, CA
02 February 2014